continued . . .

JUL -- 2018

"Fans of Western romance will be thrilled with this delightful addition to Goodman's strong list." —*Booklist*

"A wonderfully intense romance . . . A captivating read." —Romance Junkies

"Exquisitely written. Rich in detail, the characters are passionately drawn . . . An excellent read." —*The Oakland Press*

A Touch of Flame

Jo Goodman

JOVE
New York

A JOVE BOOK
Published by Berkley
An imprint of Penguin Random House LLC
375 Hudson Street, New York, New York 10014

Copyright © 2018 by Joanne Dobrzanski
Excerpt from *A Touch of Frost* by Jo Goodman copyright © 2017 by Joanne Dobrzanski
Penguin Random House supports copyright. Copyright fuels creativity, encourages
diverse voices, promotes free speech, and creates a vibrant culture. Thank you for buying
an authorized edition of this book and for complying with copyright laws by not
reproducing, scanning, or distributing any part of it in any form without permission.
You are supporting writers and allowing Penguin Random House to continue to
publish books for every reader.

A JOVE BOOK and BERKLEY are registered trademarks and the B colophon
is a trademark of Penguin Random House LLC.

ISBN: 9780399584299

First Edition: June 2018

Printed in the United States of America
1 3 5 7 9 10 8 6 4 2

Cover photo of couple by Claudio Dogar-Marinesco

For Pam Hopkins and her steady guidance

Chapter One

Frost Falls, Colorado
September 1898

Ben Madison tipped his chair until he had it balanced on its two rear legs. The top rail rested against the wall behind him, so he was of the opinion that he was not in danger of an embarrassing collapse. He stretched his long legs and casually set his boot heels on top of a keg that he'd cut in half to make the perfect stool. Ten minutes of shut-eye, he promised himself. He tugged on the brim of his pearl gray Stetson and pulled it forward to cover his eyes and the bridge of his lightly freckled nose. Positioning the hat in such a way meant uncovering more of the back of his head and exposing his carrot-colored hair to passersby who'd known him all their lives and still seemed to think they were the first to comment on it.

Nothing about being the newly elected sheriff of Frost Falls changed that.

Under his hat, Ben closed his eyes. Ten minutes, he reminded himself. There was a gentle hum of movement up and down the wide thoroughfare unimaginatively named Main Street. No one was in a particular hurry this afternoon, least of all him. He could identify the voices of the Saunders brothers deep in conversation outside the land office. Mrs. Fish, the owner of the town's only dress shop, announced to someone that she was closing for a half hour while she visited the apothecary. Ben swore he heard her turn the sign on her door from OPEN to CLOSED.

The boardwalk vibrated gently under him as folks went on about their business. No one came close, which he appreciated. Even the children returning to the schoolhouse after lunch gave him a wide berth. He made out the sounds of some playful shoving and whispered teasing, but none of it lingered, and when the schoolmaster rang his bell, it was only to call in the last stragglers.

Ben wondered about the Salt children, but only long enough to make another promise to himself he would drop in on them later, make sure they were settled, and see if there was anything he could do for their mother. As for their daddy, there was no point talking to the man while he was still sleeping off another two-day drunk in a cell. Anyway, there was only so much Ben could say to Jeremiah Salt about his behavior, and Ben reckoned that over the years, he'd said all of it. Not that anything changed for the better, not permanently, and there were times that saying something changed things for the worse. He needed to think on that, and as long as his office reeked of sour body odor, warm piss, and stale brew, he was doing his thinking outside.

Wrinkling his nose, he fell asleep.

And woke to the sound of a train whistle as No. 459 approached the station.

It was a month ago, a couple of weeks after the election results were in, that Dr. Dunlop had taken Ben aside and confided his intention to leave Frost Falls for a teaching position at the Boston University School of Medicine. Ben immediately understood what Doc's exit would mean to the town. The man had been looking after folks for better than twenty-five years, delivered most of the children born during his tenure, removed a coffee can's worth of bullets from various body parts, set broken bones, prescribed healing tinctures and poultices, took out an appendix now and again, treated gout and head colds, and knew everyone's name and their common ailments.

Doc was set on not having a fuss made over his departure, but neither could he leave like a thief in the night. His housekeeper for all the years he was in residence, who often as not was called into the surgery to assist, made no secret that she felt betrayed and abandoned, and, oh yes, there was the town to consider. Her way of expressing her disapproval and displeasure was to organize a farewell celebration of Bacchanalian proportions. The good citizens of Frost Falls mourned the loss of their doctor with dancing and feasting and plenty of alcohol, which provided the catalyst for what became Jeremiah Salt's first two-day bender under Ben's sole oversight. No one blamed Mary Cherry because it was well known that Jeremiah did not require much in the way of provocation and because Mary Cherry was so obviously crying in her beer.

Doc assured anyone who asked that arrangements had already been made for a replacement. His patients were not comforted to hear it. Who, after all, could replace him? To ease their minds, he gave them a name: Dr. E. Ridley Woodhouse, a graduate of his alma mater, the Boston University School of Medicine, where he was returning to teach. In fact, Dr. Woodhouse's father was a former classmate of his and was now a professor at the university. No one was particularly mollified by that news. What would be a homecoming of sorts for Doc was still an uncertain future for the folks who had been under his care. Even more unsettling, they were able to deduce from the information that their new physician was on the youngish side.

They either did not remember, or did not care to remember, that once upon a time, Dr. Dunlop had been on the youngish side himself.

It was when Ben accompanied Doc to the station for his departure a few weeks ago that the doctor elicited Ben's promise to meet Woodhouse on arrival and offer support throughout the transition. In his mind, Ben imagined that he would either amble or mosey—he was not sure of the distinction—down to the station so as not to give any impression of urgency or anxiety regarding the new doctor's arrival. That was impossible now. Neither ambling nor moseying would get him there on time.

Ben dropped the chair on all four legs, resettled his hat on his head, and shoved the stool aside. He jumped to his feet, wavering just a bit as he was still recovering his senses, and then started south toward the station. He had a long stride that quickly covered the planked sidewalk and he had to force himself to shorten his steps so as not to attract attention. Still, by the time he passed Maxwell Wayne's bakery, he was once again moving at what most observers would characterize as a brisk pace. He slowed a second time, took a moment here and there to exchange pleasantries with Mrs. Preston, who, judging by the warm scent emanating from the bakery box dangling from her fingertips, was carrying cinnamon buns, and Miss Renquest, who sought his opinion regarding her new straw hat. Was it sitting at the proper angle on her head? Should she have chosen a black ribbon over the royal purple? Did it complement her age? The answers were: Yes, no, and your age complements the hat. Miss Renquest was eighty-four, and she was very pleased to hear it.

Passengers were already disembarking when Ben reached the platform. He had arranged earlier for a wagon from the livery to be waiting for him. Doc had warned him that Woodhouse would arrive with trunks, bags, books, and enough equipment to support the use of a wagon. Ben supposed it was something Doc had learned in the course of corresponding with Woodhouse, or perhaps in his correspondence with Woodhouse's father. Ben had been assured that Doc had full confidence in the new doctor's skill and education, and had not made the decision to leave on a whim. Neither had Woodhouse's decision to leave Boston for Frost Falls been without serious contemplation. Ben was left with the impression that the coming and going was an exchange of sorts, a bargain made, and he wondered if that could possibly be right or good. What he knew for certain was that he had no say in it then or now and what he owed the doctors was the fulfillment of a promise made.

Ben saw Mr. and Mrs. Reynolds step down from the train, Mr. Reynolds first, then his wife. Their fearless toddler twins jumped gleefully to the platform without assistance and begged to be allowed to do it again. They were bundled up and carried off, one under each of their father's arms. Mrs. Reynolds followed, smiling indulgently and waving to Ben as she passed.

A few more passengers left the train, but there was no one he did not recognize. Had Dr. Woodhouse missed a connection? Left the train at an earlier stop? There was nothing to be done but wait, so Ben waited.

His first indication that Dr. Woodhouse was indeed on the train was when two porters appeared on the platform carrying what was obviously a heavy trunk between them. When they tried to set it down, the leather straps slipped out of their hands and the trunk thudded to the deck. Their equally guilty expressions made it clear to Ben they had instructions to treat the trunk with more care. He wasn't surprised, though, when they shrugged it off and disappeared back inside the baggage car. They came out again less than a minute later, this time carrying smaller trunks they could manage on their own. They placed the trunks beside the large one and then removed several valises and a canvas carryall. There was nothing that Ben identified as a doctor's black bag, but then Ben considered that Woodhouse might be carrying it.

It was only a moment later that his thought was confirmed. Dr. Woodhouse appeared on the steps of the car, carrying that identifying bag, and waited for a conductor to add a wooden stool to make disembarking easier. Yes, this was Dr. Woodhouse. Dr. E. Ridley Woodhouse. And it was suddenly clear why Ol' Doc Dunlop had asked for his promise to meet the train and support the transition.

Dr. E. Ridley Woodhouse was a woman.

Ben swore softly under his breath. Six weeks ago this would have been Jackson Brewer's problem. He was the sheriff then and still would be if he hadn't gotten it in his head that he wanted to retire and take his wife to Paris. Paris! Jackson and Addie had their bags packed and were ready to go as soon as the election was over and it was clear that Ben would be the new sheriff. They did not even wait for the swearing in. At the time, Ben was relieved. It meant Jackson did not have to hear his former deputy stutter through a speech he never wanted to make for a position he never sought to hold.

And now there was this absurdity.

Ben walked toward the trunks and valises and canvas carryall and stopped when he reached them. He waited for her to alight from the car and approach. He touched the brim of his hat, gave a short nod, and greeted her. She was no longer carrying her black leather satchel in one hand. She cradled it against her midriff as though it offered some sort of protection.

"Yes," she said in response to his greeting. "I am Dr. Woodhouse. You are?"

"Ben Madison. Doc asked me to look after you, make sure you get settled in, have everything you need. I'm supposed to show you the lay of the land."

"Really."

It was not exactly a question the way she put it. More like she was unimpressed. He wondered if he should have mentioned that he was the sheriff. He smiled a trifle unevenly as that thought came and went. She didn't miss it, though.

"Do I amuse you?" she asked.

"No, ma'am. Mostly I amuse myself. That's what I was doing just then." It was clear to him that she did not know what to make of that so she said nothing, just continued to stare at him from behind a pair of gold wire spectacles. Her eyes were brown, same as what he could see of her hair. Her wide-brimmed navy blue straw hat sported an extravagant pink bow on the flat crown and hid her hair and shaded her face until she lifted her chin. That small chin was lifted now and to considerable effect as she eyed him candidly. Ben had an urge to tug at his collar and clear his throat. What was he going to do when she cupped his balls and told him to cough?

He knuckled his mouth to suppress a laugh.

She arched an eyebrow. "Amusing yourself again?"

Ben lowered his fist and gave himself fair marks for presenting a straight face. There was nothing he could do about the heated color in his cheeks. It was the curse of all redheads. "Yes, ma'am. I believe I am."

"I see."

"Oh, I doubt that." He did not give her an opportunity for comment but waved a hand over her belongings. "Everything here?"

She followed the sweep of his hand, regarded the baggage, and nodded. "Yes." She finally lowered her black bag so that she was carrying it in her right hand. "Do you have some sort of conveyance?"

"Yes, ma'am. A right proper conveyance. We call it a buckboard." He pointed to where it stood at the end of the platform. He thought she was going to comment on the wagon or the restless bay mare that was going to pull it, but what she did was turn back to him and say, "You and I are of an age, I think. I prefer that you do not call me ma'am."

"Well, sure. I didn't want to seem forward calling you Ridley, and I don't know what the E stands for. Elizabeth? Eliza? Emily?"

"Exactly-none-of-your-affair."

It took Ben a moment to understand. "Oh, I see. Every-bit-your-prerogative, Ridley."

"Dr. Woodhouse."

"Yes, of course. Dr. Woodhouse." He thought he saw a breath ease out of her, but he could have been mistaken. For all that she seemed self-contained, self-confident, and more than a little self-important, maybe she'd just been holding her breath all this time. He'd give her the benefit of the doubt and see where that took him.

"I'm twenty-nine," he said.

She stared at him.

"Twenty-nine," he repeated. "My last birthday. You said you thought we were of an age. I'm aiming to find out."

"Twenty-eight."

"Huh. Then you were right. That's of an age. You can call me Ben, though. I don't fancy being called Mr. Madison."

"By me?"

"By anyone."

"All right."

It seemed there was the slightest hesitation after she spoke, almost as if she were about to call him Ben. If that were the case, she swallowed the urge and the word, and his name did not move past her lips. For all that they had a short acquaintance and she was as citified as the long pointed toes of her shoes, he would not have minded hearing his name on her lips. That had occurred to him the moment she lifted her face and he saw that she had a wide, splendidly curved mouth. She had yet to smile, to unleash its full exotic power, and he thought that was probably for the best. He'd be weak-kneed and noodle-limbed and never be able to manage to get the trunks to the buckboard.

"You're staring," she said. That splendidly curved mouth flattened in disapproval.

"Was I? You have something . . ." He pointed to the left corner of his lips and made a brushing motion with his index finger. She mirrored the same motion and he said, "That's it.

It's gone." Of course, nothing had been there, but it was a perfectly acceptable excuse for him staring, and unless he told her, she would never know he lied.

She dropped her hand to her side. "Is there anyone to assist you with the trunks? I can manage the smaller things."

"You go. Wait at the end of the platform. The stationmaster will help me." He did not wait to see if she started walking. He went into the station, asked the agent to give him a hand, and when he reappeared, she had already climbed onto the buckboard's thinly padded seat. The doctor's bag was at her side, and one of the valises was in the bed of the wagon. It was good to know she wasn't helpless. He had confidence in Dr. Dunlop when he announced E. Ridley Woodhouse was in every way a competent physician. What Ben didn't know was if E. Ridley could manage the everyday competencies that were necessary for living in Frost Falls. At the very least, she had proven she could lift and carry. It was a start.

The buckboard sagged as the largest trunk was placed on the bed. Ben didn't comment until everything was loaded and they were on their way. "What's in the big trunk?"

"Books."

He whistled softly. "That's a lot of books. We have a library here, you know."

"Medical reference books," she said. "They are hard to come by in any library outside of a university."

Ben nodded. "No bodies, then." Out of the corner of his eye he saw her head jerk in surprise and then a hint of a smile hover on her lips. "Good to know about the bodies. I was wondering."

"You were not."

He shrugged.

She said nothing for a long moment and then regarded him with a sideways look. She asked, "Did you truly wonder?"

One corner of Ben's mouth lifted just a fraction. "Truly, I did not."

She nodded once, thoughtfully. "It's as you said, then."

"What's that?"

"You do like to amuse yourself."

"I don't believe I said that I like to do it. It's more that I can't help myself. There's plenty that strikes me odd." He thought she might seize on that, but if she felt the urge, she restrained herself. Her head swiveled to the right and left as she took in her surroundings. She did not ask any questions, and Ben wondered what sort of impression she was forming. He tried to see what was so familiar to him with fresh eyes.

He raised a hand to acknowledge Hank Ketchum as the man looked up from tending to one of his horses. Hank nodded once, rather sharply, and went back to work. The livery could use a fresh coat of paint, Ben noted, and if Hank replaced the battered boards on the side visible to the public, it'd be a marked improvement. Ben didn't see it happening. The building was a reflection of the man who owned it, utilitarian and a little careworn, rich with history, full of character. It was the sort of thing that Dr. Woodhouse could not appreciate in a glance, but something she would learn soon enough.

Hank Ketchum was not the only person to give him a nod or lift a hand as the buckboard rattled on. He counted seven women gathered in front of the Presbyterian Church, all of whom looked up and offered fulsome smiles until they clapped eyes on his companion. While their smiles remained in place, stillness settled over the women, and Ben realized the set of their features was frozen. Whatever thoughts they were entertaining, he doubted that any one of them recognized that the woman he was escorting was the town's new doc.

The canted sign above the Songbird Saloon was a fixture that no one had ambitions about straightening, least of all the proprietor, who had a fondness for it since it had slipped fifteen degrees below level the same day his wife left town with a cardsharp from New Orleans.

The land office had windows that could barely reflect the sun's glare because they were in need of washing. The windows of his office were hardly any better. In fact, when Ben regarded the leather goods store, the apothecary, the mercantile, and the barbershop, he concluded that most of Frost Fall's businesses required a spit shine. Mrs. Fish's dress shop and the Butterworth Hotel were exceptions, gleaming like polished jewels in a dusty setting.

Would Dr. Woodhouse judge the town by its appearance,

or would she reserve her opinion until she met its citizens? And equally important, would the town judge her by her appearance or on her merits?

"It's precisely as he described it."

Ben turned to look at her. She appeared rather more pleased than disappointed, but he couldn't be sure that it was a compliment to the town. She could have been referring to Doc's skill at putting his observations to paper. Before he could ask for clarification, she distracted him by pointing to the butter yellow frame house on the side street past the Butterworth. He had not yet begun to turn the corner, but he did so now.

"That's it, isn't it?" she said. "The house. It's Dr. Dunlop's house."

"The way I understand it, it's your house now."

Her slim smile widened. "So it is."

"I wondered why Doc was so keen to slap a fresh coat of paint on it this summer. He hired the Anderson boys to do it for him, and he was particular that they should do a good job. I suppose that was all for you. Guess this has been in the works for longer than anyone's known."

She shrugged lightly and said nothing as Ben tugged on the reins and the mare halted in front of the house. Instead of rising, she remained seated and stared at her new home.

Ben started to rise and then lowered himself back on the seat when she didn't move. He was quiet, letting her take her fill. It was hard to tell from her profile, but he thought she looked reverent, and not for anything was he going to disturb that moment.

With no warning, her head swiveled in his direction and she nearly pinned his ears back with her sharply focused and suspicious gaze. "What did he tell you about me?"

Ben figured he knew what she was getting at, but he decided she'd have to do some better fishing for it. "Same as he told all of us, I reckon. Mainly that you had all the qualifications and that he was leaving us in good hands. Reminded us that he was a young'un once, and came here with considerably less experience and knowledge than you're bringing." He noted that his answer did not exactly calm the waters. Her dark eyes were no longer narrowed, but one of her eyebrows remained arched fractionally higher than the other. He asked,

"That's all true, isn't it? You said you were a doctor and I took you at your word. There're folks who will want to see a paper that says you are." Ben jerked his thumb over his shoulder to indicate the wagon bed. "I have to believe you got proof of that back there."

"My diploma. Yes. I have it."

"Framed?"

"No."

He looked off in the distance and spoke more to himself than to her. "Damn. Thought it'd be framed." When he looked at her again, he saw that suspiciousness had been replaced by curiosity. "Doc Dunlop had his diploma framed. He was that proud of it. Had it hanging in his office. There are plenty of folks in these parts claiming to be doctors that never studied for it. Sometimes they do all right. Sometimes they get run out of one town and move on to another."

"I'll have it framed."

He was careful not to smile. "Probably for the best."

"It used to be in a frame. I took it out to make room for other things."

"Sure. Makes sense on account of you wanting to bring all your books." He watched her purse her lips in disapproval, but she didn't take the bait.

"What else did he say?"

Ben pretended to give it some thought. "He mentioned that he and your father were at the college together and that they stayed friends all these years."

"They corresponded regularly," she said. "I don't imagine he mentioned that he was my godfather."

Ben did not have to act surprised; he simply was. "That never came up. Mary Cherry might have known. She was his housekeeper and occasional assistant."

"I know who she is. I am hoping she will agree to work for me."

"I couldn't speak to that. It never came up."

"Hmm."

Ben waited. The question was there, right on the tip of her tongue, but she was obviously loath to give it sound. "Give me a moment," he said. "I'll come around and help you down." He started to rise, but this time he stopped because Dr. Woodhouse had a tight grip on the sleeve of his jacket. He expected that she would release him as soon as he sat, and when she didn't, he was the one who raised an eyebrow. "Yes?"

"You are being deliberately obtuse."

"You're giving me too much credit. There's folks who will tell you I can be obtuse without even trying." He thought she might have growled at the back of her throat, and because he was imagining her fingers as talons, he was grateful when she released his sleeve.

The question she had not wanted to ask directly finally came out in a single burst of sound. "Did he tell you that I was a woman?"

Ben took a moment to study her. It was hard not to linger on her mouth, especially since she was worrying the inside of her lower lip, harder still not to think about nibbling on it himself. He blinked, met her eyes through the glass shield of her spectacles, and pushed all carnal thought to that mysterious part of his brain where he stored information about square roots and conjugating Latin verbs. "No," he said finally. "Doc didn't mention it. He probably figured I would be able to work that out on my own."

Chapter Two

"I suppose you think you're clever," Ridley said, and the way she said it left no doubt that she held a very different opinion.

"Clever?" he asked. A small vertical crease appeared between his dark orange eyebrows, and he seriously considered her observation. "No. I guess I don't. Just about anyone seeing you step off the train would have recognized you straightaway as a woman. Maybe Waite Givens would have had a little trouble, but that's because he has to squint something fierce to see past the end of his own nose."

Ridley huffed, but it was done delicately. She had mastered tempering her frustration, and although she felt it keenly, she refused to be riled at this early juncture and by this man. She could not imagine why Dr. Dunlop had chosen Ben Madison to meet her at the station and help her establish her practice in Frost Falls. He did not impress her as the serious sort, and she meant to be taken seriously.

She was prepared to put the question to him again, this time in a way that could not possibly be misconstrued, when he turned his back on her and jumped down from the buckboard. He looped the mare's reins around a portion of the whitewashed picket fence before he walked to her side of the wagon and held out a hand. She gave him her black satchel and alighted from the buckboard without assistance.

"So that's how it's going to be," he said, grinning.

Ridley frowned. "What do you mean?"

He handed her back her bag before she asked for it. "Oh, you know, refusing help because you figure you have to prove you can do it on your own." Ben shrugged. "Whatever *it* is."

"That's ridiculous. I ask for assistance when I need it." She pointed to the trunks and valises in the bed of the buckboard. "You'll help me with those, won't you?"

"Sure." He plucked two bags from the wagon and started walking toward the house. Under his breath, he said, "But I'm not wrong about the other."

"I heard that."

"Meant you to."

Ridley stared at his retreating back. Realizing that she was faintly slack-jawed, she snapped her teeth together and dragged one of the small trunks toward the edge of the wagon bed. She placed her black bag on top and lifted the trunk by its brass handles. It was heavier than she recalled, but she was able to heft it as high as her midriff and support its weight against her. Ben stepped aside for her on the walk as he was returning to the buckboard. He let her pass without offering assistance. There was no hint that he was amused by her insistence on self-sufficiency, but neither was there any indication that he was particularly pained by it. Whatever he was thinking, he was keeping it to himself.

Ridley decided she was just fine with that.

He'd left the front door open for her and set her valises on the floor off to one side of the vestibule. She hadn't noticed if he had produced a key to get inside or whether the door had been left unlocked. Perhaps Frost Falls was the kind of place where people never locked their doors.

Ridley was curious about the house, more so about the surgery, but she quelled the urge to explore in favor of returning for another of the small trunks. When she stepped back on the porch, she saw Ben was carrying it. That left the impossibly heavy trunk on the buckboard. There was no point in trying to move it alone, and she was not entirely sure that she and Ben could carry it together. She waited on the lip of the porch for him to appear.

He brushed past her without a word and she hurried after him. "I don't think we can manage it. Perhaps you will be able to carry your end, but I'm not sure that I can carry mine."

Ben looked to his right and left and then glanced behind him. "Do you see anyone else around?"

"No."

"Then it's up to us." He held out his right hand, palm up. "Key?"

Ridley opened her black-and-white-beaded reticule and began rummaging. When she produced the key for the brass-bound trunk, she placed it in the flat of his palm.

Ben unlocked the trunk, lifted the twin brass latches, and raised the lid. It was indeed filled with books. He picked up the first book that caught his eye and examined the lurid cover, which featured a young woman wearing a diaphanous night shift and an extravagantly large hat with more feathers than an ostrich. The feathers dipped low because she was artfully poised in a swoon over the manly arm of a gentleman scoundrel. Ben read the title aloud. "*Felicity Ravenwood Tames the Beast.*" Arching an eyebrow in dramatic fashion, he turned to Ridley. "Medical reference book?"

She tried to snatch the dime novel from his hand, but he raised his arm and kept it out of her reach. There was no dignity in jumping for it so she set her chin at a haughty angle and turned away. She began removing books from the trunk.

Ben did not join her. He read the synopsis from the back cover. "It says here that Miss Felicity Ravenwood has a startling adventure when she is abducted in the Black Forest." He looked up. "Isn't that in Germany?"

Ridley snapped, "Felicity travels the world."

"Oh. Maybe she should think about staying closer to home. Unless she is German. Is she?"

"No. Her home is in Manhattan."

"Plenty of scoundrels there."

"No doubt," said Ridley.

"I know it for a fact. My sister-in-law, Phoebe, was raised in Manhattan. Of course, she met scoundrels out here, too. Train robbery before she reached Frost Falls. Remington— that's my brother—more or less saved the day, but some say he's a scoundrel himself. Felicity Ravenwood have any adventures like that?"

Ridley's foot beat a tattoo. "Mr. Madison. Please." She watched him make a show of reluctance in surrendering the book. He placed it on top of the stack in her arms and she tucked it in place with her chin.

"Maybe you'll lend it to me later."

She sighed. "If you like."

Ben began collecting books, choosing the thicker, heavier tomes. "I'd like that just fine."

Ridley headed for the house. With the books piled so high in her arms, she had some difficulty seeing where she was going. She hesitated at the steps and then used the toe of one shoe to probe for the riser. When she found it, she climbed the first step, balanced herself, and used the same technique to locate the next step. Her mistake was thinking there were only two. She expected to be on the porch with the third, and when she wasn't, she stumbled forward and would have taken an ignominious fall if Ben had not dropped his armload of books and hauled her back.

For an odd moment, she was seized by the idea that she was still falling. The cascading thud of the books disoriented her into thinking the sound was her hitting the porch face-first. She shook her head slowly, steadying herself, and then found a similar equilibrium for her scattered thoughts.

"Thank you," said Ridley. She was aware of Ben's arm looped around her waist. Her spine was pressed solidly against him. It was rather more comfortable than not, and the longer he held her in place, the more intimate the gesture seemed. *That* was not comfortable. "I'm fine, thank you. Really, you can release me."

He did. "Careful you mind the books that I dropped. Better yet, let me get them out of your way." He stooped and began to pick them up, starting with those that had fallen in her direct path. "Go on."

Ridley hurried into the house. She was almost sure she heard him chuckling, but believed it was the wiser course to let him have his fun without commenting. She was not one for blushing. It was a blessing that she rarely showed any outward signs of embarrassment. She'd been accused of being unnaturally self-possessed, and while her ability to remain composed in difficult circumstances made her an asset in the operating theater, that same sangfroid in social settings made her seem aloof, untouched and untouchable.

Ridley set her armful of books on the stairs leading to the second floor. When Ben entered the house, she directed him to do the same. "I'll decide where I want to put them once I am familiar with the house."

Shrugging, Ben set them down and left again to get another stack. Ridley trailed behind him. It took three trips to unload enough books to make the trunk light enough for Ben to carry. Her offers to assist fell on deaf ears, so she made sure there was a clear space in the vestibule where he could set it.

"Are you sure you don't want me to unload the last of the books and carry this upstairs? You'll probably have use for it for blankets and linens and such."

It was a good suggestion, but it meant she'd have to clear the stairs of all the books that were currently blocking his path. "Just put it down for now. I'd like to think about how best to use it before it's moved upstairs."

"All right." He dropped the trunk after making sure his toes and hers were out of the way. The floor vibrated beneath his feet. "You want to look around?"

"I do." She opened her reticule and began rummaging inside again.

Ben held out the trunk key. "Here. You gave it to me, remember?"

She nodded but made no move to take it. "I'm not looking for that. But thank you. You can drop it in."

Ben did. "Kinda adds to the clutter, doesn't it?"

"Nothing in here is clutter, Mr. Madison," she said with some asperity. "Necessity. All of it."

"Uh-huh."

She ignored him. "Found it." Ridley extracted her change purse and unclasped it. She removed two carefully folded bills and some coins and held them out to him. "For your trouble."

Ben stared at her offering and then at her. He gave a bark of laughter that communicated real enjoyment.

Ridley frowned. She was certain what she was holding in her hand was a generous tip. No doorman, bellboy, cab driver, or porter would have laughed at it. Could things really be so different here? "I'm sorry," she said. "Not enough?" When she opened the change purse again, he stopped her by placing a hand over hers. The contact startled Ridley and her head snapped up. Her reaction was not enough for Ben to remove his hand so she slid it out from under his. She thrust the money and the change purse back inside her reticule and lowered her arms. "Where I come from, it is customary to tip. I'm afraid I am not familiar with how things are done here."

Ben's laughter had faded away but his grin had not. "Mostly people just help each other out. That's what I was doing and what plenty of others would have done if Doc had asked them. Save your money, and when there is someone doing a service for you, offer him a third of what you were holding out to me. You don't want to get a reputation for throwing money away. People will think you're foolish, not generous."

She nodded once. "I understand. Did I insult you?"

"Insult me? No. I don't even know if that's possible."

"Thick-skinned?"

"Dull-witted. I don't know an insult even when it's poking me in the chest."

Ridley knew that was an outright lie. He was neither thick-skinned nor dull-witted. What he was, was unflappable. She had tried to dismiss him with the tip, but he was not having any of that. He was just waiting her out, staying put until he was satisfied that she was at least partially settled.

"You're familiar with the house?" she asked.

"I am. Spent my fair share of evenings here jawing with Doc." He rubbed the back of his neck where the faint webbing of old scars puckered and made his skin tighten. "Spent some time being tended by him, too."

"Would you show me around, then?"

"It'd be my pleasure."

Ridley blinked. He was completely, perfectly sincere. She didn't quite know what to make of it. She had spent so much time in the company of people, most of them men, who said all the right things but seldom meant them. She was used to being tolerated, not appreciated, and when someone responded as Ben Madison had, there was generally an undertone that alerted her to a quid pro quo. Sometimes the undertone made her skin crawl.

That was not the case now. She could admit that she should have placed more faith in her godfather's judgment. If she made allowances for Mr. Ben Madison's rather peculiar dry sense of humor, perhaps he was the right person to have met her train.

Ben invited her to precede him into the parlor on the left. Ridley walked to the center of the cozy room and slowly turned to take in the appointments. The wide arms of all the upholstered furniture were covered in antimacassars. They might have been white once upon a time, but they were faintly yellowed now with age and what she suspected was smoke. She breathed deeply and caught the stale smell of it in the air.

"What happened to the housekeeper?" she asked.

"Couldn't say, except she took Doc's leaving pretty hard. I don't believe that she's been here since he's been gone."

Ridley kept her thoughts about that to herself. A large brushed velvet sofa the color of an eggplant dominated the room. The cushions on either end were shiny with wear. Two chairs that complemented the sofa in style, if not color, were situated so the three pieces formed a triangle where conversation might comfortably take place. The side tables were covered in a thin layer of dust that Ridley did not have to run her finger through to see. The wallpaper's true color was revealed in the rectangular spaces where paintings had once hung. There was a large area above the mantelpiece where the clusters of pink hydrangeas looked especially bright and the greenery was nearly vibrant.

Ridley pointed to the space above the mantel. "Do you recall what hung there?"

"A cityscape. Boston. I asked him about it once, and he told me that he'd brought it with him. He'd settled here, was important in the community, but he cherished the painting. I guess he cherished his roots, too. I don't know anyone who wasn't surprised when word got out that he was leaving."

Ridley nodded, and she remained thoughtful in her silence.

Ben pointed to the stove in the corner. "When it's deep winter in these parts, you'll want to fire up the wood burner, but the fireplace will keep you warm enough most evenings if you prefer it. There are folks who make a living hauling and splitting wood. I can give you some names. Mary Cherry knows them, too, if it's your intention to hire her."

"I'm sorry, but now that I've seen the neglect, I'm undecided."

"I thought maybe you were. She should've had the place shined up for you. I'm guessing Doc asked her to. I suspect she's grieving some, so maybe you can give her leave to do that before you make your decision. Doc valued her."

"Were they . . ." She did not finish the sentence and hoped he would do it for her.

"Lovers? Couldn't say. I never asked straight out. Figured it was none of my business. Folks come down on both sides of that question but only Doc and Mary Cherry know for sure. She's married, if that counts for anything. Anson Cherry hires on as a wrangler when the mood strikes him, but that's less and less as the years pass."

"So Mrs. Cherry needs the work."

"She does, but that doesn't mean there aren't others who would hire her. No one could steal her away from Doc, but there are probably some who think they have an opportunity now."

"Thank you. That's good to know."

Nodding, he led the way into the kitchen, where Ridley halted her steps in front of the iron behemoth and stared at it. "You've seen a stove before, haven't you?" he asked.

"Never one this big. How old is it?"

"No idea."

She sighed. "I don't suppose he cared since he probably never touched it. Poor Mrs. Cherry." Ridley looked around. Doc had not taken his china, though it did not appear that he had many pieces. The cupboard had enough mismatched pieces to serve three, perhaps four if someone was willing to use a bread and butter plate as a dinner plate and use a teacup without a saucer. Pots and pans were stacked on the bottom shelf of a serving cart; the surface of the oak kitchen table showed scars and stains, evidence of years of food preparation and dining. Ridley was vaguely surprised all the chairs matched.

She followed Ben through the unremarkable and little-used dining room to that part of the house that interested her more than any other, and she was not disappointed. Ridley could look past the film of dust on the walnut desk and merely appreciate it for its size. Nearly as long as the sofa in the parlor, this desk would hold her important correspondence and files and notes and current research books. All of her other books would fit easily on the built-in cases that lined two walls. She was tempted to sit in the dark burgundy leather chair behind the desk and test its fit. There were two spindle-legged chairs for patients on the other side of the desk. Like so many things, the seat covers were faded to a pale mossy green. There was no paper on these walls, and Ridley imagined they had once been painted to match the seat covers. She easily found the space where her godfather had hung his diploma, and thought she might try to have that leafy green color matched when she repainted.

The surgery had its own entrance so patients did not have to come through the house. When her father had practiced medicine outside the hospital, their home had been similarly arranged. She remembered using that entrance when she brought her dolls in for diagnosis and treatment. Her father never failed to make them better and he always had a sweet for them because they were such good patients. She decided that she would keep a jar of peppermints nearby for the children.

Ridley was just stepping over the threshold of the surgery when Ben caught her by the elbow and pulled her back. She looked at him, surprised by the firmness of his grip and the force he used to make her retreat. She opened her mouth to ask what he was about, but her question remained unspoken.

"Let me go first," he said, releasing her. He squeezed past her to enter the surgery. Broken glass crunched beneath his boots. "Didn't want you stepping on that. There's a lot of it."

Caught up in the memory of her father's care and kindness, Ridley had not noticed the shards of glass scattered on the floor. "What's broken?" she asked, bending for a closer look.

"What's not?"

"That's hardly a satisfactory answer."

Ben crossed the floor to the large white hutch. Glass panes were set in the double doors that closed over the upper half of the cabinet. Those doors, which were never locked, were flung open. The narrow shelves were almost entirely bare, but Ben knew that this was where Doc kept the medicines and ingredients for poultices and salves. Below, the hutch's locked cabinets had been forced open. The inside had been similarly rifled and laid bare. Doc's most powerful drugs were missing, and in their haste, the thieves had left a trail of broken glass bottles. Some of the glass was clear, but there were also shards of amber and cobalt blue. Powdered medicine was sprinkled over the glass.

"His medicine cabinet, I presume," Ridley said, coming to stand beside Ben.

"That's right."

"It looks as if whoever broke in dropped as much as he took."

"Looks that way."

"Do you know how much he kept here?"

"Couldn't say. Mary—"

"Yes," said Ridley. "Mary Cherry will know."

"Right again."

"We passed an apothecary. I saw it. Why wouldn't a thief go there for medicine?"

"Because this place has been deserted for a while and Mickey Mangold lives above his business and would have been sure to raise the alarm. Clumsy, not stupid. Or not completely stupid." He shook his head at the mess. "Too big of a hurry to do the job carefully."

Ridley was inclined to agree, but there were other possibilities she felt compelled to mention. "Alcohol," she said.

"Yeah, might've been liquored up."

"Or smoking the pipe. Is opium a problem here?"

"Not here. Not yet. There are parlors in Denver that cater to the opium eaters. Still, it's something to consider."

"Yes, well, shouldn't we allow the sheriff to consider it? I believe we passed his office on our way from the station."

"We did. I'll let him know. Damage is done; no reason to run after him now. I'm going to find a broom and dustpan. Try not to move. You don't want to put glass through your shoes."

"In the kitchen," she said. When he regarded her oddly, she explained. "The broom and dustpan are in the kitchen."

Ben thanked her and returned quickly with both. He held one item in each hand and asked her to choose.

"Broom," she said, taking it from him. She began sweeping in small circles while he used the dustpan to shovel some of the glass toward her.

They worked slowly, carefully, and had the floor in relatively good condition in under fifteen minutes.

"It will have to be mopped," he told her. "There's no telling how many slivers are between the floorboards or in the wood grain."

"I understand." She held up a hand to stay him from saying what she was sure was coming next. "I know. Mary Cherry."

He grinned. "Just something to think about."

Ridley took the dustpan from his hand and made a shooing motion with the broom. "I've seen the house, and I thank you for your help. I'll be fine. You should go for the sheriff now."

"I will. It might be a while before he gets here. There's no real emergency, and I know he's got a local reprobate in a jail cell. Could be he has some responsibilities there first."

"That's all right. This is hardly a priority."

"Well, it won't be at the bottom of his list. I'll make sure he's back before it gets dark."

"You have some influence there?"

"A little. I know his family real well." With that, he turned and left by the surgery door.

Ridley followed his exit with her eyes, riveted by his easy walk, the amble in his gait. When he was out of sight, she went to the door, closed and locked it, and then leaned back against it. She closed her eyes.

When that didn't diminish the ache behind her heavy lids and heavier heart, she let the tears fall.

Chapter Three

Ben's first order of business was to return the buckboard to the livery. He hoped someone other than the owner would be there to take possession of the wagon and mare, but that hope was dashed when grim-faced Hank Ketchum stepped out of the yard.

"Saw you earlier," said Ketchum as Ben jumped down from his seat.

"I know. I waved to you."

"So you did, but now I'm wonderin' who that was with you. Thought you needed this equipage for the new doc. What happened? Did he get cold feet or just miss a connection?"

"Oh, Dr. Woodhouse will be along directly."

Ketchum gave the mare a slap on the rump and she dutifully began walking toward the livery. "I can't say I blame you for giving the young lady a ride. Quite the proper miss she was."

"You could tell that from where you were standing?"

Ketchum nodded sharply. "Spine like a ramrod, that one. And the hat? Never imagined a hat like that outside of a Felicity Ravenwood dime novel."

Ben wanted to howl with laughter but he let Ketchum's observation go unremarked. He jerked his thumb over his shoulder to indicate the street behind him. "Have to be going, Hank. Jeremiah Salt is still sitting in a cell. Can't keep him there much longer."

It was hardly an exaggeration that Hank Ketchum's shoulders were set as narrowly as his eyes. When he shrugged them, as he did now, they just about touched his earlobes. "And I can't say that anyone would care if you did."

"He's got a wife and children."

"Them least of all."

Ben knew Ketchum was right, but there was the law, and drunk and disorderly did not get you a life sentence. Ben nodded shortly, touched the brim of his hat, and thanked Hank for the use of the buckboard before he headed to his office.

On his way to the livery, he'd seen the Saunders brothers standing outside his office. He acknowledged them as he passed but didn't slow to inquire if they were loitering there for a reason. They owned a good piece of the boardwalk in front of the land office for doing nothing and they frequently used it for just that purpose. He would count it as a good thing if it were a dispute that brought them across the street and not questions about his companion on the buckboard.

He slowed his steps a little as he saw that two more citizens had joined the brothers. He recognized Bob Washburn, the longtime manager of the Jones Prescott Bank, and Amanda Springer, the president of the Presbyterian Ladies Giving Circle for the last twelve years. Ben had no idea how to prepare himself for what surely was coming and, for the second time that day, wished Jackson Brewer had not got it in his head to take his wife to Paris.

When the group parted as he approached, Ben saw there was a fifth person there to greet him. Buzz Winegarten, the proprietor of the town's only saloon, was sitting in Ben's chair with his left foot propped on the stool that Ben had fashioned for himself. The foot was shoeless and sockless and wrapped in enough gauze to make it half again its natural size.

"Shall we go inside?" Ben asked. "No need to conduct business out here."

"There is," Washburn said, pushing his spectacles up the bridge of his nose. "Give it a moment."

Ben had his hand on the doorknob, but he didn't push. He waited. It was only a matter of seconds before he heard the reason the gathering had chosen to remain outside. Jeremiah Salt was making one hell of a racket.

"I'll take care of it," he said. He went inside and shut the door firmly behind him. He was tempted to cover his ears as he walked through the front office to the pair of cells at the back. In addition to his caterwauling, Jeremiah also had a lot of percussion going on. It sounded as if he was running a tin cup back and forth across the bars of his cage.

Ben waited for a natural pause in the cacophony before he entered the back room. Jeremiah's cell was littered with the detritus of his cold breakfast since he hadn't woken to eat it hot. At some point the tin plate had been hurled against the bars, and in a miscalculation on Jeremiah's part, the plate had sailed between the bars and now lay on the floor at Ben's feet. Ben kicked it aside and regarded Jeremiah rather dolefully. He shook his head to add to the appearance that he was disappointed, not angry.

"Quite a mess you made, Mr. Salt, and if you think I'm only talking about this little tantrum, you'd be mistaken."

Jeremiah Salt did not reach Ben's six-foot height, but he had powerfully broad shoulders, thickly muscled arms, and fists like anvils. He owned the forge and had been standing over molten metal most of his life, fashioning shoes for horses, hoops for barrels, rims for carriage wheels, and every other thing that folks needed. He made nails, tacks, and spindles to order. He made hinges and handles and hammerheads.

He was a hard worker, a fair-to-middling provider, and when he wasn't drinking, a decent family man. The problem was he drank often and often drank well past his tolerance. While he was friendly, even gregarious and good-natured when he was sober, he was as mean and unpredictable as a rabid dog when he was drunk.

Jeremiah stepped away from the bars, retreating until he felt the bed frame against the back of his legs. His knees folded under him and he sat down heavily on the cot. The tin cup clattered to the floor as he unfolded his fists. He bent his head and plowed his fingers into his unruly black hair. He held his head steady in a vise fashioned by his own hands and stared at his knees.

Ben was familiar with Jeremiah Salt's penitent posturing and remained unmoved. His experience with the blacksmith went back to his earliest days as a deputy when Sheriff Brewer sent him to remove Jeremiah from the Songbird. Brewer hadn't made it clear that Ben should escort Jeremiah to a cell, so Ben wheedled and cajoled and finally managed to get Jeremiah home, where he could sleep off the drink in his own bed.

After Ben left, Jeremiah gave his wife the beating he'd wanted to give Ben.

"I'm not letting you out yet, Mr. Salt. I'm not sure you're sober. Did you eat any of the breakfast I left for you?"

Jeremiah's head came up. "Why would I? It was stone cold."

Ben shrugged. "Couldn't be helped since you wouldn't get up. Figured you didn't need a lunch brought in since your breakfast was still untouched when I left."

"Yeah, about that. What kind of lawman are you, leaving me locked up and unattended? Brewer never did that."

"Brewer had me to keep an eye on you. I don't have a deputy yet. A few men have expressed interest but I haven't made my choice."

"Better not be that Springer kid."

"Jim Springer's son?"

"*Amanda* Springer's son. He's been a mama's boy from the cradle. Jim's got no stake in raising him. Never has."

"Now, you're not saying that because you heard Mrs. Springer talking outside, are you?" Ben watched Jeremiah Salt shrug those powerful shoulders and knew he was right. The Presbyterian Ladies Giving Circle was also the temperance society, and Amanda Springer was once again their leader. "I'm going to give you a broom. You can sweep your mess onto this plate." Ben picked up the tin plate, set it on its side, and rolled it between two bars. "A little work will help you sober up."

Jeremiah pointed to the pail in one corner of the cell. "I pissed away most of the drink."

"Not emptying the bucket yet," said Ben. "Getting you a broom now, and when you're done, you slide it through the bars. I won't be standing where I am now if you're holding a broom." There were some who might describe what Jeremiah did as grinning. Ben thought of it as a baring of teeth. That, more than anything else, let Ben know that Jeremiah hadn't used the bucket nearly often enough. The man was still full of piss and vinegar.

Ben retrieved a broom and set it inside the cell while Jeremiah was still sitting on the bed. "I'm going to deal with the folks who came by to see me. I'm advising you now not to make another ruckus. I feel certain the Saunders brothers are here to see me about that. Unless you want me to put one of them in charge when I leave again, you'll find another way to entertain yourself. Nod if you understand."

Jeremiah Salt nodded. He was no longer baring his teeth. In fact, when Ben left him, he looked every bit as glum as Hank Ketchum.

Ben shut the door to the cells and then invited his visitors inside. He had two chairs opposite his own behind the desk and a bench against the wall below at least twenty wanted posters and governmental notices. Amanda immediately seated herself in one of the chairs while Buzz Winegarten hobbled to the other. Dave and Ed Saunders paired up on the bench and offered to make room for the banker. Bob Washburn thanked them but decided to remain standing. He took up a position beside the cold stove and rested one hand on the top. It was a statesmanlike pose and served as a reminder to everyone present that he meant to run for the general assembly in the next election.

Ben took a seat at his desk. He moved some papers around, cleared a place to set his folded hands, and waited to see who would speak first. He had his money on Amanda Springer, but there was a reason he did not make wagers. He lost.

Dave Saunders was sitting directly below a poster that offered five hundred dollars for a man who looked suspiciously like Dave Saunders. Ben refrained from interrupting Dave to point this out.

"Ed and I came here because we could hear Jeremiah carrying on something fierce from across the street. Seemed unusual, even for him. Thought maybe we should investigate."

"Did you?" asked Ben.

"Well," Dave drawled, "we didn't. We weren't sure it was our place once we got here."

Ed spoke up. He was the younger brother, less apt to speak first but always there to support Dave. He had a cherub's round face and a bit of a double chin. His wide blue eyes lent him an innocence no man in his forties deserved. In contrast, Dave was lean and square-jawed. He also had blue eyes, but the expression was shrewd and faintly suspicious. The brothers worked well together. They married the Hoover sisters. Dave and Dotty lived above the land office. Ed and Abigail had a home on a side street not more than a stone's throw away.

"We got to talking," said Ed. "Dave and me first, then Bob here joined us. The question of your deputy came up. Or the lack of the same. Could have saved ourselves a passel of worry if you had a deputy to see to things while you're out of the office."

"Odd you should mention that. Jeremiah just expressed that same sentiment to me." Ben turned his attention to Amanda Springer. "Is your son still interested in the position?"

Amanda Springer stared at Ben, her eyes widening in equal parts shock and horror. "Hitchcock? My Hitchcock?"

"You have just the one son, don't you?"

"Well, yes, but—"

"Hitch didn't tell you he expressed interest in being my deputy?"

"Well, no, but—"

"Tell him to stop by tomorrow." Given Amanda's reaction, Ben doubted she would mention anything except her strong disapproval. "Mr. Washburn, what about you?"

"There's a bank matter I'd like to discuss, but it can wait until morning. It wouldn't be proper to talk about it in front of others. You'll be here?"

"I will."

When Washburn nodded, assured now that he would have Ben's ear, his spectacles slid from their perch. He pushed them back. "I'll see you then." He left the office and was followed in short order by the Saunders brothers.

Ben's gaze returned to Amanda and then shifted to Buzz. "What can I do for you?"

Buzz spoke through gritted teeth, pointing to his swollen foot. "I want to know when the damn doctor is going to get here. My big toe is killing me, and I can hardly stand long enough to pour drinks. I got my nephew Lincoln helping behind the bar, but I don't trust that he doesn't have his fingers in the till when I'm not looking. Could be when I'm better, I'm gonna have you arrest him."

Before Ben could formulate an answer, Amanda inserted herself into the conversation. "I also want to know what happened to the doctor. I saw you driving a woman in the direction of the Butterworth. Did she distract you from your purpose? I was under the impression that Dr. Woodhouse was arriving today."

Grimacing, Buzz looked her over in a most unfavorable way. "What's so wrong with you that you need to see the doc?"

"Nothing is wrong, and I would not entertain the subject with you if there were." She sniffed disdainfully and turned her attention back to Ben. "The Ladies Giving Circle would like to invite Dr. Woodhouse to a tea to welcome him and introduce ourselves."

"Self-important biddies." Buzz spoke out of the side of his mouth but that did not stop him from being understood.

Ben gave the saloonkeeper a quelling look that was mostly for Amanda's benefit. It would not stop Buzz Winegarten from speaking his mind. A Colt Peacemaker aimed at Buzz's head was likely to be similarly ineffective, so Ben did not bother drawing his piece for show.

"Dr. Woodhouse will be along directly," said Ben.

"That's hardly a satisfactory answer," Amanda said.

It was the second time today he'd heard that. It did not bode well that Dr. Woodhouse said it first. "I can't hurry it along, Mrs. Springer, but when I see Dr. Woodhouse, I will be certain to bring up the subject of your tea."

Buzz pressed Amanda's point. "Tomorrow? The day after that?"

"Can't Mickey help you, Buzz? He must have something in the apothecary to ease your pain."

"He has lots of things, but he won't give me anything without the doc's okay. Damndest fool notion I ever heard. I bought a bottle of Ebenezer's Elixir from the last fellow that came through town carrying a case of cure-alls. Drank it down and threw it up. Good for a purge but not much else."

Amanda blanched. Ben shrugged apologetically, but Buzz was either oblivious or uncaring. Ben suspected it was the latter.

"She's a New York actress friend of Mrs. Frost's," said Amanda, recovering her voice.

"Pardon?" asked Ben.

"That woman you were taking to the Butterworth. She's a

friend of Mrs. Frost's." She didn't wait for Ben to affirm her statement. "Young Mrs. Frost, I mean. Phoebe, not Fiona. Although her hat put me instantly in mind of Fiona Frost, so maybe she is a mutual acquaintance."

Ben said nothing and wondered how long it would be before he heard the same thing from someone else's lips. Amanda required nothing but her own assumptions to create a story worth repeating.

Amanda Springer stood, drew back her shoulders until they were squared and her bosom was a shelf. She laid a hand on Buzz Winegarten's shoulder. "Come along, you old reprobate."

"I'm the same age as you, you old biddy."

"I'll make you a poultice for that toe of yours like a wife would do if you still had one."

He gave her a sour look. "Would still have one if you'd married me."

"You should have asked me, then."

"Thought it was understood."

"In your mind. Not mine." Satisfied that she had the last word for now, Amanda slipped a hand under his elbow and helped him to his feet.

Dumbfounded by what he'd heard, Ben still had the presence of mind to hurry to the door and hold it open for them. They managed to get to the sidewalk before they started arguing again. Ben closed the door on them and waited until he could no longer hear them bickering before he let loose the bark of laughter that was lodged in his throat.

"Everything all right in there?" Jeremiah hollered from the back.

"Fine," Ben said. He poked his head through the doorway so Jeremiah could see him. "I'm going out again. You mind yourself. I'll send dinner down from the Butterworth if there's someone willing to bring it. There aren't many do-gooders who want to do good for you. You might have to wait until I get back." He ducked out before Jeremiah could offer opinion or objection.

The Salt family lived in a two-story frame house a block back from Main Street but within sight of Jeremiah's forge.

The whitewashed front had faded to gray. The sides and back of the house had never known a coat of paint. The windows were small, gray like the rest of the house, and made the neglected flower boxes attached to the sills just seem that sad.

Ben had sufficient experience with the Salt family to know that Jeremiah provided his wife with an allowance, provided she asked, and provided he thought her request was not frivolous. If there was going to be extravagance, Jeremiah was the one to provide it, and in that way he kept everyone under his large, meaty thumb.

Ben knocked on the door and waited. He could hear scurrying on the other side, a shout, and some bumping and thumping as there was a race to answer the door. It was the oldest boy, a rail-thin lad of ten with hair every bit as black as his father's, who opened the door just wide enough to peer out. The boy regarded him suspiciously, and Ben suffered the inspection without comment because he was certain Clay Salt had his reasons. When the boy nodded as though satisfied, Ben said the first thing that came to his mind. "Shouldn't you be in school, Clay?"

"Ma said I could stay on account of I asked and she said I could."

"Huh. That never worked for me."

"You probably didn't ask right."

"Probably didn't." Ben tried to look through the small opening that Clay provided, but the interior of the room was too dark for him to see inside. "Is your ma here?"

"Sure. Where else would she be?" A small hand inserted itself between Clay's legs and tugged on his trousers. Clay wriggled and slapped at the hand. Its disappearance was accompanied by a squeal. "Little ones are here. Lizzie and Ham. Hannah's in school. Ma made her go."

"I see. She didn't ask right?"

"She didn't get a chance to ask at all. Ma pointed her to the door and she left."

"Are you going to let me in?" asked Ben.

"What for?"

"I want to speak with your mother."

"She's not receiving visitors," he said rather grandly.

"She'll receive me."

Clay squinted and tried to look around Ben. He pulled a frown. "Pa still locked up?"

"He is."

"You letting him out today?"

"Depends."

"On what?"

"On whether I get to speak to your mother or not. Now step aside, Clay. I appreciate you're the man of the family when your father's out."

Clay raised his pointed chin and set his gaze firmly on Ben. "I'm the man of this family when my father's in."

"I understand," said Ben, and didn't doubt for a moment that it was true. He gave Clay a few moments to save face before he placed the flat of his hand on the door. He did not have to exert any pressure. Clay opened it for him and escorted him to the front room.

"It's Sheriff Ben," said Clay.

Lily Salt was lying on her side on the sofa, a pillow under her head and a blanket pulled all the way up to her shoulders. She was holding a damp cloth over her right eye. She murmured something, perhaps a greeting, and started to rise. Her moan was easily interpreted for what it was.

"Stay where you are, Lily," said Ben. "There's no reason you have to get up for me." He felt a tug on his trousers and looked down. Little Lizzie was pulling on his leg. Unsure what to do, he patted her on the head rather awkwardly.

"She wants up," Clay told him. "Go on. She won't hurt you."

Ben was more concerned that he would hurt her. She looked fragile, as skinny as her brother and a third of the size. Now if young Ham had been asking for the same, Ben would have scooped him up without a second thought. Ham was a sturdy boy who raced from pillar to post on chubby legs and chortled every time he bumped into something. Lizzie continued to tug and Ham was nowhere in sight, so Ben bent and picked her up. She snuggled up to him like the coquette she was, blond curls sliding over his shoulder. One of her small sticky hands clutched the lapel of his jacket. The other batted lightly at his face.

"Clay," Lily said. "Take her. Sheriff Ben doesn't need her pestering him."

Ben shook his head. "I've got her, Clay. And she's latched on."

"Stuck to you is more like it," said Clay. "She was makin' a jam sandwich when you knocked."

"Ah." He licked his lips after Lizzie made a swipe at his mouth. "Blackberry." He smiled at Lizzie while watching Lily from the corner of his eye. She had settled back on the sofa and now even her left eye was closed. "How old is she?" he asked Clay, giving Lizzie a little bounce in his arms.

Clay said, "You can ask her. She likes to tell people."

Ben did, and Lizzie announced she was three. "Where's Ham?"

"Still workin' on his jam sandwich, I expect. There's not much that comes between Ham and food."

"Maybe you should check on him while I speak to your mother. Lizzie can stay if you don't want to take her."

Clay's mouth thinned momentarily. "I know what you're doin'." He held out his arms for his sister, and Ben managed to dislodge her without too much fussing.

"Thank you, Clay."

Clay took a deep breath to puff his thin chest and regarded Ben with defiant eyes. "She's gonna tell me what you say."

"I'm sure she will, you being the man of the family and all, but I have to say it to her first." It was clear to Ben that Clay did not like that answer, but the boy accepted it just the same. When he was gone, Ben pulled a chair close to the sofa and sat. He leaned forward so he could rest his forearms on his knees and regarded Lily frankly. "How bad is it?"

She raised the compress only long enough to show him that all of the color in her face framed her swollen eye.

Ben shook his head. Lily Salt had attended school most of the same years that he had. She'd been Lily Bryant back then, and he remembered her as one of the prettiest girls in the room. Her attendance had been sporadic because she was needed at home to tend to a mother who always seemed to be ill, but he'd been in awe that she always knew the answers to everything when she was there.

When Ben accepted the position as Jackson Brewer's deputy and left the Twin Star Ranch to make his home full time in Frost Falls, he'd been unsettled by his first encounter with Lily Salt. In all the years that he'd been back and forth between the ranch and town, he'd never run into her and, in truth, never had a thought of her, and he hoped that he had not revealed his surprise on the occasion of their first meeting. He reckoned that she was three years his senior and looked as if she had a decade on him.

"What else is wrong, Lily? You don't have to show me. Just tell me."

"My shoulder's out of joint. The right one. I tried putting it back, but I couldn't set it on my own. Nothing's broken. At least I don't think it is. Got some pain in my abdomen, some bruising. I am probably going to lose the baby."

"Oh, jeez, Lily. You're pregnant?"

She smiled wanly. "Not for long."

"Is that what set Jeremiah off?"

"I don't think he even knows. I haven't told him." She chuckled humorlessly. "He's never needed a reason."

"I've still got him in a cell. I can keep him maybe another night if you don't swear out a complaint, a lot longer if you do."

She started to shake her head, winced, and then held herself still. "I can't do that, Ben. For better or worse, he's my husband."

Ben knew she was going to say that, same as she always did, but he was still disappointed each time he heard it. "You've got some family," he said. "Do you ever think about sheltering with one of them for a while?"

"My brother's living over in Harmony—the town, not the state of mind—and he's got five young'uns of his own. Anyway, I'm not sure he treats his wife any better than Jeremiah treats me."

"What about your mother? I hear she's in Denver."

"Living with her sister. I can't go there; she won't have me. She says I abandoned her when I married Jeremiah. I don't suppose she's wrong. I couldn't tell her that Jeremiah didn't like me visiting her, or that he thought she was never as ill as she made out to be. I don't suppose he was wrong either."

"What about the church? There are people there that would help."

"I don't have much left but my pride, Ben. Let me keep that."

"He's going to kill you." Ben thought she might flinch at his plain speaking. She didn't.

"Probably," she said. "You'll get him then."

"Lily!"

He waited for her to say something. She didn't, but he observed a tear leak out from beneath the compress. He sighed. "He doesn't touch the children?"

"No. Never."

Ben nodded. "All right." He sat back and then stood. "Do you have anything to take for the pain?"

"Clay wheedled some laudanum from Mickey Mangold. A few other things as well. Clay's clever that way."

While that was certainly true, Ben thought, it was also true that the druggist knew what was going on in the Salt home. Mickey might not give anything to Buzz Winegarten for his aching toe, but he'd give Clay laudanum for Lily.

"I'll be back later to check on you," said Ben. "Tell Clay to expect me and not give me a hard time at the door."

Lily's weak smile appeared again. "I'll tell him," she said softly, and in no time at all she was asleep.

Chapter Four

It was dusk by the time Ben returned to the doctor's home. He had promised to arrive before dark and he considered his promise mostly kept. In another minute or so, it wouldn't have been.

He stood on the porch, shifting his weight from one foot to the other, his thumbs hooked in the waistband of his trousers above his gun belt. His jacket was unbuttoned but not spread so wide that the tin star on his vest was visible. As far as he knew, Dr. Woodhouse had never spied it.

Ben was occupied contemplating the exact color of the good doctor's hair when the door finally opened. Deep in contemplation as he was, it startled him some to come face-to-face with Dr. E. Ridley Woodhouse again, and for a few moments he simply stared at her, but mostly at her hair. *Chestnut?* he wondered. She had removed the navy blue straw hat with the extravagant pink bow. To his way of thinking, the fussy hat was an intriguing but incongruent accessory if her intention was to be taken seriously, and he very much believed that was her intention. And just that quick, his mind lurched back to his conversation with Amanda Springer. Without preamble, he said, "You've been invited to tea with the Presbyterian Ladies Giving Circle."

"Have I?" she said, surprised. "Already?"

"Friendly town."

"I see. Perhaps you better come and tell me all of it because I think it's quite likely that the invitation wasn't meant for me."

Ben took off his hat as he stepped into the house but he didn't put it up or set it down. He noticed right off that there were no longer any books on the stairs. The vestibule was also clear of the valises and the pair of small trunks. She had managed to drag the brassbound trunk into the parlor and now it rested in front of the sofa as a utilitarian coffee table.

"You've been busy," he said. He pointed overhead to where the bedrooms were. "Unpacked?"

"Mostly. I stopped to answer the door. Would you like a cup of tea? I was going to make a pot."

His eyebrows climbed his forehead. "You got that old stove fired up?"

"No. I haven't tried, but do you recall me telling you that I have no problem asking for help?" When he nodded, she went on. "I'm asking for help."

Ben was disappointed that he couldn't oblige. "It will have to wait, I'm afraid. I have a patient waiting for you. City doctors make house calls, don't they?"

"Of course, but you're not really serious."

Ben kept his gaze locked on hers until she'd had her fill of his sober and unsmiling features.

"You *are* serious."

"Yes, ma'am . . . Dr. Woodhouse."

"All right. Let me get my coat and bag. I'll only be a minute."

He called after her, "Leave the hat. It won't open any doors for you where we're going."

She reappeared with her coat over one shoulder and her medical bag in hand. The hat was nowhere to be seen. Ben took the bag while she shrugged into her coat, then he opened the door for her.

"Wait," she said. "I don't know if I have everything I'll need. What is the nature of the patient's distress?"

"Your patient is Lily Salt. She's been on the receiving end of her husband's fists. This isn't the first time. Nothing's broken, she says, but her shoulder's out of joint, and she can't reset it herself. I think, but don't know for a fact, that she's had some belly bruising. She says she will lose her baby." He noticed the doctor's fingers tighten on the handle of her bag. "Well? Do you have what you'll need?"

"Yes. Barring some complication, I believe I do." She waved him on and closed the door behind them. "Should I lock it? I locked the door to the surgery earlier, but that was from the inside. I don't have any keys."

"I don't think Doc ever locked his doors. I'll have to think on where he might have kept the keys, if he even had them any longer. I'm not hopeful. He should've given them to me." He could see that she was reluctant to leave the house open and unattended. "Your things will be fine. I promise."

She regarded him with a skeptical eye. "You can't promise that."

"Pretend I can. We should go," he said, and was glad when she did not offer further argument. She was right, of course, he couldn't promise that, but he believed the thief was done here and was unlikely to return at least until the doctor restored the contents of the medical cupboard.

At the end of the short walk to the street, Ben waited for her to close the picket gate before he pointed to the alley behind the Butterworth Hotel. "We're going this way. It will be faster."

"Truly?" she asked, falling in step beside him. "I have the impression you are hiding me."

"I have to tell you honest, Dr. Woodhouse, that your impression is nonsense. Have you already forgotten that I paraded you down the center of town like you were the queen of the Frost Falls Festival? And then there's that invitation to the Ladies Giving Circle tea that I secured for you. I spoke to Amanda Springer herself about it, and once you're acquainted with Mrs. Springer, you'll have some idea how that pained me."

"Hmm."

"What?" Ben asked. The alley was deserted, as he knew it would be. Businesses were closing or already closed, proprietors were locking up and heading home, and what lamps lighted rooms at the backs of the shops were extinguished. It was a real shame, he thought, that dusk had already turned to darkness. Ben figured he was familiar with the suspicious expression that lifted one of the doctor's eyebrows higher than the other and curled one corner of her mouth, but he'd like to have seen it nonetheless. Something about that look tickled him.

"*Is* there a Frost Falls Festival?"

"Uh, no. But that doesn't mean there can't be. I admit I'm partial to the idea now that it's come to me."

She stopped suddenly. "Are you the town fool, Mr. Madison, or playing at it for my benefit?"

"Do you mind if I think on that awhile?" Her heavily exaggerated sigh made him grin. He kept walking, having no doubt that she would catch up. "Have a care where you step. There are ruts that'll trip you up."

"Tell me again why we are walking behind the business establishments instead of in front of them."

"Speed."

"Right. That must be it." She gravitated toward the center of the alley, where the grooves from the wheels of delivery wagons were not generally a hindrance.

"Take my arm," Ben said, making his elbow available. He wasn't sure she would accept it, so he was pleasantly surprised when she did. "That's better, isn't it?"

"If you say so."

"You're walking more confidently, so I do say so." As if on cue, she stumbled hard and would have pitched forward if it hadn't been for his supporting elbow. "You did that on purpose."

She did not respond to the accusation. Instead, she said, "Tell me about the invitation to tea. How did that come to pass?"

"There's nothing mysterious about it. Amanda Springer is in charge of every important committee in town. There's your Presbyterian Ladies Giving Circle, the temperance society, the library board, Friends of the School, and the future Frost Falls Festival Committee."

"I see."

"Do you? Mrs. Springer can smooth the way for you."

"I was hoping my skills as a doctor would do that."

"I'm sure they will . . . in time. In the *mean*time, it cannot hurt to fall in with Mrs. Springer's plans."

"I thought Dr. Dunlop chose you to smooth my way."

"He did, and I'm offering you my best advice."

"I'm not interested in joining her committees."

"Well, there goes your chance to be queen of the festival."

"I take it back," she said. Under her breath, she added, "Village idiot."

"How's that again?" asked Ben, though he had heard her perfectly well. He also heard her sigh in response but gave her full marks for not dissembling or hesitating to answer.

"You are not the town fool at all, Mr. Madison. I believe you are the village idiot."

"Maybe, but I can light that stove of yours."

"Point taken."

"And you should probably wait until you're asked to join one of Mrs. Springer's committees before you decide against it."

"Invitation only, then."

"That's right."

"I can make myself perfectly disagreeable, you know."

"That was never a question in my mind."

She chuckled. "All right. I deserved that." She paused to shake off something stuck to the bottom of her fashionably pointed shoe. For the first time, she was glad for the darkness. She did not want to know what she had dislodged. "How much farther?"

"About a hundred yards. Is that a problem?"

"Hardly. I walked miles every day along hospital corridors and I could still take the stairs two at a time when I needed to." She fell quiet for a while, then, "What precisely is wrong with my hat?"

Ben had been concentrating on where to put his feet so he didn't fall or turn an ankle. Now his head snapped up and his brow puckered. "How's that again?"

"My hat," she said. "You told me it wouldn't open any doors where we're going."

"Did I? Huh."

"You're avoiding answering my question."

"Nothing gets past you."

"Still avoiding." When he remained silent, she said, "It's the bow, isn't it? Too pink."

"Too fussy," he said. "And too pink."

"I believe I saw more elaborate hats on the way through town."

"I'm sure you did, but none of those women want to be doctors." Although they were no longer touching, Ben felt her stiffen beside him, and he knew immediately that there was nothing in the alleyway that he could have stepped in that was to be avoided more than what he had just stepped in.

"I don't want to be a doctor," she said in clipped city accents. "I *am* a doctor."

"Well, I know that's what you say." He went on hurriedly. "And I believe you without seeing that diploma of yours, but if you don't want to have to show it off everywhere you go, you'll need to think about looking the part."

"It's *not* a part."

Ben shortened his stride to match the way she had slowed her pace. He cleared his throat. "The spectacles are a good touch. They give you a studied, sober air. Do you need them?"

She sucked in a breath. "You know I have sharp implements in this bag, don't you?"

"Did you maybe not see that I have a gun?"

"I took an oath to do no harm, but I am seriously considering breaking it."

"Bet you want to hit me with that bag."

"In my mind, I am aiming for the back of your head."

He rubbed the spot she was talking about as if he could feel it. His hat tipped forward slightly. "Good aim. Strong arm." Ben righted his hat. "Look, Dr. Woodhouse, it's going to be hard enough for some folks to accept you as a doc when you're not wearing a fancy go-to-meeting, go-to-church, or go-to-tea hat, and when you are wearing the hat, folks, especially women folks, will admire it, want to copy it, and whisper about who looks best in it, but what they won't do is believe that you know a darn thing about doctoring."

Ben paused, said more quietly, "I figured you should know, I just didn't figure on telling you all of it tonight."

When she remained silent, he added, "Maybe it's different in the East, in the city, but you being a female doctor is going to take some getting used to. Doc knew it, too, and it's a disappointment to me that after all these years being a part of this community, he up and left you and me on our own. I don't know how you feel about that, you being his goddaughter and all, but I'm peeved."

She said nothing, and Ben did not insert himself into her thoughts. They were passing behind the cells at the rear of his office. He swore he could hear Jeremiah Salt snoring on the other side of the wall. It looked as if he would have to make good on his promise to take a dinner to his prisoner.

"Doc's dying," she said.

Now it was Ben who stopped in his tracks. He reached for her elbow to hold her back and was relieved when she didn't shake him off. "Say that again," he said. "I heard you, but I need to hear it again." Ben's eyes narrowed as he peered through the deep curtain of nightfall, and he observed the slow but distinct movement of the doctor's head. She was nodding as if she understood his need to hear the horrible truth one more time.

"It's cancer," she said. "Belly cancer, most likely, from his description of the symptoms. Probably intestinal, colon more specifically. Do you know where the colon is, what it does?"

"Yes. Never saw human parts, but I've shot, skinned, and dressed enough deer and elk and slaughtered enough cows and pigs to know about the parts." Ben realized he was still holding her elbow. He released her and touched his fingertips to his furrowed brow. Closing his eyes, he rubbed gently. "Jesus, Mary, and Joseph," he said under his breath. "It's a death sentence, isn't it?"

"Yes. I'm afraid so. I don't think there's anything else that would have dislodged him from Frost Falls. Maybe if you shot him from a cannon, but I have my doubts about that."

"What about that teaching position he talked about? Was that a fiction?"

"No. My father offered that to him as an inducement to return to Boston. There are new protocols for the type of cancer we think he has, and my father wants him to have the best care."

"So he really is your godfather."

"He is. I only met him twice, both times when I was very young, but we kept up a steady correspondence over the years so it is not as if I didn't know him."

"All right. I can understand better why Doc left, but what the hell was he thinking encouraging you to come here?"

Her chin came up. "I am choosing not to be insulted by your question, and I think we should go. I have a patient waiting, don't I?"

"Yes, but—" He stopped because she was already on the move. He let her go a ways before he double-timed it to catch her. "We're almost there. That's Jeremiah's forge on our right that we're about to pass, and that's his house over there." He pointed off to his left where murky yellow light from a pair of oil lamps outlined windows on the first floor. "Hannah will have come home from school by now. She wasn't here when I stopped in earlier. She's eight, maybe nine. Clay is ten. There's Lizzie, who's three, and Ham, short for Hamilton, who is four. The little ones will be pleased to make your acquaintance. I can't speak for Clay and Hannah. They are very protective of Lily."

"Why should my visit threaten them?"

"They know there could be retribution if their father finds out, and they can't depend on Lizzie and Ham to keep a secret."

"Where is the father now?"

"Jail." He couldn't tell whether that surprised her, but he did not think it did. When they reached the narrow path to the house, he led the way. "Jeremiah won't be there much longer unless Lily wants to press charges."

"So you did speak to the sheriff," she said. "I wondered when he didn't stop by and then again when he didn't accompany you."

"You'll meet him directly, I expect." And now he was grateful for the dark because he didn't have to look her in the eye. He rapped on the front door and waited. The sounds he heard coming from the interior were similar to what he'd heard before: some shouting, thumping, a squeal, and pounding feet.

"I think someone just peeked out the window," she said. "I suppose they've learned to be cautious. Oh, there's that little head again. It's the little girl. Lizzie." The child abruptly disappeared. "I think one of the older ones just pulled her away."

"Wouldn't surprise me," said Ben just as the door began to open. His view into the interior of the house was no wider than before. Clay blocked the entrance with his body. "I told your mother I would be back to check on her. Here I am."

Clay's bony chin jerked sideways. "Who's she?"

"I've brought a friend. She's going to help your mother."

"Yeah?" Clay opened the door wide enough to poke his head out for a better look. In the daylight, the sun would have given his coal black hair a blue cast, but just now it was barely distinguishable from the gloomy interior of the house. "Is Ma expecting her?"

Ben exhaled a frustrated breath. "Enough, Clay. Let us in." He was aware of Clay's hesitation and wasn't sure how the standoff would be resolved. He did not want to push his way in, but if Clay gave him no choice, Ben was prepared to put this particular obstacle over his shoulder.

Dr. E. Ridley Woodhouse stepped away from Ben's looming shadow. "Clay, is it?"

"Yes, ma'am."

"Well, Clay, your friend Ben asked me to accompany him because he's concerned about your mother. I understand she's hurting, and he thought I could help. I need to speak to her, though. If she wants me gone, I'll go, but I need to hear it from her."

Ben watched Clay step out of the way as though moved off center by a force outside himself. He thought it was probably less about what the doctor said, and more in the way of how she said it. She must have sized Clay up and gauged her approach from there. She gave the boy straight talk, not sweet talk, and the result was "Open Sesame."

The front room was dimly lit. In addition to an oil lamp on a side table in front of the window, there was a second lamp on a gate-leg table beside the sofa. Lily was still lying on her side, the compress and the blanket exactly as they had been when Ben was there. He couldn't tell if she had moved at all.

Eight-year-old Hannah was leaning over the back of the sofa. She had a brush in her hand and was gently using it to sift through her mother's hair. Lily was a redhead like her older daughter, but hers had darkened to rust years ago and the murky yellow light revealed threads of gray at her temple. Hannah paused brushing long enough to give Ben a shy, sweet smile. For the other visitor, she had a green-eyed stare that had as much to do with jealousy as it did with the color of her irises.

Lizzie was curled on the end of the sofa near her mother's feet and lay with her head against Lily's thigh. She stirred but didn't surrender her place to Ham, who was perched on the arm of the sofa like a plump bird of prey.

Ben was prepared to make introductions, but the doctor surreptitiously nudged him with her elbow, and she was the one who identified herself to the family.

"I am Ridley Woodhouse," she said, lifting her black bag from her side and holding it in front of her much as she had done upon meeting Ben at the station. "I hope I am not unwelcome, Mrs. Salt. I would like to speak to you alone, examine your injuries in private, if you will permit it."

Lily stared at her from her uninjured eye, but she spoke to Ben. "You said you were coming back, Ben. You didn't say anything about bringing somebody with you. This is a bad idea."

"I didn't say anything because we would have had this argument earlier, and I didn't see the point since I was going to do it anyway."

Lily put some effort into a wan smile. "Never could stay mad you. Don't know a soul who can."

Ben shrugged. He did not turn his head away from Lily, but his eyes swiveled sideways to the doctor. "There's some who try harder than others."

Hannah stopped brushing her mother's hair and set the brush beside the oil lamp. Her expression remained suspicious of their guest. "Doc Dunlop had a bag like the one you got. Guess that means the new doctor's arrived, but I don't see why you're here and he ain't."

"Hush, Hannah," said Lily. "I don't like your tone. There's no cause for disrespect."

Hannah clamped her mouth shut. The line of it was mutinous.

Ben thought that Ridley might set Hannah straight right then, but the doctor said nothing in defense or explanation.

What she said was, "I'll need more light. A second lamp on that table would be helpful."

Ben lifted his chin in Clay's direction. The boy did not need more encouragement than that. "How about I take the children into the kitchen? We'll play cards. Hannah, do you have a deck of cards?"

The girl's head bobbed once, but she didn't look pleased at the prospect of leaving her mother's side. Young Ham, on the other hand, was nodding excitedly. He jumped down from his perch, gave a little yelp when his bare feet hit the floor, and then danced in place on tiptoes, while his sister went in search of the cards.

"What about that one?" Ben asked, nodding toward Lizzie. The little girl could barely keep her eyes open, but he was afraid that she would cause a fuss if he removed her from Lily's side. She was attached like a burr.

Clay returned at that moment with a lamp. "I'll take her. She'll come with me." He set the lamp on the table and turned up the wick. The flame flicked and then was still. He adjusted the wicks on the other two lamps and then looked to Ridley Woodhouse for approval. "I can bring another, if you need it."

"No. This will be fine. Thank you."

Clay nodded. He put a hand on his brother's shoulder to stop the dancing. "Go on with you, Ham. In the kitchen."

Ham ducked from under Clay's hand and ran off, still on tiptoes.

Ridley watched the boy go. "Does he speak?"

"Sure. When he has something to say. Most times you can't shut him up, but this ain't one of those times." He bent over the sofa to scoop his sister into his arms. He made a comfortable cradle for her; she burrowed against his thin chest. "I'll put her to bed. Tomorrow, she won't recollect how she got there." He headed for the stairs, stopped, and turned to Ridley.

"I know who you are."

"Yes," she said. "I told you."

"No, I mean I know *what* you are. I remember what Doc said at his farewell shindig. Woodhouse. That's you. *Dr.* Woodhouse. That's your bag."

"Yes."

"I'll be darned," said Clay, and then he was climbing the stairs.

Chapter Five

Ben shuffled the cards while Hannah and Ham argued over whose turn it was to deal. Clay was silent on the matter, occasionally sharing a very adult, long-on-suffering look with Ben. They'd been occupied with cards for almost an hour, and the bickering was indicative of tiring of the activity. There was mostly silence from the front room. Sometimes they could hear the women talking, but it was muted and unintelligible. Once, they stilled and quieted when Lily's cry of pain cut through their laughter, and for a moment they could not look at one another. Guilt had them all staring at the table, even Ben, although he knew Lily would want her children to be distracted and that their laughter was as much a healing balm as anything Dr. Woodhouse could apply.

Ben stopped shuffling and squared off the deck, tapping it lightly against the table before he set it in front of him. "How about we do something else? Do you know any card tricks?" They shook their heads, and Ben feigned deep disappointment. "I have a few up my sleeve." He reached under his jacket at the wrist and produced an ace of diamonds.

Ham slapped the tabletop with his chubby little palm. "Do it again!"

Ben shook his head, but he stretched his arm toward Ham and then produced a four of spades as if he'd drawn it from the boy's left ear. Ham laughed, delighted, and clapped his hands together for an encore. Ben was slower to respond this time. He had not failed to notice that Ham flinched when Ben extended his hand. It simply could have been a natural reaction to the surprise of someone reaching for him. Or it could have been in expectation of something else. Ben held his question.

This was no time for an interrogation, and in any event, Ridley would have interrupted it because she suddenly appeared in the kitchen doorway holding Lily's compress.

"May I have a clean cloth?" she asked.

Ben started to get up, but Clay was already on his feet.

"Wet or dry?"

"Wet, please, and thoroughly wrung out." While Clay went to do her bidding, she crooked a finger at Ben and then stepped back from the threshold so he would follow her. When he stood in front of her, blocking the children's view, she opened the folded compress and showed him the crusted bloodstains. "I wanted you to know about this. I'll take it with me and wash it out. There's no reason for the children to see it."

"That was covering her eye," he said. "She was bleeding from her eye?"

"No. I found cuts on the underside of her forearms and cleaned them up."

"He *cut* her?"

Ridley Woodhouse shook her head. "She did this."

Ben stared at her.

"I'll explain later, but I'd be so grateful if we could stop at the sheriff's office on the return. It could wait until tomorrow, I suppose, but I'd rather not."

It occurred to Ben that this was another opportunity to tell her she was speaking to the sheriff, but he had no difficulty talking himself out of it. The Salt home hardly seemed the proper place. "Her husband's there in the jail. Better there's no chance of him overhearing anything you want to tell the sheriff."

"All right. Then it will have to be at my house. You did say he would come by to investigate what happened in the surgery."

"Maybe he's already been."

She looked doubtful. "I suppose."

"Right. Guess I could stop in on the way back and tell him there's one more thing he ought to know."

"Yes. He can't release Mr. Salt yet. He just can't." To press her point, part frank statement, part plea, she took a step toward Ben, lifting her chin just a fraction. The hallway narrowed, or at least it seemed that it had, and her breath caught unexpectedly when he didn't retreat, didn't waver. With her face tilted toward him, he calmly regarded her. She didn't blink. For some reason that made her feel marginally better, or just a tad less annoyed with herself.

"I'm sure he'll hear you out, but if Lily's cutting herself to make Jeremiah look worse than he is, well, he's got to know that, too."

"Don't you say that to him," she whispered. "Don't you dare. It's not true. You get him to my house and I'll do the explaining."

Ben opened his mouth to speak, but Clay appeared and inserted his hand and the damp cool cloth between them. Ridley thanked him, took it, and hurried away. Ben returned to the table.

"I think you'll be able to see your mother soon," he told them, pulling up his chair. "Seems like they're almost done. Any of you want to tell me more about what happened the other night? How it started, maybe?" Ham had taken the cards and spread them out in front of him. He turned them over one at a time and never looked up. Hannah stared at her fingertips resting on the edge of the table. Clay's expression was downright impenetrable. "No? Perhaps some other time. You know where to find me if you get to feelin' loquacious." When Ham's head popped up, Ben explained. "Means chatty. If you get to feelin' there's things you ought to say, I'm telling you to drop on by."

Having said his piece, Ben left it there on the table for them to think over. He swept the cards toward him, ignoring Ham's protest, and settled the earlier card-dealing argument by distributing the cards himself. "Queen of hearts is still the old maid, right?" When they nodded, he fanned the cards in his hand and looked them over. "And I'm calling out cheaters this time. No more looking the other way. I'm done being the old maid."

Of course, he wasn't done. To the delight of the children, especially Hannah, he was the old maid twice more before Ridley appeared again.

"You can come see your mother now," she told the children. "She's sitting up, but you have to be gentle. Her shoulder's tender and it will be for a while. She'll need help getting upstairs to bed and after that with work around the house."

They nodded in unison, full of promises as they pushed back their chairs and hurried to the front room. Ben was the last to get up from the table. "I'll help her up to bed this evening after the children say good night."

"That would be my preference, but upon reflection, I think it would be better if Clay helped and you stood back to lend a hand if it's needed."

"I can do that."

"Thank you."

Ben expected her to immediately return to the front room. When she didn't, he asked, "What is it? You have a frown line right here." He pointed to the space between his eyebrows. "Except it's on your face, not mine."

"Fool." She pressed the crease with her fingertips, ironing it out as she briefly closed her eyes. "Did you notice how the little one ran on tiptoes or the balls of his feet?"

He nodded. "That's new. Don't know where he picked it up. You should ask Lily."

"I did. She said the same thing. She noticed it shortly after her husband struck her this last time." She dropped her hand back to her side and opened her eyes. "Do you think he will let me examine his feet and ankles? I'm concerned about his tendons."

"I can hold him, if you like. Try to keep him still."

"I hoped you'd say that."

"Next time, just ask."

"Of course."

Her short reply, delivered in a voice that was barely audible but not because she was trying to whisper, told Ben everything he needed to know about her level of exhaustion. When she turned to go, he fell into step behind her. Lily was not the only one who might require a helping hand.

As it happened, Ham would have stood on his head if Ridley had asked him. He happily climbed onto Ben's lap and settled in. He giggled and shivered when the doctor ran her forefinger along his arch.

"Tickles, does it?" she asked.

"Uh-huh. Again."

"In a moment." She used the pad of her thumb to test the ball of his foot and also on his heel. When she pressed on his heel, he winced. She nodded to herself and felt for tenderness all around his ankle. That did not bother him in the least. She repeated an examination of the other foot with the same results. "Clay, will you bring one of the lamps over here? Hold it just above us so I can have a better look." When Clay complied, Ridley lifted one of Ham's feet and studied the base of his heel. "Hannah. Would you remove the tweezers from my bag and hand them to me?"

Hannah opened the bag with something akin to reverence and found the tweezers. She placed them in the doctor's palm.

"Thank you," said Ridley. "You are all excellent assistants."

From her corner on the sofa, Lily asked anxiously, "What is it? What do you see?"

"I'm not sure yet. Give me a moment." She touched the tip of the tweezers to a sliver of cobalt blue glass embedded in Ham's fleshy heel. She was not able to extract it on the first attempt. The boy howled when she dug more deeply and Ben had to hold his leg in place. Ham whimpered when she pulled it out and held it up to the light. "Hmm," she murmured. "Hannah, could I have a little bowl or saucer?"

By the time Hannah returned, Ridley had a second glass splinter waiting for her. She dropped them on a cream-colored saucer with dainty pink and blue flowers along the rim and then tilted Hannah's hand and saucer so Ben could see. The second sliver was amber glass, not cobalt. "Are you all right, Ham? I can see there are more splinters, and I imagine there are some I won't be able to see until they work themselves closer to the surface. Looks as if you took a stroll across broken glass. Does that sound right?"

Ham looked at his brother and said nothing.

Ben was not expecting a confession, and neither, did it seem, was Ridley. Lily, though, had a different idea.

"Hamilton Salt," she said, brooking no interference from anyone. "Tell me true. What did you break?"

Ham was powerless against that voice, although he did shrug as if he could minimize the importance of his explanation. "Just some old jars, Ma."

"Now where'd you do that?" Lily was no longer speaking to Ham. It was Clay who was on the receiving end.

"Down by Crider's Creek." The lamp shook ever so slightly in his hand, but the flame flickered and danced with abandon. "Came across a crate of jars and bottles, like maybe someone left them to wash out and never got around to it."

"So you took it upon yourself to make sure they never could. I swear, Clay Salt, I don't know what gets into you. And Ham right there beside you, learning such things as he should never be taught."

Clay hung his head. Ben thought Clay looked properly contrite, and likely regretted that Ham was injured, but the truth as he'd laid it out was a fragile thread and convincing only to a mother who wanted to be convinced.

Ben was grateful that Ridley asked Ham if she could keep removing the glass from his foot before Clay's story unraveled. Ham responded with the gravitas of a stoic and then squeezed his eyes shut.

Ten minutes later, Ridley pronounced she was finished. She bandaged his feet and put them in thick socks that Hannah found in his chest of drawers. "You can remove the bandages tomorrow before bedtime, but you need to keep socks on your feet. Do you understand, Ham?"

He nodded, and when she continued to stare at him with that single arched eyebrow, he said, "Yes, ma'am. I understand."

"Good." She produced a handkerchief and gave it to him. "Wipe your eyes and blow your nose. Go on."

He did and then neatly folded the handkerchief into quarters before he returned it to her. "What if there's more?"

"Then I'll remove them as well. You'll come by my office with your brother. You know where it is, correct?" She looked from boy to boy.

The answer came in unison. "Yes, ma'am."

"Doctor," she said.

"Yes, Doctor ma'am."

Ben snickered and was immediately on the receiving end of her sideways disapproval. He pressed his lips together.

Ridley snapped her bag closed and stood. "I'll come by tomorrow evening, Mrs. Salt—"

"Lily. Please."

"Lily. Tomorrow evening. Sooner if you need me. Please rest. Legs elevated. Clay, your mother needs your help now. Hannah, that means you'll need to tuck in Ham."

"Who will tuck me in?" She tilted her head and turned a coquette's coy smile on Ben.

He swallowed hard. The doctor was in the business of saving lives, and she did not let him suffer long before she stepped in to save his.

"I'll tuck you in and listen to your prayers," she said. And that was that.

Chapter Six

Ridley's steps slowed as she and Ben neared what she now understood was the rear of the sheriff's office and jail. Ben also slowed, but it was because she had, not because he had intentions of paying a call on the sheriff. She decided right then that she would force his hand.

"I am not moving until you speak to the sheriff about the Salts. In fact, I believe I will go in with you. He may be glad of a medical opinion."

Ben cocked his head to one side. "Do you really think that Doc Dunlop never gave him one?"

"No, but—"

"And do you suppose, you being a newcomer and all, that your opinion will carry more weight than his?" He saw her blink in surprise at his response. He paused, spoke more softly. "It's like this, Dr. Woodhouse, Doc probably delivered Lily Bryant, and he was there when her babies were born. You made Lily's acquaintance barely two hours ago, and it seems to me that you think you know what needs to be done. Did Lily encourage you to speak to the sheriff?"

"No."

"The opposite, I bet. She doesn't want anyone to know how badly Jeremiah hurt her this time. I'll probably get an earful when I see her again. I wasn't sure she'd let you treat her, which is why I took you there without asking her."

"Who is she to you?"

"Someone I've known since school days." He shrugged. "I might have had a little crush on her once upon a time, but she was a couple of grades ahead of me and didn't pay me any mind."

"She told me she's thirty-one."

"Yeah? Well, I'd take her at her word."

"She looks a decade older. You must see that."

"Sure. Sometimes. But she was pretty bad off tonight. You can't judge her by what you saw this evening. You'll hardly recognize her or the young'uns when you see them walking to Sunday church. Dressed to the nines, I think it's called. All of them turned out just so, looking as fine as anyone taking a pew, and the children are better behaved."

Ridley's sour look was wasted on him in the dark, but it made her feel better. "It won't be this Sunday. Or even next. I doubt she's in the habit of explaining away black eyes, stiff shoulders, and belly pain. Everyone knows, don't they? What he does to her. They know."

"They know," he said quietly. "And she probably knows they know, but it's kept hushed, exactly as she wants it."

"So there is a conspiracy of silence that, while sparing her humiliation, will most likely contribute to her death."

"That is a harsh judgment on folks who are doing what they think is best, and like I said, it is precisely what she wants them to do."

Ridley gripped the handle on her bag more tightly and turned on her heel.

"Where are you going?"

"Around the corner there to see the sheriff, and if I get a glimpse of Jeremiah Salt, all the better." It occurred to her that he might try to hold her back, so she kept her elbows close to her sides and lengthened her stride. She did not look over her shoulder when he didn't follow her.

Ridley peered in the front window of the office. It was gritty with dust but she could clearly see a desk with papers organized into neat piles above the green blotter. The chair behind the desk was empty but the seat was turned at a right angle, suggesting perhaps that someone had recently vacated it. She saw no movement. There was no one sitting on the bench; no one brewing coffee at the stove. The office looked spare and utilitarian. There were two chairs for visitors, a full gun rack on the wall behind the desk, and a score of wanted posters and notices tacked above the long empty bench.

Ridley saw that the door between the office and what she

suspected might be the cells was ajar. That gave her the impetus to step inside.

"Hello?" she called, closing the door behind her. "I'm looking for the sheriff. Is someone here?"

The voice that called back was loud and rough and rife with anger. "Yeah, someone's here. I got a pissant pointing a gun at me with no intention of using it, which anyone can tell you is a very bad idea because I won't always be in a cell, and he'll always be a pissant."

Ridley did not move away from the door. "Is the pissant someone in authority?"

"He's someone with a gun. You decide."

There was a pause, and Ridley could hear an exchange between the prisoner, who she assumed was Jeremiah Salt, and the pissant, who she assumed was the jailer, if not the sheriff. She could not make out a single word that passed between them, but she knew when it was over because Jeremiah's booming voice reasserted itself.

"Who are you, ma'am? Thought at first you might be Deputy Pissant's mama, but Amanda Springer would have her boy by the ear and halfway to home by now. Ain't that right, Deputy?"

She did not hear what the deputy said but thought it probably did not matter. "My name is hardly important," she called back. "I'm here to speak to the sheriff, but I am willing to speak to anyone holding a gun to your head."

She imagined Jeremiah's mouth snapping shut because she did not hear a sound from that quarter. She could make out footsteps but not whose they were. She heard another exchange, and although she strained to distinguish voices and words, nothing was clear. Ridley braced herself to hear the sound of a gunshot, not because she thought the deputy would shoot Jeremiah Salt, but because the deputy probably needed to get a little of his own back by proving he could fire his weapon.

The door between the cells and the office swung open and a young man, no more than twenty in Ridley's estimation, stepped into the room. He was of average height, probably five foot seven, and of medium build. His shoulders were neither broad nor narrow, and his arms fell loosely at his sides. He raised one of them now, tipped his hat, and gave Ridley a glimpse of non-descript brown hair and a better look at a round and hairless face.

Here was a man, hardly more than a boy, really, who would not catch anyone's eye in a crowd. Perhaps this was not undesirable in a lawman, but it was certainly the reason the prisoner called him a pissant.

"What can I do for you, ma'am?" he asked. He tilted his head toward the back room. "You might have been able to tell that I'm kinda busy at the moment."

"Yes. Yes, I understand." She pointed to one of the visitor chairs. "May I?" Ridley did not favor him with an opportunity to gainsay her. She was in the chair, her bag firmly in her lap, before he found his voice.

"Of course." He approached the desk but did not take the chair. "I'm Hitchcock Springer. Folks call me Hitch. And you are?"

"Ridley Woodhouse."

Hitch blinked and his mouth parted ever so slightly. "*The* Ridley Woodhouse?"

Ridley chose to purposely misunderstand. "E. Ridley Woodhouse, yes."

Hitch frowned. "I meant . . . never mind. You're Doc's replacement? The one he told us about?"

"Yes."

"But you're a woman."

"You are the second person to remark on that."

He blushed. "Sorry."

She waved his apology aside. "I came to have a word with the sheriff. I don't suppose you know where I can find him?"

"I might have an idea."

"This is important. You are his deputy, aren't you?"

"Not exactly. Not yet. But I hope to be. He told my mother to send me over tomorrow so I took it as he's interested in hiring me for the post. Thought it best not to wait until tomorrow. Wanted to impress him with my initiative."

Ridley's cheeks puffed as she released a breath to a ten count. "I think you better tell me where he is, then. I can tell you it concerns Lily Salt. That should be enough to get his attention, especially when you explain how you were holding a gun on Jeremiah when I got here."

"That? That weren't nothin'."

Ridley intended to tell the would-be deputy it was a little more than nothing, but her attention was drawn to the door as it was pushed open for the second time. She tensed, wondering if she was about to come face-to-face with Jeremiah Salt, and then wondering how she would know until he spoke. Her shoulders relaxed when she saw who it was.

Ben Madison stepped in the room and closed the door on Jeremiah's vituperations. "He has a set of lungs on him, doesn't he?" he asked no one in particular. To Ridley, he said, "Back door." A key dangled between his fingertips before he set it on the desk. "Did Hitch offer to make you coffee or a cup of tea?"

"I believe he was just about to." She stared at the key and all the tumblers clicked into place.

"I was," said Hitch. "Damn, if she didn't just read my mind." He headed for the stove. "She's the new doc, by the way. I guess you would know that if you'd met her at the station."

"Who says I didn't?"

Hitch stopped shoving kindling into the stove's maw. His eyes darted from the sheriff to the doctor while a question hovered in his mind that he couldn't quite grasp. He finally shrugged and returned to his task.

Ridley set her bag on the floor. When she straightened, she unbuttoned her coat and slipped out of it, letting it fall over the back of her chair. She folded her hands in her lap. Her eyes, sharp as glass, never once strayed from Ben Madison's face. He did not even have the grace to blush, and she knew very well that he had the complexion for it.

"You're the sheriff." It was not a question. "I suppose you were amusing yourself. You must have been because it certainly is not amusing to me."

Ben also removed his coat. He hung it on a peg by the door, and when he turned, his star was finally visible where it was pinned to his vest. He offered no defense. He sat in the chair at the desk and turned ninety degrees to face her.

Ridley was the first to look away, not because he'd stared

her down, but because she became aware of the frosted glass paperweight keeping one short stack of documents in place. Her fingers twitched and her eyes narrowed appreciably as her imagination took her to a dark place where she introduced that paperweight to the sheriff's thick skull.

Ben followed her gaze. "You're tempted, aren't you?"

"I am."

"I have to advise against it."

Her gaze returned to him. Her fingers stilled, but her eyes remained narrowed. "Unlike you, I don't surrender to every temptation."

"Hmm."

She waited, and when he offered nothing else, she said, "That's it? That's all you intend to say?"

"I'm not sure what I can tell you that will erase that murderous look in your eye."

"Try."

"Well, I'm new to the job. Been a deputy for five years, but I've only been sheriff for six weeks, give or take." He swiveled slightly in Hitch's direction. "That sound about right, Hitch?"

Hitch was setting the kettle on the stove. His brow furrowed and he did a count on his fingertips. "Yep. Seems like it might be."

"Your point?" asked Ridley.

"Just that I'm not in the habit of introducing myself as Sheriff Madison. Folks haven't quite come around to thinking of me that way, though they sure as hell voted for me."

Hitch centered the kettle and lifted three cups from a nearby shelf. "I voted for you, Sheriff." Ben gave him a quelling look and Hitch returned one of the cups to the shelf. "Um, if it's all the same to you, I'll just go in the back and keep an eye on Jeremiah."

Ben nodded. "Keep your gun in your holster and stay out of his reach."

"Yes, sir."

"Oh, and tell him if he keeps calling you a pissant, I'm going to extend his stay in Hotel Madison."

"Right. I'll do that." He shuffled his feet a little and ducked his head as he bade good evening to the doctor.

"It was a pleasure, Hitch."

"Same here, ma'am . . . Doctor." Then he was gone.

Ridley turned sharply on Ben again. "Was there perhaps any other time you might have told me? Say, when we were sweeping the surgery or the very first time I told you I wanted to speak to the sheriff?"

"It just didn't feel right to me."

"It didn't *feel* right?"

"No."

Under her breath, she said, "Unbelievable."

"Pardon?"

"I said, 'Unbelievable.'"

"What is it about me keeping quiet that upsets you the most?"

Ridley knew the answer: He'd made her feel foolish. She also knew she was not going to tell him that. "There was no reason for it. None at all. You deliberately withheld information."

"I told you my name."

"I'm beginning to question the veracity of that." It was an imprudent thing to say made worse by a supercilious tone. She did not need him to cock an eyebrow at her to know how she sounded.

Ben reached for the paperweight globe and idly passed it from palm to palm when he leaned back in his chair. "Looking back on the point of our introduction, I'd have to say I decided not to tell you I was the sheriff the moment you made it so important for me to call you 'doctor.' Something in your manner struck me sideways, I suppose, and that's when I figured you didn't need to know I was the sheriff. Not that I'm saying my title trumps yours. More likely the opposite is true since yours is academic and professional and mine is . . . well, mine is an elected office where the requirements are a certain amount of common sense and the ability to shoot straight."

"Hmm."

"The common sense trips me up now and again."

"Yes, I imagine it might . . . from time to time." Ridley noticed that he did not seem to be at all offended that she agreed with him. That prompted her to confess. "I am known to be touchy—some would say thin-skinned—about having my accomplishments disregarded as if they were of no account. I'm afraid when I stepped off the train, I was in expectation of being treated as I often am—dismissively. I have been preparing to assert myself since I left Boston. Perhaps I overplayed my hand."

"Perhaps you did. And perhaps I should have folded sooner." He leaned forward and returned the paperweight to its place on his desk. "I hear the water boiling, but I have to tell you, I'm hungry. When did you last eat?"

"I had a ham sandwich and an apple on the train after Denver."

"So about twelve hours ago. That needs to be rectified." He rose from his chair and went to the rear door, opening it just enough to poke his head and a shoulder through. "I'm going to take Dr. Woodhouse to dinner, then I'm going to walk her home. You all right here on your own until I get back?" Hitch indicated that he was. "You can come on out here and sit. Water's hot for coffee."

Ridley had her coat on and her bag in hand by the time Ben pulled his jacket down from the peg. She did not ask where they were going until they stood on the boardwalk and she was unsure which way to turn.

"The Butterworth," he said. "For my money, the hotel has the best food. It's also close to your house, and that's a bonus this evening. I imagine you're tired. Do you have a bed made up yet? Something you can fall into when you are home?"

"I found the linen cupboard. Everything I need has been left behind for me. I'll just wrap myself in a sheet and a quilt and fall into bed tonight."

"Probably a good idea." Ben pointed out the apothecary shop as they passed. "Mickey Mangold owns the place. I'll introduce you to him tomorrow, if you like. He and Doc were fast friends. As best as I could tell, an interest in medicine brought them together, but the Wednesday night poker game at the Butterworth was their glue."

"I don't play poker."

He chuckled. "Neither did they."

Ridley required a moment to understand his meaning. "Were they really so bad?"

"The worst, or the best, depending on how you look at it. They took to losing on purpose when folks who were down on their luck joined the game. Doc and Mickey could be depended upon to lose enough at the table to help someone out."

"Ah."

"Thought it was something you might need to know."

"It is, and he never mentioned it in any of his letters."

"That's not surprising. Neither of them would ever admit to it." His steps slowed and he pointed to the wide wraparound porch that was a distinctive feature of the Butterworth and a welcome mat to all visitors. "We're here," he said. "You're still hungry, aren't you?"

"Starving."

"Come on, then. It's not too late for us to get a hot meal." She regarded him uncertainly. "You're sure?"

"Absolutely."

Ridley's stomach was provoked into growling by a whiff of something her nose identified as hot apple pie. She placed a hand on her midriff and took the first step toward that heavenly scent.

Chapter Seven

"Hey, Sheriff." It was the perpetually pink-cheeked, kindly-looking gentleman standing behind the registration desk who called to Ben first. His smile was welcoming but not aggressively eager. He laid an embossed leather bookmarker on the page he was reading and closed the book.

"Hey, yourself, Mr. Butterworth. Do you have a table for us?"

"Sure, I do, but you have to make the necessary introductions." He looked to his right and left and then at the staircase. His voice dropped to a stage whisper. "Ellie's in the kitchen so this might be my only chance to know a thing before she does."

Ben grinned. "Then you will be pleased to make the acquaintance of Dr. E. Ridley Woodhouse." While Mr. Butterworth's jaw was still slack, Ben added, "You will recall, I think, that Doc Dunlop told us we could expect a new doctor and that she comes to us very well qualified."

When the hotel owner remained stupefied, Ridley took a step toward the desk and held out her hand. "I am pleased to meet you, Mr. Butterworth. Your hotel is certainly a grand establishment. It drew my eye when I passed it earlier on the way to my home. Sheriff Madison pointed it out to me, but that was hardly necessary since I was already an admirer."

If Butterworth had been standing in front of his lobby desk rather than behind it, Ben would have given him a nudge. The man who most folks agreed had never met a stranger was still faintly openmouthed and speechless. He seemed to be completely unaware that the doctor's hand was still extended.

Ben snapped his fingers with a mesmerist's flair. "I'll be

darned," he whispered when Butterworth's entire body twitched and the man blinked owlishly.

Butterworth shook the doctor's hand with more enthusiasm than was warranted, perhaps to make up for his initial astonishment. "Excellent, Dr. Woodhouse. Simply excellent. You say that Ben escorted you past the hotel today?"

"He did."

"And how is it possible I did not hear that you had arrived?"

"I can't explain it except to say he was eager to see me settled. He didn't introduce me to a soul along the way, and I recall that a number of people waved to him or called out his name. Do you find that peculiar?"

Before Butterworth answered, Ben interrupted by clearing his throat and looked pointedly at the man's hand still swallowing Ridley's. It was comical in a way. Ridley was too mannerly to extricate herself, and Butterworth was too anxious to correct a first impression to release her.

It required a second throat clearing, this time behind his closed fist, for Butterworth to get the hint. He dropped her hand as though it had suddenly scalded him, which was also rather comical. When Ben suggested dinner at the hotel, he'd had no idea he would find any entertainment beyond the doctor's company, but now, if Butterworth's reaction was indicative of how folks would take to the new doc, then Ben thought easing E. Ridley Woodhouse's transition had a silver lining.

But what did the E stand for? There was a puzzle.

Ben realized he must look amused because Ridley's lips were bunched in a way that signaled disapproval. He wondered if he should be troubled being as familiar as he was with that expression. He hadn't known her twenty-fours, and he'd caught hell from her for most of the ones that he had.

"Pardon?" he asked politely, just as if she weren't fixing him with eye daggers above the gold rim of her spectacles.

"Mr. Butterworth was asking about someone in the jail." She glanced at Butterworth. "Jeremiah Salt, was it?"

He nodded. "That's right. You still holding Jeremiah, Ben? Sure could help if you were to let him out. He was working on some new hinges for our oven door. The darn thing hasn't closed right since Mrs. Vandergrift beat it with a hammer.

Burned her bread, she said, and dared all of us to say different. She was swinging the hammer at the time so naturally we stayed quiet."

"Understandable." Accustomed as Ben was to matters like this, he was able to respond solemnly. Out of the corner of his eye, though, he saw that Ridley was unable to mask her shock. He couldn't say whether it was Mrs. Vandergrift's attack on the oven door that shocked, or whether it was Mr. Butterworth's request for Jeremiah Salt's release that appalled. He was sure he'd hear about it when they sat down to eat. "He's still there. I'm not releasing him tonight. Probably not tomorrow. You remember how he was at Doc's farewell shindig?"

"I do. Lasted two days, as I recall. Wasn't sure you were going to be able to corral him, but you're still pretty good with a lasso. Shame it came to that, but truly, I feared for my business." He turned to Ridley and explained. "Jeremiah wandered into the mercantile and knocked everything off the shelves and tables with a broom when Rodney Hennepin tried to show him the door. The sheriff here roped him like a steer and dragged him out." Butterworth's eyes darted back to Ben. "There was a time Jeremiah could hold his liquor so you'd hardly notice that he'd drunk the trough dry."

"Those days are past, I think, though he doesn't usually make a spectacle of himself."

"Thank the Lord for that."

"Maybe," said Ben. Offering no further explanation, he pointed to the restaurant. "We're hungry, Mr. Butterworth, and from what I can smell, the oven door is working well enough to produce an apple pie."

Butterworth clapped his hands together. "It is. Oh, yes it is. This way. You can have your choice of tables. We were full up an hour ago, but the locals have mostly wandered off. We have the overnight guests and a few boarders enjoying a quieter dinner."

The dining room had four large round tables, each of them capable of seating up to six diners comfortably. There were five smaller square tables with four chairs each and still three more tables set for two. Ben had seen every one of the fifty seats filled on a Sunday morning after services. It wasn't unusual for all of the rockers on the porch to be occupied as people waited for room at a table. As the only hotel in Frost Falls, the Butterworth had always had a successful trade with travelers, but it had gained popularity with the locals in recent years when the restaurant began to offer brunch every Sunday, not only once a month, and white linen tablecloths appeared on the tables with finer china and matching silverware. Now there were potted ferns at the entrance and a veritable jungle of greenery in the corner farthest from the kitchen door. The pots were given a quarter turn daily so the plants did not stray too far toward the windows on either side of them. The broad leaves were dusted and sprayed with a mist of water to keep them very nearly reflective of the sunlight during the day and the table lamps in the evening.

Because the hotel bore his name, Mr. Butterworth was generally given credit for the improvements to the restaurant, but everyone who lived in Frost Falls or traveled through it frequently knew that Mr. Butterworth's real genius had been hiring Ellie Madison.

Ben was still standing behind Ridley's chair, helping her to be seated, when the kitchen door opened and his mother rushed forward. She nimbly skirted the tables as well as the chairs that were not yet returned to their places, all the while drying her hands on her calico apron. By the time she reached Ben, which was no time at all, her hands were dry, the apron was pressed flat again, and the only thing she had to show for her excitement was the warm color flushing her cheeks.

"Mother," he said dryly. It was a temptation to step back in the event she meant to bowl him over, but he held his ground and for whatever reason that stayed her. "How did you know I was here?"

She shrugged. "How do I know anything I know? It's a gift."

"Uh-huh." More likely she had been peeking out from the kitchen to look at the diners. He did not offer that as an explanation. He pointed to Ridley, who was still sitting but looking up his mother. "Mother, this is Dr. E. Ridley Woodhouse. Dr. Woodhouse, my mother, Ellie Madison."

Ridley began to rise, but Ellie quickly disabused her of that formality. "Entirely unnecessary," she said, waving Ridley back down. "Did I hear him correctly? You're *Dr.* Woodhouse?"

"You did, and I am."

"Well, run me up a pole and call me a flag. Why, aren't you a breath of fresh air? Folks will have something interesting to talk about for a change." She eyed her son. "Did you know about this?"

"This? You'll have to be more specific."

Ellie Madison had marked her fiftieth birthday a few years back and stopped counting. She was a handsome woman, petite in stature, with auburn hair that time had faded but that was only recently beginning to reveal silver threads. Her diminutive figure was not to be underestimated in either her physical strength or in her strength of will. Ellie had both in abundance and had had occasion to prove it during her long tenure as housekeeper at the Twin Star Ranch. After more than twenty years, it had ended badly, although almost no one knew why, and so here she was, moved into town and managing the Butterworth in the same way she had been managing things all her life.

"I should cuff you," she said, setting her hands on her hips as though it were necessary to avoid assaulting him. "And don't pretend that you would arrest me because you won't." Ellie pinned Ben's ears back with sharp green cat's eyes. "Did you know she was a woman?"

Ben found enough room behind one of his pinned-back ears to give it a thoughtful scratch. "Now see, Ma, you're not the first one to ask me that today, and it's making me think people must believe I'm plum stupid. I knew right off she was a woman without her showing me any of her particulars."

Ellie pulled out the nearest chair, which happened to be at a right angle to Ridley's. She sank down onto the seat and set folded hands on the edge of the table. "I really do want to cuff him," she said in a conspiratorial fashion.

"I understand."

Ben not only heard the doctor's response, but heard the sincerity that underscored it. He could not recall that he'd ever had two women express such a heartfelt desire to do harm to his person—at the same time. And this was very different than two women fighting *over* him, which was not an unfamiliar experience but one that usually resulted in his blood being drawn when he tried to break it up. He supposed that, all things being equal, he preferred being cuffed.

Ben chose the chair opposite his mother and sat. "If your meaning was to inquire whether or not I knew our new town doctor was a woman before she got here, the answer is no, I did not. Doc Dunlop never breathed a word about it."

Ridley nodded. "It's true. I haven't met anyone who hasn't been taken aback."

"And how many people have you met exactly? I assure you we are all not small-minded."

Ridley thought about it a moment and then held up eight fingers. "You're number nine. I was never properly introduced to the stationmaster so I am not counting him, and four of the nine were children. I'm not sure how to gauge their reaction."

At the mention of children, Ellie looked at Ben with one eyebrow raised quizzically.

"The Salt young'uns. I took Dr. Woodhouse to see Lily."

Ellie nodded slowly. The eyebrow dropped but her forehead furrowed. "I heard Jeremiah was in jail. Mrs. Vandergrift's beside herself. The oven door—"

Ben put up a hand. "I know all about the oven door."

"I'm sorry. The news rattled me for a moment. It's one thing to know he's in jail, another thing to think on why that came about. No one's ever said, at least not in my hearing."

"Anything that's said is pure speculation, and that's how it's going to stay until Lily decides different."

Ellie nodded. She closed her eyes for a moment while she rubbed the bridge of her nose. "If he didn't bust up something, how did he come to your attention? It seems like you could tell me that."

"Not a word about it leaves your lips. Is that understood?"

"Yes." She clamped her lips closed.

"Hannah came and got me. It was the middle of the night. I was home, not at the office, but she knew what to do. She banged on the back door and threw pebbles at the window until she roused me and told me what was going on."

"Hannah? Little Hannah? Why not Clay?"

"He couldn't leave his mother. Lily was trapped in the bedroom with Jeremiah. Clay could hear but he couldn't see and he couldn't get in. I can only imagine that it must have been hell for him. He won't talk about it, though, and that makes me think this wasn't the worst. I don't know how it began except that drink was involved. Lily says it doesn't take a reason, and she's probably right."

"Those poor children . . . and Lily." Ellie looked to the doctor. "What about Lily?"

"I can't really speak to that," said Ridley. "She's my patient."

Ellie stiffened slightly. "Doc would have told me."

"Mother." Ben spoke sternly. "That is an outright lie and you know it. Doc never betrayed a confidence." He looked over his mother's militantly set features. "Good Lord. You don't even pretend to be remorseful."

She sniffed. "That is because I do not countenance secretivity."

"Secretivity? I don't think that's a word."

"It must be because I just said it."

Ridley had been following this exchange with interest. Now she touched a hand to her mouth and hid a grin behind it.

Ben suspected there was a grin but was unsure what provoked it. "Mother," he said, going to the bottom of the well for patience, "is there dinner to be had here or should I take Dr. Woodhouse to Brickle's or the Songbird?"

"You would be just that mean, wouldn't you?" Ellie pushed back from the table and stood. She darted away from the table, but not before she cuffed him at the back of his head. "And take off your hat. I raised you better than that." She winked at the doctor. "I really did."

A whoosh of air escaped Ridley's lungs as she sat back in her chair. She felt calm, relaxed, but not deflated. "I confess. I wasn't expecting that."

"What?" he asked, although he had a pretty good idea what she meant.

"This is why people want to cuff you. You make us work so hard to ask even the simplest question."

"Do I? I hadn't realized."

"I don't believe you, but that is another conversation entirely. I meant I was not expecting to meet your mother this evening, and it was gratifying to see that she does not suffer fools."

"I suppose you're referring to me again."

She shrugged. "There's an expression about the shoe fitting . . ."

"Mm." He half stood to remove his jacket before he swept his hat from his head. Out of habit more than necessity, he plowed his fingers through his hair to give it some semblance of order. "Would you like me to take your coat? I meant to put it up in the lobby but Mr. Butterworth was full of talk tonight."

Ridley let him help her remove her coat but would not part with her bag. It remained on the floor at her feet. A waitress wearing a black cone-shaped skirt, a white blouse with leg-o'-mutton sleeves, and sporting a stiff black bow at her neck accompanied Ben's return to the table. She took their drink orders and told them their available meal choices. Without consulting each other, they made it easy for her by ordering identical dinners: beef stew with dumplings, cucumbers dressed in vinegar and oil. Ben asked for beer. Ridley asked for coffee, changed her mind, and also asked for a beer.

Ben thought she looked vaguely guilty. "Wondering if you made the right choice?"

"Did I?"

"If beer is what you want, then you should have it. No one will think anything about it, even after they all learn you're a doctor. Doc regularly promoted the medicinal qualities of alcohol."

"As a disinfectant, perhaps."

"As more than that."

She chuckled. "All right. I don't doubt it. It's still an opinion that's widely held even among learned men." She fingered the stem of her spoon, drawing it even with the stem of her knife. "There are things I would like to discuss with you. Can we do that now?"

Ben looked around the dining room to gauge their privacy before he nodded. "I imagine that Hamilton Salt figures pretty high on your list."

"Indeed. That little boy is at the top of it."

Chapter Eight

The humor that often left its mark on Ben's smile or brightened his blue eyes was absent now. His expression was grave and the grim shadow that passed over his features made him seem older than his years.

"You realize, of course, that he had help breaking into your home," he said.

"I do realize that. Was it his father who was his accomplice, do you think? Or his brother?"

"His brother."

"How can you be sure? Didn't I hear Mr. Butterworth say Mr. Salt did damage at the mercantile?"

"You heard right. You asked me, and I'm telling you. It was Clay and Ham who made a mess of the surgery. If I press Clay, he'll give me the truth, but I'm not sure I want to shame him into taking back that story about breaking bottles down by the creek."

"He was quick with that story."

Ben thought there might have been a hint of admiration in her tone. "He was, wasn't he? And you and I know he did it for Lily. He told me Mickey Mangold gave him drugs from the apothecary, and it seemed reasonable at the time, but I should have realized that Clay wouldn't tell Mickey why he needed the drugs. Clay keeps the secret as well as Lily."

"But he told you what happened to his mother."

"Because he didn't have a choice. He was trying to prevent a murder."

Ridley's eyes dropped away. She stared at the tablecloth, smoothed the edge of it with her fingertips.

Ben said, "You have to understand that Clay could only

hear what was going on in his parents' bedroom. He imagined the worst, and he wasn't wrong to be thinking it might end with Lily's death. He couldn't intervene so he sent for me."

Ridley lifted her eyes, searched his. "Has he tried to step in before?"

"A couple of times. And yes, he's been knocked around for it, but not in an intentional way. The boy's no bigger than a minute. In my mind, I see Jeremiah brushing him away like a pesky gnat."

Nodding, Ridley said, "So Clay takes it in his head to help his mother by stealing drugs Doc left behind."

"That's what I figure."

"What accounts for the broken bottles and jars?"

"Hamilton."

"To what purpose?"

Ben chuckled. "He's four. He doesn't need a purpose." He paused, sitting back a little as their waitress delivered their beers and steaming bowls of stew. He thanked her, and when she was gone, he continued. "I can't know for sure, not without talking to Clay, but I think it's likely that when he decided to leave the house to carry out his plan, his mother told him to take Ham along. The boys are often seen about together, and it would have been hard for Lily to have Ham underfoot feeling as poorly as she did."

Ridley unfolded her napkin in her lap and pressed it flat with her palms. "The little one is a dervish."

"That's my point. Clay couldn't control him. Maybe the first bottle was broken by accident, but then . . ."

"Yes, he's four."

Ben grinned, picked up his spoon, and tucked into the stew. "Careful. It's hot." He fanned his mouth.

She stared at him as he fanned, put in mind of any number of impulsive rascals she had known. "No wonder you understand the boys so well. You have a year, maybe two, on them."

Ben took another spoonful but blew on it first. "Are you trying to insult me?"

"Not at all. I was stating a fact."

"All right. Just so we're clear, because I wasn't insulted by it. There's nothing wrong with trying to get inside the heads of the criminals."

Ridley almost choked. She swallowed hard, and her eyes watered. She blinked several times to clear them and tapped her throat with a hand. "Very well. Tell me why Ham was barefoot."

"You're not going to trip me up with that. Everybody knows the boy hardly ever wears shoes."

"Of course," she said softly. "I have a lot to learn."

Ben did not comment on that. It was true enough, but she'd said it more to herself than to him. He could tell she was deep into her thoughts and he let her keep them private. He dug into his dinner, and when he wiped the bowl clean with a thick crust of bread, the waitress appeared to whisk it away and put down a second bowl. She would not listen to Ben's protests, and he figured she had her marching orders from his mother. He sighed.

"You don't have to eat it," said Ridley, pointing to his bowl with her spoon. "I suppose that's your mother looking after you."

He nodded. "At the risk of confirming your worst opinion of me, my mother thinks I'm nine, not twenty-nine."

"Who said that was my worst opinion?"

Ben chuckled. "Who indeed." He thought he saw the doctor's mouth twitch, but it was such a narrow thing that he couldn't be sure. Ben picked up his beer and drank and spoke over the top of the glass mug. "Tell me about the cuts on Lily's arm."

"Arms."

Shaking his head, Ben set down his beer. He pushed the bowl of stew toward the middle of the table. "Is it her aim to kill herself?"

"I don't think so." She finished her dinner, and when the waitress appeared to take it away, no second bowl replaced it. "I'm not entirely comfortable having this conversation with you. As I told your mother, Lily is my patient."

"I understand, but I have a duty to look after folks, and Lily is one of my folks."

"I appreciate your desire to do right by her, but it doesn't trump my oath. Her wish for secrecy runs deep. You've explained that yourself. I've likely said too much already."

It was Ben's estimation that she had not said nearly enough.

"So that's it?" She was quiet for so long that Ben did not think she had any intention of responding.

When her answer came, her voice was hardly more than a whisper. "Perhaps we could speak in broad strokes."

Ben frowned. "How's that again?"

She did not explain. "During hospital rounds, I've seen women who present with horizontal cuts on the underside of their forearms and on their inner thighs. Most often these women have scars that indicate that the cutting is not anything new. Sometimes, depending on the husband or parents and the recommendation of the treating physician, these women are discharged to an asylum. It is rarely the cutting that brings them to the hospital. That behavior is hardly known to the people closest to them, but when it is discovered, the information is shared and decisions have to be made. I have known patients who were released to their families and were never admitted again."

"That's good, isn't it?"

She shrugged. "There is no way to know. I was unable to follow the progress of those who were released. I know the asylum offered no real sanctuary except from their abusers."

"Did any of the women kill themselves?"

"Yes, but rarely by their own hand. They were all vulnerable to mistreatment. By their caretakers. By the physicians. By the other inmates."

"But the cutting by their own hand? What do you make of that?"

"Few women will talk about it. I'm not sure that they understand it themselves or have the words to describe it, but those that can put something into words explain the self-inflicted pain as *relief.* Sometimes as release. You have to know, Sheriff, that what these women have in common is a history of abuse at the hands of a husband, a father, a brother, a mother. The crimes against these women are ugly and relentless; do not judge them harshly for wanting to find relief."

"I'm not judging them. I would never judge Lily."

"We were not speaking of Lily. We were speaking of women like Lily."

Ben nodded slowly, thoughtfully. "Broad strokes. Yes, I understand."

"How long can you keep Mr. Salt locked up?"

"This afternoon I was thinking I'd have to release him tonight, but I suppose I can stretch it another day. Maybe two. Keeping him locked away only solves the one problem. His family needs the money, and whatever else Jeremiah is, he's always provided for them. You heard that he has jobs waiting."

"Yes," she said dryly. "There's that oven door."

"I know. It's a trivial thing in your eyes, but it's business as usual. It has to be. That's for Lily's sake, too. You don't have to like it, but you do have to appreciate that it's true."

Ridley sipped her beer. "What can you do to protect her?"

"From herself? Not a damn thing. From Jeremiah? I can promise him that I will stop by regularly, but not so regularly that he'll see me coming, and I can talk to Buzz Winegarten about not serving Jeremiah past three drinks. Can't say how that will go over, or maybe I can and I just don't care."

"Are you really going to ignore what Clay did?"

"No. Wish I could, but I can't allow him to think he got away with it."

"You won't tell his parents?"

He shook his head. "Never. I can't promise they won't find out. There's Ham."

"I don't know. He might surprise you."

The edges of Ben's mouth turned down. It was more of a sad smile than a frown. "One can hope." He finished his beer, set the mug down, and pushed back from the table. "Let me walk you home. I need to let my mother know I'll be wanting something to take back to the jail for Jeremiah."

"You don't have to walk—" She stopped. There was no point arguing. For all that he was a frustration, at his core he was a gentleman. "I suppose you do."

"That's right. I do."

Chapter Nine

Ridley stood inside the doorway and watched him go. He did not turn back or even glance over his shoulder. She wondered why she thought he might. She had not invited him inside and he had not seemed hopeful that she would. They'd said good night, and except for his promise to show her how to fire up the stove come morning, they'd left it at that.

Ridley climbed the stairs to her room. She had chosen the one at the front of the house, the larger room by a few feet on each side, and the one that faced the street. Her godfather, judging by the cracked shaving mug and worn leather strop he left behind, had slept in the bedroom at the rear. It seemed an odd choice, given that the street was quiet and the windows faced south and west. She imagined that morning light would ease into the room. It would be a pleasant way to wake, though perhaps Doc required an eastern perspective to give each day a punch of light.

She did not linger on the thought. After closing the curtains, Ridley stripped to her cotton shift. In the morning she would be appalled by the careless way she discarded her clothes, but just now it was all she could manage to unfasten the hooks and ribbons and shimmy out of everything that confined her and, if the sheriff were to be taken at his word, *defined* her.

Ridley removed a sheet and coverlet from the linen cupboard and snapped them over the bed. She fell on top and pulled them close around her. It was not quite the cocoon she wanted, but it served, and only moments passed before she was asleep.

And only moments later, or so it seemed, she was sitting up

in bed, heart pounding, wide-eyed and disoriented. She looked around, frantic to make sense of her surroundings, to find something that would ground her. She heard voices, one of them very loud and grating, the other softer, but firm and vaguely familiar.

Ridley strained to identify it. The sheriff? That put her in her place better than any landmark could have. Bound as she was by the covers, she inched toward the edge of the bed and tried to stand. She stumbled before she was able to throw off the coverlet and had to yank on the sheet to keep her footing on the way to the window. Ridley parted the curtains only far enough to peek through the opening. The front porch overhang prevented her from seeing straight down and there was no activity on the street. The voices lifted again, and this time she realized they were coming from the back of the house, closer to the surgery entrance.

Ridley threw off the sheet and replaced it with her robe. She remembered that she had not unpacked her slippers, but because she also recalled the spray of glass on the floor of the surgery, she took the time to find them and put them on.

"I'm coming," she shouted, though with little expectation that she could be heard. She swept her spectacles from the bedside table and put them on as she hurried down the stairs. "Coming!" By the time she threw open the surgery door, the voices had quieted, but that was because Ben Madison was standing on the lip of the stoop with a man in a headlock. She set her hands on her hips. "What are you doing? What is this?"

"This," said Ben, nudging the man in the restraint, "is George Hotchkiss. He got himself in a tussle over at the Songbird at closing and now he thinks he needs to see the doctor." He loosened his hold on George's neck. "That sound right, George?"

George nodded. He tried to speak but his voice was strangled.

"I told him it could wait until morning, that he could sleep off whatever was ailing him in the cell beside Jeremiah, but that made him rowdier, so I explained that I'd escort him here, figuring I could talk him out of it, but you can see for yourself that I couldn't." He shrugged. "And, well, here we are."

Ridley shook her head, not quite believing what she was confronting. Sighing, she stepped aside and ushered them in.

Unfamiliar as she still was with the surgery, it took her some time to find a lamp and then light it. Ben did not release George until they were at the examination table, and then he did so slowly.

George Hotchkiss was a narrow fellow with long arms, a short trunk, and legs that seemed to extend from just below his armpits. He had a youthful countenance, more battered than bloody, and a crooked smile that indicated he was just that much ashamed. He eased himself onto the table, those stilt-like legs dangling over the side. "Think something's got broke," he said, slurring the words ever so slightly. "Want to see the doc." He looked straight at Ridley. "You fetch him and tell him what I told you."

Ben sat on a nearby chair, folded his arms across his chest, and extended his legs. He nodded at Ridley. "You fetch the doc like he said."

The look she gave him was full of lethal intent. "What's the something that's broken, Mr. Hotchkiss? Can you be more specific?"

He pointed to his nose. "I wasn't born this way. You be sure to tell the doc that."

"I'll tell him." She cupped her hands over his considerably bent and swollen proboscis. "May I?" When he nodded, she positioned her thumbs on either side of the bridge of his nose and snapped it into place. He yelped and nearly unseated himself but a moment later was breathing easier. "Anything else?"

He pointed to his right shoulder, which was another obvious injury. It sagged several inches below his left one.

"Second time tonight that I've seen this," said Ridley. "Who did this to you?"

"Holden Anderson."

"So it wasn't the sheriff."

"Nah. He didn't make it feel no better, but he didn't snap me neither."

Out of the corner of her eye, Ridley caught Ben Madison's smug smile. "Not for lack of trying, I'll wager."

"No, ma'am. Not for lack of it, that's for sure." He craned his neck around to get a look past the surgery into the doctor's office. "Now, about the doctor. He'll be along directly?"

"I have a notion he will." Ridley felt along her patient's

collarbone. The fact that he tolerated her touch as well as he did inclined her to believe it was the shoulder that was out of joint, not a broken clavicle. "It will help if you can relax."

"I'd relax a mite better if the doc were here."

"I understand." She rolled her shoulders and then her neck. "Stay loose. I can't promise this won't hurt, but—" She stopped talking to concentrate, taking him by the affected side's elbow and bending it at a right angle to his body. Gripping the elbow in both hands, she applied traction, and then moved one hand to his forearm. She rotated the elbow and repeated the process until she heard a popping sound as the ball joint found the socket.

"I'll be damned," George said, slowly rotating his shoulder. He whistled softly. "I'll be damned."

"That's a good bet," said Ben from his chair. "You about done carrying on about your aches and pains? If you're going to sling insults at folks inside the Songbird, you should be prepared for what comes after. Doc Dunlop would have had no parts of you until morning and that's a fact."

"Lucky for me that he ain't here no more and I found me an angel of mercy." He grinned toothily at his angel and blew her a kiss, humid with alcohol.

Ridley almost reared back, but she held her ground because that's what she did. Never give ground. Over the shoulder of her patient, she caught Ben's eye. "I think we're done here."

He stood. "I believe we are." He walked to the door, opened it, and gestured to George to make his exit. "You square things later with her, George. You understand? Bring her a load of wood, split the right size for the stoves. I swear I'll lock you up for being a nuisance if you don't. A couple of buckets of coal, too."

"I hear you," George muttered, ducking his head as he left. "Hear you just fine. First thing in the morning, it'll be here."

Ben pulled the door closed. "Good idea to keep this locked. There's no telling who'd try to wander in otherwise."

"When do you think he'll realize that he saw the doctor tonight?"

"Like as not, sometime tomorrow when I explain it to him. George is all right. He's got himself all twisted up over Charlie Custer—that's Charlie as in Charlotte—and he can't stand it if he thinks someone's looking at her crossways. I guess tonight it was Holden Anderson."

"It seems as if you have a lot to occupy you, Sheriff."

"Some nights, yes. Most nights, nothing at all. I'm sorry we woke you. That's what I was trying to prevent. I figured you needed your sleep."

The thought of sleep provoked a yawn. She used the back of one hand to cover it.

"Yeah," he said, watching her. "I thought so."

Ridley waved aside his concern. "I don't even know what time it is."

"Around three. Still plenty of time for shut-eye."

"What about you? Don't you sleep?"

"I was doing just that until the ruckus at the saloon."

"Oh."

He rubbed the back of his neck. "Got a bit of a crick here on account of nodding off sideways in the chair."

"What happened to your deputy?"

"I sent him home. He'll have night duty tomorrow."

Ridley thought she understood what that meant. "Then you'll be keeping Mr. Salt at least that long?"

"Yes. It seems best."

She nodded. "I wouldn't object if you offered to show me how to fire up that stove now. I'd like a cup of tea."

"You're sure?"

"I am, yes."

"All right, then. I need to bring in some of the wood you have on the stoop. Give me a moment." When he returned with an armload, he directed her to lock the surgery door and then headed to the kitchen. He dropped the wood into a galvanized pail beside the stove. "Have a seat."

Ridley pulled out a chair and sat. "I suppose you think I'm hopelessly ill-equipped to live here on my own."

"What I think is that you'll learn, partly because you have to, but mostly because you want to. I take it you had help back in Boston who did this kind of thing for you."

"Yes. Mrs. Roach was our cook. Madelyn Eddy was her assistant. There were others, too. My mother came from money. My father worked hard to meet her expectations. There was always help."

"So that's why you don't know how to start a stove. Where I was raised, my mother was the help. I picked up the temperament of a stove like this by watching her wrangle it into submission."

"I've seen it done, but I wasn't paying attention." She set her folded hands on the tabletop. "I am now."

Ben went through the steps, explaining the difference between the front damper, the oven damper, and the chimney damper, each with a particular use and importance. He showed her the ash receiver, which Mary Cherry had seen fit to clean, and warned her that when she freed the grate of ashes, she had to put on the covers over the firebox, close the front and back dampers, and open the oven damper. The steps had to be followed as a precaution to keep ashes from flying all over the room.

"Should I be taking notes?" she asked.

"Only if you think you need to."

Ridley hoped there was a book in the library that explained it all because she was certain there was no such book in her own collection. She concentrated on what he was saying about building the fire: Turn the grate back into place, remove the covers, and cover the grate with pieces of paper. Having none handy, he showed her how to place small sticks into the firebox and arrange it so it would admit air. He added the hard wood next.

"You're out of coal, but you'd add it now. I'll send Bill Olney by tomorrow with a couple of buckets for you. Not sure I trust George to remember." He looked around, spotted matches on top of the windowsill, and asked her to light one. While she was doing that, he returned the covers to their positions, opened the closed dampers, and then took the lighted match from her. As he held it under the grate, the fire was drawn toward the wood. He tossed in the match and closed the door. "That's all there is to it," he said.

"Uh-huh. I've observed surgeries in the operating theater that were less complicated."

Chuckling, Ben picked up the kettle and went to the sink, where he pumped water until he had a good clean flow. He filled the kettle halfway and set it on the stove. He brushed off his hands on his trousers. "I should be going."

She frowned. "What do you mean? Aren't you going to stay and have a cup of tea with me?"

He cocked an eyebrow at her, amusement in his eyes. "I did not want to presume that I was invited."

"I'd be a poor hostess if you weren't. You did all the work."

"Well, then, thank you. I'd like a cup of tea just fine."

Ridley rose from her chair just as he sat. "I have to get the tea. I am not entirely unpacked. I brought my favorite blend with me."

"Of course you did. I bet you brought a little china pot and one of those knitted sweaters to go over it."

"A cozy." She smiled. "Yes, I have that, too."

"Did you arrive here expecting Frost Falls to be the last outpost of civilization?"

She hesitated before answering.

"Oh," he said. "I see. You thought civilization stopped at Denver."

"Something like that."

"Saint Louis?"

Ridley nodded. "I suppose I had that notion."

He grunted softly. When she left the room to retrieve her tea and teapot, he called after her, "It's the dime novels, isn't it? If you read Felicity Ravenwood, you probably read a Nat Church adventure now and again."

"If I did," she called back, "it's because Doc recommended them to me as a means of acclimating myself."

"Of all the . . ." Ben shook his head as his voice trailed off.

"What's that you said? I couldn't hear you."

"I said—" He stopped. "Never mind. I was talking to myself. Do you need help? You sound as if you've stuffed your head in a trunk."

"Found it!" It wasn't but seconds after her eureka discovery that she reappeared in the kitchen holding the pot and cozy in one hand and a small pouch in the palm of the other. "Perhaps you think I should not be so triumphant," she said, placing the items on the table, "but there were several bad moments back there when I thought I had left it all behind."

"Of course," he said dryly, regarding her satisfied smile. "The comforts of home."

Not certain if she was the object of his amusement yet

again, Ridley cinched her robe and then went to the china cupboard and took down two cups and saucers. The saucers, with their gold leaf rims, were part of a set. The cups were not. She set them on the table, along with a spoon, and then returned to her chair, where she carefully measured tea into a silver tea ball. She placed the infuser inside the pot and replaced the lid. The water in the kettle had not begun to roll.

Ridley set her folded hands on the edge of the table and looked around the room, casting her eyes on anything . . . except Ben Madison. "Do you take sugar in your tea? I don't have any."

"I do, but I can do without."

She nodded. "I suppose I shall have to visit the mercantile in the morning and purchase the staples that I'll need. Is that the sort of thing that Mary Cherry would do for my godfather?"

"Uh-huh. Would you like me to have her stop by so you can meet her, maybe decide what you want to do?"

"No. Not yet. I want to think on it awhile."

"Makes sense. You've hardly been here twenty-four hours."

Ridley was vaguely startled to hear it. Her head came up and a small vertical crease appeared between her eyebrows. "That's true, isn't it?"

"It sure is. A lot has happened and I don't think you've had but a minute of sleep."

Ridley could not argue with that. "I'll sleep in. When word gets around that I've arrived, I don't expect to have any patients beyond a few curiosity seekers."

"Folks might surprise you."

"Will they?"

He shrugged. "Probably not."

She laughed under her breath. "I think I hear the water rolling."

He placed one hand over her wrist when she started to rise. "Give it another minute or so."

More aware of his hand on her arm than she wanted to be, Ridley sat. His hand fell away. She watched him return it to his lap. "Why do you suppose Doc chose you?"

"You mean to help smooth the way for you?"

"That's right. Why you?"

Ben shrugged. "I can think of a couple reasons, but it's all conjecture. He never spelled it out plain."

"I imagine one of the reasons is your position."

"My position? Oh, you're talking about me being a duly elected officer of the law."

"Sheriff," she said dryly. "Yes."

"Maybe. I expect that carries some weight with folks but not as much as the fact that I know pretty much everyone in and around town. More importantly, I get along with most of them. I've known Doc almost all my life, got to know him better about six years back when I was his patient, and better yet when I became Jackson Brewer's deputy, moved to town, and we became neighbors." He stood and found a towel to wrap around his hand as he picked up the kettle. "You want to take the lid off that little pot?"

Ridley did, holding it away while he poured, and then replacing it so the tea could steep. She waited for him to sit again before she spoke. "When you said you became Doc's neighbor, how did you mean that exactly?"

"Exactly?"

"Yes. Neighborly? In the neighborhood? Share a fence neighbors?"

"That's the one."

Her cheeks puffed as she blew out a small breath. This was unexpected. She couldn't have imagined that she would be having tea with him on so short an acquaintance, yet here she was sitting at the same table, close enough that she could see the fine dusting of copper hair on his knuckles, the freckles scattered across the bridge of his nose, and the subtle lift of one corner of his mouth. Her heart did an odd little skip and she spoke carefully, without inflection. "So you and Doc are next-door neighbors."

"We were. Now you and I share a fence."

"The white house with the blue shutters. That's yours?"

"Yes. The blue shutters were my mother's idea."

Ridley's brow wrinkled. "She lives with you?"

"No. She's had a small suite at the hotel since she began working there. Mr. Butterworth gave her the accommodations because he knows he has a gem in her. But here's the good thing about sharing a fence with me." His chair scraped the floor as he pushed back. "I have sugar."

Ridley stared after him as he disappeared without so much as a by-your-leave. When she realized her jaw had gone slack, she clamped her mouth shut. *Her neighbor.* Doc should have told her that. She wondered if her father knew. In all likelihood, he did, and he would have approved. She would not put it past him to have suggested something like this. It went a long way to explaining why he was supportive of her decision to leave home. Not only supportive, but also encouraging.

She had hoped he trusted her judgment. Now she was not so sure. It was disappointing to have come so far and then realize she was hardly more than a few steps beyond the garden wall. Was she supposed to be grateful for her father's oversight? His protection? Perhaps someday, but not just now.

Ridley was still musing on this Ben-as-neighbor conundrum when he returned with a cup of sugar. He set it in front of her and then nudged it closer when she continued to stare at it.

"It's sugar," he said, tapping the lip of the cup.

Ridley blinked. Feeling rather foolish for being caught so deeply in woolgathering, she spooned sugar into her cup. Once he had done the same, she poured the tea, and breathed deeply of the warm aroma that held a hint of oranges and clove.

"Deep thoughts?" asked Ben, stirring his tea. "You were about a thousand miles away by the time I got back."

"Nineteen hundred miles, give or take."

"Thinking about home, then."

Ridley couldn't see that it hurt to admit it. She raised her cup, blew on the hot surface of the tea, and nodded. "Did Doc ask you to keep him apprised of my progress?"

"No. I imagine he thought you'd do that."

"What about my father?"

"What about him?"

"Did he ask for reports?"

Ben removed his hat and hooked it on the spindle back of another chair. He pushed his fingers through his hair, first one way, then the other, so that the darker shades of orange lay crossways over the lighter ones. He regarded her at length, his mouth screwed pensively to one side.

"I'm not sure I understand your meaning," he said.

"It was not a difficult question. Did my father request reports from you?"

"How is it that you figure he could do that? We're not acquainted. Never corresponded. There is only you to connect us and that's just come about today." He corrected himself. "Yesterday, though it is surely starting to feel as if it were longer ago than that."

Ridley could concur. "You have to know my father."

"See? There's my point precisely. I don't know him."

"I'm sorry. I just thought . . ."

When she didn't say what it was that she thought, Ben filled it in for her. "That I was some sort of spy?"

"No. Nothing like that. Well, not exactly like that. No cloak-and-dagger."

Ben sat back, sipped his tea, and watched her over the rim of the cup. "I've seen this before," he said. "This is the influence of one Felicity Ravenwood. You should stop reading her adventures."

"Don't be ridiculous."

He shrugged. "Something to think about, though."

"It isn't."

"So you say. I say different."

She opened her mouth to speak and then abruptly closed it. Her eyes narrowed on his, searching his features for some hint of mischief. He was remarkably good at concealing it. His blue eyes were perhaps a shade brighter than they had been earlier, and there was a slight curl to his mouth that lifted one corner higher than the other. His eyebrows, several shades darker than his hair, were fixed in a position of serious contemplation. Now that his hat was removed, she could easily see the tips of his ears. No flush there.

The freckle dust across his nose was a beguiling feature, and she found herself staring at it in a manner that was wholly impolite.

Ben passed a knuckle over his nose. "It's the freckles, isn't it? Trying to connect the dots, I suppose."

"Not quite. Has anyone ever done it?"

"The jokers in the bunkhouse at Twin Star. I slept right through it both times, and the ink did not come off without some serious scrubbing. The freckles remained, though, so that was disappointing."

Behind her cup of tea, Ridley smiled.

Ben said, "Are you satisfied that I'll not be in correspondence with your father, and that if Doc and I trade letters, you will hardly figure in mine?"

The abrupt turnabout in conversation startled her and her smile faded. "I am." She lowered her cup and repeated herself so that he could hear her clearly. "I am."

"Good. I'm your neighbor. Not your guardian. Once you're settled in, have your practice established, I probably won't see you but five or six times a week, same as I did Doc, and that's only if you take to walking the way he did." Ben finished his tea and hauled the leanly muscled length of him out of his chair. "It's been a pleasure, Dr. Woodhouse, and I thank you for the tea. If you get a hankering for more like it, you'll want to speak to Mickey Mangold's wife. She's the one who blends the tea leaves here. If she doesn't have it, she'll get it for you." He picked up his hat, settled it on his head, and gave her a nod. "How early you figure you'll rise?"

"Eight?"

"Give yourself another hour in bed, and I'll be by an hour after that to take you around and introduce you properly."

"Ten o'clock, then."

"Lock the door behind me."

Ridley rose to see him out. He stood on the back stoop for a moment after she shut the door. She realized he was waiting to hear the lock fall in place. She turned it, saw him nod as though satisfied, and then he was gone.

What a peculiar man, she thought, and realized she was smiling as if she did not mind it all.

Chapter Ten

Hitchcock Springer appeared at the sheriff's office at the appointed hour, carrying a covered breakfast tray from the Butterworth. Ellie Madison had fed him first and then sent him off with the tray. He was tempted to take a biscuit from under the green-and-white-checked napkin because he knew there was more than one and because they smelled so darn good. He resisted because even though the tray was meant for Jeremiah Salt, Hitch thought Ben might expect that there would be something for him.

"Sheriff?" Hitch bobbled the tray as he stepped inside. The office was empty. "Ben? You around?"

The answer came from the back. "In here. You have breakfast?"

"I do. Yes, sir."

"Well, bring it on through. Mr. Salt has a powerful growl in his middle regions." Ben sat up on the cot where he had spent the night after leaving Ridley. He stretched until bones cracked, arched his spine, massaged his neck, and sucked in the aroma of hot coffee, bacon, and biscuits and gravy. "Give me a minute," he told Hitch when the young man was standing outside his open cell door. He swiveled his head in the direction of the man pacing in the adjoining cage. "You smell that, Mr. Salt? That's for you. You can't say we don't feed you right here. That's Mrs. Vandergrift's sausage gravy and biscuits."

"I smell it all just fine, but I'd be obliged if you'd release me so I could get on home, have my breakfast there, and start my work. Lily makes some fine biscuits and gravy herself."

"I don't doubt it." Ben picked up his hat, reshaped the brim, and put it on. "But Lily's not feeling well. I'm going to keep you here and let her rest."

Jeremiah Salt stopped pacing. "What do you mean, my Lily's not well? What's wrong with her?"

Ben stared at Jeremiah, wondering if he could believe his ignorance or whether it was for show. "You and I, we'll have a discussion later today about that. In the meantime, eat your breakfast and don't cause Hitch here any problems. He'll see that you get a basin of water and a cloth so you can wash up." He turned to Hitch, who was looking a shade paler than usual upon realizing he was going to be left alone to manage things. "Sorry, Deputy, but you're going to have to empty the slop bucket. Don't let him throw it at you."

Hitch swallowed hard. "No, sir."

"It'll be okay. He wants to go home so there's no percentage for him in assaulting an officer of the law. If you're finding it difficult to get his cooperation, threaten him with your mother. I'm fairly sure he's afraid of her." Ben stepped out of the cell and stood by while Hitch pushed the tray through the serving slot and Jeremiah took it away. "I'll be back around three. Keep a log of who comes and goes, write down their complaints. We'll decide what to do about them later. I'll be surprised if you have more than two visitors, three if your mother drops by."

"She'll be here," Hitch said glumly.

Ben clapped him on the shoulder. "Give her my best."

Once home, Ben set out clean clothes, shaved, washed his hair, and scrubbed away the stink of a night in jail. He had it on good authority, namely Maxwell Wayne's, who'd been sweeping up in front of his bakery when Ben went by, that today was going to be sunny and temperate. "I feel it in my bones, Ben," he'd said, and Ben didn't know anyone who didn't trust Mr. Wayne's bones to get it right.

On the strength of that prediction, Ben wore his brown leather vest with the star but left his jacket hanging by the door. He took down his gun belt from another peg and fastened it as he left the house for Ridley's. When Doc lived next door, they never stood on ceremony, and Ben was free to come and go as he pleased. Now the surgery door would be locked—or it had better be—and Ben concluded it would be best if he went to the front.

He presented himself at the door at the appointed hour, and realized that Ridley must have been watching for him because the door opened while he was raising his fist to knock.

"Good mornin'," he said, and immediately saw that it wasn't likely to be, not with Dr. E. Ridley Woodhouse looking as if she were preparing to face the Sioux at the Little Big Horn and knew the outcome as reliably as Maxwell Wayne knew the weather. Her features were set as stonily as they had been when she alighted from the train. There were tiny lines around her mouth because she was concealing all its splendor with tightly set lips. Her spectacles rested high on the bridge of her nose so that she regarded him through them, not over the top. There was no humor in that gaze, only solemn determination. It was a little frightening.

Last night when she had arrived at the surgery door, her hair had been bound loosely with a ribbon and mussed from sleep, and when she had held up the lamp, he saw there were pillow wrinkles on the right side of her face and her spectacles were slightly askew.

Nothing was askew now. She was wearing a white blouse buttoned to her neck with a black tie to close the collar. The sleeves puffed at the shoulders and were tight from elbow to wrist. A black skirt cinched her waist and fell in a stiff circle around her ankles. She was still wearing the fashionably pointed shoes but no hat. He remembered he had told her to dress the part.

This was his fault.

"You can leave your bag here," he said, pointing to where she was clutching it in front of her.

She shook her head. "I may have need of it, and I want to see Lily this morning."

"Of course."

"I'd like to check on Mr. Hotchkiss as well."

"Sure. You missed your chance when he dropped off that split wood for you this morning."

"How do you know? I didn't hear him."

"Because I ran into him and he told me."

Ridley stepped onto the porch and closed the door. "It was good of him to remember."

"I know. I had my doubts. Shall we?" Ben gestured to the sidewalk. "I thought we'd have breakfast at the Butterworth before we begin the grand tour."

At the mention of breakfast, Ridley's stomach rumbled.

"That's what I thought," Ben said. "Let's go."

The Butterworth's dining room was deserted except for a traveling notions salesman and a pair of elderly women visitors who fussed with each other so often that Ben decided they must be family.

Ridley placed her bag on the floor at her feet and unfolded her napkin. "Coffee cannot arrive soon enough," she said as Ben joined her.

"Here it comes," he said, pointing to the kitchen door as it opened. He sighed. ". . . aaaand my mother." He sat back to give Ellie plenty of room to pour. "Good morning, Ma."

She swooped down like a bird of prey but merely pecked him on the cheek. "Mornin' yourself." She nodded at Ridley. "Dr. Woodhouse. Did you have yourself a restful first night?"

"I did, yes. Thank you for asking."

"George Hotchkiss was here at first light clearing his head with pots of coffee. He had a story, too. Something about Holden Anderson breaking his nose and an angel of mercy setting it right. You wouldn't know anything about that, would you?"

"Mm, no."

"That's what I thought."

"You, Sheriff?"

"First I'm hearing about it."

"Have it your way. Steak and eggs do for you both? Biscuits?" When they nodded in unison, Ellie slipped away.

"Does she know everything?" asked Ridley when she was gone.

"Sooner or later. Mostly sooner. I'm resigned."

Ridley poured cream into her coffee, gave it a quick stir, and drank. "Perfect," she said, closing her eyes as the hot liquid slid over her tongue and down her throat.

Watching her, Ben grinned.

"What?" she asked, opening her eyes and catching him out.

He shrugged. "Just thinking I should've met you at the door with a cup of coffee in hand."

"It couldn't have hurt."

They were served soon after that and ate mostly in silence. Ben reviewed what he thought would be a good agenda but left to her to prioritize it. He was not surprised that Lily Salt was their first order of business.

Hannah answered the door. She was holding Lizzie in her arms, and unlike her older brother, she let them enter without an interrogation. "Clay's in school this morning. Ma made him go. She's in the kitchen and I'm helping her." She led them down the narrow hallway. Hamilton was sitting at the table building a card pyramid. The cards collapsed when Hannah bumped the table. Ham squealed as though wounded and swept the cards onto the floor.

Lily turned away from the stove to greet them with an apologetic smile. The smile, slim as it was, only served to emphasize her battered face. She had a long wooden spoon in her hand. A lump of porridge on the bottom side of the spoon fell back into the pot. "We are moving slowly this morning. The children haven't yet had breakfast."

Ben crossed the kitchen to Lily's side and took the spoon from her hand. He gently pushed Lily toward a chair at the table and told her to sit. Ridley removed Lizzie from Hannah's arms and Ben gave the little girl the spoon. Hannah stepped on the stool in front of the stove and stirred while Ben brought out bowls and spoons and directed Ham to pick up the cards. In short order, the chaos was diminished by Ben's choreography.

Ridley sat beside Lily. She kept Lizzie in her lap although the little girl held out her hands to her mother. "She'll be fine here," said Ridley, responding to Lily's anxious look. "Tell me about your shoulder."

Lily gave it a tentative roll and rubbed it. "It's much better. I don't know why I couldn't put it in place myself."

"Then you've done it before."

"Yes."

"Probably too many times. Experience doesn't make it easier." She played pat-a-cake with Lizzie. "Your eye is improved."

"The compress helped."

"I'm going to leave you with a tea to infuse into the water. Use it when you prepare the next compress. It will reduce the swelling but not the coloration. It would be best to apply it once an hour but at least once every two hours. Hannah?"

The girl turned around on her stool. "Yes, ma'am?"

"Did you hear me tell your mother what she's supposed to do?"

"I did."

"Then you'll make sure she does it?"

"I will."

"Thank you, Hannah."

Ben dropped to his haunches and helped Ham collect the last of the cards. He was aware of Ridley speaking more softly now. He distracted Ham to keep him from being too interested in the conversation.

"What about the other?" Ridley asked gently, her eyes lowering to Lily's abdomen.

"Cramping off and on last night." Lily's voice fell to a whisper. "Bloody sheets this morning. I think it's gone."

"I should examine you to be sure. We can go upstairs."

"Not now. Later, when the children are eating."

Ridley nodded. "Ben, will you put a kettle on?"

He rose, hefting Ham under one arm, and carried the boy around while he filled the kettle and set it on the stove. "Tea or coffee?" he asked.

"Neither. Just the hot water for now."

He didn't ask and she didn't explain. Once the children were all seated at the table with hot porridge in front of them, Ridley removed the kettle, took her bag, and followed Lily upstairs.

"Where's Ma going?" Ham asked.

Ben didn't answer. He diverted Ham with another card trick and was successful until Hannah asked if their father was coming home today.

"Would it be a good thing if he did?" asked Ben, idly shuffling the cards.

"Clay should be here when Pa comes home."

Which was not exactly an answer to his question, but he thought he understood Hannah's reasoning. Clay had established himself as their protector, and even if he could not stand between Lily and Jeremiah, he knew what to do. "Does your pa have any liquor around, maybe a bottle hidden here or there?"

Ham pointed a pudgy finger to the bottom of the china closet.

"In there?" Ben got up, opened the bottom cupboard, and found an unopened bottle of whiskey at the back alongside a third of a bottle of tequila. "Anywhere else?"

"Out back under the porch."

Ben located another bottle of whiskey there, this one half full. He carried it back in and lined it on the table with the others. He cocked an eyebrow at the children.

Hannah raised her spoon to indicate the upper floor. "At the back of Ma's wardrobe."

Ben shook his head. He wondered that Jeremiah bothered to hide a single bottle when nothing about it was a secret. "Will you be all right while I go and get it?" Hannah gave Lizzie and Ham stern looks that would have put Ben back in his chair if it had been directed at him.

"We'll be fine," she said. "You should know there are two."

Ben waited until he was on the stairs before he swore, and he did that under his breath. From the moment he asked the children about the liquor, he knew he was not going to hide what he'd done from their father. Jeremiah needed to know that he was responsible for finding and taking the bottles, not the children. Certainly not Lily. Ben figured he'd have to watch his back for a while, but at least Lily would not be an immediate target.

The door to Lily's bedroom was not quite closed. He knocked lightly but under that small pressure the door began to swing open. He grabbed the knob and pulled it back. "It's Ben. May I come in?"

"Just a moment."

As he'd expected, it was Ridley who replied. He waited, heard some rustling, a shifting of sheets and blankets, and finally a thud that sounded like something hitting the floor. He was prepared to ask if his help was needed when he got the invitation to enter.

Lily was lying on her back, a fresh compress across her injured eye. Although she was covered to her neck by a fresh sheet, he could see that pillows supported her hips so that they were raised higher than her head. Beside the bed was the thing that Ben had heard drop: a pail filled to the rim with bloody rags. His gaze did not linger, but he was grateful nonetheless when Ridley dropped an only slightly soiled pillowcase on top.

"She's been asking about her husband," said Ridley before Ben could speak. She gestured to him to come to the bedside. "I didn't know what to tell her."

"Are you going to swear out a complaint?" he asked Lily.

"You know I can't do that, Ben."

"Lily."

"I'm sorry," she said on a thread of sound. "I understand what you want me to do. The children need their father. I need him. I can't raise them alone."

"All right, then I'm letting him go in the morning. I can't keep him past that no matter how it aggrieves me. If you change your mind, send Clay around to the office."

"I won't."

"But if you do . . ."

"I *won't.*"

Ben looked to Ridley. There was no help from that corner. She offered a small shake of her head in response. "I'm taking the liquor, Lily. That's why I'm here. I understand there are two bottles at the back of your wardrobe." He thought she might protest, but she said nothing. He opened the wardrobe and bent down, moving aside some blankets and linens. The children had not been wrong. "Just so you know, Jeremiah is going to hear that I found his bottles without your help, which is God's own truth."

"He won't believe you."

"He will."

"Did you find the one under the porch?"

"Yes. And the flask under Lizzie's crib?"

"Missed it."

"Leave it. He's more likely to credit you with doing it alone if you leave something behind."

Ridley said, "She's likely right. And you said he has the forge. He probably has bottles hidden there."

Ben accepted defeat on this front as well. A muscle worked in his cheek as he set his jaw.

Ridley carried the basin of pink-tinged water to the window and tossed it into the backyard. She lifted the pail of soiled scraps of linen, removed her bag from the nightstand, and then indicated that Ben should take the empty kettle. "There is one other thing. Lily needs assistance. She must remain in bed. I have been very clear about the dangers if she gets up and tries to move around. Hannah cannot possibly manage the little ones by herself, and Clay is hardly any more suitable. I want to hire Mary Cherry to look after Lily and the children. Lily is not in full agreement, but she is my patient, I am her physician, and I rule."

Startled, Ben's head reared back a fraction. "You rule?"

"Overrule, then, if you prefer."

"You've been in town less than forty-eight hours."

"I know," she said, tilting her head in Lily's direction and giving her a conspiratorial wink. "It astonishes, doesn't it?"

"I saw that," said Ben, following Ridley out of the room. "You winked at her. What does that mean? I never understand what it means when women do that." He looked back at Lily plaintively before he stepped into the hallway and closed the door.

Ridley halted, turned, and looked at him. "She was smiling, wasn't she? Just there at the end?"

He nodded. "Yes, because you made me the butt of your joke."

"I know, and I wish I could be sorry for it, but I can't, and you played your part so well, which is really the point of the wink." She handed him the pail to carry downstairs to the washtub. "Thank you. Now, I will wait with the children while you engage Mrs. Cherry's services and bring her around. I think she will be more amenable if you speak to her."

"You *do* rule." She started to go but he stopped her. "The baby?"

Ridley cast her eyes downward. She shook her head. "She lost it sometime last night."

"I'm sorry."

She looked up, met his startling clear blue eyes. "I'm not certain that's the right response. She didn't want the child. I think she would have asked me to abort the fetus if I discovered she hadn't done so spontaneously. It never came to that."

Ben nodded. He wanted to ask what she would have done if Lily had put the request to her, but understood it was neither the time nor the place. He thought he should probably ask and answer the same question for himself before he heard Ridley's response.

"How can she stay with him?" Ben asked quietly as they made their return to the kitchen.

Resigned to the truth, Ridley's answer was also a mere whisper. "How can she not?"

Ridley had not inquired about the location of Mary Cherry's home in proximity to the Salts. She was prepared to wait as long as she had to for Ben to return, and he also had Jeremiah's collection of bottles to take to his office. The first half hour was spent cleaning up breakfast detritus, which included removing porridge from Lizzie's fine hair. Following that, she unbuttoned her cuffs and rolled up her sleeves and applied herself to scrubbing blood from the cloths she'd used to attend to Lily. She hung the cloths over the line out back and then climbed the stairs a second time to check on her patient. Lily was sleeping comfortably. Most important to Ridley was that she showed no sign of a fever.

The children were playing a game with dice, a ball, and no discernable rules in the front room. Ridley joined them on the floor and lost with alarming regularity, which delighted them and satisfied her. It was in the middle of the fifth round that Ben reappeared. Ridley scrambled to her feet and brushed off her skirt.

"We didn't hear you," she said, patting down her hair. The children had quieted upon seeing Ben, and Ridley thought her voice seemed unusually loud.

"We could hear you." He stepped aside and made room for his companion to come abreast of him in the archway. When she came out from behind him, he made quick work of the introductions. The children were all well acquainted with Mary Cherry, and they hopped to their feet—Ham dancing on tiptoes—to happily greet her.

Ridley had no difficulty understanding how Mary Cherry had so effectively been swallowed by Ben's shadow. If Ridley was being generous, Mrs. Cherry stood no taller than four and a half feet. She was a study in geometric shapes from her triangular face with its high, broad brow and sharply pointed chin. A second triangle could be drawn from her shoulders to her waist and a third from her waist to the spreading hem of her gown. Her features were tightly drawn, emphasizing careworn lines at the corners of her eyes and mouth and the permanent vertical crease between her eyebrows. She was graying at the temples and all along the center part of her otherwise black hair. There were wiry silver threads in her eyebrows, but her lashes were long and dark as onyx.

Ridley stepped forward and held out her hand. "I am very glad to make your acquaintance." When Mary ignored the overture, Ridley merely shrugged and let her hand fall back to her side. "Dr. Dunlop had a good many things to say about how you managed his house and his practice."

Mary Cherry snorted. "Managed his life is more like it."

"I don't doubt it."

"And he had mostly nothing to say about you. Now why do you suppose that was?"

"I'm sure I don't know."

"There's tomfoolery going on. That's what I think. Tomfoolery." She pointed to Ridley's medical bag. "You think that means something to me? It doesn't. I'm here because Ben asked me, Lily needs me, the children want me, and you're paying me a week's wages for a couple or three days of work."

Ridley inhaled a calming breath and released it slowly. She stood still for Mary Cherry's narrow-eyed assessment for a ten count and then told her in precise and chilly accents how things would be. Minutes later, she was sailing out the door that the sheriff held open for her.

Ben caught up to her quickly, touched her elbow to slow her down. "I don't think anyone's ever managed to get the best of Mary Cherry before, not like you just did. She was gaping at you and then her mouth snapped shut. I heard her teeth click."

Ridley shoved her bag at him. "Hold this." She rolled down her sleeves, smoothed them, and buttoned the cuffs. Taking back the bag, she resumed her brisk pace until they reached the main street on the other side of Jeremiah Salt's forge. "Where are we going?"

"Hold on," said Ben, standing his ground. "Who got the better of whom back there? I thought it was you with the upper hand, but I'm wondering now if that's true."

Ridley pressed her lips together. Her fingers tightened on her bag. "I don't like losing my temper. I allowed her to do that to me."

Ben cocked his head to one side and rubbed behind his right ear. "That was you losing your temper?"

"Do you doubt it?"

"I guess not, if you say so. You never raised your voice."

Ridley cast her eyes heavenward, shook her head.

"You were frosty, though. That was interesting. I'm more accustomed to hot tempers."

She sighed. "Please, can we go on?"

"Of course." He pointed up the street. "Hank Ketchum's livery is about the only business behind us. Depot's back that way, but you've already seen the stationmaster, so I thought we'd work our way north toward the Butterworth and come back around past the milliner's, Maxwell Wayne's bakery, and Hennepin's mercantile. The more proprietors you meet, the faster word will get around that you're here and prepared to see patients."

"All right." She began walking, this time with less measured steps.

"Do you have any objections to going inside the Songbird?"

"That's the saloon, isn't it?" When he nodded, she said, "I don't have any moral objections if that's what you're asking, but even that encounter with Mrs. Cherry does not tempt me to have a drink this early. Truth be told, seeing Mr. Salt's bottles lined up on the kitchen table has made me consider whether I will ever want a drink again. I was glad when you took them with you."

"They're lined up on my desk now. Hitch is guarding them. Jeremiah doesn't know they're there yet. That's a conversation for later today. The reason I want to take you to the Songbird is because the owner was in to see me yesterday. Buzz's big toe is the size of a sizzling sausage ready to burst its casing, and he was inquiring about the arrival of the doctor. The Songbird is also the hub for a lot of the town gossip, though there won't be a man there who will admit it. Sound interesting to you?"

Ridley admitted that it did. "Buzz?" she asked.

"Buzz Winegarten. The way I understand is that he poked a hive when he was a kid, the bees swarmed, and he's been Buzz ever since."

"Did my godfather treat him?"

"Yes. I'm not sure Buzz ever took his advice for more than a few days at a time. You'll find that happens around here."

"It happens everywhere. Frost Falls couldn't possibly be the exception. Pain prompts people to do something. They follow the instructions until the pain's gone and then they gradually go back on their promises to themselves, to their doctor, and to the Almighty."

Ben chuckled. "Sounds about right." He pointed to the canted sign above the saloon. "That's the Songbird. Won't be many inside at this hour. Buzz said his nephew is working the bar, but Buzz is probably sitting nearby keeping an eye on the money."

Buzz was indeed situated as Ben described. His chair was turned at a right angle to the table so he could not only see the transactions at the bar but also elevate his gouty foot on the seat of another chair. He looked up when the doors swung open and momentarily let in a shaft of sunlight. He was already grimacing so tightly that Ridley couldn't say if he actually squinted. There was no doubt in her mind that he was in an enormous amount of pain.

Ridley made out the presence of three customers in the dimly lit saloon, one standing at the bar with a boot resting on the brass rail, and two others sharing a table near the staircase. There was also a young man behind the bar wiping a glass with a damp towel. He set down the glass and tossed the towel over his shoulder. She thought he was following her progress as she wended her way between and around the tables but came to the amusing realization that it was Ben that he was eyeing.

The man standing at the bar and the pair sharing the table all grunted some sort of greeting. Buzz's nephew had nothing to say and looked as if he wished himself somewhere else.

"I brought the doc," Ben said when they reached Buzz's table.

"Yeah?" Buzz looked away from Ben and right through Ridley. "Where you keeping him, then?"

Ben pulled a chair away from the table, spun it around, and sat. "Your eyesight's no better than a mole's. You need to get out more, Buzz. You're staring at her. This is Dr. E. Ridley Woodhouse."

Ridley set her bag on the table. "Just Dr. Woodhouse," she said. "Your sheriff takes peculiar pleasure in making my name sound more pretentious than it is. May I examine your foot?"

Buzz actually shrank back and howled as pain radiated from his big toe all the way up to his knee. Beads of sweat appeared on his brow and across the crown of his bald head. She hadn't touched him.

Ridley lifted a chair and carefully set it down close to Buzz's aching foot. She was aware the vibration of setting down the chair too hard could give rise to another wave of near unendurable pain. She sat, looked him straight in the eye, and asked again, "May I look at your foot?"

He remained wary. "I don't like it."

"I understand." Her gaze did not waver. This was a standoff that she invariably won. It only remained to be seen how long it would take him to realize it.

"Aww, hell," said Buzz after a long minute of contemplating his choices. "Go on with you, then. But I'm warning you; I'm making no allowances for your tender sensibilities. You're gonna hear words."

"Words are fine, Mr. Winegarten, but I promise I'll try to be gentle anyway."

"Yeah? You sure you're a doctor? Dunlop never cared. Damn near took my toe off with his yanking and squeezing."

Ridley ignored that. She gently began removing the compress from around Buzz's sockless foot. He winced and moaned, but he didn't curse. She winced a little herself when she saw how tightly the skin was stretched around his toe. It was swollen on all sides, the color leaning unnaturally toward a deep shade of purple. There was tissue damage and the skin was flaking and peeling. She asked Ben for a small bucket, clean cloths, cold water, and alcohol.

Ben did not have to leave his chair. He looked over at the bar, crooked a finger at Buzz's nephew, and had everything delivered to the table.

"Why is that boy afraid of you?" she asked Ben.

"Lincoln? He's not afraid of me."

Buzz said, "He's afraid of me. Thinks I might have him arrested. And I will, too, if I catch him putting money in his pockets that I didn't give him."

"Has that happened?"

"Not yet, but I have my suspicions. His father is a thief—that's my brother-in-law—and my sister has the sense of my big toe, so there's good reason to suppose the boy's gonna turn out like a bent nail. I've alerted Ben, just as a precaution, and Lincoln knows what I did and that I got my eye on him."

"It seems as if you have it all thought out."

"Can't own an establishment like the Songbird and run it successfully without keeping an eye open. Two eyes. Have to stay sharp and watchful. That's the trick."

"I'm certain it is."

Ben's laughter came from deep in his throat.

Buzz turned his head. "What's so funny?"

"You are. She's cut away that ugly strip of dead skin, swabbed the toe with your whiskey, and is about to prepare a new compress, and you, Mr. Eagle-Eye, haven't seen fit to notice."

"Which was the point," Ridley said dryly. "Did you have to laugh?"

Ben raised his hands in a gesture of helplessness.

Sighing, Ridley riffled through the towels she was given, found a thin one, and tore it in half lengthwise. She dipped both halves in the cold water and wrung them out. From her bag she took a packet of salicylate powder and spread the grains carefully over the center of one cloth strip. She covered the grains with the second strip and then gently applied the compress to Buzz's toe, placing the medicinal center against the most swollen and discolored area.

There was no point in asking him questions now. Her patient was too aware of what she was doing to be diverted. As tender as her ministrations were, she glimpsed tears in the man's eyes that came too fast and frequently to be called back.

When she was done, she cupped the heel of his foot in her palm and lifted it another inch while she examined the area with the ball of her thumb.

"Is there a pillow, a cushion, something like that around here?" she asked, glancing over to the bar.

"Got another stack of towels here," Lincoln said. He reached under the bar and lifted them.

When he simply stood there holding the towels, Buzz said, "Well, bring them here, boy." To Ridley and Ben, he said, "What did I tell you? A bent nail."

Ridley wanted to laugh but she didn't dare. Jostling Buzz's leg at this point was tantamount to jostling a bottle of nitroglycerine. He'd feel the explosion all the way to the top of his head. "Ease the towels under where I'm holding him," she said when Lincoln arrived.

Ben got up. "I'll do it." He took the towels and settled them where Ridley directed and then watched her ease her palm from under Buzz's heel so it could rest on the stack.

Buzz sank his teeth into his lower lip but didn't cry out.

Ridley sat back, poured some whiskey over her hands, and shook them dry. When Buzz stretched his arm for the bottle, she pushed it out of his reach. "Oh, no. I believe you know better. What did Doc tell you about your condition?"

Buzz's fingers scrabbled against the tabletop. The movement did not bring the bottle a whit closer. "Damn." His shoulder slumped but very slowly. "I want to hear what you have to say first. Maybe Doc's advice was old-timey medicine."

"I doubt it, but if it was, it's because gout is an old-timey problem." She heard Ben snicker, but he quickly caught himself and cleared his throat. "Its exact cause is not clear, but we know many of the things that exacerbate the condition."

Buzz frowned deeply. "Exasperate?"

"Exacerbate. It means worsen or intensify. Exasperate is what you're trying to do to me."

Ben said, "Don't fool with the doc, Buzz. I witnessed her turning Mary Cherry into stone this morning and have no reason to think she won't do the same to you."

Buzz regarded Ridley with new interest. "Is that true?"

Ridley stood and picked up her bag. "No alcohol. Beer is

alcohol, Mr. Winegarten. You need to drink plenty of water but not tea or coffee."

"Christ," he said under his breath.

"I imagine your diet is rich in red meat, this being cattle country, but you should eat it sparingly or not at all. Rich foods, pies, custards, and the like should similarly be avoided."

"What the hell am I supposed to eat?"

"For now, vegetables and fruits as you get them, eggs, chicken, some breads. How long do your symptoms usually last?"

"A few days. Once, two weeks."

"Hmm. I don't doubt you wanted the doctor to amputate your leg."

"I just about asked him to."

"Well, I won't do it, so my advice is that you follow the regimen. I can't promise that you won't have another attack, but you may be able to prevent their frequency and duration. I'll visit you tomorrow." She slid the packet of salicylate powder toward him. You saw how I prepared the compress. You do the same every six hours. It probably wouldn't hurt to find someone other than your nephew to help. Keep the foot elevated. Don't walk around even if you think you can. Do you live upstairs?"

He nodded.

"Then you get a couple of your best customers to carry you up there, and you should do it before they've had too much to drink. I'm not coming back this evening to repair a broken head." She drew back her shoulders, nodded once to punctuate her instructions, and turned on her heel. "We should go, Sheriff."

Ben rose, spun his chair around to face the table, but waited until Ridley was through the doors before he turned to go. He grinned at Buzz as the man sat gaping at Ridley's back. "Turned you right to stone," he said quietly. "Damned if she didn't."

Chapter Eleven

Ridley wrote out her order for Mickey Mangold in neat script and blew gently on the ink until it was dry. Mr. Mangold would wonder why she needed the teas, salves, and elixirs when she had so few patients to attend, but he was too polite to ask and she would not offer the information. It was her habit to keep her bag stocked with the common items she might need and a few of the rarely used medicines as well, but she had also been studying her medical chemistry texts and been experimenting with the properties of certain medicines, especially the elixirs in which trace amounts of additives like mercury, copper, iron, and lead were suspended in alcohol, camphor, and castor oil. There was hardly any of it, in her opinion, that wasn't snake oil, and it probably would kill the snake that took it. She had spoken to the druggist about the salesmen who came through Frost Falls with their little tent shows and suitcases filled with product. Mr. Mangold did not have the same visceral reaction to these men that she did and did not see the harm in allowing them to ply their trade.

Ridley was of the mind that their very existence was a scourge that scientific medicine should extinguish. The battle was hers alone.

Ridley opened her stationery box, a gift from her parents after she announced she would be leaving home and hospital, and removed two sheets of cream-colored paper. She considered what she wanted to tell them before putting pen to paper. There was a need to strike a balance between fact and fiction. Too much of the former and her mother would be demanding that she return home, perhaps even sending her father to fetch her. Too much fiction, and her father would become suspicious, especially if he shared particulars with her godfather. Doc was the fly in the ointment because he knew the people of Frost Falls, their imperfections and prejudices, their conditions and criticisms. Her godfather must have known that in spite of the town needing a doctor, the good citizens of Frost Falls would be slow to embrace her as one. And equally slow to embrace her as one of them.

Eight weeks had passed since she stepped off the train, and Ridley was faced with the inescapable fact that she was a fish out of water.

It was disappointing that, by and large, it was her own gender that failed to support her. Swallowing her pride, she had asked Ellie where the women were seeking medical help and learned there was a doctor in neighboring Liberty Junction, a relatively short train ride away.

Word had gotten around quickly that she had treated Buzz Winegarten's gout and George Hotchkiss's broken nose and disjointed shoulder. They had nothing but good things to say about her, but their testimonials were not enough to prompt others to seek her out. Only a few people knew that she had treated Lily Salt, and not one of them was speaking.

There were curiosity seekers, of course, all of them men who arrived with a veritable catalog of complaints, some of them contradictory, just to test her acumen. She took it in stride and was often able to show them the door not long after they arrived. She diagnosed their condition as malingering, prescribed cod liver oil, which she knew they would never take and wouldn't hurt them if they did, and accepted their money just as if she'd earned it.

The sheriff directed patients from the outlying ranches her way. She also had occasion to visit them. She removed a potentially lethal piece of wooden shrapnel from a homesteader's flank when he failed to hear his son's fire-in-the-hole cry and damn near blew himself up along with the stump he was trying to remove. She treated a wrangler who had cornered a steer in a thick patch of poison ivy and not only had the telltale rash from head to toe, but had managed to breathe the oil into his lungs.

When a woman visited her office, there was a child in tow, often more than one. No one arrived without having tried

home remedies first. Ridley thought it was mostly a miracle
that the children survived concoctions that had no curative
powers and were more likely to cause alcohol poisoning in
high doses. She did her best to educate, but she couldn't insist
that she knew best. Every mother had to make up her own
mind about that.

Ridley finished her letter with an anecdote about Hamilton
Salt mastering his alphabet using matchsticks to form the letters. It was a successful endeavor until the fire. Fortunately the
sheriff had been there to smother the flames, but then, it had
also been his idea to use the matchsticks in the first place.

She closed her missive by inquiring about her godfather's
health and asking her father to encourage Doc to write to her.
Thus far, he had replied to none of her letters. She feared that
his health was following the devastating course that she knew
it could.

Ridley addressed an envelope before she slipped the letter
inside and sealed it. She pushed it to one side of her desk and
sat back. She closed her eyes. She could hear Martha Rushton
moving around in the kitchen and imagined the woman was
blackening the stove or perhaps mopping the floor. The kitchen
did not need a lot of attention because Ridley rarely used it.
She boiled water there for coffee or tea as the mood struck her
and made the occasional bowl of porridge. It was simply more
convenient to take meals at the Butterworth and it hadn't taken
long before it was her habit.

The widow Rushton wanted to be more helpful and had
offered numerous times to prepare meals. Ridley accepted occasionally, and then only to ease Mrs. Rushton's mind that she
wasn't being released from her employment. There was prec-
edent for the widow's suspicions. She was Ridley's fourth
housekeeper in two months, making the average length of stay
two weeks. It was a misleading statistic because housekeepers
one and three lasted mere days, while housekeeper two stayed
a full eighteen before her parents, fearful of what she might
see, changed their minds about her working for a doctor.

Ridley had given serious thought to approaching Mary
Cherry with a generous offer, but for all that Mrs. Cherry was
competent and had done very well by Lily Salt, she was also
sour and surly with Ridley at every turn. Ridley doubted that

any amount of money was going to change that, so in the end she applied to the sheriff to advise her.

Ben Madison had been good about not inserting himself into her life on a regular basis. She appreciated that. It made it easier for her to go to him when there was a need. They were friendly, if not friends, and if he hadn't been her neighbor, they would not have crossed paths as often as they did. Their encounters were brief. She always inquired about his job, his hours, and sometimes about Lily Salt. He asked if she was having difficulties with the natives, if she needed anything, and whether or not she had heard from Doc. Apparently his letters were also unanswered.

It troubled her some that her thoughts turned to him as often as they did. It was an unexpected distraction, one that was wholly unfamiliar to her but not as unwelcome as she wanted it to be. Ben Madison was a fine-looking man with his ambling walk, easy manner, and shock of red hair, which he mostly tried to hide. She never made it a point to run into him, but she did find herself wandering to the window at the front of the house and drawing back the curtain to see if he was coming or going down the street. Occasionally she'd see him passing her gate in the morning after he left his house, but if he ever looked in her direction, it happened when she wasn't watching.

When she needed help finding a new housekeeper, she went to Ben. He had consulted his mother, who in turn had recommended Martha Rushton. Because of the widow appellation, Ridley had expected a woman closer to her mother's age than her own, but men died early for all kinds of reasons, and Mr. Rushton had left this earth two years prior when a scratch from a rusty nail went septic. The widow had subsequently had offers of marriage, and if there had been children, she might have accepted one of them, but as she explained to Ridley, she had a little money put aside and was not needy for herself.

Ridley liked her plain speaking, liked the fact that she went about her work quietly, and did not gossip outside of the office. Gossip had been the downfall of housekeepers one and three as they both failed to keep patient confidences to themselves, and what they didn't know, they filled in with speculation.

"Martha!" Ridley called. Only a moment passed before Mrs. Rushton opened the door to the office. She was holding a blackened rag in one hand and smoothing the front of her smudged apron with the other. She was of an ample size, not heavy, only plump. She had a round face, a smooth complexion, and a hint of a double chin. Her cheeks were as rosy as polished apples, and when she smiled, her eyes were mere slits between her lashes. She wore her cinnamon-colored hair in a neat bun and covered the top of her head with a little white cap while she was cleaning.

"Yes, Doctor?" she asked. "Will you be having lunch here this afternoon?"

"Actually, I thought I would. There is some of that ham left from Sunday dinner, isn't there?"

"Four slices in the cold box."

"Then I'll have a sandwich and some of that leftover bean soup, if you don't mind."

"Not at all. It'd be my pleasure."

Ridley held up a hand to stave off what was surely the widow's palpable excitement. "I have a letter I want to take to the station first. I thought you might want to tidy up in here while I'm gone."

The housekeeper's eyes darted to the window behind Ridley. "You're going out? In that?"

Ridley turned and confronted the outdoor scene that had Mrs. Rushton concerned. It was snowing. Again. The ground was layered with twenty inches of snow in the open and four-foot drifts against the house. What was falling now would easily add another two inches in the next hour. The wind was calm, which Ridley knew by now to count as a blessing.

"Did you have difficulty walking here this morning?"

"No, but the snow wasn't falling then. Maxwell says half a foot of new snow by morning."

"Hmm. Mr. Maxwell Wayne would do well to allow me to treat his rheumatism and stop predicting the weather."

"That's not going to happen."

Ridley screwed her mouth to one side, chuckling. "I have to agree." She pushed herself up from her desk. "I expect to return within the hour. If anyone comes to the surgery, you explain that." The widow nodded, and Ridley did not miss the compassion in her dark eyes. "Someday, Mrs. Rushton, there will be patients crowding the surgery."

Tongue firmly in cheek, tone as dry as chalk, Mrs. Rushton said, "I wondered about your experiments. You're planning to bring back the plague, then."

Ridley's eyes brightened with humor. "My thought exactly."

Laughing quietly, the women parted ways.

The lack of wind was deceiving. Ridley discovered that as soon as she stepped out of the house. She had arrived with outerwear that she believed would be suitable for the frigid winter climes of Colorado, and subsequently marveled at her ignorance after the first snowfall. Her fur-trimmed pelisse, appropriate for short walks in her Beacon Hill neighborhood, carriage rides to and from the hospital, and ice skating on the waterfront, was wholly inadequate for the icy temperatures that characterized winter in Frost Falls. When she learned that Frost Falls was named after its founder, not its weather, she was sure the lore had it wrong.

Ridley was now dressed to manage the elements if not tame them. Her cloak, as recommended to her by the local dressmaker, was constructed of brushed navy wool. It closed with three glossy satin frogs and had a hood that could be pulled up over her head and lowered across her forehead. She wore heavy woolen socks over her stocking feet and a pair of boots with laces made especially to accommodate the presence of the thick socks. The tradespeople of Frost Falls might not require her services, but she certainly required theirs.

Ducking her head against the cold, Ridley forged on. The boardwalk had a clear path because the business owners made certain there was room for those brave enough to venture out. She did notice that the path was steadily narrowing as more snow began to accumulate. Her breath was visible upon exhalation and the lenses of her spectacles were fogged over before she was halfway to her destination. She supposed that was what accounted for her running headlong into the only other pedestrian on the walk.

"Hey!" Ben caught Ridley by the elbows and set her away

from him, steadying her at the same time. He ducked, cocking his head, trying to get a better look at her face, the only part of which was visible being the frosty tip of her nose and a pair of indrawn lips. Ben slipped two gloved fingers under her chin and lifted. "You still have a pair of eyes behind those spectacles, don't you?"

She was tempted to stick out her tongue but was afraid it would freeze to her lips.

"Here," he said, taking the spectacles by the earpieces and gently removing them. He used one end of his scarf to wipe away the condensation and then held them up to look through them. "Well, they're better than they were." He drew her into the protective alcove of Hennepin's mercantile and replaced them.

Ridley looked at him through the lenses and then over the top of them. He looked very fine from either perspective. "Thank you. I'm off to the station to deliver a letter for mailing."

"Ah. Then by all means, 'Damn the torpedoes, full speed ahead.'"

Ridley thought that was an accurate description of what her father called her single-mindedness and her mother referred to as stubborn to a fault. "Where are you going?"

"Nowhere in particular. Looking in on folks. Miss Renquest, eighty-four if she's a day, doesn't always have enough wood and she surely can't step outside to bring in any. Thought I'd sit with her a spell."

She had always known that he was kind, but that he would seek out Miss Renquest to sit with her touched Ridley unexpectedly. "Mrs. Rushton is making lunch. It's leftovers but I know there will be plenty. Will you join us? Sit a spell?"

There was no hesitation. "I'd like that just fine."

She nodded once, satisfied. "Drop by after you visit Miss Renquest. We'll keep the soup hot."

Chapter Twelve

Ben arrived at Ridley's door carrying half an apple pie. "Dessert," he said, stomping his snow-covered boots on the porch before he stepped inside. He handed Ridley the pie. It was wrapped in a large gingham napkin, and in spite of the temperature out of doors, warmth lingered in the fragrance. "Compliments of Miss Renquest." He unwound his scarf and shrugged out of his coat. Small clumps of wet snow clung to the lamb's wool collar.

"You can hang your things there," she said, pointing to the coat rack in one corner of the vestibule.

Ben stuffed his gloves into a pocket of his coat and then hung the coat up along with his hat. He plunged his fingers through his thick thatch of hair to give it some order. "You sure this isn't an imposition?"

"Hardly. I invited you, remember?"

He did; it was just that she had never done so before and he had made a powerful effort to keep distance between them. Some days the closest he got was when they were in their respective homes. Her surgery was hardly more than spitting distance from his kitchen, and if she was late going to bed, he sometimes saw her turn back the lamps. Ridley had never asked him to stay away or given him any indication that she noticed, but Ben believed he was doing right by her, supporting her independence in a way she could tolerate. If he was lucky, she'd never know about his spies.

"I thought we'd have lunch in the dining room," said Ridley. "It's almost never used."

Nodding, Ben followed her. The table was already set with a pair of striped placemats and mismatched dishes. There were only two settings. "Mrs. Rushton isn't joining us?" He craned his neck to see into the kitchen.

"I encouraged her to go home. It was snowing harder when I got back than when I left, and I could tell she was worried about the walk back."

"Oh."

Ridley laughed. "Are you concerned about being alone with me, Sheriff?"

"No."

"Well, you should be. Other than exchanging a few words in passing, I haven't been engaged in conversation for almost a week. I could easily talk your ear off if you only nod occasionally and pretend interest."

"That wouldn't be much of a conversation, though, would it?"

"Point taken. Please, sit down. I'll bring in the soup. It's only bean. I hope that is all right."

"Sounds good." He called after her as she sailed into the kitchen. "I appreciate the invitation. My mother sent down some shepherd's pie, but Hitch devoured it while I was at the livery settling a dispute between Sam Love and Hank Ketchum. Hank's wife showed up at the office and said I had to go right away before her husband did something foolish."

Ridley reappeared carrying a tureen. She set it on an iron trivet and ladled soup into Ben's bowl and then her own before she sat. "There's tea brewing," she said. "I thought we'd have it with our pie." She spread her napkin across her lap. "So did you arrive on time to settle the dispute?"

"I got there in time to keep Hank from taking a buggy whip to Sam, but as for their dispute, I'm no Solomon. It'll have to wait until the judge comes around or they get someone they can agree on to mediate. Mediation isn't likely. They don't agree on the color of the sky at the moment. Sam claims Hank sold him a horse that he knew was going to come up lame and Hank says Sam's a fool and that no one can know a thing like that."

"What do you think?"

Ben paused in the act of lifting a spoonful of soup to his mouth. He raised an eyebrow at her. "Oh, no. I'm not saying. That's not the kind of thing where I can safely take sides.

Hank boards my horse and Sam cuts my hair. Best to keep my own counsel."

Ridley nodded, smiled, and began to eat. "I saw Lily Salt on Tuesday. She looks well."

He frowned. "I didn't know you visited her."

"I didn't. I saw her in the mercantile with Lizzie and Ham in tow. She was a bit harried but otherwise well." Her eyes narrowed a fraction. "You look concerned. Is there a problem?"

"No. No problem." He thought she probably saw the effort he made to clear his face. He wished he could have done it smoothly and not raised her suspicions. "I think I mentioned before that I'd like to know if you pay a call on Lily Salt."

"You did. And it was my contention then and now that you have more important things to occupy your time."

"I never said I would try to talk you out of it."

"No, but you would want to accompany me, and that seems excessively interfering. It is also hardly part of your job."

"It's part of the job if I say it is."

"Hmm." She ignored him and drew another spoonful of soup.

"Look. You are not Jeremiah Salt's favorite person. It would be better if you didn't poke the bear."

Ridley pointed to the trivet under the tureen. "Mr. Salt made that for me at my request. You might not have noticed, but he fashioned a W into the design. It was very clever of him. So, you see, I've already poked the bear. He and I have an understanding."

Ben set his jaw. If his spoon had been in his mouth, he would have bitten it off. "When did you do that?"

"I'm not sure. Weeks and weeks ago. Not long after you released him, if I recall."

So much for his clever web of spies, Ben thought. Someone should have reported to him that she had been within twenty yards of Jeremiah Salt. If she requested that he make the trivet for her, then she likely visited him again to pick it up. He knew about neither time. He shook his head. He was firing them, beginning with Hank Ketchum, who surely should have been a witness to one exchange.

"Tell me about your understanding," said Ben.

"He won't touch his wife again except in the most loving way, and I won't have cause to end his miserable life."

"You said that to him?"

"Words to that effect. It's an understanding, not a contract."

"Dr. Woodhouse."

"Ridley. You can call me Ridley."

"I wish you hadn't done that."

"I needed a trivet."

Ben gave her a sour look. She was as impervious to that as she was to every other admonishment. He changed the subject. "Did Dave Saunders come by to see you? Maybe a week or ten days ago?"

"The ingrown toenail. Yes. Did you refer him?"

"I did. He was hobbling over to my office twice a day when things were slow and couldn't seem to talk about anything else. He wouldn't let his wife touch it after she threatened to cut it off."

"That's Dotty, right? Ed is the one married to Abigail."

"That's right."

"And Abigail is the one who is expecting."

He nodded.

"I heard that from your mother. I hoped she would come to see me. Abigail, that is. Not your mother. I believe Abigail will be using a midwife to deliver this child, but I understand that Doc attended her before."

"I'm not sure I can explain her reasoning other than familiarity."

"That occurred to me as well. When you mentioned that you were going around this afternoon to check on folks, see they had what they needed, it got me thinking that I could do the same. The initial introductions were helpful, but I need to do more. People are wary of me, especially the women. I think I need to make myself familiar, just as you said."

Ben didn't think he had said that exactly, but he was not going to quibble. "That makes sense. Did you accept Amanda Springer's invitation to join the Ladies Giving Circle?"

"I accepted her invitation to a meeting, but I was not invited to join. I'm sure you could have had that same information from your deputy if you'd asked."

"I did ask. Hitchcock is largely deaf to his mother's voice. He didn't know anything about it."

Ridley set down her spoon. "Do you keep an eye on me?"

"What?"

She shrugged lightly. "It's something I've been wondering for a while now. Do you look out for me? I know you refer patients, and sometimes I wonder if it might not be at the point of a gun, but of late I've had the sense that perhaps you know more about my comings and goings than is warranted by your position."

"Now, what would give you that sense?"

"Little things. The way Mr. Winegarten often steps out of the Songbird when he sees me passing. He's always interested in where I'm going, what I've been doing."

"He's friendly," said Ben. *And not very subtle*, he thought. "He's grateful for your attention to his foot."

"Hmm. I wonder."

"That's slim evidence."

"There's more. Mrs. Mangold is peculiarly interested in my activities when I visit the apothecary. She blends my teas for me and has as many questions as there are leaves in one of her little wooden boxes."

"Dolly has a curious nature, I suppose. I wouldn't make too much of it."

"That's what your mother said, too."

"Well, there you have it. My mother and Dolly are peas in a pod."

"Perhaps, but your mother seems genuinely interested. Dolly's questions are more perfunctory and at the same time more pointed. It's odd, is all. It's as if she's working hard to speak to me."

"That does seem odd."

Ridley nodded, looked at Ben's empty bowl. "More soup or shall I bring the sandwiches?"

"Sandwiches."

She rose, removed their bowls, and went to the kitchen.

While she was gone, Ben lifted the warm tureen and examined the trivet. Jeremiah's work was good, although the piece was hardly as exacting in detail as some of the things he made.

He was not hampered by the exact dimensions of a wheel or the breadth of a horse's hoof. He wondered at Jeremiah's reaction when the doctor had come around. The man had plenty to say about her when he was released, and none of it was fit for repeating, especially not to E. Ridley Woodhouse. Jeremiah stopped short of threatening her but skirted the edge with more delicacy than Ben could ever have expected.

Jeremiah swore he had no memory of raising his fists against Lily, and Ben was inclined to believe him. Jeremiah had stared at his hands as if they could give evidence to his innocence, when in fact, his knuckles still had blood in the creases where he pounded the door until Lily let him in the bedroom. Lily bore the only evidence that he had pounded on her. Ben had explained that to Jeremiah. He did not mention the loss of a child, only that Lily's injuries required a doctor. That did not bother Jeremiah until he remembered that Doc was not the physician who attended his wife. That lighted Jeremiah's short fuse because sobriety did not make him a less jealous man. Ben disabused him of the notion that a young male physician had attended Lily, but upon hearing that the new doctor was a woman, the fuse sparked again.

Ben didn't understand it, but it was not something that he could ignore.

The collection of bottles that Ben showed Jeremiah had almost no impact. The news that Ben had a conversation with Buzz about not serving Jeremiah more than a couple of beers was greeted with silence, but not the kind that communicated agreement. Once again, Jeremiah placed the blame on the doctor.

Ridley returned with two plates and a ham sandwich cut on the diagonal on each. She sat and encouraged him to eat. "You haven't really answered my question."

"You asked 'more soup or sandwiches.' I said sandwiches."

"Ah, there is the Ben Madison who endears himself to the people of Frost Falls."

He grinned. "I do, don't I?"

"And makes your mother want to cuff you."

His grin grew more profound. "That's true, too."

She cast her eyes at the ceiling and shook her head. "Are you keeping an eye on me?"

Ben sighed. "More or less."

"Which is it? More or less?"

"More. I have help." He picked up half of his sandwich. "I still get to eat this, right?"

"I think my brain must have been iced over when I invited you to lunch."

"Probably, but what accounts for you letting me in?"

"The apple pie."

He chuckled and took a bite of his sandwich. "What do you hear from Doc?"

"Nothing. He doesn't return my letters."

"How many have you written?"

She held up three fingers. "What about you?"

"One letter. No reply. You don't suppose he's—"

"Dead? No. At least not when I received my father's last letter a few days ago. Doc is teaching and appears to be enjoying himself. Perhaps he doesn't want to think about us."

"Maybe."

"I asked him about Jeremiah Salt. Really about Lily. I'd hoped for some advice, something I could do to move her."

"I thought you were resigned."

"I don't know that I'll ever be resigned. I understand it. It's not quite the same thing. I suppose I still want it to be different. I worry a little more every day that goes by and he doesn't hit her."

"I don't understand."

"It will happen again. He'll hit her. Nothing we did—taking his alcohol, promising that he'll go back to jail, threatening to end his miserable life—none of that will matter because I don't know if he can help himself. I don't think he wants to. The pressure will build and he'll have a drink. One. Two. A dozen. And he'll imagine some slight that will justify his actions and then Clay will send for you and you will send for me and it will begin again. I've always imagined a balloon in my mind. It's being slowly blown up, so slowly that you almost don't realize it's happening, and then it's big enough to alert you to its presence but not alert you to how much pressure it can bear. You know it will burst. It has to. And of course, it does. That's when the relief comes. Immediately afterward and it lasts only a short time. Another balloon is already starting to rise. There is always another balloon."

Ben said nothing, studied her face. She had not spoken passionately, but rather matter-of-factly. There was nothing in her expression to hint of personal knowledge, and yet he could not shake the sense that her words came from her own experience, not the experience of others.

Ridley said, "Lily and the children live with the knowledge that it will happen again. It would not be out of the question for one of them to provoke him simply for the temporary relief it brings."

"Control the explosion," Ben said quietly.

"Yes, something like that."

"You seem to know a lot about it." Ridley shrugged and Ben watched her cast her eyes to her plate. She had eaten only a few bites of her sandwich. He suspected that her appetite had fled. She was silent for so long that he did not think she meant to say anything, but he had learned how to be silent longer, and his patience was rewarded in the end.

A slim crooked smile lifted her lips briefly. She did not look at him. "I don't suppose I shared any of those thoughts without the knowledge that you might ask for more. I'm still wondering if I'm prepared to tell you."

He almost said then that she didn't have to, which was true, but not what he wanted. She was a private person. It was the thing most remarked upon by other people. She struck them as mannerly but not quite friendly, willing to listen, not willing to share. It was not that she was disliked, only that she was unknown. As well as the introductions had gone when he escorted her around town, she had not made connections on her own or followed up on the ones she made with him. He was encouraged by her invitation to lunch and her thinking that she should get around to see people whether or not they had need of her.

It was a good beginning, he thought, a better one than she had when she stepped off the train. This was something she came to on her own, and the first real sign that she did not want to be as insular as she appeared.

Ridley pushed her plate away and lifted her eyes. She did not look directly at Ben but at a point just past his shoulder. "I think it's better if I don't leave you to your imaginings. I don't know what they are precisely, but I doubt that you've hit the nail on the head." She took a shallow breath, sipping the air as though from a soupspoon. "The balloon in my family is my mother."

Ben felt the hairs stand up on the back of his neck. He wondered if he gave away his surprise. She was correct that he had not hit the nail on the head. He had been about as far from the nail as one could get and still make it a family affair. He expected to hear it of her father, a brother—although he didn't know if she had any—a male cousin, perhaps an uncle. He remained quiet, waiting to see if she would add more.

She said, "It's all right if you don't know what to say. I'm not sure that there is any one response more appropriate than another." Ridley finally looked Ben in the eye. Her gaze was candid. "Besides the help, who never spoke out under the threat of losing their positions, I can only think of two people outside the family who know what went on for years inside it. One is my mother's physician. The other is my godfather."

"That is a small circle."

"Indeed. The Salt family is an open secret. It was very much closed in my family. One is not better than the other. Neither prompts change."

Ben nodded and kept his focus on her. She deserved that.

"My mother can kindly be described as unpredictable. At times she is a dervish, spinning from activity to activity, full of grand notions without the ability to see even one to completion. That energy doesn't wind down. It ends abruptly, in a bout of despair so deep that she cannot rise from her bed. You might think that the melancholia would be welcome by her children because she remained in her room, but she would summon us, ask us to bring her a tray, and then throw the teapot at our heads or try to stab us with a knife because something wasn't the way it should be. Anger was the thread that ran through all her moods. We ducked. We cowered. We circled her as though she were a wild animal, and in some ways she was exactly that."

"Who is 'us'?" asked Ben.

"I have an older brother and a younger sister. Henry Austin and Grace Elizabeth."

"Your father? He didn't take measures to protect you?"

"My father was frequently the target of her rages when he

was home, so I suppose that was protection of a kind. He had an office in the house, but my mother's temper was not restrained simply because there were patients present. He eventually worked only out of the hospital. The servants watched out for us, intervened when they could. Father eventually hired a companion for her, a nurse who acted as a lady's maid and a watchdog. It was mostly a satisfactory arrangement. Father arranged for Henry's escape by sending him to boarding school. Gracie and I fended for ourselves. Like Clay and Hannah, there are but two years between us. I'm afraid I was not the protector to Gracie as Clay is to his sister."

"Jeremiah doesn't go after the children."

Ridley shook her head. "Don't be so sure. Maybe he doesn't, but I would not make that statement so confidently. It is difficult for an outsider to understand how confused and complicated the feelings are toward one's tormentor. It was not unusual for any of us to protect Mother, perhaps more than we looked out for one another or ourselves. Father would threaten to send her away. It terrified her, but it did not change her. She couldn't change, and Father's threats were empty because he knew the sentence he would be imposing if she went to an asylum."

Ben imagined that keeping the family secret was also a factor, but he said nothing. It was something she knew whether or not she could say so.

"When I boarded the train in Boston," said Ridley, "Mother accompanied Father to the station to see me off. It still shames me that when she went to throw her arms around me, I flinched. I cannot say that she noticed. I hope she didn't. My father, though, did, and he turned away rather than acknowledge what had happened." She fell silent for a moment, and when she spoke, she was no longer looking at Ben. Her voice was hardly more than a whisper, as what she said was meant for her ears alone. "I don't think I've ever despised my mother the way I despised Father just then."

Ben let her words lie there. She had no need of a response.

Ridley's cheeks puffed as she blew out a soft breath. Her brief smile was apologetic and self-effacing. "Well, that was rather more than I thought I was prepared to say. I'm sorry."

He shook his head. "I'm not."

"Hmm."

"Ridley. It's all right."

"I understand why you say that, but for me it's as if I've broken a sacred vow." She laughed a bit unevenly. "It isn't out of the question that I will be excommunicated from the family."

"They'd have to learn about it first, and they won't hear it from me."

She hesitated. "I'm sorry, but I have to ask. You won't write anything about it to Doc?"

Ben was also sorry that she had to ask, and he was reminded that whatever trust there was between them, it was a fragile thing. "No," he said. "I won't."

She nodded slowly as though absorbing the promise. "Then I suppose we should have pie."

"I suppose we should."

Chapter Thirteen

Ridley began her rounds the following morning, bracing for the cold and the wind and the occasional chilly reception. As it happened, there was only one cool welcome, and it came from Amanda Springer. In spite of Mrs. Springer's involvement in promoting temperance, her strong advocacy five years earlier for a Colorado woman's right to vote, her leadership on the library board, the school board, and three other charitable causes, she was not a champion of professional working-women. She made her opinion clear at the Ladies Giving Circle, and she was supported by her loyal followers, who may or may not have given the matter any thought before it came at them front and center.

Ridley had confronted this resistance before. Her mother, and her mother's circle of friends, embraced similar opinions. It was the hospital work that elicited her mother's most fervent objections. That was the purview of men, she announced, men who had a taste for the stink and the blood and the disease. Men who could tolerate wretched poverty, she pointed out, because where else could the poor apply for help? Ridley's interest in medicine did not trouble her mother as much as Ridley's intention to use it. It was this that was incomprehensible to Henrietta Ridley Woodhouse.

Amanda Springer was not so different, although she had never been inside a hospital in her life and had no concept of what might be encountered there. Mrs. Springer simply did not trust that a woman could be as learned as a man. She would have thought the same if Ridley were a lawyer, an accountant, a minister, or an engineer. Ridley knew better than to argue her qualifications. If Amanda Springer's mind was going to be changed, it would be because Amanda Springer changed it. Ridley simply let her be, shared the small cakes she had brought, and encouraged Amanda to talk about her son. Hitchcock was a subject that warmed Mrs. Springer to glowing.

Ridley made ten visits the first day, a dozen the next. By the third day, she realized word had gotten around and people were expecting her. She had a basket of penny candy treats for children, and small loaves of nut bread for the men and women who lived on their own. Before she set out, she read through the files that Doc had left behind. She memorized salient points and knew something about each home she visited whether someone had seen Doc days before he left or years earlier. She was careful to keep her inquiries casual and usually waited for something medically pertinent to come up in conversation before she asked any questions. She listened to family histories, rich with medical lore, discovered what home remedies were most favored and which ones were applied with near lethal consequences.

She treated those who offhandedly complained about an ailment and cautiously dispensed advice to those who were ill but still too wary to ask for help. On the evening of the fourth day, Frankie, one of the Fuller children, arrived at her surgery with a frantic request for her to attend to his parents and his siblings. She had seen Big Mike and Louella and their three children in the morning that same day, and there had been no reason then to suspect anyone in that healthy and lively bunch would have need of her soon, but she took one look at the boy's cherry red cheeks and grabbed her coat and bag.

Louella Fuller was only slightly responsive when Ridley reached her. Mr. Fuller was out cold and the children appeared to be sleeping.

Ridley hustled young Frankie back out of the house, although he was desperate to help, and sent him to fetch the sheriff. She threw open the windows and the doors at either end of the home, and made a pallet of blankets on the front porch before she carried the first child outside. Ben and Hitch appeared as she was carrying out the youngest child in her arms. She stopped Ben when he would have taken the child from her and managed to convey in the small shake of her head that there was nothing to be done for the little one.

Ben and his deputy brought Louella outside first and half dragged, half carried Big Mike out afterward. At Ridley's direction, Hitch gathered all the blankets he could find and brought them out to keep those who could be helped warm. Ridley knelt beside Louella and held her hair out of the way when she began to vomit over the side of the porch. It was not long after that Big Mike stirred and began to heave. Hitch ran for a bucket and came back with a bowl. Ridley could hear the deputy begin to retch in sympathy with Big Mike. She looked around for Ben and didn't see him. Frankie was huddled under blankets with his brothers and sister. It was the little girl who had succumbed to the noxious gas, but Frankie did not realize it yet.

Ben's sudden appearance at the front porch startled Ridley. He came from the yard, not from inside the house. "It was the stove," he said. "They had a fire going because of the cold, but the covers were off the firebox and the closed dampers just pushed the poisonous gas back into the house. It's fixed now." He found Frank's towhead as the boy peeked out from under a mound of blankets. "How are you doing, Frankie? Head still hurt?"

The boy nodded but very slowly.

Ridley asked Ben, "Did he tell you what happened? I was not able to understand much of what he was saying when he came to get me."

"He had a powerful urge to piss, he said, and a powerful headache to go with it. He felt woozy, stumbled out of the house to relieve himself off the back porch, and when he came back in, he felt worse than before. Tried to rouse his mother, then his father, and when he couldn't, he went for you. He says you came round to see them this morning. Is that right?"

"Yes."

"That's why he thought of you."

"I wondered why he didn't go to his neighbors first."

"He did, but Henry and Emma are elderly and didn't hear him knocking or calling for them. He ran straightaway for you after that."

Ridley said nothing. She continued to stroke Louella's back as the woman remained doubled over, moaning occasionally.

"What do you need?" asked Ben.

"A place for them to spend the night. I think it would be better if they went somewhere else."

"Of course."

Ridley patted Louella lightly on the back and then stood. She stepped off the porch and walked around to the side of the house. Ben followed. "I have to tell Big Mike and Louella that their daughter is dead. I'm not sure that Louella will voluntarily leave the house. I think she'll want to stay with Emmilou. You have enough cots at the jail for Big Mike and the boys, don't you?"

"I think we can do better than the jail. If the Butterworth doesn't have a room for them, there are plenty of families who will take them in. Hitch's mother, for one."

"All right. Will you carry Emmilou back inside? Maybe Hitch could take the boys to the Butterworth and I'll catch up with them there after I speak to their parents."

It was after midnight by the time Ridley returned home. She had tried to discourage Ben from escorting her, but she failed to have any influence on his decision. It was difficult to argue with him since he lived next door and was headed that way himself, but it did not keep her from trying. He simply grinned at her in that maddening way of his and rolled over her objections by never addressing them at all. He never really argued so he never lost an argument. It was frustrating and just a little unnerving.

Ben opened the gate for her. She expected he would remain outside the fence, but he dogged her footsteps right up to the front door, and then she lost her mind right there because she invited him in for tea.

"Coffee, if you prefer," she said, her hand on the doorknob.

"Tea's fine. I like yours."

Ridley wondered what she was doing even as she was taking his coat, hat, and gloves and hanging them on the coat tree beside her things. She must have revealed some of her doubt because Ben asked if she was all right, and the proof that she wasn't thinking clearly was when she told him that yes, she was perfectly fine. She wondered if perhaps she hadn't breathed more than her share of noxious fumes this evening.

"Why don't you sit?" asked Ben. "I'll make the tea. I know where everything is."

Ridley didn't try to think why that was; she simply accepted that it was probably true. She sat and watched him make himself at home in her kitchen. "I guess you don't have anyone spending the night in a cell," she said.

"Nope. Dixon Wells was the last and he just needed one night to see the error of his ways."

"Was he the one who tried to steal one of Mr. Ketchum's horses from the livery?"

"He was. And fortunate that his effort was so clumsy that he got caught and not shot." Ben filled the kettle with water and put it on the stove. He stoked the fire, set the covers and dampers, and then removed the tea canister from the shelf. "I'm sorry there was nothing you could do for Emmilou," he said quietly.

"So am I." She stared at her folded hands in her lap. "Louella and Big Mike are heartbroken. There is nothing I can do for them either."

"What about your heart?"

"Hurting. Emmilou crawled all over me this morning, rooted through my pockets like a piglet for the candy she knew I must be hiding. She reminded me of Lizzie Salt. Same fine hair, same sticky fingers, and laughter as bright as a rainbow. So, my heart's hurting. Not shattered, but bruised." She looked up at Ben, uncaring that her lashes were damp. "No one would have survived without Frankie."

"Hmm."

"What is it?"

He was quiet while he spooned tea leaves into the tea ball. "Frankie is the one who set the covers and took care of the dampers. He's done it hundreds of times. Tonight he did it wrong. That's a terrible burden for a twelve-year-old to carry on his bony shoulders."

Ridley lifted one hand to her mouth and held it there. She stared at Ben above her fingertips.

"You didn't know." It wasn't a question.

She shook her head.

"You're still correct," said Ben. "No one would have survived without him."

Ridley lowered her hand and set it on the tabletop. "Poor Frankie," she whispered.

"When did you know what the problem was?"

"When I saw him. His skin was unnaturally flushed in a way the cold could not account for. His speech was slurred and his story was confused. I've seen it before. Every winter there are entire families who die from insufficient ventilation, especially in the poorer areas of the city. Has it happened here before?"

"Not here, not in my memory, but a few years back there was a family in Liberty Junction that perished. Seven in all, I think. It's not that people don't know how to prevent it; it's just that someone forgets, gets careless. It's an accident I expect happens more often than I care to contemplate."

She nodded, knuckled the corner of her right eye, and gave Ben a watery smile when he passed a handkerchief to her.

"I like what you're doing," he said. "Getting out on your own. Meeting folks so they know you, know what you can do. That's why Frankie came to you tonight. A week ago he wouldn't have done that."

"He might have tried harder to rouse his neighbors. If not Henry and Emma Blackwell, then someone else who would have known what to do."

"Maybe. Maybe not. Frankie made the right decision when it counted most. Let's just leave it at that." The water began to rattle as it boiled. Ben pushed away from the stove and grabbed a towel to lift the kettle. He poured water in the teapot and let it steep while he got cups and saucers from the china cupboard. "These still don't match," he said, setting them down.

Ridley laughed low in her throat. "I realized I didn't care. Is that wrong? Should I care about cups and saucers?"

"Not a question I'm qualified to answer. Probably you should ask my mother . . . or Amanda Springer."

She laughed again, this time with genuine amusement. "Maybe Ellie. I know what Mrs. Springer would say."

Smiling conspiratorially, Ben poured tea and sat. "Long day."

She nodded.

He was quiet while he added sugar to his tea and stayed that way while he warmed his hands around the cup. "I'd like to ask you something, Ridley, if you don't mind. It'd be personal, so you're not obligated to answer."

"I'm not telling you what the E stands for in E. Ridley Woodhouse."

"No, it's not that, but if you want to volunteer . . ."

"I don't."

"Well, I was thinking along different lines, although I admit I'm still curious about the other. I started a list."

"You did not."

"I did." He shrugged. "I'm not terribly proud of it, but it beats counting sheep when I can't sleep."

Ridley stared at him, trying to gauge how serious he was. It was impossible. The familiar curl of his upper lip was absent. His blue eyes had taken on a remoteness that made them impenetrable. His jaw was set so that his features remained as still as if they had been cast in marble by a fine hand. "If there is something that explains the odd turn of your mind, I missed that lecture in medical school."

"You probably shouldn't dwell on it."

"Trust me. I wasn't going to." It was a lie, but Ridley thought she managed to sound believable. The real truth was that he continued to fascinate her in a manner she found discomfiting and oddly exciting. "Do you still want to ask me that question?"

"Mm-hmm."

When he didn't go on, she said, "Well?"

"I was wondering if you're lonely." He paused. "Are you?"

Ridley blinked. She removed her spectacles and cleaned them with his handkerchief, and then examined the lenses against the lamplight. Everything she did was in aid of gathering her wits. His question was wholly unexpected. She carefully repositioned the spectacles and then returned his handkerchief to him. "Ever?" she asked finally. "Am I ever lonely or am I lonely now or am I lonely since I came to Frost Falls? You must endeavor to be clearer."

A shadow of a smile crossed his features. "You get all haughty when you feel cornered, do you know that? A little stiff in the spine, maybe a little in the neck as well. At least you don't claw and spit, so there's a blessing."

"I was simply asking for clarification."

"And you don't back down. No retreat. You just hold your ground. There's a lot to admire about that."

"Now you're being patronizing."

"I hardly know what that means."

"Liar."

"Hmm." His quicksilver grin came and went. "Have you been lonely since coming to Frost Falls?"

"I'm under no obligation to answer. You said that."

"I did, and I stand by it."

"Why do you want to know?"

"I guess I thought if you were, then maybe there's something we could do about it."

"We? You and I?"

"And just when I think your grasp of the English language is superior to mine, you require a definition for 'we.' Strikes me as odd, but for the purpose of illumination, yes, you and I, that's the 'we' to whom I am referring."

Ridley's mouth opened. There was an audible click as she snapped her teeth together.

"I know," he said. "Sometimes I surprise myself."

Ridley found her voice. "Did you just proposition me?"

"Did it sound as if I did?"

"Yes."

"I find in these matters you should trust your gut, so if you think that's what I did, I probably did. There is no sense in me trying to say otherwise if I'm not going to be believed."

"You really are a most peculiar man."

"That's not a bad thing, is it?"

"No," she said after a moment. "But maybe it's not a good thing either."

"Huh. I'll have to think on that."

Ridley sipped her tea and regarded him thoughtfully over the rim of her cup. "I have been lonely," she said. She watched his eyebrows lift. They laddered his forehead as they climbed. She liked that she surprised him. It was clear that Ben hadn't expected her to answer. "You might find this odd, but I am less lonely here than I was in Boston. My brother and sister are married and have homes of their own. I saw more of my father at the hospital or at the medical college than I did at home. He spent most of his time there or at his club. My mother was not good company, and I think you comprehend why I avoided her even when she was of a moderate temperament. My colleagues at the hospital, all of them men, were not particularly friendly, and they were less respectful than they were friendly. Being my father's daughter gave me some protection from unpleasant overtures, but it could not insulate me completely. Do you understand what I'm saying?"

"They made advances."

"Yes. Politely stated. I learned quickly that not one of them had any particular romantic interest in me. Their very particular interest was in making my situation so uncomfortable, so unbearable, that I would leave of my own accord. It didn't happen that way, not the way they planned, but it happened. In truth, it happened on my terms. So you see, Sheriff Madison, your proposition is suspect. If your desire is to run me out of Frost Falls, you should just say so. We'll be clear and we can dispense with the advances."

"I might have propositioned you," he said, "but I'm pretty damn sure I did not make an advance." He paused, frowning. "Unless brewing a cup of tea for you is a romantic gambit. Is it?"

Ridley pursed her lips. She was not entirely certain whether her disapproval was real or for effect.

"You get up to some odd notions, Dr. Woodhouse. I'm not trying to run you out of Frost Falls. Those colleagues of yours were damn fools if they thought you'd cower and cut. Are you sure none of them had a romantic interest?"

"I'm sure."

Ben cocked his head and scratched behind his ear. "See? That doesn't make a lick of sense to me. Was there something wrong with them?"

Ridley pushed her spectacles down a notch and stared at him over the wire frames. "Only that they harbored real fears that I would perform more competently than they did. They gave no credit to the fact that I studied harder, worked longer hours, and—most damning of all—that I listened to my patients. This is where being my father's daughter worked against me. If my accomplishments were brought to anyone's attention, it was seen as favoritism."

Ben nodded, his features set thoughtfully. "So they were just about as dumb as a sack of hair."

She couldn't help but smile. Still, she felt it was incumbent upon her to correct that impression. "Most of them were quite brilliant. It was more that they couldn't make room for me."

"Hmm."

Ridley added more tea to her cup and half a spoonful of sugar. "So now you know."

"Do I? I'm not sure what I know. Maybe that you've got reasons to be suspicious of a man when he shows some interest in you, but that's an awfully big brush you're using to paint all of us the same color."

"Is that what you're doing, Sheriff? Showing an interest in me?"

Ben sat back in his chair, stretched his long legs under the table, and folded his arms across his chest. His eyebrows puckered, creating a thin vertical crease between them. "Damn, but I thought I was. Not sure why you had to ask. What am I doing wrong?"

"I'm not certain that you're doing anything wrong. You've just made a bad choice."

"Now, see? I don't believe that. Sure, you're about as wary as a feral kitten that's got its tail yanked too many times, but that doesn't mean you can't be interesting to someone."

"What? As a pet? As something you can congratulate yourself for taming?"

"Huh. Hadn't thought about it like that." His eyes remained steady on hers. "Anyone ever tell you that your mind's a tad twisted?"

"Of course not."

"Must be because you ran them off."

"I do *not* run people off. You're sitting there, aren't you?"

"Yeah, but you already know I lack good sense."

Ridley ignored that. "A lighted stick of dynamite wouldn't dislodge you."

"Wouldn't take dynamite."

"No?"

He shook his head. "No."

Ridley felt an unfamiliar tremor in her fingers. She quickly set her teacup down before he saw it dance in her hands. She thought she might have been too late because he was watching her intently and a slim smile lifted the corners of his mouth. His pupils were larger than they had been a moment earlier, but the way he looked at her was anything but vague or sleepy. She was put in mind of studying a slide under a microscope. He seemed just that fascinated.

Ridley felt her heart flutter and resisted the urge to place a hand over it. She reminded herself that she was not given to dramatic dime novel gestures even if her favorite heroine was. It occurred to her that she should stand, break the hold he had over her just then, and on the heels of that thought came another: It wouldn't take dynamite to dislodge her either.

Chapter Fourteen

Ben sat up, unfolded his legs and arms, and stood in a single fluid motion. Ridley's head came up as he took a step toward her. He was not certain of anything except that she was thinking too much. He curled his fingers around the wrist that hovered protectively beside her teacup and gave it an almost imperceptible tug. Still staring at him, she rose to her feet. He gave her a moment to step back, to remove her hand from his loose grip, to say something that would put him literally and figuratively back in his place, but the moment passed and nothing like that happened.

Ben bent his head, touched her mouth on a slant. Her lips were warm but not particularly welcoming. He nudged them. Her mouth parted as she took a sip of air and he carefully pressed that small advantage, touching the tip of his tongue to her upper lip, making a sweep of the sweet, soft underside. This time it was no sip that she took; her swift indrawn breath was more gasp than whimper.

He kissed the corner of her mouth and turned her head so that he could place his mouth against the hollow below her ear. Strands of hair that had escaped the anchoring combs tickled his cheek. Not for the first time, he caught the fragrance of lavender and wondered that it still clung to her hair, her skin, and the sensitive cord in her neck, which she invited him to explore with his lips and tongue.

He returned to her mouth. Her lips were damp now, parted, and definitely welcoming. She met his kiss with pressure and intent. Her hands climbed to his shoulders while one of his came to rest at the small of her back. He pressed the base of her spine. She shivered and he felt her fingers dig deeper into his vest. He liked the idea of her fingertips as an imprint in the scarred and beaten leather.

Her breathing quickened, but then so did his. He ran his tongue along the ridge of her teeth. She bit down very gently, and his skin was suddenly too tight for flesh and bone. He pushed back, deepening the kiss, and then the fingers on his shoulder were not so much holding him as holding on. Ben pushed aside the cups, saucers, and teapot. Placing his hands on either side of Ridley's waist, he squeezed and lifted her onto the table. He parted her knees and stepped between them; the drape of the skirt of her gown was a better than adequate barrier, which he decided was proper for the time being. He was certain he'd find out what she thought, but that would be later, when she was showing him the door.

In for a penny, in for a pound. The old adage wound its way through his head and seeped into his blood as he cupped her bottom and brought her to the edge of the table. Her thighs hugged him.

He set his forehead against hers, breathed her in. They bumped noses. He knocked her spectacles askew. Her hands abandoned his shoulders and flew to her face. Out of habit, she began to straighten the earpieces, but he stopped her and did it himself. He drew back just enough to examine his handiwork. Her eyes seemed larger than usual behind the lenses.

Ben spoke quietly. He put his question to her as if it were an intimate one. "Do you need them for everything?"

"Mostly for close work," she said, responding in a similar vein. "It's easier to wear them all the time."

That explained why she was often looking over the top of the rims when she wanted to take the long view.

"Are you going to remove them?" she asked.

"Hadn't thought I would. I like them. Why?"

Ridley shrugged and looked away.

"Why?" he asked again, dipping his head to catch her eye. "Is that what *they* did?"

"Mm." She looked at him then. "Why do you suppose they did that?"

"Couldn't say, except . . ." He curled his mouth to one side as he considered her face. "Maybe if you take them off for a moment." When she obliged, nothing about his expression changed. Her brown eyes were just as large, just as luminous. "They might have thought they looked more appealing if you couldn't see them clearly. How many fingers am I holding up?" He showed her three. When Ridley choked back a laugh and batted his hand away, he slipped it around the back of her neck. "They were idiots," he whispered against her mouth. "Idiots."

Ben took the spectacles from her, carefully folded the stems with his free hand, and set them aside. His mouth never left hers. When she took her next audible breath, it was his air that she breathed. He liked that, would have told her so if he hadn't thought it would hasten his departure. She would toss him out regardless, sooner or later. He preferred that it was later.

His fingers sifted in the loose tendrils of hair at the base of her neck. Earlier this evening, it had been wound in a tight chignon fixed with combs and pins to the back of her head. The shape of the chignon was softer now. Too many strands had come free of their moorings and were curling against her temples and behind her ears. Occasionally she tucked them back but the attempts at order were halfhearted at best. She had more care for her patients than she did for her appearance.

The tendrils slipped between his fingers like satin ribbons. He couldn't hold them; he didn't try. His fingertips brushed her nape. She shivered again, all satisfaction and heat, and rolled her neck in a way that suggested she wanted more of the same.

Ben placed his lips against her skin and sipped. She moaned softly. A heartbeat later, he felt her stiffen. He did not think it was what he was doing that had prompted that reaction. Rather it was her response to liking it. He hesitated and then raised his head. A rosy flush tinged her cheeks— something he did not see often—and it struck him that she was embarrassed.

"Enough?" he asked.

"Mm. Perhaps too much."

"All right." He ducked his head, placed a swift kiss on her slightly parted lips, and then backed away.

Ridley slid off the table without help. "I believe that was an advance."

"Infinitely more subtle than Pickett's Charge but worthy of being called an advance."

"I never know what you're going to say."

Grinning, he rubbed thoughtfully behind his ear. "I hardly know myself."

Ridley pressed her lips together, shook her head.

"Guess I'll get my coat," he said. "Show myself out."

"Probably for the best."

"I don't know about that, but I'm going to do it anyway." Ben pushed in his chair and started toward the front of the house. He was unaware that Ridley was following him until he turned to put on his coat. He raised an eyebrow but didn't speak.

"I think it would be better if that didn't happen again," she said.

Ben did not pretend he didn't know what she was referring to. "Is it all right for me to have a different opinion?"

"You're entitled."

"But you don't think I should."

She sighed. "I don't think you understand."

Ben finished buttoning his coat and removed his gloves from his pocket but didn't put them on. "You care to explain?" He took his hat off the rack and settled it on his head. When Ridley offered nothing, he started to open the door. Cold air swirled into the vestibule and she immediately hugged herself, but for some reason he did not think she was merely reacting to the temperature. He paused, suddenly sure that she was working up the courage to speak.

And she did. "Because when you walk through that door, I will be lonelier than I was when I asked you in for tea."

Chapter Fifteen

Ridley closed the door on Ben. She was relieved that he understood she was not issuing an invitation. What she said was true, but it wasn't his responsibility to relieve her loneliness. The fact that he suspected she was lonely made her feel vulnerable and vaguely out of sorts with him. She did not appreciate the way he sifted through her thoughts as though he were panning for gold, and she especially did not appreciate when he showed her a nugget.

She went to the front window and drew back the curtain only enough to watch him most of the way from her house to his. He followed the walk, which was shoveled clean. He'd sent Clay Salt around to clear a path from her front steps to the street every time it snowed, and since Clay would not accept any money from her, she had to assume that Ben was paying the boy. Ben ran his hand along the top of the picket fence as he walked. It was easy to imagine him as a young boy with a stick in his hand rattling fences as he went along.

She let the curtain fall back and turned away from the window. Her image of him was a false one. He hadn't grown up in Frost Falls but on the Twin Star Ranch outside of town. She'd heard that from him and more from his mother, but Ellie in particular seemed uncomfortable sharing anything from the near quarter of a century that she'd spent there. Taking her cue from Ellie, Ridley rarely asked Ben about his experiences or his relationships at the ranch, and while he showed no such reticence were she was concerned, she believed she should not rattle his fences.

In time he might fill in the gaps in the knowledge she had gleaned from Hitch and Buzz and George Hotchkiss when he delivered wood and coals. Mrs. Springer had volunteered tidbits, none of which were asked for, about the Frost family in general, and Ben Madison's connection to them specifically. She wished she had heard about them from Ben directly, because it wasn't that she wasn't interested, only that she'd grown up in a family that embraced secrets and she was reluctant to pry into someone else's.

Ridley extinguished all the lamps except for the one she carried to her bedroom. She set it on the side table, drew the curtains, and began to undress. She washed her face, brushed her teeth with baking soda, and crawled between the sheets. She lay there for twenty minutes, counting sheep, making a list of all the names she could think of that began with the letter E. She wondered if Ben had thought of Evangeline or Esperanza, neither of which was her Christian name, but should be included on his list. When she returned to counting sheep *and* naming them, she gave up and threw off the covers.

She told herself she wasn't lonely. She was angry, or at least more angry than lonely. He shouldn't have kissed her and she shouldn't have let him. Sitting up, she grabbed a pillow and hugged it to her chest. Her face was hot. Her feet were cold. There was nothing about her at the moment that felt quite right. She fumbled around for her slippers, threw the pillow to the side, and retrieved her robe from the back of the rocking chair.

She recalled that there was still a generous slice of rhubarb pie remaining in the bottom of the cold box. Picking up the lamp, she retraced her steps to the kitchen, and almost jumped out of her slippers when someone pounded on the surgery door. There was a shout, a voice that she did not recognize, and then more pounding. She wondered if Ben could hear. If he had already found the sleep that she couldn't, then probably not.

Ridley approached cautiously, setting the lamp on the table to avoid dropping it. The door rattled in the frame. The knob twisted. There was pressure from the outside, a thump as a shoulder was thrust against the door.

"Who is it?" Ridley called from a few feet back. "I'm not opening the door until you tell me who you are and what your business is."

"You know goddamn well who I am, Dr. Fancy Bitches. Britches. Dr. Fancy Britches."

Ridley took a calming breath. "Is that you, Mr. Salt?"

"Goddamn right it is." He slammed the door again with his large meaty fist. "You gonna open up, Doc?"

"What do you want?"

"I want to see you."

That was not an answer that was going to get her to open the door. "Are you ill, Mr. Salt?"

"I'm freezing is what I am. Damn cold out here."

"I understand, but are you ill?"

He put his shoulder to the door. It shuddered but did not budge.

"Is it someone else that brings you here? Lily? The children?"

"I have a powerful burning in my chest. Hot. Like I swallowed a poker."

Ridley did not know whether she could believe him. "Have you been drinking?"

Jeremiah didn't answer, but he did stamp his feet.

The floor under Ridley vibrated. She called to him again. "Have you been drinking?"

"Not so you'd notice."

That meant that he'd tippled a bottle at least once. Probably quite a few more times than that. "What do you think I can do for you?"

"You're the doc, ain't you? You got to figure it out."

Ridley inched closer to the door. She wanted to get a look at him through the side window but was afraid if he saw her, he would seize on the idea of breaking the glass.

"I'm tellin' you, Doc, my chest's on fire. I know about fire. If I swallowed a bullet right now, it would melt before it got to my gut."

Ridley couldn't be sure that he wasn't talking about harming himself. She went to stand beside the window and carefully lifted the curtain so she could peek outside. Jeremiah Salt looked like a man who was hurting. She couldn't make out his particular features, but his silhouette was bent double. It explained why he had not slammed into the door again. Now that she was close enough, she could hear him moaning deep in his throat, as much groan as growl. Surely a wounded bear could not sound as pathetic . . . or present more danger.

Ridley went to the cupboard and opened the drawer where she kept her surgical instruments. There was very little there that was not a weapon sufficient to cause serious injury. She chose the implement that fit neatly in her palm and closed the drawer. She removed the key from the windowsill. "I'm going to open the door, Mr. Salt, but you need to know I have a very sharp scalpel at the ready, and I won't hesitate to use it if I feel threatened."

"I ain't threatened you yet, Dr. Fancy Britches."

She hesitated, her key poised at the lock. "To be clear, I said I would use it if I *feel* threatened. Whether you think you've threatened me counts for nothing. Do you understand?"

"Jesus."

"Do you understand?"

"Yes, dammit, I understand."

Ridley took a deep breath, turned the key, and opened the door. She expected him to charge into the room so she stepped back out of the way. Her patient's entrance was less dramatic than that. He stumbled a little as he crossed the threshold but managed to get to the examining table without faltering a second time. "Can you sit up there?" asked Ridley, moving the lamp out of the way.

Jeremiah Salt braced his arms on either side and lifted himself onto the table. This was not accomplished without noisy effort.

Ridley watched him out of the corner of her eye as she retrieved her stethoscope. She slipped the scalpel into the right pocket of her flannel robe. "Can you sit up straight? Pull back your shoulders?" Apparently this required Herculean effort because he groaned mightily and placed one hand on his breastbone.

It was impossible for Ridley not to react to the sour odor of spirits on his breath. She suspected that if she held a lighted match near his mouth, he could easily throw a flame across the room. She held up her stethoscope but did not apply it yet. "Why aren't you wearing a coat, Mr. Salt?"

He looked down at himself and then at her. "I'll be damned."

"Probably. No hat. No scarf. No gloves. No wonder you were freezing."

She placed the stethoscope at four different places on his chest and listened. She did the same at his back. He breathed in and out on her command and she avoided the fumes. Coming around the table to face him again, she said, "Tell me about your symptoms, because there is nothing wrong with your heart."

"Didn't say there was, did I?"

"No, but chest pain can mean a lot of things. Sometimes it points to a problem with the heart."

He pressed fingers the size of sausages against his sternum. "Burns like the devil. Right here. I can taste the heat."

She nodded. "When did it start?"

"This evening."

"Can you be more specific?"

"Could have been around the time I heard about the Fullers." Jeremiah's rheumy eyes narrowed on Ridley's face. "The way it was told to me is that there was something wrong with the dampers on that stove. There are womenfolk who heard Louella complaining about them, and those same womenfolk know I fixed them for her. Cast her new ones and replaced them myself. And now her little girl's dead and there's fingers pointing at me, like maybe I made them while I was drinking, like maybe I didn't know what I was doing."

"I'm not certain you heard correctly, but regardless, your response was to start drinking."

"And there you go. Pointing a finger."

Ridley watched his hands tighten on the edge of the table. She couldn't tell if he was steadying or restraining himself. She slipped a hand inside her pocket and touched the scalpel. She ignored his comments and continued her investigation of his symptoms. "Has this happened to you before, Mr. Salt?"

"Not like this. Not so I think I'm gonna die."

"You're not going to die." She watched his broad features wrinkle as he grimaced and swallowed hard in quick succession. His reaction had nothing to do with what she said. He was fighting off the volcanic rise of acid from his stomach to the back of his throat. Ridley was not terribly sympathetic but neither did she judge him. "What did you do when you experienced this before?"

"Don't know. Probably just went to sleep."

Ridley doubted that. More likely, he passed out and the symptoms vanished in time. "I'm going to give you something that will ease the burning." She turned her back on him to go to the cupboard, where she measured out a teaspoonful of sodium bicarbonate. She carried it back and held the spoon out for him to take.

He stared at it. "What is that?"

"Sodium bicarbonate. Baking soda."

Jeremiah Salt frowned deeply. "Lily waggled a spoonful of that at me."

"You could have saved yourself a trip in the cold if you had taken it."

"Maybe. And maybe I'd be dead. My wife's trying to kill me."

Ridley found that the spoon was suddenly difficult to hold steady. She was reluctant to address his last comment. It was put to her in such a matter-of-fact tone that she suspected he was not trying to goad her into reacting; he believed it. "Here," she said, carefully holding the spoon out to him. "Take this."

"Maybe you're trying to kill me, too."

"Mr. Salt, you came to me."

"Yeah? Well, you could be in league with Lily and Louella Fuller and that damn busybody Amanda Springer. You all want me dead."

"Please, I don't want to regret letting you in here. Take this. It's only baking soda. Every home has some. Your stomach can no longer accommodate your drinking. I would venture to say that it's the same for your liver, but that's a wait and see." When his mouth remained as mutinously closed as a child refusing peas, she carried the spoon back to the cupboard and set it down. "If there's nothing you will permit me to do for you, then you may as well leave. You obviously are not in as much pain as you would have me believe, else you would not refuse the cure."

"Why did you tell people it was my fault?"

Ridley frowned, unable to follow. "I don't understand your question."

"About the Fullers. Why did you say it was my fault?"

"I said no such thing."

"I repaired those dampers. They fit the way they were supposed to."

"I'm sure they did."

"Then why'd you say different? Get people all stirred up and looking at me like I murdered that little girl. My own wife. Regulars at the Songbird. That little girl was my Lizzie's age. Did you know that? Just my Lizzie's age."

Ridley watched him press a fist against his chest and suck in a breath as the heat rose again. His ruddy face glistened with sweat. His upper lip was dotted with beads of it. He used his flannel shirtsleeve to mop his brow. Ridley wondered if there was anything she could say that would cut through his alcohol haze and decided that there wasn't. She held her tongue.

"You should go back where you came from," said Jeremiah. "People say you're a troublemaker, and I don't disagree. It takes some work to be a busier body than Amanda Springer, but I think you've managed."

Ridley backed away when he slid off the table. She expected him to cross to the door, but he didn't. He rounded the table, keeping one hand on it for support, and approached her medicine cupboard. "What are you doing?"

He looked back over his shoulder and growled at her. "Taking the hemlock. That's what you want, isn't it?"

"It's baking soda. Not poison."

He shrugged. "I guess we'll see." He lifted the spoon close to his nose, sniffed, and then put it in his mouth.

Ridley might have laughed at the face he made if the circumstances had been different. She had considered mixing the soda with water to make it more palatable but a dry dose would neutralize the acid more quickly. "Don't spit it out," she warned him. "Swallow all of it."

White powder dusted his upper lip and the groove directly below his nose. He set the spoon down and swiped at his mouth and nose with the side of his hand. "That it?" he asked.

"That's it," she said.

He nodded, wavered slightly on his feet. "Now about that other thing I was saying."

Ridley backed the rest of the way to the door and set her hand on the knob. "I suggest we leave that discussion for later."

"Doesn't surprise me."

"Do you need help getting home? I can get the sheriff; he's just next door. He'll escort you, see you return safely. He might have a coat you can borrow."

He snorted. "Have it all thought out, don't you? Probably want me to go home by way of the jail. Well, I ain't doing that."

She lifted her chin and set her shoulders. There was no intention on her part to act aggressively, but in hindsight she reflected that Jeremiah Salt saw it that way. She only had a moment to prepare for his assault. He crossed the room with a speed and steadiness that she could not have predicted. Ridley did two things at once: She pushed open the door leading to the stoop and yanked the scalpel out of her pocket. Neither of those actions gave him pause.

Acting on instinct, she ducked and spun, eluding his outstretched hands. Leaving by the surgery was no longer a safe exit; she would have to back through the door and he would be on her. Ridley ran for her office instead, skirting the table and then shoving it in his path. The obstacle was only temporary, but it gave her time to flee through her office and the kitchen. She charged toward the front door and was glad that she had never gotten around to having a key made for it. She did not have to fumble with the lock. She flung it open, ran to the lip of the front porch, and jumped. Although the path was clear of snow, there were still icy patches that she was able to avoid in daylight. That was not the case now. One foot came down firmly on a dry land; the other did not.

Her arms worked like windmills as she tried to restore her balance. In the end, there was nothing to be done except surrender to gravity. Ridley tried to make the fall as painless as possible by throwing her weight sideways so she could land in a pile of shoveled snow. She was only partially successful. Scrambling to her feet was an ungainly exercise. The stitch in her side made her gasp for breath. She was still on her knees when she glanced behind her and saw that Jeremiah Salt was on the porch. He also jumped off the porch but aimed for a snowbank. It slowed him down but he didn't fall.

Pressing one palm firmly against the sharp pain in her side,

Ridley ran awkwardly for the gate. Her other hand tightened into a fist. It was the first she realized she no longer held the scalpel. It was pointless to search for it. She slipped through the gate and closed it behind her. He was nearly on top of her.

"Ben!" she shouted, running toward his house. "Ben Madison! Wake up!" She grabbed a handful of snow as she hurried up the path to his porch and packed it between her palms. She spun around and let the snowball fly. It was luck, only luck, that it landed squarely on Jeremiah's nose. She took another handful, packed it, and while he was still scrabbling at his face, she tossed it at one of the second-story windows in Ben's house. It missed the window but thumped solidly against a blue shutter. She was on the first step of the front porch when Jeremiah caught her by the waist, squeezed, and lifted her off her feet. He threw her in a pile of shoveled snow. She wasn't hurt, but she couldn't get up. Thrashing only made her sink deeper. She stilled and looked up at the deep shadow that was Jeremiah's face.

"He's not there," he said, pointing to the sheriff's house. "I saw him duck into the Butterworth before I came here. Most likely chatting with his mama. Hardly matters that it's the middle of the night. That's how rumors get started around here. Ben with his mama; Hitch with his. Ugly things get said and passed along."

Not by Ben, she thought. Jeremiah might be right about Hitch. She turned her head in the direction of the hotel. Had anyone heard her? There was no one at any of the windows.

Jeremiah followed her gaze. "He didn't see me, in case you're wondering."

Ridley looked back at him. "What do you want?"

"You came to my business and threatened me. I'm returning the same. I want you to stay away from me, from my family. Find someone else to sweep your damn walk. I don't want you near my boy, either one of them. That goes for my daughters, too, and I especially don't want you talking to Lily. I know you run into her now and again. She tells me, so there's no good denying it."

"Is there anything else?"

"You take back what you said about those dampers. You make people understand I had nothing to do with what happened to the Fullers."

"I never—" She stopped because he was bending over her, reaching for the collar of her robe. He fisted the material and yanked her into a sitting position. He was breathing heavily, snorting like a bull. She recoiled at his moist breath. "Whatever you want," she said.

"That's right. That's better." He let her go, dropped her back into the snow. "It would not be good for you to go back on your word." He scooped some snow into his hand, made a loose ball, and with no warning of his intention, shoved it against her mouth. He held it there while she sputtered and squirmed and pushed at his arms, but he would not be moved. Ice worked its way between her teeth and into her mouth. Jeremiah Salt backed away when he was ready. "Bicarbonate of soda, eh? Does the trick."

Ridley spit snow and swiped at her mouth. "Go," she said when she could speak. "Just go."

He shrugged. "Sure. Why not?"

She watched him stumble, but he righted himself quickly and made his exit without a humiliating fall, not that he could be humiliated, she thought. In his current state of mind, embarrassment was unlikely to be his companion. Ridley was not confident that he would recall anything that he had said or done this evening. He would be a walking, talking *tabula rasa*. A blank slate.

Ridley was finally able to push herself upright but moving was not without considerable pain. Once again, she placed a palm over the spot where the pain was centered just above her hip and then ignored it. She found the porch step and used it to support her as she got to her feet. Once she was standing, she paused to catch her breath. There was never any question in her mind about what she would do next. The lamps burning in the windows of the Butterworth's dining room beckoned. Ben beckoned her, not because he was the sheriff, but because · he was Ben.

Chapter Sixteen

Ben shoved away from the table and stood when he saw Ridley framed in the dining room entrance. She was standing, but only barely, and shivering so hard it seemed that her bones might break. His eyes fell from her pale face to the hand pressed against her right side. Runnels of blood slipped through her fingers. "You're bleeding."

Ridley offered a wan, apologetic smile. "Yes, I think I am. It's nothing, really. Just a—"

He knocked over a chair as he leapt forward and caught Ridley before she dropped to the floor. He eased her down. His mother was standing behind, looking over his shoulder. "Ma! Something to staunch the bleeding."

Ellie yanked on a white linen tablecloth. A vase of flowers toppled. She caught it in one hand and held out the tablecloth in the other. "Use this until I find something better." There were no guests in the dining room, but Mr. Butterworth was in his office at the back, tallying the day's profits. The cook had left for home and her helpers with her. Ellie had been preparing to retire to her suite when Ben arrived. "I think there is something you can use in the kitchen."

Ben removed Ridley's hand from her wound. He couldn't see a thing except that she continued to bleed. He untied the belt of her robe and lifted the flannel. He winced because it was Ridley, but he had seen worse. He carefully tugged on her cotton nightgown and found the rent at the center of the blossoming blood. There was only a small tear in the fabric, but when he tore the material for a better look, he saw that the wound was not a puncture but a slice at least six inches long.

From what he could tell at first glance, it was not terribly deep, but neither was it a grazing wound.

Under his breath, he said, "What the hell?" and pressed a balled-up corner of the tablecloth to the cut. His mother had hurried off in the direction of the kitchen and he called out to her just as she was coming through the door. He expected her to be carrying towels, napkins, or bandages the hotel might have on hand. Instead she was waving a pair of scissors at him. He feared for her life, then his own, as she wended her way around tables and chairs and bumped into most of them. He could not recall that she had ever looked so frantic. She generally met every sort of complication or crisis with a composure that could make a person believe she had ice in her veins. He knew better, but what he observed now was something else again.

Ellie knelt beside Ben and lifted the part of the tablecloth he wasn't using. She began cutting it into strips, snipping and tearing, until she had a dozen pieces of cloth suitable for bandages. "I couldn't find anything back there. I think Mrs. Vandergrift sent all the towels to the laundry. You would think . . . never mind. These will do."

Ben tossed the bloody ball of cloth to one side and took a clean strip from Ellie. He folded it several times, making a pad, and pressed it to Ridley's injury. "Are you all right?" he asked his mother. "You seem . . . I don't know . . . discomposed."

"Out of practice."

"I guess there's not much call here to set a bone or fix a scrape."

"Not much, and there was always Doc to call on." Ellie lifted Ben's hand a few inches so she could see the wound then replaced it. "What in the world did she do?"

He shook his head. He didn't know if she had done it or if it had been done to her. "How about holding this? I'll give you a fresh bandage and then I'm going to get a basin of water and clean her up a little. Is there an empty room?"

"Second floor and straight ahead at the top of the stairs. Are you going to take her up there?"

"No, I'm going to take her back to her surgery. I'm taking blankets from the room."

"Of course. I should have thought of it."

Ben did not comment. He rose, headed for the kitchen, and set a kettle on the stove. While the water was heating, he went in search of Mr. Butterworth, found him in his office, and explained the situation. Butterworth volunteered to get the blankets so Ben could return to the dining room. Ben stopped in the kitchen, checked the temperature of the water, and found it sufficiently warm to use. He poured it into a pot and carried it out.

"I think she's coming around," said Ellie.

As though on cue, Ridley moaned. Her eyelashes fluttered.

Ben said the first thing that came to his mind. "She's not wearing her glasses." He knelt beside her and set the pot on the floor. He could hear Butterworth pounding down the stairs. As far as he was concerned, the man could not arrive soon enough. He dipped a linen strip in the pot until it was soaked, wrung it out, and made another pad.

Ellie put aside the one she was holding over Ridley's wound and widened the rent in the nightgown so Ben could begin cleaning the area. "Not too hard," she said. "You warmed the water, didn't you?"

He gave her a look he knew she would recognize and correctly interpret as *back away.*

Ellie held up her hands, palms out. "All right. I was merely trying to be—"

"Helpful. Yes, I know. I could use a couple more damp pads."

Mr. Butterworth dropped an armload of blankets on the seat of a chair. He was out of breath but still able to make audible commiserating noises at the back of his throat. "Has she been able to tell you what happened?"

"Soon," said Ben, but he wasn't sure he was speaking the truth. "Spread a few blankets across her legs. Tuck her in."

Butterworth did as instructed while Ellie made a pillow and slipped it under Ridley's head. She folded another blanket and laid it across Ridley's chest and shoulders. Ben had wiped away enough blood by then that they could clearly see the injury.

"Stitches," said Ben, shifting his attention to Ellie. "She'll need them. You think you can still do that?"

"It's been a while, but yes, I can stitch her up."

"All right. What about you, Mr. Butterworth? Can you help me move the doctor to her surgery?"

Butterworth nodded. "We can make a blanket sling."

"Good." Ben set a clean pad over the wound and fixed it in place by sliding two cloth strips under her and tying off the ends. He heard her moan softly and ignored it because he couldn't stomach the thought that he was hurting her.

Butterworth and Ellie went after their coats. Ben retrieved his from the back of the chair where he had been sitting. His eyes never left Ridley as he put on his hat. He thought she might have stirred, but when he hunkered down beside her and placed a hand on her shoulder, she didn't acknowledge his presence.

That changed when they moved her outside. The cocoon of blankets was no real barrier to the cold. She shivered hard inside them and paradoxically fought to be out of them. Ben thought they might drop her before they reached the street. It was the hand that Ellie placed on Ridley's brow and then at the crown of her head that seemed to calm her. Ellie stayed with her until it was time to open the door and then she led the way through the house to the surgery.

Ben and Butterworth set Ridley on the table after Ellie moved the lamp. She offered to start a fire in the corner stove. Mr. Butterworth volunteered to do the same in the kitchen. Ben tossed his hat on a chair but kept his coat on. He bent, put his mouth close to Ridley's ear, and whispered, "I have questions."

He felt her nod as she slowly regained consciousness. "Ellie's stitched more than her share of wranglers and sassy cowboys. She has a steady hand and there's hardly ever a scar. That's a mixed blessing for the cowboys. Some would prefer to show them off." Ben straightened. He watched her eyelashes flutter and then rise to half-mast and hold steady. "You all right with that?"

She nodded again. "I want to see."

"Of course you do."

Ellie turned away from the stove, holding a lighted match. "Let her be, Ben."

Ben saw Ridley's mouth turn up at the corners. He gave her

an apologetic smile, although he didn't know if he was apologizing for himself or his mother. "How's that fire coming?"

Ellie put the flame to the kindling and kept the door open until she was certain the fire caught. "How about you find a needle and some thread for suturing while I get this poor child out of her wet robe and soiled gown. Did you notice that she looked as if she dove headlong into a drift? The snow's just beginning to melt."

Ben had noticed a number of things, none of which he wanted to discuss until he had spoken to Ridley. Maybe not even then. He wanted to respect the doctor's dedication to her secrets. What happened this evening might surely be one of them.

He went to the medicine cabinet while his mother began to attend to Ridley. It was hardly surprising to find that the drawers were organized. It took no time at all to locate what he needed. He put the curved needle, thread, and snips beside the lamp. "I'll get a clean gown for her and see if she has another robe."

"I could use another lamp," said Ellie.

"I'll tell Mr. Butterworth." By the time Ben returned, Ridley was modestly covered with blankets from the hotel. Only her wound exposed. Her nightgown and robe were spilling out of a pail on the floor. A second lamp had been added to one of the windowsills. Mr. Butterworth was holding a third lamp above Ridley to give Ellie the best light possible.

Ben had been able to find only two nightgowns. He had to choose between green-and-white-striped flannel and dainty pink posies on calico, neither of which suited her. He chose the flannel because it was warmer and now he laid it over the back of the chair that held his hat.

He watched his mother thread the needle with the surgical thread. "Do you think she should have something for the pain?"

"I already gave her laudanum—that's all she asked for—and cleaned the wound. Now, if you're going to be full of questions, you should take yourself off somewhere and just sit. Mr. Butterworth is going to stay with me because he's making himself useful."

Ben considered his options, nodded once, and more or less

did what his mother suggested. He grabbed his hat and left the surgery by its entrance. He noticed small clumps of snow on the stoop and wondered if someone had come calling today. He did not recall that Ridley had mentioned a visitor. She had been out most of the day paying calls on others, and he knew that the widow came and went by the front door, not the back. He filed the observation away. The doctor would have to tell him if it was important or nothing at all.

He went down the steps and followed the narrow path Clay Salt had cut through the snow to the front of the house. It was too dark to see how well the path was used, and Ben imagined that Clay's hard work had obliterated most every footprint. Now he was adding his own.

Ben stood at the foot of the front steps and tried to get a sense of what happened. There had been no indication inside the house that Ridley had cut herself—or been cut—there. He'd seen no blood trail when he and Butterworth carried her to the surgery, but he had noticed that the table was not positioned in the room in its usual fashion. It had been moved to a peculiar angle and the lamp sitting on it was lit. That had struck him as odd since she would have extinguished it unless she was in the room. He was certain that she was headed for bed when they parted ways, and if she hadn't been able to sleep, it was more likely she would have gone to her office to choose a book or settle herself on the big sofa in the front room.

Curious.

He began to walk the path to the gate and had taken only a few steps when he felt something underfoot that wasn't a paving stone or a patch of ice. Whatever it was pressed against the sole of his boot. Ben stopped, felt for the object again, and toed it forward. He bent, scrabbled to find it, and finally was able to grasp it in his fingers. He picked it up and carefully examined the length of it. He held it up to the light of a fingernail moon and saw it for what it was.

It made no sense that Ridley had carried a scalpel outside. The razor-sharp blade accounted for her injury though it offered no explanation for the why of it. Ben pocketed the scalpel and continued on. He intended to make straight for the Butterworth as he thought Ridley must have done but paused when something drew his eye to the left, to the path that led from her house to his. He followed it. Clay shoveled snow into neat piles, sometimes patting them down with the shovel scoop. Ben had asked him about it, and the boy explained he was building walls on either side of the path to better show the way. Those walls did not seem so well made at the moment. Parts of Clay's construction had fallen in. Ben could not recall that it had been that way this morning.

He continued on the path, turning at his gate and starting toward the house. Even at night it was impossible to miss the impression in the mound of snow beside his steps. He went inside, lit a lamp, and carried it out. He set it on the edge of the porch to free his hands. There, in the drift's depression, he saw evidence of Ridley's injury. Some of the drops were as small as red rosebuds. Some were meandering crimson rivulets. He was able to identify her bloody handprint in the snow and on the edge of the first step. He imagined her trying to hoist herself to her feet.

Ben picked up the lamp and carried it down the path, across the front, and up to her porch. He could make out blood splatters that he hadn't been able to see before. They stopped exactly where he had found the scalpel.

He knew things now that he hadn't known before, but he still did not have a complete picture. He returned to the surgery.

"Oh, good," said Ellie. "You've brought another lamp. Hold it up, will you? Relieve poor Mr. Butterworth. His arms are beginning to shake and the dancing light is no help at all."

Ben took Mr. Butterworth's place at the table.

"I could have stood there longer," said Butterworth.

"I have no doubt," said Ben. "Go on. Sit down. I can see that she's almost done."

Ellie spoke to her son without looking up. "Where did you go?"

"I wanted to take a look around outside." He looked at Ridley. Her lashes were no longer at half-mast. Her dark eyes were wide but vaguely unfocused. "I found this." He reached into his pocket and pulled out the scalpel.

Ellie did not look up. "Careful, Ben, you're bobbling the lamp."

From across the room, Butterworth asked, "Is that a scalpel?"

"Yep."

"That's what she used?"

"I'm not certain she used it in the way you're thinking, but it's what sliced her open." He turned his gaze once more on Ridley. "Am I right?" There was a small, nearly imperceptible nod. Ben nodded in return and pocketed the instrument.

Ellie finished making the last fine stitch and secured the thread before she snipped the excess. "There," she said, straightening to examine her work. "I can't say how my suturing compares to our patient's, but I know it's every bit the equal of Doc's." She waved Ben away. "You and Mr. Butterworth can entertain yourselves in the kitchen while I ready the doctor for bed. I'll call when I need you."

Ben and Butterworth removed themselves. The hotel proprietor had questions, but they were easily diverted because Ben had very few answers. In a short time Ellie was calling them back. Ellie led the way upstairs to make sure the bed was prepared, and after Ridley's halfhearted protest that she could walk, Ben followed with her in his arms. Butterworth brought up the rear, carrying a lamp in each hand.

Ben placed Ridley on the bed and Ellie covered her. Butterworth, ever conscious of the lamps, set one of them on the nightstand. "Someone should stay with her," he said. "Ellie, if you need—"

"I'm staying," said Ben. He spoke in a voice that brooked no argument.

Ellie nodded as if there were nothing at all unusual about the arrangement. Butterworth puffed his cheeks and made little tsking noises. He looked and sounded as if he'd captured a chipmunk in his mouth.

Ellie touched her son's elbow as she passed and then took Butterworth's arm. "Come along, Abraham. You and I will return to the hotel and have hot cider with spices and a dash of whiskey, and we will go on as if this evening never happened."

Ben turned to watch his mother lead her employer out of the room, his mind occupied by one absurd thought: How had he not known his mother was sleeping with Abraham Butterworth?

Chapter Seventeen

Ben waited until he heard his mother and Butterworth leave before he went downstairs and secured the door in the surgery. It was then he remembered that when he had walked out earlier, it had not been locked. It was as good an indication as any that the doctor had had a visitor this evening.

He stopped in her office long enough to make a book selection and then headed back to her room. He moved the rocker sitting beside the corner stove to her bedside and adjusted the wick on the lamp so he would be able to read. The fire in the stove needed his attention so he added kindling and wood from a large intricately woven basket. He recognized the basket as Mrs. Love's handiwork. Her husband sold them from his barbershop. It made him smile to think of how many things Ridley must have purchased to demonstrate goodwill as she made her rounds.

He got the fire going, warmed his hands, and then found a blanket he could tuck around him while he was sitting in the rocker. Taking his chosen book from the nightstand, he opened it and began to read, glancing back at the cover from time to time for a clue that Felicity Ravenwood really did tame the beast. In spite of his interest, he nodded off before he had the answer.

"I hope you won't tell me how it ends," said Ridley. Her voice was weak, weary, but perfectly understandable. It jerked Ben to attention.

"Have you been playing possum long?" he asked. He closed the book in his lap. "I swear you were sleeping soundly a moment ago."

"Maybe more moments ago than you think. You were sleeping at least that long."

"Was not."

"Were so."

He chuckled. "Maybe I was." He set the book aside. "Is there something I can get for you?"

"Yes, but I have a feeling that she's gone."

"My mother? You want Ellie?"

"Not exactly."

He frowned and pushed a hand through his hair. "I don't under—" He stopped because he suddenly *did* understand. "Oh. Well, do you have a pot or do you want me to carry you outside?"

Ridley pulled a hand out from under the covers and pointed to the screen in the far corner of the room. "Behind there."

Ben threw off the blanket and stood. When he took a step toward the bed, she jabbed a finger at the screen again. Ben shrugged. "Guess I'm bringing the pot to you."

"Don't talk," she whispered. "Please, don't talk."

"Right," he drawled. "No talking." He slipped behind the moss green damask panels, where he found an oak cabinet with a pitcher, a basin, and soap on top, an oval mirror above it, and neatly folded towels and washcloths on the shelves below. There was a small dressing table against the wall cluttered with hairpins, combs, ribbons, atomizers, cobalt blue pots of cream, bath salts, and a handheld mirror. Ridley's surgery was infinitely more organized, but then, Ben reflected, she cared about that. The commode was an oak chair without the decorative carvings of the cabinet. He removed the chamber pot from under the seat and carried it to the bed.

Ridley was already sitting up with her knees tucked under her. Ben could see that getting there had not been without difficulty or pain. "I would have helped you." She merely held out one hand for the porcelain pot and used the other to wave him away.

"Laudanum," he said. "Downstairs." Then he left, closing the door behind him, and didn't hurry to find the medicine. By the time he returned, Ridley was lying down again, and the pot was on the floor at her bedside. He took it away, emptied it in the outhouse, and rinsed it out when he came back in. Too late he realized he had gotten the order of things to do wrong, because Ridley had dosed herself with the laudanum and had taken more than she would have advised her patients. He pocketed the bottle before he sat down.

"Thank you."

He paused as he was reaching for his book. "Don't talk."

She turned her head only that fraction necessary to catch his eye. "Right," she said in a credible imitation of his drawl. "No talking."

He smiled, nodded, and picked up the book. It wasn't long before he heard her snore softly, abruptly. It happened twice more, and then she was quiet.

Ridley carefully pushed herself upright, caught her breath, and leaned back against the headboard. She pulled a pillow out, plumped it, and then stuffed it behind the small of her back. The effort required to do that small task made her grimace and reinforced her thinking that she was useless.

She pushed back the covers and raised her nightgown to examine the state of her wound. She shook her head when she saw how long it was and recognized her good fortune that it wasn't deep. The area had been thoroughly cleaned and Ellie had closed the wound with sutures as fine as any Ridley could have done. With proper care, there might not be a scar. Ridley could understand why a cowboy might want to show off a scar as a badge of courage, but this particular scar pointed to nothing save her stupidity. She was not proud. She didn't know if she could feel more foolish.

Ridley pushed her nightgown back in place and pulled up the covers. There was no question but that she would have to get out of bed, but she was not prepared to do that just yet. She looked over at the empty rocking chair. Felicity Ravenwood's adventure was back on the nightstand. She wondered if Ben had finished reading it or had been merely pretending an interest. The blanket he had tucked around him was lying at the foot of her bed. His coat was thrown over the trunk. He must have shed it when the room became warm enough for his tastes. Flames still crackled in the stove. It couldn't have been very long ago that he had added wood and stoked it, which made her wonder about his current whereabouts.

Ridley dismissed the thought that he had gone home or returned to his office as wishful thinking, and this was borne out when her bedroom door swung open and he appeared on the threshold. Any idea she had about sending him on his way fled when the full rich aroma of freshly brewed coffee wafted into the room.

Ben carried in the tray and set it across Ridley's lap. He poured her a cup of coffee and placed the pot on the nightstand. "Mrs. Rushton says you take cream so I brought some." He pointed to the dainty china pitcher. "And sugar. I know you like your sugar."

Ridley waited until her rapidly beating heart resumed its normal rhythm before she spoke. Then she said what was surely the most ridiculous thing. "Mrs. Rushton's here?"

He nodded. "At first light. She was surprised to see me, but I told her about the Fullers, your late night, and that you weren't feeling well this morning when I came by to check on you."

"She didn't find that suspicious?"

Ben shrugged. "Folks find me easy to believe. You can tell her what you like later, but first you should try out your story on me."

Ridley added sugar to her coffee, stirred, and then added cream. She stirred again before she lifted the cup to her mouth. The fragrance was so heady, so welcome, that she closed her eyes to appreciate the moment before she sipped. "May I have my breakfast first?" she asked.

Ben moved from the bed to the rocker. "By all means." He stretched his legs and propped his heels on the side rail. The rocker stopped moving. "I already ate, in case you're interested."

"I wasn't."

"The widow was. She wouldn't hear of me waiting to take my breakfast at the Butterworth. You should let her cook for you more often. It gives her pleasure, and she's a good cook."

Ridley knew better than to suppose Mrs. Rushton had put the sheriff up to his little speech. This was all Ben Madison.

She picked up a buttered triangle of toast and bit off a corner. "I'll think about it." She expected him to comment and was grateful when he didn't. She ate a quarter of the scrambled eggs, most of one of the toast triangles, and drank all of her coffee. She refused a second cup.

Ben took the tray from her and put it on the floor. He sat back in the rocker and resumed the position of watchful waiting.

"There are some things I remember from last night," she said. "I recall, for instance, that you showed off my scalpel. Where did you find it?"

"A few feet from the bottom step of your front porch."

She considered that, nodded slowly. "I slipped on a patch of ice. Head over bucket. It must have been then that I cut myself."

"That's where I found the first evidence of blood."

"Well, there you have it."

"No, not quite, but you're making a good first effort at avoiding the details."

Ridley used the napkin to dab at her mouth and then dropped it over the side of the bed so that it floated to the tray. "I'm sure I don't know what you mean."

"Now, that's disappointing."

Ridley would have liked to hold his stare, but she was the first to look away. "You probably would like to know why I was carrying the scalpel."

"I'll make this easier for you, Doc. I know you had a visitor last night. No, I didn't hear anything because I went straight to the Butterworth after I left you. But I do know the surgery door was open, which suggests that you opened it for someone. A good start would be telling me who came by."

She hesitated. "I don't want you to do anything, at least not the thing you'll want to do."

"There's nothing about that that I like. I'm not making any promises."

Ridley would have been surprised if he had. "It was Jeremiah Salt."

Ben's heels slid off the bedrail. He leaned forward in the rocker and rested his forearms on his knees. "Go on."

"He'd been drinking, but that wasn't the problem, or not the only problem. He was having chest pains. I had to let him in. That's when I knew for certain that he had been drinking. I gave him a teaspoonful of sodium bicarbonate because the pain he was feeling was heartburn. He refused to take the soda at first, accused me of trying to poison him. He made the same accusation against Lily. Then he went on, accusing me of spreading a rumor that he was responsible for what happened to the Fullers."

Ben's head snapped back. "What?"

"He told me that people knew he repaired the dampers on their stove and that I said he hadn't done it correctly, and the dampers didn't fit properly, and that's what caused the gas to circulate back into the home. He was beside himself with fury, talking out of his head. I denied having said anything like that, but I don't think he really heard me. He accused Mrs. Springer of the same thing. In fact, he accused all the women in town of conspiring against him. It was frightening, and there was no reasoning with him."

"So you took out your scalpel."

"I'd done that earlier, before I let him in."

"Jesus." Ben pressed four fingers against his brow and rubbed. "Did it occur to you at all that maybe you shouldn't have let him in?"

"I thought he was going to break the door down."

Ben's hand dropped away from his forehead. "Jesus," he said again, this time more softly than before.

"And he said he was in pain. I couldn't ignore that. It turned out to be true. When he finally took the bicarbonate, his symptoms disappeared within minutes."

"All right. What happened then?"

Now it was Ridley who rubbed her head. "I'm not certain. Some of it's confused. I think that's when he told me I'd better set everyone straight, take back what I'd said about the dampers, which I couldn't convince him I never said in the first place. He kept insisting that I do something about the rumor, make it go away. There was no point in continuing to try to defend myself. I asked him if he needed help going home. Perhaps I shouldn't have done it, but I reminded him that you were next door. I offered to get you."

"I see. He took exception."

"Mm. I didn't know what else to do. He believed I wanted to send him to jail and that I was a threat. It seemed that he was going to make a grab for me and that's when I took the scalpel out of my pocket. I ducked and ran for the front door. You already know I fell. I got up and kept running. I swear I didn't know I'd cut myself."

"You ran toward my house."

"I thought you'd gone home."

"I wish I had."

She waved that aside. "Don't start blaming yourself and making me sorry I'm telling you anything. I think I got to your front steps. It doesn't really matter. He caught up to me and dumped me in a drift."

"I saw that."

She frowned.

"I looked around while my mother was stitching you up. Put some things together in my mind. So I understand that when you fell, the scalpel got turned on you, but what about Jeremiah? Did he hurt you?"

"No! No. He didn't." She hesitated, looked away, recalling the humiliation of having a packed handful of snow stuffed in her mouth.

"Ridley. The truth."

"That is the truth. I very stupidly threw a snowball at him. He took the opportunity to get some of his own back." She held her breath. When Ben didn't press, she went on. "Maybe it was then that he made me promise to correct the gossip. I told you, it was confusing. That might also be when he told me to stay away from Lily. He wants you to find someone else to shovel our walks. He doesn't want Clay anywhere near here."

"All right. That's the least of it. I'll find something else for the boy to do and someone else to do the shoveling."

Ridley nodded. "There's another thing."

"And that is?"

"I want you to find a way to see Lily. I have to know that she's not been hurt. Jeremiah showed extraordinary restraint when he caught me. He's never showed that kind of restraint with Lily. I'm afraid for Clay as well. What if Jeremiah's motive in stopping Clay from working here has nothing at all to do with what he imagines is our influence on the boy and is simply so neither of us has an opportunity to *see* him?"

"I agree with you about Lily. I'll ask Mary Cherry to pay a call on her. That will raise the least suspicion. I'll talk to the schoolmaster later this morning and find out if Clay attended. Now, about Jeremiah . . ." He raised his eyebrows. "Nothing to say?"

"He didn't hurt me," she repeated. "Yes, he shoved a handful of snow in my mouth. But truly hurt me? I panicked."

"Because you felt threatened."

"My injury was self-inflicted. An accident. Nothing more."

"Why are you defending him? Protecting him?"

Ridley pressed her lips together. She breathed in through her nose and exhaled slowly through her mouth. "I suppose you think you can say that after what I told you about my mother, but if I still had a fork in my hand, I swear I would stab you."

Ben glanced to where his coat lay draped over the trunk at the foot of the bed. He left the rocker to pick it up and fished in one of the pockets. He produced her scalpel. "Better than a fork," he said, laying it gently in her lap. "Be careful you don't hurt yourself." He returned to the rocker and set his boot heels once again on the side rail.

Ridley stared at the scalpel, fingered it. She set her jaw and felt a muscle jump in her cheek. "You shouldn't tempt me."

"Probably not, but notice that I'm not standing within reach either."

"Maybe I'm good at darts."

"Are you?"

"No." She put the scalpel on the nightstand. "It still has my blood on it."

"Yes." Ben cupped the back of his neck and kneaded the muscles. "Look, Ridley, when I asked you why you were protecting Jeremiah, well, I didn't mean anything by that. I wasn't thinking about your mother. Not at all. I was just trying to understand why you don't want to do anything."

"I apologize."

"Accepted. Now explain yourself."

"I want to know about the rumor," she said. "Don't you?"

"Sure."

"I truly believe it was the catalyst for Jeremiah taking his first drink."

"The way you spoke before, I didn't think he needed something to provoke him."

"He doesn't *need* it, but if it presents itself . . ." She shrugged. "He might have started drinking tonight regardless of what he heard. The death of Emmilou Fuller could have tipped the scales. He made a comparison between Emmilou and Lizzie, so he was thinking about that as well. Alcohol or no, the little girl's death tore at him. I think we should try to learn who said he was responsible for what happened and how the news reached him so quickly."

"He blamed you. I don't like that."

"He blamed other people, too."

"You said he was talking out of his head."

She sighed. "It's true. He was."

"Tell me again about you trying to kill him."

Ridley looked at him sharply. "Let's be clear. That's what he said, not what I was trying to do."

A slim smile lifted one corner of his mouth. "I know."

"He accused me of wanting to poison him when I presented him with a spoonful of the bicarbonate. He accused Lily of the same thing."

Ben pinched the bridge of his nose, rubbed it gently as he thought. When his hand fell back to his lap, he asked, "What do you think? Could he be right?" He put up a hand before Ridley answered. "Before you puff up and take offense, I wasn't asking about you. I was wondering about Lily."

She nodded, smoothed then folded the blankets across her lap to give her something to do with her hands. "You've known Lily most of your life. Aren't you in a better position to judge?"

"Perhaps. Then again, knowing her as I do, as I have, I'm not sure I have a clear perspective for seeing this. I can't imagine Lily doing anything to hurt Jeremiah, but then I think Jeremiah could provoke one of God's own angels to do murder. What's that expression? In wine, truth."

"In vino veritas."

"Hmm. So there's that."

"Maybe," she said quietly. "And maybe there's nothing to it at all."

Ben dropped his feet to the floor and pushed himself out of the rocker. "I can't put off getting to the office any longer, and then there's the obligatory visit to see Ellie. She'll want to know how you're doing. You might have a visit from her later today. That'll be something she'll need to do. *Need* to do. You understand?"

Ridley nodded.

"All right, then. I'll send up the widow to help you with whatever needs helping."

She smiled. "Yes. Please."

Ben picked up his coat and put it on, but he didn't make a move to leave. He stood perfectly still. His eyes grazed her face and it was as if he could feel the contours of her cheekbones, her chin, even the delicate bridge of her nose in his fingertips. They tingled. "I've been thinking about what you said about that other thing."

"Really? Because I have no idea what you're talking about."

"No? Well, I probably shouldn't say so, but it occupied a lot of space in my mind."

"Still no idea."

"Hmm. Wish that were different because this is going to come at you out of the blue."

Ridley's head came up. Her eyebrows puckered as she tried to read his intent. Her lips parted, which as it turned out, was what he had been hoping for. He swooped. His mouth covered hers in a hard, swift kiss. The back of her head bumped the headboard.

"Sorry," he said, but he was grinning. "I'll call on you later." Then he was gone.

Chapter Eighteen

Ben went home, cleaned up, and changed clothes. He stopped at the hotel, not only to apprise Ellie of Ridley's condition, but also to check on the Fullers. Louella had already gone home. The undertaker had been notified and was going to help her prepare Emmilou's body. There would be a viewing in the afternoon. Big Mike and the boys were heartbreakingly silent at a table in the dining room. The breakfast that had been laid out for them was hardly touched. Ben sat with them briefly, offered his condolences, and uncomfortably accepted their gratitude for what he'd done. Ben thought of Emmilou and wished he could have done more.

It was when Ben was leaving the Butterworth that he realized Big Mike hadn't asked him to pass on his thanks to Dr. Woodhouse. There was a simple enough explanation for that. Big Mike expected to see the doctor later today at the viewing, and he would not be alone in that expectation. Folks would have the presumption that she would be there.

Ben hunched his shoulders against the whipping wind and swore with real feeling. There was no one around to hear him, but he wouldn't have cared if Mrs. Springer and her ladies were circling him like buzzards over a carcass. There were curse words that needed to be said from time to time, and this one didn't blacken his soul; it lightened it.

Hitch stood at attention when Ben walked into the office. "At ease, Deputy," Ben said, amused. "Does your mama know you're thinking about a military career?"

"Oh, but I'm not . . . not, that is . . . no, I haven't said a word."

"Then I won't either."

"I'm happy here, Sheriff."

"Good to know." Ben went to the stove, removed his gloves, tossed them on the bench, and held out his hands to warm them. He looked over his shoulder at his deputy. "As you were, Hitch. Go on, you can sit in my chair." He shook his head as Hitch dropped like a stone. Had Hitch always had such a large Adam's apple, or was it noticeable now because the young man was swallowing so hard? "Something on your mind?"

"Um, no." He frowned deeply, which set his narrow features along comically crooked lines. "Not that there's nothing on my mind, because you've got to believe I'm always thinking, but sometimes there's not much important about the thoughts."

"I see." Ben turned back to the stove and unbuttoned his coat. He threw it on the bench beside his gloves. The hat stayed on. "Did you talk to your ma last night?" he asked. "I noticed we had a fair number of folks who showed up at the Fullers to see what was going on. Don't recall if I saw your parents there."

"They were there. That's not a problem, is it? I didn't spend but a minute here or there with them, and I did everything you asked."

"I wasn't questioning your performance."

"Oh."

"I was asking if you spoke to your mother. Seems that you did."

"You've probably noticed that she's hard to ignore."

Ben kept his back to the deputy. "I have. So what did you say in that minute you spent with them here and there?"

Hitch shrugged. "Can't say for certain. She probably asked what happened and I probably told her."

"Sounds about right. You remember what you might have said?"

"Told her it was the stove. I might have mentioned Frankie."

"Huh." Ben poured himself a cup of coffee. No milk. No sugar. Black as tar. "Do you think you might have said something about the dampers?"

"Could have. Is it important?"

"Might be."

"I saw Ma talking to Frankie. She had him close, an arm

around his shoulder like she was protecting him. That'd be something she would do. Maybe he told her more than I did."

Ben found that explanation believable. Amanda's sole intention might have been to give comfort, but it was likely she got something in return.

Hitch said, "Did you know that Jeremiah Salt made those dampers for Mrs. Fuller?"

"Huh. How do you know that?"

"I suppose my mother told me. Father hardly said a word, so she must have said it."

"I looked at the dampers. They weren't the problem."

Hitch stopped turning in the chair and adopted a defensive posture. "I didn't say they were."

"I know, but someone is saying that, and Jeremiah got wind of it." Ben gave him an abbreviated version of Jeremiah's late-night call on the doctor. He stressed the rumor and did not mention Jeremiah's threats or his paranoia.

"I don't think I put that thought in my mother's mind," said Hitch. "Didn't have it in my own. Frankie?"

"It's beginning to look that way. I need to think about it. First up, though, I need to encourage Mary Cherry to pay a call on Lily."

"I can do that," said Hitch.

Ben was not certain what Hitch was volunteering for. "I don't want you to visit Mrs. Salt. Jeremiah won't like that. If you can talk Mary Cherry into going, that would be helpful."

"Oh."

"That's what I thought. Never mind. I'll go see her. You can make rounds, let people know you're here. Keep what I told you under your hat, but if you hear anyone say something that perpetuates the rumor, nip it. All you have to say is that there was nothing wrong with the dampers. Think you can do that?"

"Be happy to."

Ben nodded and jerked his thumb toward the door. "I'll see you later."

Hank Ketchum looked up from mucking stalls as a side door opened and Ben walked into the livery. He didn't waste words on a greeting when a grunt would do, and then he bent to his task.

"Always good to see you, Hank," said Ben. "Funny how I can depend on it being colder in here than it is outside."

"You're welcome to go."

"Yeah, well, I wanted to look in on Macbeth."

"Damn stupid name for a mare. Have I told you that?"

"Every time I come by. Anyway, she's Lady Macbeth."

"Then you should call her that instead of letting folks think you're queer in the head."

Chuckling, Ben went to Macbeth's stall and put out his hand. The mare nosed it, tossed her head, and rubbed against it. "Good girl. I miss you, too. What do you think about pulling a buggy this afternoon? Maybe that nice one Hank has over there that no one's using." He picked up a brush hanging by a leather loop at the stall's entrance. "Hey, Hank, is that buggy spoken for?"

"Nope."

"I want to rent it, then. Just for the afternoon. I'll pick it up around one." He took Hank's grunt as agreement and stepped into the stall to give his mare the attention she deserved.

Ben had not walked down to the livery for the express purpose of attending to Macbeth or renting a buggy. He went there because his route took him past Jeremiah Salt's forge. Jeremiah was there, standing a safe distance from a glowing furnace. He had a long-handle pincer in his hand. What it held was deep in the flames, and Ben watched him slowly turn the tool, softening the metal, making it malleable. Jeremiah looked over as Ben passed. Ben tipped his hat in acknowledgment. Jeremiah nodded back.

And that was that.

Ben finished grooming Macbeth and helped Hank finish cleaning the last two stalls. He didn't expect any thanks, but he knew the buggy would be polished and ready to go at the appointed hour, and whatever Hank charged him would be reasonable.

Mary Cherry was standing at the bench in his office, studying the wanted notices when Ben walked in. "See anyone you know?" he asked.

"Always surprises me when I don't." She turned to face him. "I did what you asked. Just got here, in fact."

Ben dropped into the chair behind his desk. "And?"

"And I don't know what I think. Lily was tight-lipped, but maybe no more than usual. Clay and Hannah are both in school. I suppose that's good. The little ones weren't talking, not even to each other."

"That doesn't sound right." He pulled off his gloves one finger at a time and dropped them on his desk. "What was Lily doing when you got there?"

"Reading a story to the children."

"So she was sitting down."

Mary's nostrils flared slightly and her lips thinned. There was as much disapproval in the look as there was concern. "I took two quart jars of chicken noodle with me just to keep things ordinary. I've done it before."

"That was a good idea."

"I don't think it helped."

"Did she get up?"

"No. That worried me, but the children were like burrs on horsehair. There was no moving them. I put the soup in the kitchen, chatted a little while afterward. She might be hurting, but she's not saying, and I couldn't see anything."

"What did you chat about?"

"The Fullers mostly. Not so the little ones would understand. I asked her if she might stop by their home later today. She was definite that she would not."

"All right. I appreciate your help, Mary." He unbuttoned his coat. "I understand you're working for Mrs. Springer now."

"I am. She's a pill, but then, so was Doc."

"You hear anything from him? He hasn't written to me."

"I haven't written him."

"You're still angry?"

"Angry doesn't begin to describe it. The man left me. Maybe I shouldn't take it so personal, but after years working at his side, it felt wrong. It felt hurtful." She shrugged. "I'm tending to other things now."

Ben hesitated, wondering what he could say and still keep Doc's confidences. It wasn't even Doc who had confided that he was ill; it was Ridley who shared his secret. "Maybe it's not such a good idea to leave it that way. Couldn't hurt to write to him."

"So you say."

"And maybe you could try a little harder with Dr. Woodhouse. She's not the devil's handmaiden."

Mary's features did not alter a whit. "So you say."

"I know you've made up your mind that you don't like her, but that's as far as it goes, isn't it?"

"What does that mean?"

Ben reconsidered his approach. He couldn't ask what he was wondering. "When did you hear about the Fullers?" he asked instead. "I don't think you were there last night."

"I wasn't, but I was late at the Springers. Her nibs is having a ladies' tea and I was making tarts. I finished up just as him and her returned. Couldn't get out of hearing the whole of it, the whole of it being what she said. He went straight to bed. Looked proper sad."

"We all were."

"Not so's you always know it. You ever notice how some folks smile when they're telling you bad news? It's like they don't know what to do with it. Makes them Nervous Nellies, smiling foolishly in the face of tragedy."

"What are you saying, Mary?"

"Not saying anything. Making an observation." She repositioned her hat on her head and wound her brushed wool scarf around her neck. "I brought you some soup, too." She pointed to where the quart jar sat on top of the stove. "It'll keep warm there. Don't know what got into me, making enough to feed the town. I'm going to send my husband to the Fullers with more."

"That's real thoughtful."

She headed for the door, paused, and turned to him. "I guess you heard about the dampers on Louella's oven by now."

Ben's heart hammered once. He did not let his interest get away from him. "Might've. What did you hear?"

"Seems Jeremiah replaced the dampers and they didn't fit proper. Could have been at the root of the problem, and that's a damn shame."

"Huh. How'd you come to hear that?"

"Mrs. Springer, but she had it straight from Dr. Woodhouse. This is what I'm saying, Ben. Doc Dunlop would have known better than to share something like that. Mark my words, there's trouble for you."

Chapter Nineteen

"Wait!" Mrs. Rushton called after Ben as he began to climb the stairs to Ridley's rooms. The widow's plump arms were outstretched imploringly. Her entreaties thus far had had no impact. When she'd tried to block his way, he simply picked her up and put her aside. She stuttered and sputtered after that, but then she found her voice. "You can't go up there! I tell you, she's resting. That's on your orders! Do you remember anything you said to me this morning?"

Ben paused on the stairs and looked down at her. She'd changed her stance and now her arms were resting akimbo. She had her hackles up and looked as if she might charge the hill. "Mrs. Rushton, you are performing your duties admirably and making me regret I was so firm with you earlier, but I hereby rescind those orders, at least as they apply to me." He took a page from Ridley's book and said, "I'm the sheriff and I rule."

"Hah!"

"Overrule," he said. "I overrule myself." He did not think she was impressed. She pointed a finger at him and wagged it to great effect.

"You be careful up there. Don't make me regret that I voted for you. A lot of women did, you know, and I am acquainted with all of them."

Ben grinned, gave her a small salute, and then hurried the rest of the way up the stairs. He thought the widow might be nipping at his heels, but when he turned at the top of the steps, she was already on her way back to the kitchen.

He knocked lightly on Ridley's door before he poked his head in the room. She was sitting in the rocker, a stack of medical books beside her. It was interesting then that she was reading what he'd left behind. Felicity Ravenwood's adventures were hard to resist.

"Too late," he said when she closed the book and tried to slip it between her hip and the rocker. "Already saw it." She wrinkled her nose at him, and for a moment, he thought she might stick out her tongue. She appeared to think better of that because he only glimpsed the very provocative tip. "Are you as far as the part where Felicity—"

"Don't you dare say another word."

He made a show of clamping his mouth shut.

"What do you want?" she asked. "I heard you arguing with Martha. I don't like you bullying her."

"I didn't think I was . . ." He lifted his hands and turned over his palms in a guilty gesture. "Maybe I was. I'll apologize on our way out."

"*Our* way out? Ben, I have twenty stitches in my side because your mother has a deft and dainty hand. I've hidden them from Martha and I've managed the pain with some powders instead of more laudanum. I've moved around a little to keep from getting too stiff, but I don't think I'm ready to leave the house just yet."

He rolled right over her objection. "Emmilou Fuller's been laid out in her home."

Ridley dropped Felicity Ravenwood on top of the medical tomes. "Of course. I just need a few minutes to get ready."

Ben did a quick translation and thought a half hour was probably fair. "I'll wait downstairs. Holler when you're ready to come down. I'll help you."

"First, I don't holler. Second, I need your help now."

"Um, maybe we should call Mrs. Rushton back in here?" He inched backward in what he thought was a surreptitious manner. She caught him out immediately. Worse, she smirked. "You cannot be that shy," she said. "I was laid out like a Christmas turkey in my own surgery last night, fit for stuffing and stitching. You saw a great deal of me then."

"Actually—" Ridley put up a hand, stopping him before he began. He wondered if she would believe that he'd left the room fairly quickly and set his mind to discovering what had happened instead of giving in to carnal curiosity. Besides, she wasn't at her best just then. He knew better than to say that so he simply closed his mouth and regarded her expectantly.

"You cannot be unfamiliar with a woman's form," she said. "I know there's a brothel in town two blocks off the main street. Did anyone tell you I visited the women? It seems that Hitch is a particular favorite, but they were of the opinion that you take your pleasure out of town. Harmony, is it?"

"Can we pretend that you've embarrassed me and get started?" He liked it when she blinked owlishly at him over the top of her spectacles. "Where did you find those? You didn't have them last night when you came to the hotel."

"I didn't find them. These are an extra pair. I have several. I suspect I lost the others in that drift in front of your house."

"I'll look for them later."

Ridley placed her hands on the arms of the rocker and began to rise. The effort was slow and torturous. She did not have to ask for help. Ben was at her side before she was halfway to her feet. He put a hand at her back and steadied her at the elbow. She grimaced until she was standing and then she took a careful breath.

"Thank you," she said. She looked at him sideways. "I'm sorry about what I said. I don't know if I was trying to embarrass you, though. Goad you, maybe."

"Well, I felt a mite goaded. I took it as a sign that you're feeling better."

She chuckled and her body instantly seized on a sharp intake of air. "You can't make me laugh. It hurts too much."

"Point taken, and I'm thinking maybe this isn't such a good idea after all."

"Oh, no. You're not changing your mind now, and I'm certainly not changing mine. Let me get behind the screen and I'll tell you what I need as I go."

"So there's no chance I'm going to become more familiar with your female form?"

She swallowed another chuckle but not without feeling it. "Stop it, Ben. I mean it. You can let me go. I can make it on my own now."

His dropped his hands but stayed close. When they reached the screen, he moved aside a panel so she wouldn't have to squeeze into the small space, and then replaced it once she was on the other side. He heard water splashing into the basin and the sound of her wringing out a washcloth.

"I brought a buggy," he said. He heard her gasp and was tempted to look over the top of the screen. "Are you all right?"

"You scared me. I didn't realize you were still standing there. Go sit down. I swear I'll call you when I need you."

Scratching behind his ear in the way he did when something didn't quite make sense, Ben went to the bed and sat. The rocker looked inviting but that was mostly because Felicity Ravenwood would have been within reach. He resisted the urge and chuckled under his breath because he felt so good about it. Dr. E. Ridley Woodhouse prompted him to experience things a little off-kilter. He liked it.

"Is Evangeline on your list?" she called from behind the screen.

"Pardon?"

"Your list," she said. "The one you're making so you don't have to count sheep."

"Oh, that list. I'll have to check. I think I have Evangeline."

"And you have to have Emmilou."

He sobered. "I already do."

"Good."

"I don't suppose . . ."

"No, neither one."

"Eve?"

"No."

"Were you named after anyone in your family?"

"No."

"Who had the naming of you? Your father or your mother?"

"My mother's mother. She meant well."

Ben saw Ridley's hands rise above the screen as she shed her night shift over her head. She laid it over the top, where it slid between two of the partitions. He waited and caught sight of a lacy chemise. It slithered down her outstretched arms and disappeared. A surprisingly frilly petticoat followed. There was some more movement, and when his gaze dropped to the space between the screen and the floor, he watched a pair of wide-legged drawers suddenly appear as a drift of snow at her feet. One dainty foot found an opening in a leg, and then the other searched out the second opening. Ridley must have lowered herself carefully because it seemed like a long time passed before her fingers grasped the drawers by the waist and began to pull them up as she straightened.

There was a lot Ben couldn't see, but that didn't seem to matter. On the contrary, the experience was curiously erotic.

"All right," she said. "I need you."

No wonder she didn't have to holler. He was moving toward her like a moth to a flame. That gave him pause when he thought about it. It was not a particularly kind image. The moths usually died beating their wings helplessly in and around that flame. He shook out his arms as a precaution before he moved behind the screen.

Dr. E. Ridley Woodhouse—it was important right now to keep that in his mind—was indeed dressed precisely as he'd imagined. The fine, filmy chemise had lace edging at the neckline. There were matching tiers of it on the hem of her petticoat and evidence of the same at the bottom of the drawers where they peeped out. She must have seen the drop in his eyes because she smoothed the petticoat and the lace frosting disappeared. That was a shame.

"Yes?" he asked. "Do you need help with your gown?"

Ridley pointed to the stool at the vanity. A tailored brocade corset lay open on the stool; pink ribbons trailed over the side. There were lace frills at the bottom and a garden of rosettes trimming the top.

Ben couldn't have imagined this. It was becoming more difficult to think of her as Dr. E. Ridley Woodhouse.

"I need you to tie that off for me," she said. "I can't manage."

"Do you have to wear it? Doesn't seem that fashion should be your concern right now."

She sighed. "Of course you would think that. It's not fashion that concerns me. I need it for support. It will keep everything, and I mean everything, in place."

"Oh. You're not bandaged?"

"Yes, I'm wearing a bandage. This is an additional precaution. Please don't make me go on."

"Sorry."

"You know how it works, don't you?"

Ben picked it up, held it open in front of him, and looked it over. "I figure it's not so different than saddling up a mare."

"Yes, I'm sure you're right," she said dryly.

He looked her over again. "There's considerably less girth to you."

"You overwhelm me with flattery. No wonder you have to pay for women in Harmony."

"Hah. A lot you know. They pay me." He made a circling motion with his finger. "Turn around before you snap at that bait. Your mouth's open like you mean to."

Ridley clamped a hand over her injury and gave him her back. "I can't help it that I find you ridiculously amusing, but there will be retribution."

"There's never been any doubt in my mind. Lift your arms a bit so I can get this contraption around you. Is this what they're calling a bust improver now?"

"It's a corset, just a corset."

"Oh. Mrs. Fish. You know her, right? The dressmaker." When Ridley nodded, he said, "Well, she was telling me about these bust improvers. I guess they have bands in them where you can insert pads to present an illusion of—"

"Girth?" she asked.

Ben chuckled. "Something like that. I was thinking of bountifulness."

"I'm sure you were. You have to pull tighter. Here, let me put my hands on the wall. I can brace myself."

Ben didn't like it but he did as she asked. The corset ribbons were slippery in his fingers. He dropped them more than once as he crisscrossed the laces and pulled. "Better?" he asked.

"Yes. I'm thinking about you and Mrs. Fish discussing women's undergarments. How does that come about exactly?"

"Exactly? I'm not sure I know. I just like to hear people talk about what they're interested in. That day Mrs. Fish was looking over some fashion plates in a catalog when I stepped in to say hello. We got to chatting; she got to sharing. It happens like that." He pulled on the laces again. "That has to be tight enough because I'm not squeezing you so you can't breathe."

"It's good. Tie it off." When he was done, she pushed away from the wall. "Much better." She lowered herself to the stool. "My stockings are in the top drawer. Do you mind helping me put them on?"

Oh, he minded. He minded plenty. What he said was, "What color?"

"Any pair of black ones will do. The black garters as well."

He found them and knelt in front of her. "You're going to need help with your shoes, too, aren't you?"

"Mm-hmm."

"All right, Cinderella. Let's do this." Ben thought if he had been removing her stockings and garters, he would probably have lingered. She had smooth knees, shapely calves, and nicely turned ankles. Yes, he definitely would have lingered. What he did now was the opposite of that. The stockings were on, the garters in place, and those fashionably pointed shoes tied up with neat little bows. He was a goddamn paragon of integrity, that's what he was, and he didn't thank her for depending on it. "Is that it? Your carriage is waiting."

"You sound surly. Are you?"

"I'm impatient."

"That would be a first." She waved him away. "Go on. I can manage the rest." When he didn't move, she pointed to herself. "I'm still in my altogethers."

"Yeah. I see that." He backed away and slipped to the other side of the screen.

"You can hand me the black gown from the wardrobe," she said. "The one with the satin frogs on the left side of the bodice. I can get into that."

Ben found it and passed it over the top of the screen. There was some mildly colorful language as she wrestled with the gown. It amused him that she even cursed in pastels.

He bent so he could see what was going on below the screen and was in time to see the skirt of the gown fall into place. When she didn't appear immediately afterward, he stood and peeked around the screen. She was sitting at the vanity again, facing the mirror. She had a brush in one hand and was staring at a defeated reflection. She lifted her eyes and caught his. "I'll get the widow," he said.

"I've never asked her to dress my hair before. I manage this on my own. She'll be suspicious and she'll argue with you again. She'll argue with me. If she blocks the door, I don't think we're getting through."

"She tried blocking the stairs. I picked her up and moved her aside."

Ridley smiled. "There's a picture. She might do it again just for the thrill."

That convinced him to help her. That, and the twinge at the small of his back. Martha Rushton was not a tiny package. "What do I need to do?" he asked, taking the brush from her hand.

"Goodness, you worked on a ranch that raised horses. Are you telling me you never brushed out a mane?"

"I have, but making another comparison to a horse didn't seem wise."

"Well, it's probably a good thing it came from me, then. My plait is already falling apart. Just remove the ribbon and separate the braid. You can just brush it out. Give it a twist after that and secure it against my head with the combs I'll give you."

"You don't want another braid? I know how to do that."

"You'd still have to put it up and secure it."

"Okay." He slipped off the ribbon and held one end between his lips as he gently brushed out the braid. When he'd finished, her hair rippled down her back like a waterfall at night. It seemed a shame to wrap it up, but then he was optimistic that he'd get to see it like this again. He dropped the brush on the vanity and began to overlap thick ropes of hair. Once he'd tied it off, he took the combs she held up for him and anchored the braid to the back of her head. "Are you going to wear a hat?"

"A shawl for inside the house. My cloak and hood outside of it."

"Then this will work." He picked up the hand mirror and held it up so she could see the back of her head. "Don't make too much of that. Sam Love does the same for me after he's cut my hair."

"I did wonder. You have unexpected accomplishments that have nothing at all to with raising horses."

"Huh. Maybe I do." He laid the mirror back on the vanity. "Is your shawl up here?"

"In the wardrobe. My cloak and gloves are downstairs."

Ben was already on his way to retrieve the shawl. She was

waiting for him outside the screen. He wrapped it loosely around her shoulders and adjusted it so she would be able to cover her hair when she was inside the Fullers' home.

"Sam does this for you, too?"

"I've watched my mother," he said wryly. "And the ladies over in Harmony."

"Of course."

Ben let her walk to the door under her own steam, but when they reached the top of the stairs, he took her elbow while she gripped the banister with her free hand. He heard the widow pounding across the front room before she appeared in the vestibule.

"She looks like death," said Mrs. Rushton. "Paler than. It's probably a sin to say so, but little Emmilou will look better lying out than the doctor does right now."

Ridley grimaced. "You should have stopped after 'it's probably a sin.'"

"Don't I know it. It's a failing of mine, but it's moving me to take action. I'm going with you to pay my respects. It's not as if you need me anywhere else at the moment and I want to do right by the family. They're good people."

Ben said, "The buggy only seats two."

"That's all right. I guess I know how to drive a buggy. You can walk beside or ahead. Makes me never mind to me."

He felt Ridley's slender frame begin to vibrate. She was making a heroic effort not to belly laugh, when he imagined what she wanted to do was howl. He wanted to howl as well but not because he was amused. Out of the corner of his mouth, he said, "If you laugh, I'm letting go."

That sobered her. "I need my cloak and my gloves, Martha. Would you be so kind?"

The housekeeper removed the cloak from the coat tree and found the fur-trimmed gloves in an inside pocket. She had the cloak open for Ridley by the time she reached the bottom. Ridley stepped inside the brushed woolen warmth while Ben got his coat off the same rack. Mrs. Rushton closed the cloak, fastened the frogs, and smoothed the material over Ridley's shoulders. "Do you want the hood up?"

"Please." Ridley put on the gloves.

"I surely wish you would tell me what's wrong. You're moving like an old woman. A *very* old woman."

"I told you that I strained myself last night when I moved the children."

"Uh-huh," she said, getting her own coat. "And I told you I didn't believe it." She opened the door, gloves in hand, and was still shaking her head as she reached the sidewalk. "Have a care. There are icy patches under this last layer of snow. Thought Clay would come around, but I haven't seen him."

"I'm taking care of that," said Ben, helping Ridley down the steps. There was no rail for her to hold. "Clay won't be back. That's the word from Jeremiah."

The housekeeper pursed her lips. "Hateful man. I guess that's what makes it easy for folks to think the worst about it. No one ever questioned his work before, but something like this calls it into question."

"You heard?" asked Ridley. "Already?"

"Stopped at the butcher's before I came here. Amanda Springer was there haranguing her husband."

"That says it all," said Ben, guiding Ridley around the patch of ice that the widow pointed out.

"Don't it just."

"No," said Ridley. "Wait. That doesn't say it all. Did she mention that I was the source of the accusation against Mr. Salt?"

"She might have said something like that." Mrs. Rushton offered that information reluctantly. "I didn't believe her, and I told her so. She didn't like that, but I've disagreed with her before. It's not as if she can turn me into a pillar of salt, no matter how much she'd like that."

"But you aren't asking me if I *did* say it."

"Now wouldn't that just be a waste of my breath. It makes no kind of sense that you'd court Jeremiah Salt's wrath even if you were one to speak out of turn. I've noticed that you keep your own counsel. I don't have to look any farther than you're standing from me right now—barely standing, I can say confidently—to know the truth of that."

"All right," said Ben. "I believe that covers it. Let's get to the buggy." He helped Ridley in first and then escorted Mrs.

Rushton to the other side and made certain she could step up. He reached for the reins, but she took them on her own.

"I swear to you that I can drive a buggy."

"Just have a care with my horse. She knows my touch."

"What's her name?"

"Macbeth. Lady Macbeth."

"Lord. You call her Macbeth?"

"Uh-huh."

"Well, I'm calling her Lady and she'll do just fine." She snapped the reins; the buggy wheels hesitated over a mound of snow and then jerked forward. "There we go. Try to keep up."

Keeping up was not a problem. Mrs. Rushton couldn't exactly go hell for leather in the snow. Ben thought she was also being cautious because of her companion. When he caught a glimpse of Ridley's face, he was put in mind of that pillar of salt the widow mentioned earlier. If it were not so important that Ridley make an appearance at the Fuller home, he never would have pressed.

It was not a long trip. Yesterday she had run most of the way, Frankie weaving on his feet behind her. He suspected that in a few days, she would be able to make the walk on her own, even though as a doctor she might not advise it for a patient.

There were people spilling out of the house, mingling on the porch with cups of coffee, tea, and hot chocolate in hand. They began to separate when they saw Ben and the buggy and realized who might be inside it. Ben took the reins and tethered them. Mrs. Rushton stepped down without his help. Ridley waited for him, and as soon as she alighted, the path to the front door began to clear. Men tipped their hats. The women acknowledged her with a slight bow of the head.

Ben felt Ridley falter but he doubted that it was her wound that caused her discomfort. She had not expected her arrival to be greeted as something outside the ordinary, but Ben had suspected there might be a stir. It was a solemn occasion, but there were also thanks to be expressed, and while no one spoke, gratitude was there all the same.

Because Ridley looked as if she hoped the ground would swallow her whole, he said, "You can breathe. You're queen of the Frost Falls Festival."

Chapter Twenty

"I should have stuck my elbow in your ribs," Ridley said when Ben climbed in the buggy beside her. "Better yet, in your mouth. Someone could have heard you make that ridiculous comment."

"Someone did. You. And I've been wondering if you've always had this violent, retaliatory streak? Have we ever had a conversation where you don't threaten?"

Ridley gave him a sour smile. "Probably not, but I'll let you think on why that might true."

Ben chuckled, snapped the reins. "Lay on, Macbeth."

"I believe the quote is, 'Lay on, Macduff.'"

"Yes, but her name is Macbeth. The other would confuse her."

"Of course," she said dryly. The buggy began to move forward. Ridley put a hand on Ben's forearm. "Wait. Where is Martha?"

"I did wonder when you'd notice. She stayed back to help with the repast. I heard her tell you."

"Oh, did she? I don't remember."

"You were sitting beside Louella. You had your hand in hers, and the two of you hadn't exchanged a word in minutes. You sat there, not sharing her grief exactly. More like you were absorbing it. It's not surprising that you don't recall the widow speaking to you."

Ridley bowed her head a fraction. "I felt her sorrow all the way to my marrow. Her heartache . . . it's profound."

"Emmilou was the apple of her eye. Big Mike's, too. A little girl coming as she did after those boys. She was a blessing to them."

Ridley swiped at a tear at the corner of one eye. She sniffed, removed a glove, and swiped at another tear with her fingertip. "Do you have a handkerchief?"

"In my pocket." When she was not moved to explore, he unbuttoned his coat enough to reach inside and fish out his handkerchief and hand it to her. He shivered slightly and closed his coat. "Are you all right?"

"Yes. I tried so hard not to cry in there. It felt wrong somehow to be comforted by the one who needed comfort."

"Big Mike cried."

"So he did. I saw you were speaking to him. What did you say?"

"Not much. Asked him if he needed help with the burial expenses. I have a small fund for that, and folks will pass a hat. He was grateful. I guess no one had brought it up."

"It's not an easy thing to talk about."

"Yes, well . . ." Ben's shoulders lifted and fell inside his heavy coat. He looked down at his sleeve when Ridley placed her hand once more on his forearm.

"I imagine you said everything exactly as it should have been said," she told him. "It's remarkable really. I don't think you know how to shy away from what's difficult. I wonder sometimes if you even know that what you do is difficult for others. That family didn't need another worry. It was good of you to relieve him of that burden."

"You keep going on like that and I'm going to ask for my handkerchief back."

She patted his arm and gave him a watery smile when he shifted in his seat to look at her. She glimpsed evidence that he could have used the handkerchief just then, but he blinked once and turned his face into the bitter cold. Ridley said nothing, but she moved infinitesimally closer to him. If what she did was absorb grief, then she could absorb his as well.

"Do you want to go back to your room?" Ben asked as he took Ridley's coat from her. "It's probably better if I help you up before Mrs. Rushton returns."

"She's coming back?"

"That's her intention."

Ridley couldn't help it. Her shoulders sagged as she released an audible sigh. "I suppose I hoped she would—"

"Go home from there?"

"Yes," she admitted. "I'm not ungrateful for her help, but there is so much fussing. I think I'd just like to rest."

"And on the other hand, when you need something, it must be a relief to know she's here."

"Precisely. It's simple really. Everything must be on my terms."

He chuckled. "I'll keep that in mind. It won't change a thing, but I'll keep it in mind." He held out an elbow. "Up the stairs?"

"Aren't you going to take off your coat?"

"I have to leave. Easier to keep it on."

"But—"

"I'll be back. Probably before the widow. You said you wanted to rest."

"I do. You're restful." She ducked her head and looked toward the stairs. "I'm sorry. I don't know why I said that. I shouldn't have because it's not as if you're always restful. Sometimes you're provoking."

"Hmm. We'll sort it out. But right now, stairs."

They were halfway to the top when Ben decided that acting as Ridley's escort was taking too much damn time. He turned, looped her arms around his neck, and lifted her. He initiated the gesture, and when she didn't offer a single word in protest, he knew this was one of those things on her terms.

Once they were in her bedroom, he deposited her behind the dressing screen, and took her clothing as she carefully placed it over the top. She required assistance with the corset. Removing it was considerably easier than lacing her into it. He told her that.

"Not restful," she said.

Ben grinned behind her back because that was safe. He helped her with her stockings and garters while she removed the combs from her hair. She drew it forward over her shoulder and tied it with a black grosgrain ribbon. The ribbon drew his eye, lying as it did against her white chemise. A moment later, something else drew his eye. Droplets of blood dotted the chemise where it lay over her injury.

"That's not good," he said, pointing to the stain.

Ridley looked down at herself and plucked at the material. "Darnation."

That made him smile. "You should really try to do better." When she looked at him oddly, he explained, "Cursing. I can teach you."

"I don't doubt it," she said, her expression wry. She turned to the basin and dampened a cloth. Just as she was lifting the chemise to apply the cloth, she asked him to get her another. "And a fresh nightdress. You can put them on top of the screen."

Which meant that he was not going to get behind it again while she was in any state of undress. Damn, but she was the very opposite of restful. He put the garments where she wanted them and collected the stained chemise, her petticoat, and the corset, which he now saw had similar bloodstains.

"Are you all right?" he asked.

"Yes. The bleeding has already stopped. Most everything's in place."

"What does that mean, 'most everything'?"

"My innards aren't outwards."

"Good to know. Anything else?"

"A couple of broken sutures. I can repair them myself."

"This is the real reason you can't be left alone."

"Thread and needles are in the cabinet. The laudanum, too. I was trying not to use any more, but—"

"Enough. This is me holding up my hand. Is there anything else you need? I'm going to wash out these garments as best I can. You don't want Mrs. Rushton finding them in their current condition. Can you wait?"

"Yes."

Ridley was lying in bed when he returned holding a tray with the items she'd requested. Ellie Madison was right behind him. Ridley began to push herself up, but the look Ellie gave her sent her sinking back. Taking her cue from Ellie, Ridley gave Ben a similarly reproving look. He didn't have the grace to sink anywhere.

"I didn't hear you leave," she said.

"That's because I didn't want you to. Ellie is going to have a look and stitch you up. She is unhappy that you insisted on going to the Fullers, but I explained about you being headstrong."

"It's all right," Ellie said, laying a hand on Ridley's shoulder. "He's lying to you. He told me it was his idea."

"It was a good one, and I didn't have an objection."

Ellie sighed. "No one ever does, not that it would matter to him. Wears a body down with nothing but silence."

"I've noticed."

Ben set the tray on the nightstand. "I'm leaving now so you can talk about me behind my back. I prefer it that way. Besides, I have undergarments to launder." On that parting shot, he disappeared into the hallway.

"He's lying about that, too," said Ellie. "He brought them over to the hotel so I could take care of them. They're clean and drying in the kitchen."

"I must have fallen asleep. I didn't think there could have been enough time for so much to be done."

"And that's how it should be. Now let me look at the damage." She waited for Ridley to roll back the covers and then gently lifted her nightdress. She peeked under the fresh bandage that Ridley had wrapped around herself after she had cleaned the wound. "Not so bad, is it?"

"I told him that."

"I'm sure you did."

"I was going to fix it myself."

"Uh-huh. I heard." She patted Ridley's hand. "I have every confidence that you could have done so, but can't think of a single reason as to why you should." She reached for a teaspoon and the small amber bottle on the tray. "Here, I'm going to give you some laudanum and then give it some time to work. I'm going to make the repairs and hope you'll show more respect for my work in the future."

"Yes, ma'am. As long as I don't have to attend another viewing."

Ellie smiled. "Understood. Open up."

Ridley lifted her head and accepted the spoon that Ellie aimed at her mouth. She licked it clean, which earned her Ellie's approval.

Ellie hitched her hip to the side of the bed. "How is Louella? I was at the home early on. The hotel staff brought refreshments and I paid my respects, but I couldn't stay as long as I would have liked. It seemed as if there'd be no lack of visitors, but I still hated to go."

"Mrs. Fuller is . . . was . . . deep in grief when I sat with her. She hardly spoke. I didn't expect anything else."

"Nothing changed, then."

"No, probably not. Probably not for a long time."

"She still has the boys to look after. There's no crawling into a hole and living there."

It sounded harsh to Ridley's ears, but she did not doubt that it was true.

Ellie asked, "Was Amanda Springer there?"

"Ben didn't tell you?"

"No."

"Hmm. Mrs. Springer and I exchanged words."

"I hope you mean to tell me more than that."

"I thought I could avoid her. You know about the rumor, don't you, that I supposedly said that Mr. Salt had some responsibility for what happened to the Fullers?"

"I heard."

"As best as I can tell, that rumor was Mrs. Springer's invention. Maybe Frankie said something to her and she misunderstood. That's as gracious as I'm prepared to be. Ben might know more but we haven't spoken about it. He was going to ask around this morning."

"Then I'm sure he did."

Ridley nodded. "There was no reason for Mrs. Springer to corner me in the kitchen, but that's what happened. I naively thought she was going to apologize or at least offer an explanation for speaking out of turn as she did, but she expressed concerns that I was the one who spoke disparagingly of Mr. Salt's work. It was the oddest thing, but she almost convinced me that I had done exactly that. I had a difficult time keeping my feet under me and not because of my injury. She twisted my head right around. I can't recall if I talked to her last night. I'm not sure any longer if I knew she was there."

"Then you've finally, truly, met Amanda Springer. She has no shame, but that is because she believes what she says. There is no lying with intent to deceive. Her truth is as she sees it."

"So there is no unraveling it."

"Unlikely to happen, but most folks eventually come to an

opinion on their own. She has her acolytes, of course. You probably know who they are by now."

"Hmm." Ridley's eyelids felt heavy. She could feel that the medicine was beginning to take hold. It was a struggle to keep her eyes open. "Mary Cherry," she whispered.

"On the fringes of that group of followers."

"She doesn't like me."

"She was devoted to Doc."

"Mm-hmm." Ridley yawned abruptly. Her eyes closed. "Think I'm ready now."

Ellie smiled. "Let's get this done."

Ellie found Ben sitting in one corner of the wide sofa with his boots propped on the trunk that was being used as a coffee table—and now apparently as a footstool. "Down," she said, looking pointedly at his boots.

Ben's feet hit the floor and he sat up. He did not admonish her in turn for speaking to him as if he were a misbehaving puppy. "How is she?"

"Fine. Sleeping. I doubt I'll be the one removing the stitches. She can manage that on her own and it's safe to say that she would prefer it that way."

He nodded. "There's tea brewing. Can you stay and have a cup?"

"No, I have to get back to the hotel. I expect there will be a steady flow through the dining room as people leave the Fullers'." Her brow pulled together as she regarded him curiously. "And since when did you start drinking tea?"

Ben rubbed the spot behind his ear with a forefinger. "I guess maybe around the time Dr. Woodhouse came to town. I don't mind it so much. She has particular instructions for Mrs. Mangold on how to make the exact blend she wants. It's just chemistry, she says. I think it's alchemy."

Ellie chuckled low in her throat. "You like her, don't you?"

"Sure."

"No, I mean you *like* her."

"I know what you mean. My answer's the same."

"I swear, Ben, sometimes you are such an aggravation to me that I have to light a candle in church."

"Are you Catholic now? I thought they light candles."

"Aggravating," she said under her breath.

He stood, walked over to her, and kissed the cheek she proffered out of habit. "Thanks, Ma. I appreciate the help."

She nodded. "Just see that you do right by her. I like her just fine, and don't think I won't choose her over you if it comes to that. Always thought I might like a daughter."

"Good to know."

"I'm serious, Ben. Don't test me."

"Uh-huh."

She cuffed him on the back of the head and he helped her on with her coat, thus reestablishing the order they favored.

Chapter Twenty-one

Ridley healed without incident over the next week. There was no infection, no fever. She was able to see patients who came to her as they trickled in. Mrs. Washburn, the bank manager's wife, had a raised rash across her back, buttocks, and belly that was causing her great distress. Ridley suggested a stronger dose of calamine lotion, oatmeal baths twice a day, and having her husband remove all traces of wool from her clothes cupboard.

Mrs. Washburn was delighted with the result—and a doctor's recommendation that she purchase new clothes. Doc Dunlop was not likely to have suggested that.

Ridley treated several patients for frostbite. George Hotchkiss was one who returned, this time with two blackened toes on his right foot. She wished he were back to have his nose reset and his shoulder realigned. There was no choice but to amputate the toes to save the foot. His livelihood was cutting and hauling wood; he needed to be able to walk to be able to work.

There were patients with head colds and coughs deep enough to rattle their bones. She took her time with everyone who came through the surgery and chafed at the restrictions the sutures continued to present.

It was on the evening of the ninth day following her injury that she decided it was time to remove the stitches. Early on she had chosen not to keep the wound bandaged. In the hospital she had observed that covering the site of an injury might protect it from outside influences, most all of which were invisible to the naked eye, but that keeping it uncovered also had healing properties. Wounds did not seep and pucker; the sutures stayed in good condition, kept the skin closed, and were easier to remove.

Ridley examined her skin. Pressed gently along the line and did not find it particularly tender. She had been fortunate when she sliced herself through her robe and nightdress that she had not forced threads of either garment into the wound, where they would have festered.

Ridley stood at the medicine cabinet, surgical scissors in hand, nightgown rucked up to her waist, while she carefully snipped the sutures, when she heard the front door open. There was only one person who would venture into her home from that direction at night and without knocking.

"Stay away!" she called to him. "I'm operating. Not a step past the kitchen."

Ben draped his coat over the newel post and set his hat and scarf on top. Using the coat rack just now seemed too damn hard. "I don't think you have a patient in there," he said. "But I saw the lamps were burning so I backtracked to your front door."

"I'm removing the sutures. I've confirmed my own good health."

"Ah." He wandered through the front room, the dining room, ignored the kettle humming on the stove, and found what he wanted in the drinks cabinet in her office. Ridley kept a limited selection of spirits in her office, but what she had accumulated was better than what Doc Dunlop kept there, or perhaps it was merely better than what old Doc had been willing to share.

Ben removed a tumbler from the cabinet and poured three fingers of fine Kentucky bourbon into it. "You want a drink?"

"I have water on for—oh, you mean alcohol. No, thank you. Are you in my office?"

"I am."

So much for telling him to go no farther than the kitchen. "I'm almost done."

"No hurry." He sat down in the soft leather chair behind her desk and leaned back. There was a small painted footstool under the desk. He nudged it with his toe until he had it situated at the right distance and then set his heels on it. Stretched out, tumbler cupped in his palm, he closed his eyes. He breathed in the faint but familiar scent of Doc's cigars. The smoky aroma still clung stubbornly to the pores in the leather, but now there was more than a mere hint of lavender occupying the same space. He breathed that scent in, too, and wondered what Doc would have made of it.

It was sometime later that he finally raised the glass to his lips and drank.

Ridley stepped quietly into her office. Ben's fingers were wrapped loosely around a tumbler that was tipped dangerously close to spilling. She approached and took it out of his hand. He didn't stir. It frightened her a little, this careworn expression that shadowed his features. Sleep was a restorer, a healer, but in Ben's face she saw that he slept with heavy sadness.

She sipped from his glass. The bourbon slid warmly down her throat and put a little heat in her belly. She set the tumbler down and padded to the kitchen, where she removed the kettle and steeped a pot of tea. Ben woke abruptly when she returned to her office, but she knew it was not because of any sound that she made. Something else had jerked him out of his sleep.

Ridley elbowed some files and books out of the way so she could put down the tray in her hands. "Do you want some? I only brought the one cup. I thought you—"

"You thought right." He reached for the tumbler and drew it toward him.

Ridley belted her robe closed. The bloodstain was gone now and the rent in the material had been repaired as neatly as the rent in her flesh. She smoothed the fabric and sat. "What is it?" she asked. "There's something."

"Hmm." Ben pinched the bridge of his nose between a thumb and forefinger and rubbed. He closed his eyes. When his hand dropped away from his face, he drank.

"Ben?"

"Doc's dead."

She stared at him. Her lips parted as though she had words at the ready. She did not.

Ben finished his drink and poured another, this one merely

a generous splash. He held the tumbler between his palms, rolled it, but didn't drink. "I probably could have said that better. Eased you into it."

"No. Sometimes quick is better, even less painful." She didn't know if that were true just now. The depth to which she felt this loss stunned her. This was a man who had always been on the periphery of her life. A godfather who remembered her birthday and always had kind words and encouragement for her accomplishments was still an insubstantial presence. Correspondence gave her glimpses into the man he was, his sincere dedication to his profession, his love of Frost Falls, and yet in so many ways she scarcely knew him. He was her father's dear friend and that, more than anything, was what tethered them.

Ridley spoke quietly. "Did I ever tell you that Doc was in love with my mother?"

"No."

"Hmm. He was. I overheard my parents arguing about it when I was, oh, five or six, I think. Mother had just thrown a vase at Father's head. Behind a closed door, of course, but I was standing on the other side of that door and later I saw spilled water and broken glass. I still remember how the roses smelled strewn across the carpet. I gathered them up and took them away, and I thought of how things might be different if Mother had agreed to marry Father's friend instead of Father." Ridley looked away, embarrassed by her confession. She laughed shortly, without humor. "Did he ever speak of my mother?"

"No. Not to me."

"I think she might be the reason he left the city. I'm more confident that she was the reason he returned so few times. Her refusal turned out to be his good fortune. I imagine that troubled him."

"Why did your mother turn him down? Do you know?"

"I suspect it was because my father looked very fine on her arm. Doc had a more, um, humble countenance."

"He had a face like a peach pit."

Ridley shook her head. "That was unkind."

"That was how he described it to me. The ravages of acne, he said."

"Yes, well, it would have been important to my mother, probably the deciding factor as both my father and Doc had similar prospects for their practices." She picked up her teacup and stared at the milky liquid as though it held answers to questions she had never thought to ask. When she looked up, Ben was watching her. She spoke quietly. "How did you know?"

"Know?"

This time she finished the thought. "How did you know that he died? I don't have a letter or telegram. Nothing from home. How did you learn it?"

"Ellie."

"Ellie? How is that possible? I thought it might be Mary Cherry, but Ellie? It never crossed my mind."

Ben shrugged, sipped his drink. "Surprised me as well. She never said a word. I guess that's the way Doc wanted it. She's known for a while that he'd been ill."

"Will there be an announcement? Perhaps something in the paper?"

"Yes. Mother plans to write something. Doc, true to form, provided her with some words."

She frowned slightly. "I understand that Ellie knew from Doc that he was dying, but how did she learn he had died?"

"Your father."

"My father? Again, how is that possible?"

"An arrangement Doc made with him. I think it was Doc's intention that Ellie come to you with the news, but she told me first, and I said I would do it."

"Who is going to tell Mary Cherry? Someone should."

"Ellie is going to fall on her sword." Ben finished his drink and moved the glass to the desk. "Once Mary knows, word will get around. The obituary in the paper is to keep the record straight."

Ridley watched him close his eyes again. "Ben?"

"Hmm?"

"Were your mother and Doc . . ."

He raised an eyebrow but did not open his eyes. "I should make you finish that sentence. I did, you know, when I asked my mother."

"Did she cuff you?"

He gave up a short laugh. "No, but I could tell she was considering it. The answer, by the way, is no. She and Doc were friends. Good friends as it happens, but only that." There was a pause with a purpose. Ben opened his eyes and found hers. "Like us."

Chapter Twenty-two

Like us. Ben's words, spoken so simply, had the depth of still waters. Ridley did not look away. Couldn't. Her heart thundered against her ribs, and there was no quieting it. She pressed her lips together.

"Nothing?" he asked.

"I don't know what I'm supposed to say."

Ben dropped his feet to the floor and sat forward in Ridley's chair. "Truth? I don't know what I expected." He shook his head, rubbed his brow. "Doc's dead. I sat here and I could still smell his tobacco. I never picked up a taste for it, but we'd sit here some evenings, chewing the fat about this and that, and he'd puff smoke rings and I'd clean my gun. I suppose I've missed that."

"I'm sorry," she said. "You were more his friend than I ever was. You knew him far better."

"I wonder. I'm learning that there's a lot Doc didn't share with me. I didn't know how much he valued my mother's counsel. He never breathed a word about you. He left folks scratching their heads, wondering what kind of burr he'd gotten under his saddle that made him take off the way he did. And Mrs. Cherry? He owed her something more than an abrupt departure."

"Maybe he felt he had done enough. Maybe he felt as if he was the one who was owed something."

"Maybe."

Ridley did not think he sounded convinced, but then neither had that been her intention. "Animals that sense they're dying often go off on their own. Perhaps that's what Doc wanted. Not to be alone precisely, but to be away." Ben's gaze held her still, his eyes stark with grief. "What can I do?" she asked, and when he said nothing, merely continued to stare at her, she came to the answer on her own.

Ridley broke the plane of his gaze by rising to her feet. She moved like a sylph when she skirted the desk and came to his side. She held out her hand. His answer would be there in what happened next. If he slipped his fingers in hers and tugged, she would go where he took her, sit in his lap and curl into him, and she would set her head on his shoulder and cradle his grief in her heart, but if his fingers threaded in hers and he stood, it would be his tacit agreement to follow where she led, and it would be no time at all before he knew she meant to take him to her bed.

Ben took her hand.

Ridley held her breath.

He stood.

Her heart stuttered. Her smile was wistful; it did not falter. She backed away from the desk and drew him forward. "Bring the lamp," she said, and he did.

In her bedroom, she pointed to the nightstand. He set the lamp there. Light flickered and chased shadows on the wall and then was still. Ridley turned back the covers. It seemed the practical thing to do and the movement hid the faint trembling in her fingertips. When she turned away from the bed, she saw he hadn't moved. He stood there, his arms at his sides, his feet set easily apart, his shoulders relaxed. His head was cocked; the expression in his heavily lidded eyes was unreadable.

Ridley gestured to the bed. "Why don't you sit there?"

Ben sat.

Ridley inched closer and nudged his knees. This was what he had done when he'd set her on her kitchen table. It seemed so long ago now, and this would be different. She meant it to end differently. When his knees parted, she slipped between them, took him by the wrists, and set his palms against her hips. She released his hands, and when they stayed in place, she took it as a good sign. Ridley cupped his face and tilted it toward her. She lowered her head and brushed his lips. His mouth was warm but not mobile, not at least while her lips were against it. It was when she drew back that she saw them lift, and the shape that defined them now, the expression that she had not been able to read earlier, was amusement.

Of course it was.

Ridley started to draw away, but he caught her wrists and held her fast.

"No," he said. "Don't go."

She twisted her wrists but not very hard, and he didn't release her. Her gaze fell away from his. "I wish you weren't so easily amused. I wish I didn't so easily entertain you."

Ben applied fingertip pressure to the delicate blue webbing on the undersides of her wrists. "You overwhelm me, Ridley. That's what you do, and if it seems as if I am amused, it's because that's all that's left to me when you take away every other sense, especially the common one."

She stole a look at him and murmured something unintelligible between the lips she had pressed closed.

Ben released her. Without asking permission, he unbelted her robe and opened it enough so that when his hands rested on her hips this time, there was only her thin cotton shift between his palms and her skin. "I could get used to warming my hands here," he said. His thumbs made passes up and down across the fabric. He did that until she looked at him again. "Are you still itching to cuff me?"

"Maybe not as much as I was a few moments ago."

"That's something. Will you sit beside me?"

Ridley stepped out from between his legs and sat. Her hip brushed his when the mattress dipped. She did not move away.

Ben hoisted his left calf over his right knee and removed a boot. As soon as it hit the floor, he reversed his position and did the same with the other. He bent, took off his socks, and dropped them inside his boots. He didn't wiggle his toes. He stretched them. They splayed wide and drew Ridley's attention. "Monkey toes," he told her as she stared at his feet. "I could climb anything when I was a boy. Doc told me they were unnatural. You have an opinion?"

"You might be the missing link."

"Yeah, he said that, too." Ben set his bare feet on the cold floor. "Maybe we could lie down."

"In a moment." Ridley took off her robe. She helped Ben remove his jacket and then his vest. He tossed each of them at the rocker. The jacket landed on the seat. The vest overshot the mark and landed on the floor. Smiling, Ridley raised the covers, lifted and curled her legs to one side, and slipped under them. She scooted sideways to make room for him but not so far that she would have to stretch to reach him.

He unbuckled his gun belt, handling it with considerably more care than his clothes, and slid it under the bed. He stood, slipped his suspenders over his shoulders, dropped his trousers, and kicked them away. When he turned, Ridley was watching him. She looked interested, not embarrassed.

Ben shifted his weight from side to side. "I suppose you've seen a lot of . . . well, I figure there won't be any surprises."

Now it was Ridley who was amused. "The toes were surprising." She removed her spectacles, carefully folded the stems, and handed them to him. "Nightstand, please."

Ben put them aside and crawled in beside her when she held up the covers for him. The mattress depressed again, this time toward the middle, and they both rolled toward the center of this gravity.

Ridley raised her head and then rested it on his shoulder. The curve felt right. With her ear against him, she could hear the steady beat of his heart. It was the most natural thing to slide an arm across his chest. In time she would finger the buttons on his shirt, but not just now.

Ben's hand found her braid. He unwound the loose plait and threaded through the heavy strands. Her hair was lustrous in the lamplight. "What color do you call this?" he asked.

"Brown."

"No. I'm serious."

"It's brown, Ben. There's no dressing it up. It doesn't have enough red in it to be auburn, not enough polish to be chestnut, not dark enough to be coffee or cocoa. It's brown."

"Russet," he said.

"Yes, exactly like a potato."

He continued to sift her hair. "You don't think much of your looks, do you?"

"I'm not vain, if that's what you mean."

"No, you're not that, though when you stepped off the train, the hat made me wonder."

Without any hint of rancor, she explained, "My mother

chose it. She said it would keep men from staring at my face and finding me wanting." She felt more than heard Ben's sharp intake of air. "That's who she is, Ben. Who she always will be."

"But—"

"I appreciate that you might want to flatter me, but it's not necessary. I am going to sleep with you regardless."

"Jesus," he said softly.

Ridley shrugged. "I know I'm not as ugly as the proverbial mud fence, but I also accept that I am not more than the sum of my parts. So, my hair is brown. My eyes are—"

"Intense," he said. "The color is the least interesting thing about them."

"Well, yes, because they're brown. My nose is—"

"Aristocratic," he said.

"Narrow. I was going to say that it's narrow." She touched the bridge. "And I have a bump that ruins the line in profile. My mouth is—"

"Splendid," he said. "I thought so from the first."

"It's too wide. There is barely room for it on my face."

"So you say." He turned his head. "Is that why I have to surprise a smile out of you?"

"I look like a clown when I smile."

"Your mama told you that. I'm beginning to know her voice."

Ridley fell quiet for a time, then, "I thought I was going to comfort you."

"You have. You are."

"I'm glad of that, but it seems to me that you are returning more than I'm giving."

"Comfort can be mutual. It probably should be."

"Mm." She slid her hand to the middle of his chest, found his shirt buttons, and idly began to follow the line of them with her fingertip. "You didn't kiss me back," she said. "Earlier. You were sitting on the bed and I was standing, and when I kissed you, you didn't kiss me back."

"I have every intention of making up for that lapse."

"But why was there a lapse?" She felt his chest rise and fall and then she heard him sigh. "I did something wrong, didn't I? And you don't want to tell me."

Ben stopped her from fiddling with his buttons by laying his hand over hers. "It wasn't like that at all. I told you, you overwhelm me."

"No, there was something else."

"Sometimes it's better if you just give up the bone."

Far from being offended, laughter sputtered on Ridley's lips. "It's been said that I am stubborn to a fault."

Ben's mouth lifted in a wry twist. "No. Really?" He held her hand still when her fingers scrabbled at his shirt. "Shh. If you must know, and it seems you must, then I didn't kiss you back because I recalled what a good student you said you were and how hard you worked and applied yourself, and it occurred to me that I might be the subject of new experimentation. I couldn't decide whether I should be flattered or frightened."

Ridley slipped off Ben's shoulder and raised herself on an elbow. She waited until he turned his head. "I only wanted to give you ease."

"I know that," he said. "It's what I wanted, what I still want, but I needed to be sure I wasn't taking advantage."

"I'm twenty-eight years old, Ben, and a doctor. You can hardly take advantage."

"I can, and the fact that you don't understand that proves my point."

"Now you're speaking nonsense."

"Nonsense," he repeated. "That sounds about right. The one sense you didn't steal from me." He patted her shoulder and invited her to return.

She did. "You're restful," she said. "Have I told you that? You make it easy for me to clear my head, slow my mind. I didn't expect that would be true of a man who wears a badge and carries a gun. It's nice."

"Doc said something similar once. Told me it was the only reason he tolerated me."

Ridley smiled. "Sometimes I can't quite get a sense of who he was day to day. I think he must have led a quiet life. I know he helped others outside of what he did for them as patients and accepted no accolades for it. As far as I can tell, his intimates were you, Ellie, and his companion at cards, Mr. Mangold. I'm not sure that Mary Cherry belongs in that small circle, though I believe she wishes she might have been."

"I guess no one's told you that Doc was a curmudgeon."

"He was?"

"Yep. It got worse as he got older, and it was no secret that he didn't suffer fools. You have to understand that sainthood was not conferred until word got around that he was leaving."

"A curmudgeon," she said quietly. "Imagine that."

"You didn't get a hint of it in his letters?"

Ridley shook her head. "I can't recall that he ever complained. I suppose the person I knew the most about was Mary Cherry, although he wrote primarily about her responsibilities and not much about her."

"They fought regularly," said Ben. "But don't think they didn't enjoy it. I wouldn't be surprised if that's what Mary Cherry misses most. She liked to think she could order him around. He liked to prove she couldn't. Did he tell you that?"

"No."

"He probably didn't want to scare you off."

"He couldn't have, but he didn't know that." Ridley's palm settled over Ben's heart. The steady beat comforted. "I want to be here."

"I know."

"I don't think you do. I want to be *here*." The corners of her mouth lifted a fraction when she felt his heart thump once. It immediately resumed its steady rhythm, but that thump was telling. "Uh-huh," she said softly. "This would probably be a good time for you to kiss me. You won't be taking advantage. I swear."

Ben circled her wrist with his fingers, squeezed. When she turned from her side to lie on her back, he rolled with her. His face hovered above hers. Ridley's eyes were wide and watchful. The dark centers were growing but there was nothing vague about her focus. She was taking all of him in, and when he began to lower his head, she did not close her eyes.

He was not surprised when she lifted her head to meet him. Her lips parted on a soft exhalation as his mouth touched hers. The pressure of the kiss pushed her back against the pillow. She freed her hands. They came to rest again at the base of his spine. Her fingers splayed. Through the fabric of his shirt, he felt the tips of every one of them make small impressions against his skin.

She tasted like tea and sugar. Or he imagined she did. Her mouth was warm and moist and it moved under his. He did not imagine that. She was not in the least tentative. If she had made a study of kissing, then she had learned her subject well.

He raised his head only that distance necessary to see her face. Her eyes were still open. One of his eyebrows kicked up. He didn't have to ask the question.

"I don't want to miss anything," she whispered.

It was extraordinarily uncomplicated to her. That worried him some. Knowledge, the kind she gleaned from books, did not make her worldly. She would disagree with him if only for the sake of advancing her argument. That didn't bother him because he knew he was right, and that made him responsible.

Equally quiet, he said, "Don't be afraid to feel."

"I'm not afraid."

In some ways she was predictable and Ben had counted on that. When she closed her eyes to prove her point, he swooped. He kissed the space between her eyebrows where the vertical crease often appeared when she was worried. It was there for an infinitesimal moment; he erased it with his lips.

He kissed her temple. His breath stirred her hair, and fine strands of it tickled his mouth. She hummed her pleasure. "You like that?" He gave her no opportunity to answer. His lips slanted across hers. Her mouth parted. He traced the ridge of her teeth with the tip of his tongue. She bit down gently and then sipped. His tongue was in her mouth, swirling, teasing, licking. She might have shivered, but Ben knew that he did. He was undone before her fingers plucked at the buttons of his shirt, but it was when she slipped her hands beneath his fleece-lined undershirt and placed her palms flat against his naked chest that he forgot to breathe.

Did she know? It seemed that she might have because the roar of blood in his ears was not enough to mute her wicked laughter.

He called her a witch, and when he kissed her again, it was because he wanted to enjoy her splendidly smug smile. She had earned the right to it.

Ridley's fingers walked the length of his spine as if she were practicing piano scales. She stopped when she reached the back of his neck, that place he often massaged when he was deep in thought or just pretending to be, and it was here that she could feel the contradiction in his skin. A fine web of scar tissue lay like a veil across oddly smooth flesh.

"It must have hurt horribly," she said against his mouth. Her fingertips stopped their exploration when he sat up suddenly. He moved too quickly for her to stop him. "What are you—" She didn't finish because it became clear what he was doing. He shrugged out of his shirt and then pulled his undershirt over his head. He tossed them both in the direction of the rocker. Neither made it.

He sat motionless, waiting for her verdict. His shoulders and back were exposed to the lamplight. He let her see the extent of the damage. The worst was at the back of his neck where his hair had literally been on fire. The flames had licked him under his collar and spread across his shoulders. His skin was taut and shiny and unnaturally pink almost as far as his shoulder blades. Ben knew it could have been so much worse, but did she?

He would always remember the whore who retched into a chamber pot when she saw the scars. Ben had to remind himself that it had been early days yet when the scars were still tender and angrier looking than they were now. That had described him as well. Tender and angry.

He felt her move behind him. She was sitting up. One of her hands alighted on his shoulder. A moment later her lips were at the crook of his neck.

"Do you want to tell me?" she asked.

Ben didn't know how it was possible, but her breath felt as cool as aloe against his skin. Her touch was a healing balm. "Not now," he said. "Later."

"Of course," she whispered and kissed him again. "Whenever you like." She kissed him at the hollow behind his ear. The skin was tight there as well. Was he aware that he often rubbed that spot when he was in full consideration of a problem? Probably not, but it made her smile because she suspected that she was often the problem he was considering. She put her lips to his ear. "Lie with me."

Chapter Twenty-three

Ben took her down with his mouth against hers. It was a mutual surrender except that Ridley's idea of giving in was pushing back. She pressed against him, wound her legs around his, tangled the blankets until they were trapped in a chrysalis of cotton and wool. She marked her territory with kisses, planting them like flags along his jaw, his neck, and his shoulders. She had the subtlety of a marauder, and Ben was fine with that.

Ridley's nightgown was rucked up around her thighs. A niggling sense of modesty prompted her to try to push the hem to her knees. Ben stopped her, made her laugh at herself, and then she was helping raise the hem higher. His palm curved around her inner thigh. It struck her how nicely it fit there. She was not a believer in fate, but it seemed to her that this was meant to be.

Her breasts felt full, heavy. She drew his hand toward them. Her thought was that his palm would fit nicely there as well. She didn't find out, not just then. Instead of covering her breast as she encouraged him to do, he stopped short and used his thumb to tug at the loose ribbon that closed the neckline of her gown. It required only a few passes before the material parted. Anticipation made drawing air difficult. In the end she simply held her breath.

He nudged the material aside, exposing one pink-tipped breast to the lamplight, but it was not his hand that closed over her aureole. It was his mouth. Ridley resumed breathing but only because Ben's humid mouth and the damp tip of his darting tongue made her gulp great drafts of air. Her rib cage swelled with that indrawn breath, her breast lifted, and the suck of his mouth drew a guttural cry. It was at once too much and not enough. She felt an ache deep in her womb, a contraction that she recognized as emptiness closing in. Her heels searched for purchase against the mattress. She rose, arched into him as much as she was able. Without words, she told him what she wanted until he showed her that she wanted something else.

Ben's attention wandered from her breast to the hollow of her throat and then to the curve of her neck. He sipped her skin, laved it with his tongue, and kept her restless and wanting under him.

His mouth retraced a line from the underside of her jaw to the shallow valley between her small breasts. He slid the parted neckline to the other side and gave his full attention to the swollen pink rosebud he had neglected earlier.

If Ridley thought she was going to come out of her skin, it was no different for him. She'd found the drawstring to his drawers, yanked, and then frustrated both of them because of the knot she made. He rolled her nipple between his lips. Her fingers scrabbled with the drawstring to make it right. Ben lifted his head and looked her in the eye. "Get it done," he said. His voice was barely recognizable to either of them, coming as it did from deep in his throat, but the message was intelligible. His flat belly retracted when her knuckles brushed his skin. He put his mouth to her breast again, drawing on the nipple in a way that made her toes curl and her fingers go still. He stopped, waited for her to catch her breath and begin to work the knot before he lowered his mouth once more to her breast.

"Hah!" Ridley produced a throaty cry when she loosened the knot. Her fingers dove beneath Ben's drawers and he produced a cry very much like her own, though there was perhaps a thread of relief running through his.

His erection had been pressing against her thigh since he first put his mouth to her breast, but her gown and his drawers and the occasional awkwardness of their position made for a volatile mix of frustration and heady anticipation. Whatever mystery Ben's body held for her, Ridley ended it by curling her fingers around his penis. It swelled, throbbed in her hand. She understood the mechanics but had no use for them now. Dr. E. Ridley Woodhouse preferred the miracle.

Her knees lifted on either side of his hips and she cradled him between her thighs. Ben levered himself on his elbows. He dipped his head, kissed her. He did not intend to linger there, but he did. He nudged her upper lip and nibbled gently on her lower one. He made the kiss slow and long and deep.

Ridley's thumbnail scored the underside of his erection. His breath hitched. She released him to push his drawers past his hips and then regarded him expectantly. He was hot and heavy against her belly. "I'm ready," she said when he lifted his head. "I *am*."

Ben smiled crookedly. "All right, but only because I want to be convinced."

She didn't know exactly what he meant until he pressed for entry. There was more discomfort than pain, but there was a lot of discomfort. She sucked in her lower lip, bit down.

"Uh-huh," he said. He heaved away as best he could under the tangle of blankets. Her knees collapsed as he snapped and straightened the covers. A moment later he disappeared under them.

Ridley watched his head move. There was his mouth at her shoulder and again at the soft underside of her elbow. He trailed a line of kisses down the center of her abdomen. She knew where he was going. She wished he would get there.

Ben lifted her thighs and settled between them. Her calves rested against his back. He lowered his head, found that sweet, sensitive kernel between her lips, and flicked it with his tongue. He did it again and again. Her hips rose and she pressed her heels hard into his back. Her fingers fisted in the sheets. She breathed shallowly and quickly, sipping the air in fractions of a full breath. Her lungs never felt quite full. She felt light and light-headed. It never once occurred to her to ask him to stop.

She hovered on the edge of pleasure that was so sharp it was almost painful, but he cared more for her than to make it that. He held her when it felt as if she would shatter and eased her into feeling whole once she was still. He gave her time, but not too much, and then pressed his entry for the second time.

It was not that there was no discomfort for her; only that she did not mind it as much. Her eyelids were heavy, her gaze slumberous. This was in contrast to her limbs, which felt weightless. She knew her body would accommodate him. It was biology, the way it was meant to be, but she'd held him in her hand and so it seemed more fantastical than simply the usual course of nature.

Her gaze widened when pleasure began to stir again. That was unexpected. Ben's thrusts were measured, powerful yet restrained, and there was a tautness to his features that bore evidence of his self-possession. If he saw her surprise, he gave no indication of it. If there was a smug smile behind the set of his jaw, he was clever enough not to reveal it now.

From beneath the dark fan of her lashes, she watched him. From inside her body, she felt him. She ran her hands up and down his arms. His muscles bunched under her touch. The same thing happened when she caressed his shoulders. He stretched, arched, plunged. The cord in his neck became defined.

Ridley felt heat blossom in her belly. It was softer this time around, spiraling instead of rising. There was warmth in the tips of her fingers, in her toes. She rubbed the sole of her foot against Ben's calf and pressed her trimmed nails into his shoulders. Inside, she contracted, not because she thought about it, but because she didn't. Ben moaned and she recognized his pleasure in the sound. She contracted around him again, this time on purpose. He growled and that pleased her as well, and when he came deep, pushing into her hard, and finally shuddered as she had earlier, she was there to ease him down and into the cradle of her body.

Ben lay heavily on top of her, full of agreeable lethargy. His breathing slowed, became inaudible. His heart ceased to thrum and resumed its normal rhythm. He lifted his head and began to ease away from her.

"No," she whispered. "Don't. Not just yet."

"Ridley."

"A little longer. It's nice this way."

He gave in because she was right. A minute passed and then another, and when she didn't ask him to move or push him away, he realized she was asleep. It was encouraging, he supposed, that he hadn't suffocated her.

Ben rolled sideways and then left the bed. Except for an abrupt little snore, she didn't stir. Grinning, he held up his drawers in one hand and crossed to the dressing screen, where he ducked behind it. He scrubbed his face at the basin and stared into the mirror above it. He was still grinning, stupidly, he thought, but then he was a happy man and allowances could be made for that. Ben wondered if he would feel differently after he had time to reflect on how things might have changed between them.

He completed his ablutions, tied off his drawers, and padded barefoot to the corner stove. He added some split wood to the meager fire and waited for it to begin its burn before he returned to the bed. The room was cold enough to raise goose-flesh on his arms. He slipped under the covers. Ridley attached herself to him like melting wax, and she was about as warm.

That was all right, then. He closed his eyes.

Chapter Twenty-four

"Ow!" Ben swatted at Ridley's hand and rubbed his arm where she had just pinched him. "What was that for?"

"You were sleeping."

"Yes. So were you."

"Not for a while."

Ben looked at the oil lamp to gauge how long it had been burning. He guessed he had slept for at least a few hours, certainly longer than he'd meant to. "There are kinder ways to wake someone from a dead sleep."

Ridley propped herself on an elbow and shrugged one shoulder as she looked down at him. "I kissed you," she said, tapping her forefinger against his lips. "Right here. You wrinkled your mouth as though I were a pesky fly."

"Clearly you should have tried again."

"I did. I was rebuffed three times. It was humbling."

"You don't sound humbled."

"Time heals some wounds and revenge heals others. I pinched you harder than I had to. That helped."

Ben's mouth twisted wryly. "I'll just bet it did." He raised his arms outside of the blankets and stretched. His yawn was so prodigious that his jaw cracked and he had to work it side to side. "Sorry."

She shook her head and knuckled his stubble once he settled his jaw in place. "You make it seem . . . I don't know . . . as if this were not the first time we woke up in the same bed. I thought it would be awkward."

"I imagine that pinching me helped that, too."

"We should decide on a better way of waking you in the future."

Ben was encouraged. "You can always say my name. That's surprisingly effective."

"Oh. Of course." She hesitated. "I think I must have embraced some romantic notions."

"I blame Felicity Ravenwood."

Ridley nodded; her eyes were grave.

Ben caught her hand, threaded his fingers through hers. "Ridley, I was teasing. I don't object to romantic notions. I've been known to have them."

"Have you really?"

"Mm-hmm. I used to wash Amelia Trainer's slate when we shared a desk. I carved her initials in the side of the schoolhouse. The heart was sadly lopsided but recognizable."

"That *is* romantic. How old were you?"

"Ten or eleven. You need to know that Bob Coffield liked her, too, and he was blamed for it. I didn't speak up so he got the punishment and the girl. They live over in Stonechurch. Five children, the last I heard. I like to think my cowardice led to their courtship."

"Huh. I suppose you can justify anything when you've had a long time to think about it."

"That's right." He looked over his shoulder toward the window. The curtain was pulled closed, but he could tell that outside it was still dark. Curious, he asked, "What was so important that you couldn't let me sleep?"

"I thought you might want to go home before it's morning and someone could see you."

"Uh-huh. Do you want me to leave?"

"No, not if you'd like to stay, but I don't want anyone happening upon you. I have an appreciation for how news is spread in Frost Falls and it isn't Drew Abernathy's weekly paper."

"Do you have any idea what time it is?"

"When I looked, it was a bit past two. That was just before I woke you." Before he asked, she added, "I consulted the pocket watch in the jacket you so carelessly discarded."

"Oh." Ben wondered when he had last slept so soundly. He hadn't heard or felt her leave the bed. "All right, but it's not necessarily less likely that I won't be seen at this hour."

"I know. I've thought of that. That's why you should exit

through the surgery and enter your house through the back door."

"You're suggesting stealth."

"I suppose I am."

"I see. And who do you imagine is walking around out there at this hour?"

"Anyone staggering out of the Songbird."

"Yes, of course," he conceded with a laugh. "But who else?"

"Your deputy takes a stroll when he's on night duty."

"Damn, but you've given this some thought."

"I had time," she said dryly. "And then there are the hotel guests who can't sleep and stand at the windows. You might have noticed that some of those windows face your house and mine."

"They are probably more interested in your bedroom window."

"Be serious."

"I am."

Ridley sighed. "Ben, people expect to be able to find us when they need us. Someone comes looking for you far more often than me, but there's an expectation that we will respond to whatever the need is. You only have to recall Hannah Salt coming to get you at her brother's request or Frankie Fuller running here to ask for help."

"That's a fair point, but no one's ever come looking for me and been quiet about it. I'm confident that one of us would hear something. I would then make a stealthy exit, appear at my front door minutes later, and no one would be the wiser. And if someone comes for you, I don't have to do anything except pinch you awake. You can manage your patient and I can go back to sleep."

Ridley fell silent, considering. "Is it as simple as that?"

"What I know is that it doesn't have to be complicated." He smiled when the space between her eyebrows puckered. "You're not convinced."

"I want to be, but the more I think on it, the less certain I am that there is any circumstance in which you can be stealthy. You're very straightforward. I don't think you'd mind at all if you were caught sneaking between our houses."

"I'd mind sneaking around, and I'd mind getting caught, but that's not what you meant. I wouldn't care for myself if we were found out, but I'd care plenty for what folks would say about you."

"Ah, yes, the stain on my reputation. Did you know I bled?"

Ben stared at her. His eyes widened fractionally. He understood how her thoughts leapt from the first thing she said to the question she asked, but that did not mean he was prepared to talk about it. If she thought he was straightforward, then how in God's name would she describe herself? He had an image of a train coming at him full throttle.

"I've made you uncomfortable," she said.

"It was unexpected, is all. There was always plain speaking about women in the bunkhouse, but I never figured I'd hear the same so plainly from a woman. To answer your question, yes, I knew. I got up to wash. You'd already fallen asleep. I saw there was some blood. Is it because you were a virgin or did I hurt you?"

"You can ease your mind. You didn't hurt me. I didn't think at twenty-eight there would still be any evidence of virginity, so that was interesting."

"Uh-huh. Interesting."

She chuckled, dropping her elbow and laying her head on her arm. "You're staying, then?"

"Mm-hmm."

Ridley inched closer, snuggled. "Martha usually arrives at seven thirty."

"This time of year it's hardly light by then. I'll be gone or hiding under the bed." He turned his head, kissed her brow. "Do you remember how to wake me?"

"Ben."

"Good. Go to sleep."

And she did.

In the morning, Ben left the surgery a full five minutes before the widow arrived. That was too close for Ridley's comfort, but then she hadn't tried very hard to stop him when he tumbled her back in bed. He drugged her with leisurely kisses, the kind that muddled her brain and made time both relative and unimportant. He whispered outrageous things in her ear, only half of which she understood, and he made her laugh, slowly tracking a line from her belly to her breasts and calling it stealthy. She lifted her nightgown, hugged him with her knees, and sighed deeply as he entered her with the caution of a thief.

He took care with her and moved with an almost hypnotic rhythm that she followed in like measure. Her breasts swelled. She touched them when he didn't, and when she saw his eyes darken as he followed the movement, she did it again. The second time was as much for his pleasure as it was for hers.

He came noisily and then so did she, but her release was very close to a shout of laughter. In between moments of catching her breath, she said, "My name's not Ernestine. That's what you called out, isn't it?"

"I did. Are you certain that's not it?"

"Quite certain. You intend to amuse yourself with this for a while, don't you?"

"I do."

She couldn't help but grin. "I think I will look forward to that."

He swooped to kiss her splendidly curved mouth and then rolled out of bed to finish dressing. He wished her well before he left. He also called her Evelyn.

Shaking her head, because what else could she do, Ridley rose and put on her robe and slippers. When Mrs. Rushton arrived minutes later, Ridley asked for water for a bath. They dragged the tub into the kitchen and took turns filling it. While they waited for multiple kettles to boil, the housekeeper poached an egg and made toast and gave Ridley the weather report as she had it from Maxwell Wayne.

"When is the thaw?" asked Ridley.

"April. Not much chance of seeing grass or scrub more than a few days at a time before then."

"I don't remember Doc saying anything about this much snow in his correspondence."

"If you wanted someone to come here, would you mention it?"

Ridley saw her point. "Probably not. It's beautiful, though, even if it is relentless."

"Speaking of relentless, Mary Cherry's been pestering me about Lily Salt. She thinks you need to see her."

"You're only telling me now? How long ago did she say something?"

"I guess it's been a few days. You weren't well, so I told myself to wait until you were. We both know Lily can't come here, and it won't do for you to see her in her home."

"If Mrs. Cherry is asking for me, there must be something concerning her. Did she tell you what it is?"

"No, only that Mr. Salt is suspicious of her visits and she doesn't dare risk Lily's well-being by going again."

Ridley pushed her plate away. "Let me think on it," she said. "I'm going to get towels, soap, and a washcloth. A hot bath is good for thinking."

Mrs. Rushton shook her head. "I'll get everything for you."

Recalling that she'd left her bed unmade and that the whole of it smelled like sex, Ridley held up a hand. "No, I'll do it. You put on another kettle so I can rinse my hair." She left before the housekeeper could argue. Once she was in her room, she stripped the bed, shoved the sheets under it to be dealt with later, and made up the bed with fresh linens. She was halfway down the stairs when she realized she had none of the items she meant to get.

Mrs. Rushton looked her over with a keen eye. "You're flushed, Doctor, and I would have to say a little out of breath. Are you sure you're well enough for a bath? Perhaps at the basin would be better. It's been a slow recovery, I think. Maybe that's not a fair assessment given that you've never been clear about what you're recovering from."

"I told you it was a lung ailment."

"That's not specific, and you told me that because you forgot you'd already said you'd sprained your back carrying the Fuller children out of their house. So what is it?"

Ridley pushed a chair close to the tub and set the towels, washcloth, and soap on the seat. "Have you been thinking it's consumption?" When the housekeeper said nothing, Ridley knew she had stumbled on the truth. "Oh, my dear Martha, I wish you had told me that was your fear. I wouldn't have allowed you in the house if I thought you could acquire my illness. I would not have seen patients. It's *not* tuberculosis."

Mrs. Rushton nodded. "I shouldn't have allowed my imagination to get the better of me." The housekeeper regarded her hopefully. "And you're sure you're feeling better?"

Ridley thought about her activities last night and again this morning. She was glad she wasn't one for blushing. "Much better," she said, and looked the widow straight in the eye when she said it. "May I have some privacy?"

Mrs. Rushton was immediately about her business. "Of course you may. Let me add a pail of cold water. You can't put your toe in there yet. You'll scald yourself."

Ridley waited. As soon as the housekeeper left to go about her other tasks, Ridley stepped out of her slippers, removed her robe, and pulled her nightgown over her head. She would have dived into the tub if such a thing were possible. Instead she stepped in, got accustomed to the heat, and carefully lowered herself. The space was small, but she was used now to bathing with her knees drawn toward her chest. Water was displaced by her entry so it rose high enough to lap at her breasts.

In a tub like the one in the bathing room adjoining her dressing room at home, she would have been able to stretch, rest her head against a folded towel set against the lip, and have that thinking time she needed to address the problem of Lily Salt. She did not have that luxury now. The water would grow cold with a speed that always astonished her, and the length of the tub did not lend itself to relaxing.

Ridley grabbed the soap and washcloth from the chair and began to apply both. Intent on her task, she didn't hear anyone at the surgery entrance until Mrs. Rushton came hurrying through the kitchen, begging her pardon, and disappearing into the rear of the house.

Ridley stopped what she was doing, cocked her head, and listened. The banging was insistent, reminiscent of Jeremiah Salt, and Ridley made an attempt to be heard over the top of it. "Don't let anyone in until you know who it is." The next thing she heard was Mrs. Rushton offering the visitor entrance, a seat in Ridley's office, and a cup of tea.

Mrs. Rushton reappeared, mouthed the name of their visitor, and set about making that promised cup of tea.

Ridley called toward the office. "I'll be with you in a few minutes, Mrs. Springer. Are you here for yourself or someone else?"

"It's James."

Ridley continued scrubbing. Amanda was the only one who called her husband James. He was Jim to everyone else. Ridley plunged her head underwater and then soaped her hair. "What's happened to him?"

"He's lost his mind."

Ridley looked over at Mrs. Rushton, who shrugged helplessly. "How's that, Mrs. Springer?"

"He's taken it into his head that he wants to tend bar at the Songbird. He says he doesn't want to be a butcher any longer. He thinks he can find someone to manage the shop or sell it outright. That was my father's business. I don't want him to sell it."

Mrs. Rushton helped Ridley rinse her hair before she disappeared with the tea service. Ridley rose, towel dried her hair, and then fashioned a turban for it. She stepped out of the tub and moved closer to the stove while she dried off and dressed. She walked into her office while she was belting her robe. Ignoring Mrs. Springer's astonished expression at her attire, Ridley sat behind her desk.

"I'm not sure what it is you think I can do," said Ridley, setting her folded hands on the desktop. "It seems to me that speaking with an attorney should be a consideration."

"Oh, indeed I shall, but there is also the matter of my husband becoming completely deranged. Can you imagine him behind the bar at the Songbird? I am the president of our temperance society, the leader of the Presbyterian Ladies Giving Circle, and a voice for reason in our community. He will make me a laughingstock."

As Ridley suspected, this was about all the ways Jim Springer's decision was going to affect his wife. Ridley was not entirely unsympathetic. "I understand, but I am less clear about how I can help."

Amanda pointed to the diploma on the wall. "That says you're a physician graduated from a reputable medical college. I've had my doubts, but I am willing to set them aside. Doc would have known what to do. Do you?"

Did she? Ridley wondered. "When did your husband bring this to your attention?"

Amanda considered the question as she raised her teacup to her lips. "I think the first time I heard him say that he wanted to do something else was when he realized Hitchcock had no interest in taking over the shop."

"So that would have been a year ago? Two?"

"A year, I think. That sounds about right, but my son's fascination with being a deputy will wane, and then he'll be prepared to be reasonable."

"I see. You said the shop was your father's?"

"Yes. Father offered James work there when we were married. The plan was always that he would own it one day. My father wanted to be sure James could provide for me and our family."

"What work did your husband do before you were married?"

"He was a wrangler for Harrison Hardy at the Double H."

Ridley nodded. She had been to the Double H before the weather turned. Mr. Hardy had lumbago. "He gave that up to have a family with you."

"He gave it up to *court* me. My father insisted. Father did not approve of Buzz Winegarten. He was my other suitor."

Ridley was fascinated in spite of herself. "And now your husband wants to work for Buzz?"

"I told you, he's lost his mind. There must be something in your medicine cabinet for what ails him. I put my quandary to our druggist, and Mickey said I should get a recommendation from you. I don't put much store in some of the snake oil he sells, so here I am." She set her empty teacup down with enough force to rattle the saucer. The look she gave Ridley was both expectant and challenging. "Well, Dr. Woodhouse, what are you going to do?"

Chapter Twenty-five

Ridley walked into the sheriff's office and could barely close the door quickly enough to suit her. There was no wind to speak of, no falling snow, the sun was shining, and she could not recall that she had ever been quite so cold. She stood at the entrance, shivering inside her cloak, and looked around for evidence that someone was in the building. The coffeepot on the stove gave her hope.

She pushed back her hood and lowered her scarf to her chin so she could speak. "Ben! Hitch! Anyone here?" She heard some movement in the rear where the cells were and was relieved when Hitch appeared holding a mop and bucket and came loping forward to greet her.

"Hey, Doc. I was doing some housekeeping. Sheriff likes me to keep the place tidy."

Ridley's eyes darted to the mop and bucket and then back to Hitch. A slim smile touched her lips. "So the job is not merely about arresting scoundrels."

"No, ma'am." He set the bucket down and leaned the mop against the wall. "Sheriff expects me to make a decent pot of coffee, too. Would you like some?"

"I would actually." She went to stand next to him at the stove and warmed herself while he poured. She removed her gloves to wrap her hands around the mug he gave her. "Where is the sheriff?"

"At the Fullers' or Miss Renquest's place. He wanted to stop by and see how they were faring. Here, let me take your cloak and scarf. You don't want to stay bundled up in here. You'll freeze when you go back out."

Ridley was grateful for the help. She did not want to give up her mug. It was a better hand warmer than any fur muff she had ever owned. "Thank you. Did you know the sheriff hired young Frankie to shovel his walk and mine?"

"Didn't know. I thought Clay Salt had that job."

"He used to, but his father took exception. Now it's Frankie."

Hitch poured a cup of coffee for himself and invited Ridley to sit when she could tear herself away from the stove. "Sheriff's always finding ways to look out for folks. It's a shame about Clay." He dropped into one of the chairs most often used by visitors and pointed to the chair behind the desk. When Ridley seated herself, he said, "I don't figure him for being away much longer; of course, he can find the long way around to wherever he's going."

"That's all right, I came to see you."

Hitch started visibly. "You did?"

"Mm-hmm." She took her first sip of coffee. "This is better than decent."

"Thank you, but if you don't mind, I'd rather you didn't take the long way around to say what needs to be said."

"Right. Well, your mother came to see me this morning." Ridley watched Hitch lose all color in his face. "She's fine," she assured him. "I imagine you're surprised because you know she doesn't particularly favor me."

"On account of you being a doctor," he said quickly.

"I understand, but the fact that I *am* a doctor is the reason she came by. The truth is she'd have a better chance of getting what she wants by consulting a witch doctor. Oh, and a lawyer."

"Oh, Lord," he said, closing his eyes and rubbing his brow. "She's plum lost her mind."

"Look at me, Hitch." She waited for him to recover before she went on. "She hasn't lost her mind, but she is afraid. Do you know what your father told her he wants to do?"

"Sure. He wants to tend bar at the Songbird. Only reason he's a butcher is because he wanted to marry my mother and that's what he had to do to get her. He was a wrangler at the

Double H, but he hadn't done that very long, and he always said it was no kind of sacrifice to take a job in town to be able to see his girl. That's what he called her. His girl."

"And now he wants to do something else entirely," said Ridley. "Do you think you will change your mind about taking over the shop?"

"Change my—hell, no. She put that idea in your head, didn't she?" He put out a hand. "Did I curse? I think I might have cursed. Begging your pardon. No, I'm not going to be a butcher. I worked in the shop after school when I was a kid. Had my fill of it then and Pa knew it. This job suits me. Besides, I just learned to make a decent pot of coffee."

Behind her mug, Ridley smiled. She lowered it to the desktop. "All right. You don't have to convince me, but you do have to find a way to persuade your mother. Tell her what you're doing now, what you're learning. Maybe not so much about the housekeeping and the coffee, but you could tell her how you answer complaints and settle disputes and break up the occasional fight without getting yourself hurt. Show her you're competent. The sheriff thinks you are or he wouldn't keep you on. Your mother thinks you're still a child who doesn't know his own mind. Share things with her that will give her an opportunity to see you differently."

Hitch looked doubtful.

Ridley said, "I know you think your mother is set in her ways, Hitch, but given the proper motivation, she's capable of changing her thinking. She came to see me, didn't she? You only have to remember that."

Ridley waited beside the butcher shop's front window while James Springer took care of his customers. There were only two when she came in, but Mary Cherry entered shortly afterward. Ridley offered to let her go ahead.

Mary's thank-you was nearly inaudible. She kept her head down. After taking a few steps forward, she stopped, turned, and then set herself squarely in Ridley's path to the counter. She thrust her sharp chin forward, and though the act spoke of defiance, the wobble spoke of distress.

Ridley confronted Mary Cherry's red-rimmed eyes and the profound sadness in their depths. She wanted to take the older woman's hands in hers and offer comfort where before she had merely offered her place in line, but because she didn't think the gesture would have been welcomed or even accepted as sincere, Ridley kept her hands at her sides.

Mary's voice quavered when she spoke. She kept her voice low, a mere whisper, so as not to be overheard. "He should have told me that he was gravely ill. Don't you think he should have told me that?"

"I do," Ridley said gently.

"Why didn't he?"

"I don't know."

"I can't think about anything else since Ben came around this morning. Doc's dead. How can that be when I didn't know he was sick?"

"I am so sorry, Mrs. Cherry." She saw Mary's eyes narrow. Grief was replaced by accusation. Ridley wanted to take a step back but the window was behind her.

"You knew. He told you."

Ridley did not deny it. "Yes. He was my godfather. You know that my father and he were friends of long standing, and I was coming to fill the position that had been his for a quarter of a century. So, yes, he told me."

Mary pressed a gloved fist against her mouth and swallowed a sob. She looked right and left to see if anyone noticed.

"Let me help you," said Ridley. "I'll purchase whatever it is you need and you can leave. Do you have a list?" Ridley thought she might hear objections but none came, further proof that Mrs. Cherry was distraught. She took the paper that she was given and glanced at it. "I assume this is for you and your husband."

Mary nodded. "Mr. Springer takes home what's needed there."

"All right. Go. I can manage this." When Mary simply stood there, Ridley stepped away and opened the door for her. "Go on." Once she was gone, Ridley could acknowledge that the encounter had gone better than she had expected. That had to have been Ben's influence. He must have spent considerable time consoling Mary Cherry before he went about any of his other duties, probably before he had breakfast. For some reason that made her smile. He might not have sought the job, but he certainly took the responsibilities seriously.

"How can I help you?"

Ridley's head came up when she realized Mr. Springer was speaking to her. She walked up to the counter. "I was wool-gathering," she told him.

"That's allowed." He wiped his hands on his apron. "Was that Mary Cherry you were talking to?" When Ridley nodded, he asked, "Everything all right? I saw her leave. She doesn't work for my wife on Thursdays. I don't know why except that she never worked for Doc on Thursdays. I understand the Sabbath, but Thursdays? She's peculiar but there always was a good heart there."

Ridley found an opening to speak when Jim Springer took a breath. "Everything's fine. I have her list here." She handed it over. "And I promised Mrs. Rushton that I would bring home a good soup bone. Ham or beef, it doesn't matter."

"Got just the one for you," he said, looking over Mary's list. "This weather cries out for a hearty soup."

"Indeed."

Ridley had always thought Jim Springer had an amiable countenance. His easy smile kept his mouth turned up, and his eyes were bright and perpetually crinkled at the corners. His hair was receding, which gave him a high professorial brow. Sometimes he wore his spectacles pushed against his forehead, but right now they were settled where they were supposed to be across the bridge of his nose with his sandy-colored eyebrows puckered above the gold-plated rims. Before she lost him to his work or a customer entered the shop, Ridley launched into the real purpose of her visit, relating his wife's visit to her office that morning and then her own visit to the sheriff's office.

When Ridley had finished, Jim whistled softly but he offered no reply. He set about filling Mary Cherry's order. He wrapped the steaks and chops in brown paper, tied both parcels off with twine, and held up the soup bone for Ridley's approval. At her nod, he wrapped and tied it. He pushed everything toward her and gave her the price.

"Have I overstepped, Mr. Springer?" she asked, handing him the proper coins. "Are you not going to say anything?"

He dropped the money in the till and closed the lid. "I think we can agree that it is my wife who overstepped; at least I hope we can. I have not lost my mind, Dr. Woodhouse. On the contrary, I believe I have come to my senses."

Ridley didn't disagree. "Then you have to make her understand that."

"Do you think I haven't tried? That's insulting."

"No, of course, I know you've tried, but perhaps you have to try in a different fashion."

"I'm listening."

"Mrs. Springer explained that this business was her father's. I had the impression that when he died, he left the shop to you, not his daughter. Is that right?"

"Yes. He was old-fashioned in his notions that a woman should not own property."

Ridley managed not to roll her eyes at that sort of thinking, but it was a narrow thing. "Have you considered selling your wife the shop?"

Jim snorted. "Amanda does not want to be a butcher."

"No, I'm sure you're right, but she could manage the money and the books and the ordering and all the other details that you take care of in addition to the butchering. You could advise her on a good butcher, but the hiring and everything else would be her responsibility. There's hardly a pie in Frost Falls that doesn't have her thumbprint. School board. Library board. Giving Circle. Quilting bees. Welcoming committee. And no, I haven't forgotten the temperance society. My point is that she has the skills and the experience; she needs the property to make it all her own. Keep the business in the family, at least for now."

Jim was silent, considering. "Mrs. Fish has her own business," he said finally. "So does Mrs. Palmer. Mickey's wife works side by side with him in the apothecary. You more or less have your own shop."

She smiled. "More or less."

"Maybe I should give her the place, make a gift of it the way her father did me."

"No. She should buy it if for no other reason than to prove

she wants it. You can sell it to her for one dollar or a hundred. The amount is less important than the deal."

"Hmm. What about the temperance society? She thinks her friends will be sniggering behind her back if I serve drinks at the Songbird."

"I can't say what her friends will do, but it's up to you to give her a better reason for choosing to tend bar over all the other jobs you could have pursued."

He shrugged. "I heard about Buzz not trusting his nephew so I spoke to him and he made me a good offer."

"A better reason than that," she said. "I understand you've been making noises about doing this for years."

Jim blew out a long breath as he thought.

Ridley took pity on him. "Maybe you want to work at the Songbird to keep an eye on Buzz Winegarten. I heard he was your wife's suitor at the same time you were trying to court her."

"Yes, but that was years ago. I don't suspect him of—"

Ridley interrupted. "And perhaps you got wind from the sheriff that she offered to make a plaster for Mr. Winegarten's gouty toe right there in Ben's office."

Jim's eyebrows rose halfway to his former hairline. "She did?"

"So you heard."

"Oh. I see. What else have I heard?"

"Anything you like. Ask Mr. Winegarten if you need ideas. If he wants you in the Songbird, he'll be happy to help, and he's just ill-humored enough that he won't mind tweaking your wife."

Jim Springer reached in the till and took out the exact amount that Ridley had given him and then added a quarter. "Here. Take this. I don't imagine that Amanda thought to pay you for your time this morning, and I am learning that it's worth quite a bit."

"You're kind to say so." Because she doubted that anything would come of arguing with him, she took the coins and slipped them in a pocket inside her cloak. When he pushed her purchases toward her, she took them in the crook of her arm and thanked him. She turned to go but he called her back.

"One more thing, Dr. Woodhouse. Do you mind telling me

exactly what kind of medicine you studied at that big Eastern college?"

She smiled, puzzled. "The usual kind. Why?"

"Because you didn't make me choke down some foul-tasting concoction and I feel better than I have in years."

Chapter Twenty-six

Satisfaction that she had done what she could warred with concern that perhaps that she had done more than she should. She was no novice at dispensing medical advice, but this was different, and Ridley knew it. It was her experience with people who truly lost their minds that made her want to do something to help the Springers, none of whom was anything but sane.

She would have to wait and see, something she was not terribly good at.

Ridley wanted to deliver Mary Cherry's parcels first, and she was moving in that direction when she remembered how close Mary lived to the Salts. Did she dare visit Lily on her own? The question had barely formed in her mind when the answer came back to her. Not only could she not risk a visit for both their sakes, but she had left the house to carry out specific errands and was not in possession of her medical bag. Lily would have to wait, but seeing Mary again would give her an opportunity to learn more than Mrs. Rushton had been able to tell her. Feeling more hopeful than she had only minutes earlier, Ridley crossed the street to the Jones Prescott Bank. She had meant to stop at the bank prior to seeking out Hitch, but it had gone right out of her head as she was walking to the sheriff's office and thinking deeply about what she wanted to say to the deputy. Some days she could not keep two disparate thoughts in mind simultaneously. She blamed the December cold.

The Jones Prescott Bank had rather a grand entrance relative to the businesses around it. Situated on the corner of

Golden and Main, the bank had stairs that hugged the corner and led up to the impressive double-door entrance. Ridley pulled on one of the large brass handles harder than she needed to. It was always surprising when the doors swung open so easily. She supposed the bank did not want to make it difficult to take anyone's money.

She walked in, smiling, prepared to greet people who were no longer strangers to her. A few steps into the lobby she was aware of a charged atmosphere, the kind one could expect during a lightning storm. The hair on her back of her neck crackled. Her smile faltered then disappeared.

Her gaze was drawn first to Mr. Washburn standing behind the teller cage. He was unnaturally still, his carriage not merely correct but exact. As bank manager, he did not customarily make transactions so his presence behind the cage was telling of itself. He never once glanced in her direction. His attention was all for the man—an outsider to Ridley—who was leaning casually against the counter, knuckling his scrub beard and smiling with a hint of derision.

Ridley met his eyes when they shifted toward her. She smiled as though his attention were a greeting. She had already determined that she must act as if nothing was wrong when, in truth, nothing was right.

She counted five people in the lobby and two bank employees in addition to Mr. Washburn. The bank tellers flanked their manager but neither had the stoic bearing of Praetorian guards. Ridley thought it was not out of the question that their knees would buckle sometime in the next few minutes.

Ridley's eyes shifted left. Dolly Mangold stood within arm's reach of another man Ridley did not know. The way the druggist's wife was clutching her reticule and surreptitiously eyeing the man at her side helped Ridley understand that this second stranger was in league with the first.

What gave her hope was the man standing near the bank of windows on her right. He was holding a young boy in his arms, talking to him quietly, acting as if he had not seen her walk in or that it was unimportant that she had. At Ben's elbow was a striking dark-haired woman, presumably the child's mother, who was clearly pregnant and clearly pissed. Ridley had the oddest inclination to grin at the murderous expression on the woman's face, and she could not dismiss the urge as a nervous reaction because she was not in the least anxious.

Even now Ben was a restful presence. She watched him heft the boy in his arms, ruffle his dark hair, and give him a finger poke in his chin. Ridley had the impression that whatever Ben was saying to the child was meant in equal measure for his mother. The boy, who could not have been more than four, was chortling; his mother was not.

Ridley's attention was arrested front and center when the stranger at the counter crooked a finger at her and beckoned her to come closer. She did, but stopped within a few feet of him, close enough now to see that Mr. Washburn was placing money in a leather bag.

"You here to make a withdrawal?" he asked.

Ridley heard an accent that she couldn't place. There was more twang than drawl in his speech. He had a broad face and a square jaw and wore a hat with a flat crown and a wide brim that covered his hair and shaded his eyes. He hadn't shaved in several days and his bristle was as much gray as it was black. She suspected his hair was the same salt-and-pepper mixture but that it was the result of graying prematurely and not because he was significantly older. She estimated his age in the middle years of thirty. His dark eyes were watchful, belying his casual stance, but they were not cruel or forbidding. Here was a careful man, she thought, and wondered that he had made no attempt to conceal his face. Was he truly so confident of not being caught or looking for notoriety in the form of a wanted notice?

"Yes," she told him. Her voice was steady, and she was justifiably proud of that. "A withdrawal."

"Then we have that in common," he said. "I'm here for the same."

Ridley gave a small start when the relative quiet of the bank was interrupted by a loud and harsh spasm of coughing. She turned her head because the sound had not come from the stranger but his accomplice. She saw Mrs. Mangold recoil as the man's hacking could not be suppressed by the handkerchief he stuffed against his mouth. When he finally stopped, he wiped spittle from his lips and stuffed the handkerchief under his sleeve. Ridley avoided appearing interested in what she had glimpsed. The bloodstains on the white cotton were a mixture of old and new, crimson and rust. The blood was telling but she saw other things that supported her diagnosis. She suspected he had a mild fever because he had unbuttoned his coat when no one else had, and there was a sheen of sweat across his upper lip. In contrast to his friend at the counter, this man did not fill out his clothes though he shared the same broad features. She could surmise that he had been losing weight. Ridley saw hollowed-out cheeks and shadows under his eyes. He looked as if he had ten years on his companion, but she suspected that he was the younger of the two.

There was no conclusion that she could draw but that he was dying.

Mr. Washburn held up the leather bag to show he had filled it. He had to clear his throat to garner the attention of the man standing on the other side of the cage.

The man looked over, nodded, and said, "Now the safe." He jutted his chin in the direction of his accomplice. "You go with him. Better draw your gun. Never met a banker I trusted."

The dying man nodded once, removed his gun from its holster with a steady hand, and gestured to Mr. Washburn to precede him into the office, where the safe was located.

The stranger turned so he could lean back. His gun remained holstered and he rested his elbows on the counter. Ridley thought it was rather insulting to the bank employees that he did not see them as a threat, but then they were hardly breathing behind the teller cage. She followed his eyes as they swiveled to Mrs. Mangold.

"Ma'am, you need to sit down. The excitement's just about over. There's a bench behind you and I'm suggesting you avail yourself of its dubious comforts. Lie down if you think you have to, but please disabuse yourself of the notion that I am going to wrest that reticule from your death grip. It's tempting to know what's inside but it ain't worth the tussle."

Ridley watched him turn his sights on the other woman in the lobby. He said, "And you, ma'am, I'd surely like to hear what's got you so peeved. You need to take a page from your man's book and settle down so you don't scare the little one or deliver your baby on its head."

"Peeved?" she said, thrusting her chin at him and curling her hands into fists. "Peeved is what I am when my husband leaves his trousers on the floor and pulls his socks over the bedposts."

Ridley looked on in astonishment as a scarlet flush crept over Ben's face. "Ah, Phoebe," he said. "Did you have to tell everyone about the socks?"

The woman called Phoebe gave him a withering look. Ridley thought she might cuff him on the back of the head. She probably had in the past, for Ridley now understood this was Phoebe Frost, the sister-in-law that Ben had spoken of on her first day in Frost Falls and hardly a word since. She also recalled that this wasn't Phoebe's first experience with robbery. If she was here, where was Ben's brother? Why wasn't Remington Frost saving the day again? It was frustrating that she didn't know more. Ben kept so many of his cards up his sleeve that she should call him out for cheating.

"What I am," said Phoebe Frost, "is as purely pissed as a cat that's had its tail pulled once too often. This is that once-too-often moment. You understand what I'm saying, mister?" Her son began to cry. There was no whimper to warn of the impending wail. He opened his mouth and *howled*. Phoebe clapped a hand over the ear closest to her son's alarming cry. "See? Now Colt's pissed." She stepped in front of Ben and held out her arms to take him. When she stepped back and away, Ben had his gun drawn and aimed squarely at the man who meant to take the bank's money. *Their* money.

It was no accident that Colt stopped crying as abruptly as he started. His performance deserved applause, but no one offered any because the silence was so welcome.

"Hands up," Ben said calmly. "High. Higher." When the man opened his mouth to speak, Ben shook his head. "Don't. I'll shoot you where you stand, and sure, it'll bring your friend, and then I'll shoot him. I don't much like shooting folks, but I'm good at it. Keep that in mind. Now grab the bars behind you. Todd? Gary? You have something back there to tie his hands to the cage?" When they shook their heads and looked at him helplessly, he glanced around.

"I have something," said Ridley. She produced the parcels she was holding under her cloak. "Butcher twine. It's strong." Before Ben stopped her, she moved to the far end of the tellers' cage and set the packages down. Mr. Springer had double knotted the twine on the parcels, and she cursed under her breath as she struggled to undo them.

"Pass the twine to Todd and Gary," Ben said when she was done.

It was an unnecessary instruction since she had no intention of tying the man herself. She dangled the twine through the bars, and when it was taken, she picked up her packages and backed up a safe distance.

She would never be able to say with certainty precisely when it all went wrong, but she could certainly say that it did. Perhaps it was when Gary Cunningham couldn't steady his fingers to manage a knot or when Todd Lancaster dropped his length of twine on the floor. It might have been when the hacking cough of the dying man in the back fairly vibrated the walls or when young Colt decided he'd had enough of being held and heaved himself out of his mother's arms. Certainly Phoebe's mighty groan as Colt launched himself off her belly could have accounted for some of the disturbance, and Dolly Mangold sliding sideways off the bench in a dead faint contributed to more of the same.

Ridley had years of experience standing her ground and she called on it now to remain perfectly still. She needed to remain outside the notice of everyone, especially outside Ben's notice, because everything that was happening was leading to a particular end. *A bad end*, she thought, and the best she could hope for was that Ben would emerge uninjured and that she would keep her wits.

As expected as the gunshot was, it was also surprising because it came from Mr. Washburn's office. Phoebe lost her balance as Colt dove under her skirt and between her legs. She landed awkwardly, mostly on her backside because she was trying to protect her son. Ben did not give any indication that he wanted to help her, and Ridley could only suspect what that cost him. His attention was all for the man whose hands had never been secured and was now diving sideways and reaching for his gun at the same time.

Ben fired. He didn't miss, but neither did he shoot to kill. The bullet found its target in the man's thigh. He was still falling, still grappling for his gun, when Ridley decided she'd had enough.

She clobbered him on the head with the soup bone.

Chapter Twenty-seven

Phoebe Frost sat beside her husband on the bench in Ben's office. Remington had taken her hand over an hour ago when he walked into the bank and found her sitting on the lobby floor rubbing her backside, and he had hardly let go since. Their son was sitting in one of the chairs in front of Ben's desk, swinging his legs back and forth while he drew pictures on the backs of wanted notices that his uncle Ben had given him. Occasionally he held up a drawing for approval and after receiving the appropriate accolades, he happily returned to his important deputy work. He wore a star on his jacket to prove he was a lawman now.

"I'm telling you, Remington," said Phoebe. "She was like Samson, if Samson was a woman, smiting that Philistine with the jawbone of an ass."

"Yes," said Ben from behind his desk. "If the jawbone of an ass had been a soup bone." He added dryly, "Although I think Phoebe's right about our robber being a Philistine. I don't know anyone from Ebensburg who isn't."

Remington's dark eyes narrowed and darted between his wife and Ben. Nothing about the look he gave them made them sober. "I suppose you two think that's amusing."

Phoebe could not stifle her smile. She dropped her head to her husband's shoulder and made an attempt to console him. "I'm fine, Remington. You're good to worry, but I'm fine." She drew his hand toward her belly. "Here, feel for yourself. Little Winchester is better than fine. He's snug."

Remington kept his palm in place, fingers splayed, until he felt the baby kick. "He's restless."

"He's always restless."

Ben said, "You're not really going to name him Winchester, are you?"

"No," said Remington.

"It's still under discussion," said Phoebe.

"There's no discussion," said Remington.

"Winnie if she's a girl," said Phoebe.

Ben asked, "What about names that begin with E? Did you ever think of that? Probably lots of good names there." He was saved from having to address their identically incredulous looks when the Philistine in one of the cells shouted that the doctor was killing him. The accusation was followed by a mild reprimand that made them all smile.

Remington said, "Now *that's* amusing."

Ben pushed away from his desk and stood. "Sounds as if she got the bullet. Maybe she'll let me look in on her now."

Colt stopped swinging his legs and sat up straight. "I want to see."

"I'm sure you do," said Ben. "But no." Ben looked over at Phoebe and Remington and asked with a perfectly straight face, "That's the right answer, isn't it?"

Remington pointed in the direction of the cells. "Go before you lose uncle privileges."

"If you two name that baby Winchester—"

"We're not," said Remington.

"Winnie if she's a girl," said Phoebe.

Ben stared at them, shook his head. "Never mind. I'm going." He was fairly certain they were exchanging grins as soon as his back was turned. Under his breath, he said, "Name that baby Winchester and he's going to need this uncle's protection. That's a fact."

Ridley's head came up as Ben walked in the back. She eased up on the pressure she was applying to her patient's wound. "What's a fact?" she asked.

Ben stopped at the cell's entrance. "Would you name a child of yours Winchester?"

She blinked. "It's all right with me if you don't always say what's on your mind."

"Okay."

"But I suppose if the baby's father is named Remington, and the first child is Colt, Winchester is not out of the question."

"Winnie if she's a girl."

"Well, I'd have to draw the line there."

He nodded. "I suggested they think of names that begin with E."

"Did they look at you as if you had gone slightly mad?"

"It's like you were there."

"Can you hold this pad in place for me? Mr. Gordon's wound is clear. The blood flow should be slowing soon."

Ben stepped up to the cot where Tom Gordon lay with his injured leg elevated on the pillow meant for his head. Ignoring all of her patient's protests, Ridley had cut away one leg of his trousers and drawers to expose the wound. Ben placed his hand over the pad so Ridley could remove hers. She wiped her bloody hands on a towel she'd wrapped around her waist.

"Where's Hitch?" asked Ben. "You didn't want me back here but you let him help you. So where is he?"

"Let me say I know why that young man will never be a butcher."

"What does that mean?"

"I can tell you all about that later. He's out back. The blood made him queasy."

"It made me queasy," said Tom Gordon.

"Shut up," said Ben, and then to Ridley, he added, "I didn't hear him leave. You should have called for me."

"He only walked out a few minutes ago, and I insisted. He'd done enough." Indeed, it was Hitch who fetched everything she needed from the surgery so she could operate in the jail rather than transport Mr. Gordon to her home. "You made a good choice when you hired him."

"I got lucky. It wasn't exactly a thoughtful decision. I chose him because Jeremiah Salt told me not to. We should keep that between ourselves." He looked down at Tom Gordon. "You repeat that and I'll put another bullet in you."

"Repeat what?"

"Good. We have an understanding, then." Ben turned his head to the adjoining cell and regarded the man lying on the cot. He was turned on his side facing the opposite wall. Two wool blankets covered him to his shoulders. "How's your other patient?"

"Resting. I gave him some codeine to ease his cough. He's

exhausted. He'll sleep well into the evening and shouldn't cause you any trouble." She began to clean her instruments in the water bucket that the deputy had fetched for her. "I'm still confused about what happened in Mr. Washburn's office. Have you had the whole story from him?"

After escorting his prisoners to their cells and sending Hitch to the surgery with Ridley's list, he left Remington in charge and returned to the bank to get Mr. Washburn's statement. No one was more surprised than Ben when Mr. Washburn had emerged from his office unscathed. Not only was he uninjured; he also raised his arm to show he was now holding the gun that had been previously held on him. It hardly mattered that his hand was shaking. He wore an expression of triumph right up to the moment he saw Mrs. Mangold curled in a fetal position on the floor, Mrs. Frost sitting on her backside with her son just beginning to emerge from under her skirt, Ben holstering his Peacemaker, his bank tellers crouched behind the counter, the stranger laid out cold on the floor, bleeding from his thigh, his gun half drawn, and Dr. E. Ridley Woodhouse neatly folding butcher paper around what looked to be an astonishingly large soup bone. That was when the bank manager returned to the relative sanctuary of his office and politely told the robber to vacate his chair.

He sat.

He was still sitting in his office when Ben came back for his statement. Ben confiscated the gun that was lying on the green blotter, and once it was out of Mr. Washburn's sight, it seemed to Ben that the man breathed a little easier. The story wasn't hard to extract after that.

Mr. Washburn explained it simply. When the accomplice, whose name they now knew was Michael Gordon, younger brother of Tom, began to convulse with another bout of his bone-shaking cough, the gun fired. Until then, Mr. Washburn had no idea the weapon was poised to shoot. It was only that the younger Gordon's aim was so wildly off that the bank manager escaped injury. The bullet sank into the back of the open safe; the gun fell on the floor and Mr. Washburn was able to recover it first. It was at that point that Michael Gordon asked Mr. Washburn to kill him.

"I'm dyin' anyway," he said. "And I'd rather not hang. Go on. Shoot me."

Ben watched Ridley's expression as he repeated Michael Gordon's words. He couldn't tell what she was thinking, only that she did not appear surprised. "Did he ask the same of you?"

She nodded. "He says it would be a sin to kill himself and his brother won't do it for him. Neither said so, but I think you'll find out that if their robbery had been successful, they would have headed to hot, dry climes. Arizona, perhaps. New Mexico." Her eyes shifted to Tom Gordon. He appeared to be sleeping, but she couldn't be sure. "What I think is it didn't really matter to them if they were successful. He drew on you because you promised to shoot him. You told him you would shoot his brother, too. What they couldn't do, you could."

"Jesus," Ben said softly. It made an awful kind of sense when he heard her say it. He applied more pressure to the pad he was holding over Tom Gordon's wound. The man's eyes opened wide and he growled. "Just so you know, I don't like being used that way."

"Stop that, Ben," Ridley said. "This is precisely why I asked Hitch to help me. Here. Give me that pad." He did and she tossed it in a pail filled with other bloody cloths. She gave him a gentle push out of the way and examined the wound. "I need to clean this again and give him a few stitches. We'll know in a day or so if it's going to fester. I think I removed all the threads, and you were good to miss the femoral artery and vein."

"Sure, because I had time to think about that."

She sighed audibly. "Why don't you go outside and check on Hitch? Bring him back and you can return out front and visit with your family."

"Yes, ma'am."

When he was gone, Tom Gordon rubbed the lump on the back of his head and asked, "You ever think of walloping him with a soup bone?"

"All the time, Mr. Gordon." Then she set about going to work.

* * *

Hitch volunteered to remain at the jail so that Ben could accompany the others to the Butterworth for dinner. Ridley was dismayed to realize she still was in possession of Mary Cherry's butcher order and Mrs. Rushton's soup bone. Ben solved that problem by snagging one of Sam Love's boys as he was leaving his father's barbershop and giving him a few pennies to make the deliveries. Ridley wanted to take her medical supplies with her, but Ben promised that Hitch would bring them around when he was relieved of duty, and ignored all the noises she made about not being satisfied with that answer.

"Did Ben ride roughshod when he was a ranch hand?" Phoebe asked Remington as he held out a chair for her. "I'm not recalling."

"Always had a gentle hand," said Remington. "Even as a deputy under Jackson Brewer."

Phoebe eyed Ben. "So this is a consequence of your newly elected position?"

"It's not that new," he said, sitting down on Ridley's right.

"How like you to remark on the least important part of my question."

"How like you to point it out."

Colt sat on his knees in a chair squeezed in between his parents. His attention shifted between his mother and his uncle and then came to rest on his father. "May I have pancakes?"

Remington cocked an eyebrow at Ben and Phoebe. "The boy knows what's important. Are you done?"

They spoke in unison and unapologetically. "No." It was Ben who added, "But we can certainly make peace over pancakes."

Colt clapped his hands and grinned in a way that showed off almost all of his baby teeth.

Ridley wanted to join him; she was enchanted. "How old are you?"

He held up four fingers.

"So many?"

"How many pancakes can you eat?"

Now he put up both hands and spread his fingers.

"Oh, my. Won't you get a bellyache?"

He shook his head, looked pointedly at his mother's belly, and patted his own. "I'll get a big belly. Like Mama."

Ridley's eyes widened a fraction.

"Don't worry," Phoebe said. "He knows there's a baby in here, not a stack of flapjacks."

"Winchester," said Colt. "Winnie if she's a girl."

Ben gave a shout of laughter. Ridley smiled. Remington looked at Phoebe over their son's head. "See? This is your doing."

Before Phoebe could respond, Colt said, "I hope she's a boy. Horses whinny. Papa says so."

Phoebe turned to meet Remington's eye. "And *that's* your doing."

"Right," he said. A waitress was wending her way toward their table. "I think we should order."

They did. Only Colt and Ben ordered pancakes. Everyone else asked for chicken and dumplings. No one wanted to talk any more about the events at the bank, but the same was not true for the diners around them. They buzzed like worker bees and stole glances at the table.

It was not until their meals arrived that Ridley dared to ask, "Do you suppose they know about the soup bone?"

Phoebe laughed with genuine amusement. "Oh, Dr. Woodhouse, you can depend on it."

Remington agreed with his wife. "Frost Falls is growing steadily but it's still a small town where word of mouth is as important as the weekly paper."

Ridley released a long sigh. "Boston wasn't so different. It's probably the same everywhere. What do you imagine people are saying?"

Ben said, "You're probably being compared to Felicity Ravenwood."

Ridley found his boot under the table and set her heel hard on his instep.

"Ow!"

Phoebe didn't have to ask what that was about. She regarded Ridley approvingly. "Good for you, Dr. Woodhouse."

"Ridley, please."

"Ridley. Good for you. He's not wrong—we all love Felicity—but he shouldn't have said so. People will respect you for what you did. You can trust that's what they're saying. But honestly, you should be prepared to receive more soup bones than your housekeeper can use in a year."

"It's a tribute," said Remington.

"I'm telling you," Ben said, "queen of the Frost Falls Festival." He quickly moved his foot out of the way.

"Is there going to be a festival?" asked Phoebe.

"Only in his mind," Ridley told her.

"And you're the queen?"

"Again, only in his mind."

"Ah." Phoebe stopped eating to cut more pancake triangles for her son. She also nudged the little pot of syrup out of his reach. "Well, I think it sounds like a good idea. Once I have this baby, I might be moved to organize it."

Ridley could not decide if Phoebe was serious and hoped to God she wasn't. "When is the baby coming?"

"Doc told me it would be after Christmas, but probably before the New Year."

"So only a few weeks, then."

"Yes," said Remington. "And she got it in her head this morning that she had to take advantage of this break in the weather to come to town."

"Presents," Phoebe whispered. "I ordered things months ago for everyone at the ranch, and maybe"—she winked at Ben—"a person or two right here in town."

"Phoebe," said Ben. "You don't—"

"Oh, do be quiet. You'll spoil my fun."

"Yeah, but now I have to get something for you," he said, injecting a modest amount of whine into his voice.

Remington caught Ridley's eye as Phoebe and Ben continued to poke at each other. He spoke over the bickering and directly to Ridley. "It's better if you ignore them. Ben and I grew up together, but the way these two carry on, you'd think they were siblings."

"Anyway," Phoebe was saying, "that's why I was at the bank. I had a substantial withdrawal to make."

"Substantial?" asked Remington. "This is the first I'm hearing of it. This morning it was just a withdrawal."

Before the conversation went sideways again, Ridley asked the question that had been on her mind since she identified

Phoebe Frost in the bank. "Why is this the first I'm meeting you?"

Phoebe cast her eyes at her son's plate and began cutting more triangles. "Hmm. I don't come into town often. I think I mentioned that it was several months ago that I placed orders."

"Yes, you mentioned that. I've been here months." Ridley's gaze moved to Remington and settled there. He had a dark, steady stare, and he didn't look away as Phoebe had done. He looked nothing at all like Ben, with his coal black hair and slanted eyebrows. "I've known about the Frosts nearly from the first. People like to talk about you. Most people. Ben hardly ever says a word. I bet you've been to town on more than one occasion. The sheriff's introduced me to almost everyone around. I've been to a few of the outlying ranches. It strikes me as curious that you and I have never crossed paths."

Remington nodded, glanced at Ben, and said, "The easy answer is that we embarrass him, or maybe that he's embarrassed by us."

"I don't believe you. What's the not-so-easy answer?"

Phoebe said, "We set him on fire."

Chapter Twenty-eight

Ben pushed his plate away. "For God's sake, Phoebe, you did not set me on fire." He darted a sidelong look at Ridley. Her eyebrows had climbed her forehead. "They did *not*."

Remington's expression was wry. "This is how embarrassment becomes a factor."

Ridley didn't think Ben looked embarrassed. He looked annoyed, perhaps on the verge of getting riled. She said quickly, "I shouldn't have asked. Obviously there is a lot I don't understand. I didn't mean to corner you, or rather I did, but I didn't expect it would be so uncomfortable. Forgive me."

The look that Phoebe gave Ben was mildly reproving. "There is nothing to forgive," she told Ridley. "In fact, I would be quite relieved if you agreed to attend me at Winchester's birth. It would mean coming out to Twin Star."

Ridley did not have to think about it. "Yes. Of course." Out of the corner of her eye she saw Ben and Remington exchange looks that she could not interpret. "What is it?"

Remington said, "Agreeing now to being at the birth doesn't commit you to being there when the time comes."

"I don't understand."

"The weather," said Ben. "Remington can't be certain that anyone will be able to ride in to get you if the weather turns. It's also possible that you could be snowed in after you arrive. You wouldn't be available to your patients here in town."

Phoebe wiped Colt's sticky face with a napkin she dipped in water and removed the spoon he was tapping on the tabletop from his equally sticky hand. "Take him, please, Remington. It's your fault I don't have a lap." She dropped the damp napkin on Colt's empty plate and pinned Ben back in his chair with a brilliant emerald green stare. "Do you have reservations about Dr. Woodhouse coming out to the ranch?"

"No, but—"

"Then you do," said Phoebe. "If you have to qualify 'no,' then you have reservations."

"Did you not hear me say that the weather could be an obstacle to her getting there or getting back?"

Ridley said, "And it could be no problem at all. It's my decision and not your concern."

"You're right." Ben saw immediately that surrendering his position so quickly did not ease the minds of either woman. They were both frowning. He looked to Remington for help, but his brother was pretending to be occupied in a finger game with Colt. He exhaled deeply. "All right," he said finally. "There are objections from other quarters."

"What does that mean?" asked Ridley.

"He's talking about Fiona," said Phoebe.

"Mrs. Frost?"

"Yes, the *other* Mrs. Frost."

Remington lifted Colt and passed him without ceremony to Ben. "Make yourself useful," he said, and then addressed Ridley. "Fiona is my father's wife, but in her defense, Ben's also talking about my father. Thaddeus has it in his head that you're too young and too inexperienced to be at Phoebe's bedside when his grandchild is ready to be born. Experience colors his reasoning."

"I see," said Ridley. "Then he doesn't object on account of me being a woman?"

"No. Fiona would have already kicked him to the barn if he'd said something as foolish as that. Look, none of this is Ben's doing. He asked me right off when I saw him after you arrived if Phoebe and I would think about you attending her. He said there were women planning to see the doctor up in Liberty Junction or engage a midwife. He thought it'd help you gain acceptance if you were there when Phoebe delivered. I didn't disagree, but I let him know Thaddeus's opinion, and—"

Phoebe interrupted. "And you decided that your father's opinion was more important than mine."

"No," said Ben over the top of Colt's head. "We decided that peace trumped conflict." He looked sideways at Ridley.

"That's why I didn't introduce you when they were in town. Remington and I figured we could avoid this conversation."

Remington offered a wry observation. "You see how well that turned out."

Phoebe's frank gaze shifted to Ridley. "Has it been your experience that men generally are of limited intelligence in these particular matters?"

"Yes."

"Hmm. Mine also. I've often marveled that they can find socks in the sock drawer."

Remington said, "That's unfair. One has nothing to do with the other."

Phoebe reached for his hand, squeezed it, and feigned an adoring glance. "We are not done here, you and I. We will continue this conversation on the ride home."

Ridley frowned. "Surely you're not leaving this evening. It's already dark."

"They're staying at my place," said Ben. "If you hear shouting from that direction, it means that the conversation Phoebe plans to have started early."

"We don't shout," said Phoebe.

"She gets very quiet," Remington told Ridley. "You might want to drop in if you don't hear anything."

Ridley smiled because she knew he was attempting to lighten the mood. She did not feel light at the moment. In spite of telling herself that she was not really at the center of a family argument, that what Phoebe objected to was having no voice in something that concerned her so greatly, it was difficult to embrace the notion. It made her stomach churn.

They got up from the table when Colt announced that he was tired. No one needed to see him yawn to prove his point. Ben helped him into his coat, got his own, and then hoisted his nephew on his shoulders. Colt leaned forward and crushed Ben's hat. Ridley was struck by the fact that the man who set such store by his hat that he fiddled with the brim every time he put it on did not cringe when the crown collapsed.

Ridley bade them all good night when they reached her gate. Ben offered to walk her to the door, but she told him there was no need. She stood on her porch, watching them cross to his house. Colt waved to her, no doubt prompted by one of the adults. She waved back and went inside.

Mrs. Rushton had long since gone, but the housekeeper had left a note on the kitchen table informing her that she had taken delivery of two soup bones, one ham, and one beef, and they were in the cold box on the back stoop. Laughing, Ridley set the note aside. So it had begun. For the first time since coming to Frost Falls, she felt part of the whole, not apart from it. Perhaps she would be queen of the festival after all.

Before she started planning her speech and what she would wear in the parade, Ridley thought she better take in the state of her surgery. While she was prepared to find it in a sad condition after sending Hitch to retrieve the items on her list, what she discovered was something more than that. It looked as if he had ransacked the room. She was taken back to the moment she had first visited the surgery after Clay and Hamilton Salt had been there. At least Hitch hadn't broken anything. She supposed that was a blessing.

She circled the room, straightening the chairs and the examining table, taking inventory of the drawers and cabinets before closing them, rerolling bandages and restacking towels, righting a bucket lying on its side, and replacing the lids on the canisters of soap, wads of cotton, and toothpicks. It seemed Hitch had left no stone unturned.

Ridley carried a lamp to her office and set it on the desk. She removed a leather-bound journal from the middle drawer, opened it to a blank page, and began making notes on the Gordon brothers, detailing Michael Gordon's symptoms related to consumption and the surgery she performed on his older brother. Assuming the men were found guilty, a judge might take Michael Gordon's medical condition into account when passing sentence. She made her journal entry with that in mind, though she was less certain that she was doing the dying man any favors. It wasn't that he was not prepared to die, only that he didn't want to hang. Ridley didn't have a good answer for the problem; she could hardly recommend a firing squad. As for the other Gordon, she thought she'd done her work well enough that he would walk to the scaffold without a limp. Years of hard labor were not out of the question; he was healthy enough for that. She would always choose life over death, but it was impossible to know what a judge would decide.

She finished her work, sat back, and removed her spectacles. Closing her eyes, she rubbed the bridge of her nose. Images from the day appeared in her mind like photographs in a stereoscopic viewer. She could see them in great detail but only for a moment. There was Amanda Springer sipping tea and announcing in no uncertain terms that her husband had lost his mind, and her son sitting at the sheriff's desk saying much the same thing about his mother. She saw Mary Cherry's grief shimmer in front of her like a watery reflection and Jim Springer's thoughtful turn as he considered his wife's fears. As though she were a spectator rather than a participant, she watched herself accept the neatly wrapped soup bone and step out of the butcher shop, and then she was in the bank. She could hear the air crackle and feel the hair rising at the back of her neck. The images began to pass more quickly. They were a blur right up until the moment Tom Gordon dove toward her, his hand on the butt of his gun. It seemed that he was coming at her slowly, ruthlessly, but she had no fear for herself. She was never his target. He had Ben in his sights, only Ben. The bullet he meant to deliver was for the man sworn to protect them all.

Ridley could not let that happen. She swung the soup bone with all of her might. She watched the trajectory of her arm, felt the recoil in her shoulder when she connected, heard the dull thud of bone on bone, and then . . . nothing. The quiet was absolute for as long as it lasted. The image shifted and she saw Mr. Washburn coming out of his office. The look of triumph on his face as it dissolved into stupefaction would always have the power to make her smile.

Chuckling softly to herself, Ridley replaced her spectacles and chose a book on the advanced practice of assisting at childbirth to carry to the front room. She curled in the corner of the sofa closest to the stove and loosely pulled an afghan around her. The illustrations captivated her more than the text, but after half an hour they were not of sufficient interest to keep her eyes open. She told herself she only had to stay awake long enough for Hitch to arrive with her medical bag and mis-

cellaneous supplies. Ridley looked at the mantel clock for the
time and assured herself he couldn't be much longer.

She never felt the book slip from her hands or heard it drop
to the floor. Likewise, she was unaware that the deputy quietly
entered her home when she did not respond to his knocking,
saw her sleeping on the sofa, and left what he was charged
with returning—along with a meaty soup bone that he took
from his father's shop—on the floor of the vestibule.

Chapter Twenty-nine

It was still dark when Ridley woke. The oil lamp had not yet extinguished itself, and Ridley could make out the time. Two hours gone, but it wasn't terribly late. On any less eventful day, she would only now be preparing for bed. She wondered what had happened to Hitch.

She uncurled her legs, raised her head, and rolled her shoulders. She was stiff all the way to her toes. Throwing off the afghan, Ridley bent and retrieved the book that she'd dropped and placed it on the trunk. Later, she promised, she would read more when her bed was not calling to her.

She walked through the house, turning back lamps, checking the flue, and came across proof that Hitch had been there when she stood in the vestibule. She also found his gift. It would serve him right if she clobbered him with it the next time she saw him. To keep it from spoiling, she took the bone to the back stoop and placed it with the others in the cold box, then she headed for her room.

Halfway up the stairs, she stopped. Somebody was clamoring for her attention at the surgery door. She could have only just missed seeing the person when she was on the stoop. Sighing, moved to wonder if it was a fact of the medical profession that people would always require her attention when she was sleeping or preparing to, she retraced her steps to the surgery.

"Who is it?" she asked through the door. "And what do you need?"

"It's Remington. Phoebe's going to have—" He grabbed the door when Ridley began to push it open. "A baby."

Ridley stepped aside. "Come in. Calm yourself." She pulled

the door shut behind him. He was not wearing a hat, and his thatch of dark hair had been plowed many times with his fingers. He did it again now, and she thought of how Ben did it in a similar fashion, only with Ben there was generally improvement. Remington's hair was standing up six ways from Sunday.

"You don't understand," he said. "It's now. The baby's coming now. I think it's all been too much today. The excitement of the robbery. She fell on her backside at the bank, you know."

"I remember. Let me get my things and we'll see what's what. You go back and sit with her. I promise I'm right behind you. Oh, and put a kettle on."

"Right." He took a step forward and then halted, looking vaguely perplexed. "Coffee? Tea?"

"To clean my instruments in the event I need them." She gave him a push and then he was gone.

True to her promise, Ridley followed quickly, though she suspected that Remington had vastly exaggerated the speed at which Phoebe was going to introduce Winchester—or Winnie, if she was a girl—to the world. Thaddeus Frost was correct in that she did not have a lot of experience with deliveries, but she had assisted at enough of them to know that the husbands and loved ones were often more frantic than the mother.

She also knew that for as long as women had been delivering babies, the risks had never been substantially reduced. Everyone knew someone who had lost a wife, a mother, a sister at childbirth or shortly after. It accounted for much of a woman's anxiety as her time neared and the effect on her husband was no less real. But, Ridley reminded herself, Phoebe had delivered a healthy baby four years ago, and she appeared to be in good health now. There was no reason to believe there would be complications, only reasons to prepare for them.

Ridley let herself into Ben's home by the back door. Remington was waiting for her in the kitchen. The kettle was on. She was prepared to ask him why he wasn't with his wife, but he stopped her by speaking first.

"My mother died of childbed fever," he said. "My sister died not long after she was born, my mother a few days later. I was five. I wanted you to know. Doc understood and wouldn't let me near Phoebe until Colt was bawling as loudly as a new-born calf. He called me a lunatic. My father called me a drunk, but then so was he."

Ridley nodded. "I understand," she said gently. "Would you like to have someone with you? You could go and get Ben. I think he'd want to be here. He can leave his prisoners for a few hours."

"I don't think it will be a few hours."

"It will be fine," she assured him. "Bring the kettle upstairs after the water boils and then you can go."

Ridley found Phoebe sitting up in bed, a pillow at her back and two others on each side of her that she was using as arm-rests. Her hair was brushed back from her face and wound in a coil at the crown of her head. She looked like royalty.

"I chose the wrong room at first," Ridley told her as she removed her coat and put it aside. "Colt didn't stir so I think whatever excitement there has been thus far, he's unaware of it."

"The only person excited here is my husband, and it is not in a good way."

"He told me about his mother."

"That's something at least. He was insane when I went into labor with Colt, and my father-in-law didn't set a better ex-ample. That has a lot to do with his opinion regarding you."

"That's clear to me now." She approached the bed. "How long ago did your water break?"

"It happened when we were walking from the hotel to Ben's."

Not so long ago, then, Ridley thought. "And you didn't say a word," she chided.

"I couldn't, not then. Remington would have handled the news badly. I envisioned him insisting that you attend me right then and there, so I excused myself when we reached Ben's and took care of it. Remington's used to me having frequent and urgent needs. The baby dropped Saturday a week ago."

"I bet you didn't mention that to him either."

"No, he wouldn't have brought me to town, and you and I both know it's not a sign that labor's imminent. Colt sat on my bladder nearly a month before he showed himself."

"What about this labor? When did it begin?"

"Just around the time I cleaned myself. It was hardly more

than twinges at first. I couldn't have hid it from Remington otherwise, and frankly, I didn't recognize the pain for what it was. I *did* fall this afternoon. It didn't seem out of the question that the back pain I felt was related to that."

Ridley thought it was just as likely that Phoebe didn't want to believe she was in labor. This thought was confirmed when Phoebe regarded her with a hint of anxiety in her features. "What is it?" asked Ridley.

"Is it too early? Can my baby live?"

"You told me Doc calculated that you're due between Christmas and January first. That's only fifteen or so days from now. I'll make sure your baby's lungs are clear and that Winchester or Winnie has a healthy cry, maybe one to rival Colt's."

Phoebe's smile was a little uncertain, a little watery. "I want to hear that cry." The smile became a grimace as a contraction seized her uterus.

Ridley counted out the length of the contraction. Forty seconds. She asked, "How long between contractions?"

"Fifteen minutes, I think. I'm not sure. I told Remington there was time. I had a long labor with Colt."

"I don't think he could hear you, and you probably shouldn't compare this labor to Colt's. The progression can be very different. I'm guessing that your husband knows that."

"Hmm. He took out books from the library."

Ridley chuckled. "Of course he did."

"They raise horses at Twin Star. Did you know that?" When Ridley nodded, Phoebe continued. "He's been present at the births of hundreds of foals, and helped with more than a few distressed mares. I'm quite certain there wasn't anything in those books that experience hadn't already taught him. And the illustrations? I thought they were disturbing. I made him return the books."

Ridley thought of the medical text she had been reading earlier. She was glad she'd left it behind. "Remington is bringing me hot water to sterilize my instruments. Afterward, at my recommendation, he's going to the sheriff's office to get Ben. I hope that's all right with you."

"God, yes."

"Good. We'll wait for him and then I'll have a look at you."

Remington arrived when Phoebe had just begun another

contraction. He stood at the foot of the bed as pale as salt, the kettle in one hand and a large basin under an arm. Ridley pointed to the washstand in the corner but wasn't surprised when he didn't move. She mentally counted out the seconds. This contraction was no longer than the previous one. There was definitely time for Remington to leave and return with Ben.

When it was over, Phoebe sipped air through pursed lips. She smiled at her husband, although the effort was stiff. "In the corner," she said when he continued to stand there staring at her. "Like the doctor said. The things you're carrying. Not you."

He nodded and still didn't move.

"You're making me nervous, Remington. A woman preparing to give birth does not want to be looked at by her husband as if he's memorizing her face. I *will* be here when you get back and for years after that."

"You're beautiful," he said. "I love you."

"And I love you, you ridiculous man."

Remington nodded again, this time with a slender smile edging the corners of his mouth. He carried the kettle and basin to the washstand and then returned to Phoebe's bedside opposite the doctor. He touched her cheek with the back of his hand. "Ben won't let me drink too much."

"I'm counting on it." She caught his hand, moved it to her mouth, and pressed a kiss against his knuckles. "I love you," she said again.

"I'm counting on it."

When he was gone, Ridley took her medical bag to the washstand to give Phoebe time to compose herself. In truth, even if she hadn't needed to clean her instruments, she would have required the distraction. Seeing them together touched her more profoundly than she could have imagined. She had only ever witnessed an approximation of that affection in the relationships between her father and his occasional mistresses. Marital infidelity aside, it was still not an example she wished to emulate. Her father had found ease from his volatile marriage in arrangements that were as comfortable as his slippers and as orderly as his library.

Ridley appreciated comfortable slippers and order to her bookshelves, and it pained her to think that once upon a time, she might have been satisfied with that tidy life. Watching Remington and Phoebe together was a revelation, but so was being with Ben on any given day . . . or night.

Ridley gripped the corners of the washstand, steadied herself. She knew something about a contraction just then. This one squeezed her heart.

Chapter Thirty

"Doctor?"

Ridley snapped to attention. "Yes?"

"That last time . . . I think I soiled myself."

Ridley cleared her throat, found her voice. "It's all right. Perfectly normal."

"Maybe, but it's still mortifying." Phoebe smiled crookedly. "I put a towel under my backside in anticipation of all this normal. That's something I learned the last time. I could use some help."

"Of course." Ridley's approach was straightforward. Her efficient handling of the mess, the cleaning, and the changing made what had to be done marginally less discomforting for Phoebe. She slid a fresh towel from a stack in the linen cupboard under Phoebe's bottom. "You need another shift," she said as Phoebe drew the blankets up to her naked shoulders. "I don't suppose—"

"We didn't plan to spend the night," Phoebe said.

"Maybe one of Ben's shirts?"

"No!"

Ridley laughed at the vehemence of her reply. "All right. I'll go next door and bring back a couple of mine."

"Will you check on Colt again, please?"

"Of course." Ridley looked in on him twice, once before she left and once when she returned. Both times he was burrowed so deeply under the covers that only the top of his head showed. He slept through both interruptions.

Phoebe took the shift that Ridley handed her and slipped it over her head. When she emerged, the other shift was already hanging on the wardrobe door and Ridley was taking off her coat. "Tell me about Colt," she said.

"Sleeping soundly. Tell me about your contractions. You should have had one while I was gone."

"There's no point in lying, is there?" With a mildly guilty expression, Phoebe held up two fingers.

Ridley's eyebrows lifted. "Two of them? How long? Please tell me you counted."

"Fifty seconds each, give or take a few."

"And in between? They must have been close together."

"I don't think you could have been out of the house when I had the first one. I heard you coming up the stairs when the second one was ending."

Ridley estimated the interval at about six minutes. She began setting her instruments out on a clean towel.

"It's happening faster than before," Phoebe said. The anxiety that tugged at her features earlier was now a note in her voice. "Should I have known that? I didn't. I thought it would be the same." She closed her eyes. "Lord, I should have read that book Remington brought home."

Ridley washed her hands and then carried the towel with the instruments over to the bed. She placed it at the foot. "There are many ways a woman experiences labor, and a woman who gives birth multiple times can have a different experience each time. She can also have a labor similar to the ones before, but that does not seem to be the case here. That doesn't mean there's something wrong; it only means that it's different."

Phoebe pressed the heels of her hands into the pillows on either side of her. Her fingers curled. Her eyes, already closed, were squeezed tight.

Ridley counted. When the contraction passed and Phoebe sank back against the headboard and opened her eyes, Ridley said, "Sixty seconds."

"Are you certain? It felt like forever."

"I don't doubt it. Here's what I know, Phoebe, and every textbook, every mother-to-be, confirms it. Babies are born on their timeline, not ours. This one's eager, but that's not exactly surprising when there is a family like yours waiting to welcome him—or her."

"Do you really think so?"

"I really do." And with that last assurance, Ridley began her examination.

"Well?" asked Phoebe when Ridley emerged from under the sheet and she could finally lower her knees and scoot back toward the head of the bed. She was nearly sitting upright when another contraction laid her back. She pressed one hand to her belly; the other squeezed the corner of a pillow. She folded her lips together and muffled the cry that sounded as if the baby were lodged in her throat.

"Don't push," said Ridley, and when Phoebe stared at her with evil intent, she merely smiled back. "You're not the first woman to consign me to one of the lower circles of hell. Do you know Mary Cherry?"

Phoebe gave a shout of laughter that quickly spiraled into a groan. She panted, catching her breath after the final wave of the contraction rolled through her. She tried to relax, find a comfortable position. She couldn't. "Well?" she asked. "Did you see anything interesting? My tonsils?"

"No, but I think I found your sense of humor."

Phoebe's short laugh ended in a snort. "It seems you did."

"Your cervix is dilated to about the diameter of a lemon slice. That's good. I thought the opening might be bigger given the frequency and duration of your contractions."

"The size of a slice of lemon. I don't want to push a baby through there."

"No, you don't, and your baby will thank you for it."

Phoebe nodded. "Will you look out the window and tell me if you see my husband?"

"Of course." Ridley went to the window that faced the front street. The Butterworth Hotel blocked much of her view of the main thoroughfare. "Nothing. Would you like me to go outside and look? I could see more if I walked to the corner."

"Would you?" She sighed. "I sound needy, don't I?"

"Nonsense. I'll go right now." Ridley didn't think about her coat until she was outside. She hugged herself rather than go back inside and took the diagonal path to the corner of the cross streets and the hotel. Ben and Remington were coming abreast of the Songbird when she saw them.

Ridley waved and waited. Ben was stripping off his coat

before they reached her, and because he did not look as if he would entertain an objection, she let him put the coat around her shoulders.

Remington didn't pause as he passed her. He'd begun to lengthen his stride as soon as he saw Ridley. His pace was now double what it had been. He called back to Ridley over his shoulder. "What's happened? Is it Phoebe? Is it the baby?"

She hurried after him, Ben at her side. "She's fine. They're both fine. She asked for me to see where you were. She wants you there, lunatic or not."

Remington took the front steps in a single leap but slowed as he crossed to the door. "She wants me?" He raised an index finger, pointing to the upper floor. "There?"

"I don't know about that." Ridley caught up to him, slightly out of breath. "She wants to know that you're in the house, I think. It probably seemed as if a long time had passed."

Nodding once, Remington went inside. By the time Ridley and Ben were there, he was almost at the top of the stairs. Ridley started to follow, but Ben caught her elbow and held her back.

"He needs time," said Ben. "He'll want to see for himself that what you said is true."

Ridley nodded. He was right. She returned his coat.

"What about you?" he asked.

"Me? There's nothing wrong with me." She watched him make his own assessment, blue eyes grazing her rather warmly from head to toe.

"There certainly isn't."

"Are you flirting?"

"Not very well, if you have to ask." He threw his coat over the newel post and tossed his hat on top. "You took my breath away this afternoon. Did I tell you that?"

"No. Did I?"

"Uh-huh. You probably saved my life, or if not mine, then Phoebe's or Colt's. I don't know where Gordon's bullet would have gone. Did you think at all?"

"No."

"So it was blind luck."

"I think it might have been. I'm fairly sure my eyes were closed at the end."

He sighed, nodded. "I wish you had it in you to be a little dishonest."

"I know. I'm sorry."

Ben sank his fingers into his hair, separating the strands with deep furrows. "Can I at least depend on you not to do something so brilliantly reckless in the future?"

"Yes, you can depend on it."

His expression was immediately suspicious. "You're lying, aren't you?"

"Yes, but only to prove to myself that I can."

He kissed her. Hard. Her splendidly wry smile made it a moral imperative. She raised her hands, placed them on his shoulders, and then moved them to the back of his neck. She laced her fingers against his web of scars, rose on tiptoes, and kissed him back.

Ben seized her at the waist, pulled her to him. Her breasts flattened against his vest. He would have let her crawl inside his clothes if she could have, burrowed under his skin if such a thing were possible. His hands moved to the small of her back; her fingers wrapped themselves in his hair.

The moment, the kiss, could easily have lasted this side of forever. The wanting was clear. The need was evident. The hunger was real. The opportunity, though, was miserably mistimed.

Ben drew back the fraction necessary to whisper against her lips. "Later, Edwina. I swear I mean to have you." He felt her warm chuckle at his mouth. "Not Edwina?"

"No." She lowered her heels to the floor and let her fingers drift from his hair to his shoulders and then down his arms. "Not Edwina."

"All right." He brushed her lips, set his forehead against hers. "I still mean to have you."

"I hope so. Do you think we've given Remington enough time?"

"You didn't hear him at the top of the stairs?"

Ridley reared back and set herself from him. "What? You're making that up."

Ben held up both hands. His eyes were full of mischief. "I swear I'm not. Don't worry, he knows I've kissed girls before."

Ridley let him know she was not amused. She shouldered

right past him to reach the stairs, but she didn't fight him when he caught her on the first step, spun her around, and offered what she imagined he thought was a contrite expression.

"Don't pretend you're sorry when you're not," she said.

"I'm a little bit sorry. I told you I wouldn't mind for myself if we were found out. Do you remember? I said I would mind for you. And I do, but only because you're distressed. It was Remington who saw us. He's hardly the town crier. You can expect that he'll say something to Phoebe, but she's not going to tell anyone."

"Hmm." Ridley's gaze faltered; she looked away. "Sometimes I take things too seriously, myself included."

"Sometimes." He paused, bent his head to catch her eye. "And sometimes I fail to see when things *are* serious."

She shook her head. "No, you don't. I never think that. You merely wear a different suit of armor than I do."

Ben said nothing. She had captured it exactly. His hands fell to his sides.

Ridley turned and mounted the steps. She felt his eyes on her back all the way to the top.

Chapter Thirty-one

Remington and Phoebe were whispering when Ridley walked into the room. That ended abruptly. Remington, who was sitting at his wife's side, his head bent toward hers, immediately sat up straight. They wore identically innocent expressions, the kind that guilty children everywhere produced when caught with their hands in the cookie jar.

Ridley cut through the pretense. "I know you know." She appreciated they had the grace not to ask her what she meant. Their simultaneous sighs were rather amusing. With that out of the way, she was all about the business at hand. "How are you, Phoebe?"

"Doing well, I think. Remington thinks so, too."

Ridley sat on the bed opposite Remington. She removed a stethoscope from her medical bag, fixed the ear tips in her ears, and placed the bell against Phoebe's rounded abdomen. She moved it around until she found where the baby's heartbeat was the strongest. Keeping the bell in place, she removed the ear tips and offered them to Remington. His disbelief and subsequent hesitation were charming. "Go on," she encouraged him. "You've probably put your ear to your wife's belly before. This is like that, only better."

Remington looked sideways at Phoebe. "You don't mind?"

She smiled, shook her head.

He took the ear tips, inserted them, and listened, fascinated by the steady beat of his child's heart. He reared back slightly when the baby kicked and he felt the vibration through the ear tubes. Grinning, he handed the ear tips back to Ridley. "Thank you."

"You're welcome." She dropped the stethoscope back in

her bag and then asked Phoebe about her contractions. There had been no change. "Your labor's stalled. That happens sometimes. Your cervix needs to soften and stretch. It will." She noticed that Phoebe took this information in stride. Remington had gone a little pale. "Are you going to be all right?" she asked him. "You can leave anytime, but you can be certain I will call for Ben to escort you out when Phoebe's ready to deliver."

Phoebe said, "Ben's assistance will not be required."

Remington did not contradict his wife.

She found his hand, squeezed it. "Stop thinking about those illustrations."

"I can't. They're burned like wood etchings at the back of my eyelids."

"You know what would help?" said Ridley. "Some of my good whiskey. I'm not inviting you to get drunk, only suggesting that in moderation those images might fade." When Remington didn't move, she shrugged. "Or you can sit right here." She caught sight of Phoebe's pinched features, a precursor to the next contraction. "And here we go."

Phoebe squeezed Remington's fingers bloodless. She drew her lips inward, pressed hard, and managed not to draw blood. Pain was a rolling tide. She squeezed her eyes shut, tried to breathe when Ridley reminded her, and dug her heels into the mattress to shift positions. There was no ease to the pain, but a minute later, when it had run its course, she felt loose jointed and separate from her body. It was lovely. Her grip on Remington's hand relaxed. She laughed a little jerkily when he slipped his hand out from under her fingers and shook it.

Ridley laid a damp folded cloth across Phoebe's perspiring brow and then gently wiped her face.

"I hate it when you tell me not to push," Phoebe told her.

"Do you remember I said your cervix is open about the diameter of a lemon slice?"

"Yes."

"Well, to accommodate the baby, it needs to be dilated to the diameter of a"—Ridley paused while she considered her analogy—"the diameter of a doughnut. A fat doughnut."

"A fat doughnut," Phoebe repeated, as she looked at her husband. He was significantly paler than he had been before.

"Go on, dearest. Have that medicinal whiskey like the doctor suggested. And when Ben says you've had enough, you've had enough."

Remington nodded, kissed Phoebe on the cheek, and exited the room muttering "doughnut" under his breath.

Watching him go, Phoebe sighed. "He's a comfort to me until he isn't. It was definitely time for him to go. He was done in by the doughnut."

Laughter bubbled on Ridley's lips. A moment later, Phoebe joined her.

"You hear them?" Remington asked Ben when he reached the front room. "Where's your liquor? They're laughing at me, and you don't want to know what about. I wish I didn't know. I was satisfied with the mystery, and then I read that damn book, well, mostly looked at the illustrations, and what I didn't know, Dr. Woodhouse just explained. You'd think breeding horses all these years would prepare a man for the facts, but it's different when it's facts about your wife. You'll see. Where'd you say your liquor was?"

"I didn't," Ben said. "I'm pouring you a drink right now."

"What?" Remington pulled in his focus. Ben was indeed standing by a drinks cabinet holding a glass in one hand and a bottle in the other. "Is that yours or the doc's? She said she had some good whiskey at her house."

"The doc's," said Ben. He handed Remington the glass and then poured a drink for himself. "I went next door and stole it."

"Good." He tipped the glass against his mouth and took a large swallow. "Smooth," he said when it reached the pit of his stomach. "Better than what you usually have on hand."

"I know. Her liquor selection was a revelation. I thought she only had a taste for blended teas." He shrugged. "I guess you never know. Have a seat, and don't knock back what's left of that drink. I'm pouring. You're not."

Remington dropped into a large overstuffed chair. He slumped, stretched his legs, and rolled the glass between his palms. "Talk about something," he told Ben. "Whatever you like."

"Better if you talk. Your mind won't drift. Tell me about Thaddeus and Fiona. How are they?"

Remington knew that Ben was right and he launched into a story about his father wanting to make Fiona a gift of one of the new mares, but finding out that the particular chestnut he had chosen was as single-minded as Fiona herself. None of the hands thought the mare would accept Fiona in the saddle Christmas morning. The mare had thrown everyone at one time or another, and Thaddeus was understandably reluctant to let his wife mount her.

"That's why I finally gave in and told Phoebe we could come to town. Thaddeus asked me to choose a saddle for Fiona, and I said I would. I was at the leather goods store when all of you were at the bank." He raised his glass but only took a sip. "Have I thanked you for looking out for my family?"

"About five or six times. And they're my family, too."

Remington nodded and said quietly, "I wish you wouldn't be a stranger at the ranch. Phoebe and I have our own place, you know that. You could—" He stopped because Ben was already shaking his head.

"I won't sneak around Twin Star to visit you. It wouldn't only feel wrong; it'd be wrong."

"Only in your mind."

"Maybe, but there it is."

Remington eyed Ben over the rim of his glass. "How's Ellie?"

"She has nothing to do with me not going out to the ranch."

"I didn't say that she did. I was inquiring about her health."

"Uh-huh." When Remington continued to stare at him, Ben decided to let it go. "In that case, she's well. Grieving about Doc's passing. She was a better friend to him than I knew."

"I thought we might see her at the hotel."

"No, you didn't."

"It's been a long time, Ben. I can understand that she would want to avoid Thaddeus and Fiona, but Phoebe? There's no need. Phoebe championed her. She was the one who could see events through your mother's eyes."

"What about you?"

"Me? For all intents and purposes, Ellie raised me. I loved her. I suppose there for a while I thought I felt differently, but time passes, and I learned that nothing's changed."

"Maybe you should tell her that. I could, but she wouldn't believe me."

"Maybe I should." He took another sip of his drink. "You know, Ben, if she really wanted to get away, she would have gone farther than Frost Falls."

"I know. But then she wouldn't be able to punish herself in quite the same way." He leaned forward, bottle in hand, and refreshed Remington's drink and then his own. He placed the bottle on the table between them but closer to his side. He sat back and rested his head against the back of the sofa. "I like it here," he said. "I missed the ranch more when I was Jackson's deputy than I do now that I'm sheriff. I had more time on my hands then, I guess, less responsibility. Did Thaddeus put Jackson up to recommending me for the job?"

"You know better than that."

"Hmm. I guess I still wonder."

"Well, he didn't. He approved. So did I. The election was up to the people. We didn't stuff any ballot boxes."

Ben chuckled. "Jackson might have. He was dead set on getting to Paris. I don't think there was anyone except his wife who didn't think it was a damn fool notion."

Remington started to reply but he cut himself off when he heard Phoebe's cry drift down the stairs. The tips of his fingers turned white on his glass.

Ben didn't like the sound any better than Remington. He kept one eye on the bottle so Remington couldn't take it and run. "You remember Lily Salt? She was Lily Bryant when you knew her in school."

"Huh?" Remington required a moment to get his bearings. Ben's conversational diversion gave him whiplash. "Yeah. Sure. Jeremiah's wife. I don't see her around much when I'm in town. What about her?"

"Jeremiah's been whaling on her. I took Ridley to see her early on, but Jeremiah won't have any part of that now. I spoke to Mary Cherry this morning about Doc's passing, and once she got her thoughts together, she told me that she thinks Lily's in a bad way again. Nothing she could see, and nothing Lily would say, but Mary's got a nose for that sort of thing. I can't dismiss it."

"There are children, aren't there?"

Ben held up four fingers just as Colt had done earlier in the dining room.

"Damn. Does he wallop on them?"

"Clay—he's the oldest—says no. I'm not sure I can believe him. There are no visible marks. I've talked to the schoolmaster, but that man comes from the spare-the-rod, spoil-the-child line of thinking, so I don't know if he's a reliable source. He has a switch hanging beside the blackboard. Hurt my backside to look at it."

"What are you going to do?"

"I want to talk to Ridley first and hear what she knows. Mary said she spoke to Ridley's housekeeper about it a few days ago, so it might have gotten back to Ridley by now. There's almost no way either one of us can lay eyes on Lily if she doesn't leave the house or if I don't put Jeremiah in jail. So far, the wily bastard hasn't given me cause."

"No public drunkenness? That doesn't sound like Jeremiah. I recall Jackson joking about giving him exclusive rights to one of the cells."

"We didn't arrest him all that often," said Ben. "If he didn't harm anyone or destroy something or no one pressed charges, I usually escorted him home on the sheriff's say-so. God only knows how many times I put Lily in danger when I dropped him off on his doorstep."

"You feeling guilty?"

Ben nodded. "Some. I didn't know what I didn't know."

"Rock and a hard place. You do what you can and sometimes you can't even do that. I'm sorry, Ben."

"Hmm."

Remington's head snapped toward the staircase when Phoebe cried out again. "Jesus, that tears me up. How long since the last time we heard her?"

"I don't know. Five minutes?"

"Five minutes. The doc said Phoebe's labor was stalled. Does five minutes sound like it's stalled to you?"

"Hey, you're the one with the experience."

"I was drunk."

"Well, you said yourself that you read a book."

"Yeah, but I didn't exactly bone up, and I mostly looked at the pictures."

"How'd you graduate law school? Those books have pictures, too?" Ben added a finger of whiskey to Remington's glass when he held it out. "Last time I'm filling it, so go easy."

Remington ignored him. "Maybe I should look in on Colt. The boy sleeps like the dead, but those sounds that Phoebe's making could raise Lazarus."

"I'll go," said Ben. He stood and swiped the bottle from the table, gave Remington a knowing grin, and headed for the stairs.

Colt was blissfully unaware of what was happening down the hall. Ben straightened the boy's blankets where he had kicked them off and added some coals to the stove. He stood outside the door, listening in the event he had disturbed his nephew but he heard nothing.

Ben started for the staircase, backtracked, and went to stand at his bedroom door. It was ajar a few inches; he nudged it open a few more. Ridley was telling Phoebe to relax, close her eyes, and think about holding her baby in her arms. Did she favor a girl or a boy this time? Ben didn't hear Phoebe's reply, but he wondered what she said. He hadn't thought to ask either Remington or Phoebe if it mattered.

He stepped back. The floor creaked under his boots. He paused, tried to retreat again, but this time the door opened and Ridley poked out her head.

"I thought it was probably you," she said. "Colt would have barged in and Remington wouldn't have come close. What do you want?"

"Nothing. Um, I came up to look in on Colt. He's still sleeping, by the way."

"Uh-huh."

"You, um, don't suppose I could see Phoebe?" He added quickly, "If she says it's all right, that is. It would set Remington's mind at ease if I could make a report. It'd set my mind at ease, too."

Ridley's head disappeared from the opening as quickly as a turtle retreating into its shell. She placed her fingers in the door to stop it from closing but also to keep Ben from nudging it back open.

Ben realized that she was pantomiming his request because he couldn't hear a word she was saying. When she reappeared, it was to open the door wide enough to usher him inside.

"How is he?" asked Phoebe. She pushed back damp strands of hair that had escaped the knot on her head and come to settle against her temples and one cheek. "I see you're carrying a bottle. I suppose that tells me something."

Ben went to the foot of the bed and held it up. "Better than half full," he said. "I took it for safekeeping purposes."

"Uh-huh. And left my husband alone with every other bottle you have in your cabinet. Where is your head, Ben Madison?"

He grinned good-naturedly. "Clearly not attached to the rest of me. How are you?"

"Ready to have this baby."

Ridley said, "Phoebe's started hard labor. She'll be ready to push soon."

"She's only started hard labor?" asked Ben. "What was that before?"

"Mm," Phoebe murmured. "Apparently a picnic, so says the doctor."

"I did not say that."

Phoebe's fingers curled and her back stiffened. "One of you come here. Quick." Ben reached her first. She grabbed his hand. "Here we go." Once again the contraction seized her breath. Her nostrils flared and creases appeared at the corners of her eyes and mouth.

"It's time," Ridley said. "You can push."

Phoebe did.

Ben thought she might twist his fingers off but complaining just then would not have been wise. By his count, the contraction lasted a full ninety seconds. When it was over, Phoebe went limp.

Ridley pointed Ben toward the door. "Go on. Tell Remington that Phoebe is doing excellently. Whether you want him to know that you were here is up to you."

"Oh, I don't think I'm going to mention that."

Phoebe had a drawn smile for him, weak but knowing. "Coward."

"That's a fact." He left the room.

Chapter Thirty-two

According to Ben's pocket watch, Winnie Frost arrived at six minutes after three in the morning, making her officially a Friday's child, good and giving. Remington was able to see his wife as soon as she delivered the afterbirth and Ridley had mother and daughter spit-shined and polished, all of it done to Phoebe's exacting directions.

Ridley left the parents and the new arrival on their own and carried out a pail with the placenta and an armload of soiled linens. Ben pulled out the washtub and showed her where she could dispose of the afterbirth. When she returned to the house after taking the opportunity to finally relieve her bladder, Ben was pouring a bucket of cold water into the tub. It looked to Ridley as if he had already made several trips from the sink pump to the tub.

"Do you have a washboard?" she asked.

"Of course. In the pantry. The soap's in there as well."

She retrieved both. She was preparing to kneel at the tub when he stopped her with a look.

"Sit down," he said. "In a chair, not on the floor. I can do this." At her raised eyebrows, he said, "Did you think I took my laundry to the hotel for my mother to do?"

"Not exactly."

Ben dumped soap flakes into the water and swished them around. "What do mean, not exactly?"

"I thought she came over here and picked up your laundry." Ridley threw up her hands, laughing, when Ben sprinkled her with soapy water. "I apologize."

"Good. People who live in glass houses . . ."

"What do you mean?"

"You have a housekeeper."

"Oh. And you have a good point."

Ben started to scrub. Ridley covered her mouth to hide a yawn. "You could leave now," he said. "Get some sleep."

"Not just yet. I'd like to look in on Phoebe and Winnie one more time."

"They really named her that?"

"Mm-hmm. Your niece is Ophelia Winchester Frost."

"I'm going to call her Ophelia."

Ridley chuckled. "Good luck. I'm not sure that she'll ever answer to the name. At least at the ranch."

"Why Ophelia? Do you know?"

"One of Fiona's favorite roles, according to Phoebe. That's when I realized that Fiona Frost was formerly Fiona Apple, the toast of the New York stage. I saw her perform once when I was young. Father took us all to the city. He had a speaking engagement at one of the university hospitals and we had a holiday." She smiled a little crookedly. "It's a good memory."

Ben glanced up at her in time to see that crooked smile before it faded.

"What is it?" she asked, self-consciously raising her fingers to her lips.

"Hmm?"

"You're staring at my mouth."

"It's a lovely mouth." When that lovely mouth pursed disapprovingly, Ben merely grinned. "Still lovely."

Ridley leaned over and flicked water at him. "Please don't retaliate," she said when he sat up. "I don't have the energy for a full-out water battle."

"You are fortunate. Neither do I." Ben returned to scrubbing. "Maybe you should check on Phoebe and little Feely now. You're going to fall asleep in that chair."

Ridley didn't stir. "Feely? That's your idea of a proper nickname?"

He shrugged. "I'm trying it out."

"Try harder."

"Fifi?"

Ridley ignored that. "Where was Ellie this evening?"

"We're talking about that now?"

"I'd like to, yes. I noticed that she didn't come out to the dining room while we were there. I found that odd. She makes a point to stop by my table when I'm there, whether or not I'm with you."

"She has responsibilities outside of the dining room. She was probably busy doing other things."

Ridley's raised eyebrow was lost on Ben. He didn't look up. She also noticed he was scrubbing just that much harder. "Earlier tonight I asked Phoebe if she might like to have another woman attending her in addition to me."

"Another woman?" Ben posed the question with a certain amount of cynicism. "Or did you specifically ask her about Ellie?"

"Ellie."

"Then you should have said that right off."

"I've upset you."

Ben stopped scrubbing. He sat back on his heels; his hands folded over the lip of the tub, gripping it. He was quiet and he did not look up. Finally, "Besides declining your suggestion, what did Phoebe say?"

"I thought she was candid. She told me that Ellie was unlikely to agree, and it would be unfair to put her in that position. She also said Ellie's presence would be a problem for Fiona."

"That's all?"

"Yes."

Ben reached for the towel he had dropped in the water, lifted it, and began to wring it out. "It sounds as if Phoebe was straightforward. So what is it that you want to know?"

"The why of it all. Phoebe showed me the forest and none of the trees. Why would Ellie refuse? Why would it upset Fiona if she didn't?"

When Ben finished wringing out the towel, he tossed it on the table and chose another. "Did you ask her?"

"Yes. She said I should speak to you."

He sighed deeply and started scrubbing again. "Of course she did. You know my mother worked at Twin Star for better than twenty-five years."

"Yes. She told me."

"And that she came there when Mary, Thaddeus's first wife, was confined to her bed during her pregnancy with Remington's sister?"

"I didn't know that. That's the sister who died?"

"Mm-hmm, Mary died soon after she gave birth. Remington was five, I think, or thereabouts. Ellie was there for the grieving and the comforting. She stayed on. She was more than a house-keeper, less than a wife. In effect, she raised Remington. I was born at Twin Star. Remington was six then. Thaddeus raised me right beside his son. I idolized Remington, followed him around, pestered him. We fought, scrapped in the yard, and I wouldn't let anyone say a word against him even if they were bigger, older, or stronger. He looked out for me." Ben smiled a shade wistfully. "No question that he had an easier time of it. In every way that mattered to us, we were brothers."

Ridley winced in sympathy when Ben scraped his knuckles against the washboard. She waited patiently while he shook out his hand, afraid to pose a question or insert a comment that would make him think better of finishing his story.

"We are *still* brothers. Nothing that's ever been said made a lick of difference to us. Sure, we had to sort out some things, but there was never any doubt that we'd see eye to eye in the end. It didn't even take very long. No scrapping, no shoot-out. We're not Cain and Abel. Hell, we're not Jacob and Esau."

Ben finished scrubbing. This time he passed the towel to Ridley to wring. "If you're going to sit there, I guess it wouldn't bother me much if you helped."

She took the towel and twisted it over the washtub while he went to work again.

"There've always been whispers about me being Thaddeus's bastard. I didn't like hearing that much because of what it said about my mother. I wasn't aware of it when I was a kid. I got wind of it when Remington went east to college and was no longer around to beat the snot out of someone who said it. My response to the comments was different. I didn't do anything. I figured fighting was the surest way to keep the rumor in everyone's mind. I didn't ignore it exactly; I shrugged it off. There were lots of things that'd get my fists up, but not that. Besides, Ellie talked about my daddy as I was growing up, and it didn't matter that I never knew him. I had a picture of him in my mind. Why would I believe what some thin-skinned, thick-witted kid said to me when my mother told me different?"

Indeed, Ridley thought. *Why would anyone?*

Ben went on. "What I didn't understand, what no man at the ranch understood, but what Fiona figured out about ten seconds after being introduced to Ellie, was that my mother was in love with Thaddeus Frost and had been for a very long time." He looked up at Ridley. "You're not surprised."

She shook her head.

"Damn, why aren't women surprised?"

Ridley was wise enough not to try to answer what was essentially a rhetorical question. She tossed the towel she'd finished in the pile and held out her hand for another.

He gave one to her. "Fiona wasn't correct in all her assumptions, but she had the gist of it, and her being at the ranch, being Thaddeus's New York actress wife, raised about as much stink as sheep huddled in a rainstorm. Ellie did some things that caused their own kind of stink. Thaddeus had to make a decision, choose between his wife and the other woman who loved him. You know what he decided. Ellie's here. Fiona's at Twin Star."

Ridley said, "Did you leave with her?"

"No. I stayed back for a while. Didn't really think about going at first. I loved the ranch. I still do, I guess, but I'm also glad to be here. I have property in my name at Twin Star. Thaddeus settled a big parcel on me, same as Remington, and I could go there, build a homestead, but I'm not ready. Remington and Phoebe made a place for themselves, and it's good. I'm not sure it suits me any longer. Lately when I've been contemplating on it, it's occurred to me that the land might be something I could pass on to a son or a daughter."

"That's a lot of contemplation," she said quietly.

"Yeah, I guess so." He bundled a soiled sheet and pushed it under the water. "That can soak."

Ridley looked at the pile of wet linens on the table and the empty space beside Ben. "That's the last of it."

He nodded and rose to his feet, brushed himself off, and rolled his shirtsleeves back into place. "I'll hang this on the line in the morning."

Ridley shook her head. "Mrs. Rushton and I will do it." She recognized the breadth of Ben's fatigue when he didn't argue.

"I'm going to make some coffee before I head back to the jail," he said. "You want some?"

"No, but thank you."

He nodded once and went about filling the kettle and measuring the coffee. He stood at the stove, his hip against the oven door, arms folded across his chest. For a long time, he just stared at the floor. When his head finally came up, his clear blue eyes settled on Ridley. "So, are you going to ask?"

She didn't pretend she didn't know what he was talking about. "You said that in every way that matters to you and Remington, you're brothers. That resolves it in my mind. Whether or not you and Remington have the same father is a detail, one you can share with me or not as you like, but I don't have a need to know."

Ben said nothing, went back to staring at the floor. Finally, at the end of a long sigh, he told her, "Truth is, no one knows. There's no certainty here. Ellie *was* married to the man she claimed was my father. He may well have been because he came around trying to reconcile with her when she was living at Twin Star. Thaddeus was so deep in grief then that he doesn't remember the visit, but he's admitted that he had relations with my mother around that time." He looked sideways at Ridley. "There you have it."

Ridley remained pensive. "I imagine Ellie wants to believe Thaddeus fathered you."

"Mm-hmm. Her husband drank too much, came and went in her life, provided financial support when he remembered he was married, and died before she told him he was a father. That's the way she tells it now. Hard to know if she's fabricated a new history for herself or if that's how it really was. Thaddeus never claimed to be my father, but sometimes he called me son in that friendly, affectionate way of his. I was family. Still am, though there's some awkwardness now. Most of that rests with me. There's a share that's Fiona's. She thinks of Ellie when she looks at me, but I don't attach any blame to her for that. It'd be hard for anyone to do otherwise, and Fiona, well, she's not exactly the forgive-and-forget sort."

"So you stay away," said Ridley.

"Uh-huh. Thaddeus always looks for me at the office when he's in town. That's comfortable for both of us. In the last few years, he's started to ask after my mother. He hasn't been in the Butterworth since she took a job there. Neither has Fiona."

"What would your mother do if they showed up?"

"What she did when we were there. Make herself scarce."

"What does Thaddeus think about you being sheriff? Has he told you?"

"He's never had a problem saying that I make him proud." Ben pushed away from the stove when the water boiled. Once his coffee was made, he sat at the table. "He also never had a problem kicking my ass when he thought I needed it—that's in the figurative sense. Thaddeus never laid a hand on Remington, or me, but there sure were times when that would have been the easier punishment." When Ridley regarded him curiously, he explained, "A thrashing hurts, but then it's done. We all took turns with chores like chopping and mucking stalls except when Thaddeus's idea of a good lesson was to take everyone else's name off the rotation except yours. What I learned is that if you chop wood for a week, you can hardly lift the shovel to muck the stalls, and if you have to weed the garden for a month, then your back's so stiff you can't keep your seat on a horse. He was diabolical."

Ridley smiled. "I had to stand with my nose in a corner, sometimes for hours."

"I take it back," said Ben. "Nothing I had to do was as hard as that."

"I've never mucked a stall in my life." She said this in the manner of a confession.

He laughed. "I can take you down to Hank's livery. Let you get a feel for it."

Ridley's features sobered. There could be no mistaking her sincerity. "Take me to Twin Star instead."

Chapter Thirty-three

"How are you boys doing?" Ben asked when he checked on the Gordon brothers. It wasn't dawn yet and there was probably no good excuse for waking them up, but he didn't like thinking about Ridley's request, so this suited his mood. Besides, he deserved to get a little of his own back after these two troublemakers disrupted the peace and dignity of his town.

Ben watched Michael Gordon turn over on his cot and huddle under the blankets. It did not appear the man woke, but there was enough movement to assure Ben the man was still alive. Tom Gordon opened one eye, stared at Ben, and then cursed him roundly.

That was more or less the reaction that Ben was looking for. Whistling softly to himself, he returned to his office and made himself as comfortable as he could in his chair by leaning back and propping his feet on an open drawer. He closed his eyes. His experience rounding up cattle on the range, spending nights in the open if it was clear, or under the chuck wagon if it wasn't, usually served him pretty well. He was accustomed to being able to fall asleep easily and wake just as quickly when something stirred.

The sleeping part wasn't happening now, and every crackling ember in the stove kept him alert. He understood the problem was that his mind was too damn busy for sleep, and that it was Dr. E. Ridley Woodhouse's fault.

Her voice still echoed faintly in his mind. *Take me to Twin Star instead.* She had put it to him sincerely. She understood the gravity of what she was saying. Nothing about her expression changed while she waited for his reply, and he didn't answer immediately, although he knew what the answer would be.

That's why it surprised him when he said, *We'll see.* He was sure he'd meant to say no. He'd left the door open on the subject when he'd meant to close it. Hard. Ben rubbed the back of his neck. How the hell had she made him do that?

He didn't believe for a moment that she was satisfied with his answer, but when she had time to consider it, she'd realize the enormity of what she had wrested from him. He hadn't given her time to think about it. To avoid any chance of further discussion, he'd swept his coffee cup off the table, dumped the contents in the sink, and asked her rather curtly to make his good-byes to Remington and Phoebe. She didn't follow him to the door; it only felt as if she were dogging his footsteps.

Maybe it would have been better if she had. Now she was dogging his thoughts.

"Hey, Sheriff!"

Ben sat up, dropped his boots to the floor. He consulted his pocket watch. Almost an hour had passed since he sat down. He didn't know when he had fallen asleep, only that he had, and now that he realized it, he was not happy about being awakened.

"What is it?" he called back.

"My brother. Come see for yourself. Hurry. Somethin' ain't right."

Ben responded to the thread of panic in Tom Gordon's voice. He rose and worked out the kinks in his bones as he walked back to the cells. Tom was standing at the bars that separated his cell from his brother's, all of his weight on his uninjured leg. Michael's cot was in the middle of his cell, well outside of Tom's reach. That didn't stop Tom from trying to get at him. He had twisted one of his blankets so he could put it between the bars and snap it in his brother's direction. As Ben watched, the tip of the blanket flicked the edge of Michael's cot.

"Okay," said Ben. "Stop that." He waited for Tom to pull back the blanket and then indicated Tom's cot. "Toss it over there." Tom threw it behind him without looking. Most of it ended up draped over the side of his cot. "What do think I can do for him?"

"Hell, I don't know. Not really. His breathing's out of rhythm. Short breaths. Long breaths. Rasps when he takes in air. I've been sleeping alongside him for a long time, so I know when he's not right."

Just then, Michael Gordon's lungs seemed to explode with another coughing spell. It had the rat-a-tat speed and power of a Gatling gun. Gordon's shoulders bounced and he drew his knees toward his chest, but he didn't throw off the blankets or make an effort to get up. When his coughing subsided, he was as still as stone. His brother said his name several times. It had no effect.

"Maybe you could bring that doctor here," said Tom. "Or give him some of that medicine she spooned down his throat earlier. That helped him. At least he wasn't coughing his fool head off for a while."

Ridley had left the codeine elixir in the event Michael Gordon's coughing returned, but Ben did not tell Tom. He had enough experience under the former sheriff's watchful eye to tread cautiously. It wasn't out of the question that the brothers were carrying out the first stage of an escape plan.

"I'm not going after the doctor," he said. "She's already put in plenty of time here with the pair of you." While he was speaking, he walked around the corner to the supply closet and chose the broom with the longest handle.

"What are you going to do with that?" Tom asked. He took a step in Ben's direction, but as soon as he put some weight on his injured leg, his face contorted with pain. He stayed where he was.

Ben didn't answer. He'd observed Tom's effort to walk toward him and considered that the man was overplaying his hand. If he was hurting half as much as his expression seemed to indicate, then it had been a heroic gesture to leave his bed. Ben turned the broom so he was holding the working end of it. He inserted the broomstick through the bars, slipped it under the blankets at the foot of the cot, and used it to maneuver the blankets out of the way. Every part that the prisoner wasn't clutching to his chest remained where it was; the rest fell over the side of the cot.

Ben didn't care about what Michael Gordon was holding. He wanted a good look at his feet. When Ben saw the man wasn't wearing his boots, he turned his gaze on the brother. "Where are they?"

"Under his bed."

Ben dropped to his haunches and saw the pair was indeed under the cot. Perhaps the brothers were not preparing a quick getaway after all. He stood and poked Michael hard in the center of his arch. The prisoner's leg recoiled. Ben did the same to the other foot. This time he hit a ticklish spot. He knew that because Michael Gordon began to squirm and tried to kick the broomstick out of the way, but it was the short bark of laughter that was the most telling.

The laughter didn't last. It couldn't. Another spasm of coughing cut it off. Ben withdrew the broom and set it against the wall. He didn't try to talk until there was quiet. He addressed Tom Gordon, not Michael.

"So what was your plan? Get me inside your brother's cell because I'd think he was too weak to be a threat? Maybe he'd knock me out, take my gun, let you out. Where did you imagine you'd be going? Your horses are boarded at the livery, and Hank Ketchum would shoot you as soon as look at you if you tried to take them away. He's probably already up, looking after his place, and if he's not, he sleeps with his shotgun."

Tom Gordon's confession was a careless shrug. He limped back to his cot and sat down.

Ben watched his progress across the cell. "Looks like your leg is already on the mend."

Michael Gordon had pushed himself into a sitting position. His shadowed, sunken eyes cast a sardonic sideways look at Ben. When he spoke, his voice was little more than a rough whisper. "Think you're pretty damn smart, don't you?"

"I don't think much about it. If I can get my left foot in my left boot, I figure the other one's for my right foot. You decide if that makes me pretty damn smart." He glanced at Michael's toes still twitching inside his heavy woolen socks. "I notice you're not wearing your boots."

"Shut up," Michael said.

Ben went on as if there had been no interruption. "So why aren't you wearing them? Did the left foot in the left boot stump you?"

"Leave him be," said Tom Gordon.

"All right," Ben said. He leaned back against the wall beside the broom and waited.

Tom Gordon spoke wearily. "Truth is, that deputy of yours helped him out of his boots when the doc was treating him. Doc said to make him comfortable and that's what the boy did."

"Well, there you go. I thought he'd removed them to maybe persuade me he wasn't trying to bolt. Guess I had it more complicated in my mind than it needed to be."

"Guess you did," said Tom.

Michael Gordon reached under his cot, yanked out a boot, and pitched it hard at Ben. It bounced harmlessly off the bars and thumped to the floor.

"Feel better?" asked Ben.

"Go to hell." He fumbled for the second boot, couldn't quite grasp it, and in frustration he leapt from the cot and charged the cell door. "Go to hell!" He managed to spit out the words before a racking cough dropped him to his knees. His hands curled around the bars; he pressed his perspiring forehead against them.

Ben stared down at the top of the man's head. "I can give you some of the doc's medicine if you still want it." When Michael Gordon nodded tiredly, Ben disappeared into the office to get it. He stopped short when he saw Remington lounging in his chair. "I didn't hear you come in."

"It sounded as if you were occupied so I thought I'd leave you alone and make myself at home." He extended an arm. He held a medicine bottle between his thumb and forefinger. "I think this is what you're looking for."

"It is." Ben took the bottle, measured out two teaspoons into an empty tin cup. "I'll be right back."

Ben returned to the cells and pushed the tin cup through the bars several feet away from where Michael was on his knees. "There's a dose in there that should help you rest for a few more hours. Take it or don't. It's up to you." He looked over at Tom. "Don't call me back here again. I won't come until your breakfast's arrived. You understand?" He waited until he had affirmative nods from both of them before he rejoined Remington.

"You can't have forgotten your wife gave birth a couple of hours ago," he said, dropping into one of the visitor chairs. He rubbed the back of his neck. "So naturally I'm puzzled as to what you're doing here. Does Phoebe know you're gone?"

"She kicked me out. Said I was staring at her."

"Were you?"

"I prefer to think I was attentive."

"Uh-huh. Probably with a chair pulled right up to her bedside. Hovering like a hummingbird."

Remington puffed out his chest. "More like a papa eagle."

"Yeah, because you have the beak for it." Ben grinned because Remington was already self-consciously touching the bridge of his nose. It struck him how childhood taunts could still niggle after so many years. It made him think of Ridley's mother's cruelties, and then it made him think of Ridley. "Did the doctor finally go home?"

"She did. Stayed awhile to look in on Phoebe and the baby. Now *there's* someone who hovers like a hummingbird. We were lucky to have her tonight."

"This afternoon, too."

Remington agreed. He leaned back and looked at Ben down the length of his nose. "So . . . you want to tell me what's going on with you and the doctor?"

"No."

"Saw you kissing her. Didn't see her pushing you away."

"Answer's still no."

"Thought there was something between the two of you at dinner. Phoebe had the same opinion, but she noticed it in the bank first."

"Not talking about it," said Ben.

"Well, that won't stop me from speculating, and you can be sure it won't stop my wife. Last few years she's just been itching to put you with some gal."

"Thanks for the warning, and Dr. E. Ridley Woodhouse is not some gal."

Remington's dark eyebrows puckered over equally dark eyes. "What's the E stand for?"

"Exactly-none-of-your-affair."

"What?"

Ben held up his hands, palms out. "That's what she told me when I asked her."

Remington looked past Ben's shoulder to a point beyond it as he thought back. "Right," he drawled. "You asked Phoebe and me if we ever considered names for Winnie that begin with the letter E. Is this what that was about?"

Ben shrugged.

"Hmm. Interesting."

"It's not," said Ben. "Not really."

"Do you think it might be Eustachia? That'd be a name I wouldn't want on the tip of anyone's tongue. Or what about Edda? Elvira? Eos, the goddess of dawn? Eris, goddess of strife and discord?"

"Now you're just showing off."

"Humor me. I hardly ever get to bring up Eos and Eris at the ranch, and I spent a lot of time in college learning the Greeks."

Ben contemplated throwing something at his brother, but he would have to reach for the paperweight and he was too tired to make the effort. "Leave it," he said instead, but in his mind he was going to add every one of those names to his list. "Have you had any sleep at all?"

"Dozed off for bit. You?"

"The same."

"Oddest thing," said Remington. "I woke up thinking about Lily Salt."

"Huh?"

"I was thinking about her situation, what you told me earlier. I have an idea of something that might help. Wanted to lay it out for you, see what you think."

Ben thought that whatever Remington had in mind was infinitely preferable to further probes about Ridley. "I'm listening."

Remington dropped his chair forward and sat up. "I have work for Jeremiah. Real work. Not something made up for this. I didn't think I'd have time to talk to him about it, but with our departure being delayed, I realized I could have that opportunity tomorrow—I suppose that's today now. Morning. Afternoon. Whatever works better for you and the doctor. I can keep him occupied for at least an hour while the two of you visit Lily. The Salts still live close to the forge, don't they?"

"They do. We'd have to circle around and enter from the back. Hard for him to miss us if we went in the front. You sure you can keep him busy?"

"I wouldn't have suggested otherwise. And if there's a lull in the conversation, I can bring out the Greeks."

"Yeah, that will interest him."

Remington waved Ben's wry observation aside. "Phoebe got it in her head, oh, maybe a month ago, that she wants a fancy weather vane on the roof of the house. She drew some pictures. I don't have them with me, but I imagine she could re-create them. Probably has four new ideas by now. Everything she showed me is a complicated whirligig. Not sure any of them will spin in the wind."

"You didn't tell her that, did you?"

Remington regarded his brother as if he'd lost his mind. "Hell, no. You know as well as I do that if I so much as hinted it was going to be a bust, and it turned out that the thing *did* work, well, she'd be unbearably smug."

"She has a great smug smile."

"She does, doesn't she? I don't plan on telling her that either. She might turn mean."

Ben chuckled briefly and then sobered. "Afternoon would be better. That'd give Phoebe time to make the drawings. Neither one of us has the talent for it. Might as well give Jeremiah something to work with. That will keep him occupied."

"We're going to do this? Will the doc agree?"

"We are and she will."

"Are you courting Eulalie?" asked Remington. "Or just being neighborly?"

"Still not talking about it."

"Hmm. So what do you think about Eleanor? Like your mother."

Ben's response was good-natured, but firm. "Shut up, Remington."

Chapter Thirty-four

Hitch arrived with breakfast from the Butterworth for the prisoners, and Ben was finally able to go home and get some real sleep. He appropriated the bed where Colt had spent the night and dropped off immediately. When he woke around noon, he discovered sticky dabs of oatmeal in his hair and went in search of his nephew. Colt heroically chose being tickled breathless over helping Ben wash his hair.

Ridley walked into Ben's kitchen just as Colt was panting for air even as he was asking for more of the same. She watched Ben pick up his nephew and toss him over a shoulder and carry him away. A few moments later she heard a thump as Ben tossed the boy like so much baggage on the sofa in the front room. She also heard Remington tell his son—and possibly Ben—that that was enough. Ben returned to the kitchen without Colt and stopped dead only a few steps in.

"When did you get here?" he asked.

"Just as you were carting your nephew out of the room. I want to look in on Phoebe." Her eyes narrowed as she looked at him more keenly. "What do you have in your hair?"

"Oatmeal."

"Ah."

"The evidence suggests that Colt crawled into bed with me after breakfast. It also suggests that Remington was lax in cleaning up his son and keeping an eye on him." He went to the sink and bent over it, picking out small clumps of oatmeal and flicking them away. "Have you and Remington spoken?"

"Yes. When I came over to look in on Phoebe and Winnie. Both doing well, by the way."

"I figured they were because Remington's recovered his wits."

"Has he? He's been calling me Eustachia. Sometimes Eris. That's the Greek goddess of strife and discord."

Ben ran his fingers through his hair several times to be certain he'd removed all the oatmeal before he turned and put his back to the sink. "Of course you would know that. Did you tell Remington?"

"I did. He seemed unusually pleased."

"I bet. I guess it means that studying the Greeks was not a complete waste of his time." His features shifted suddenly as he became suspicious. "It's not Eris, is it? Your name, I mean."

"No, Ben, it's not Eris. It's not Eustachia either. Is puzzling out my Christian name a competition now?"

"Might be," he muttered, looking away.

Amused, Ridley said, "Phoebe said the two of you are boys when you're together."

"She's probably not wrong," said Ben.

"Which is a rather backhanded way of saying that she's right. It must pain you to say so."

"She gets smug."

Ridley laughed. "I won't mention it to her, then. Now, when are we doing this? Martha is going to come over when we leave to keep an eye on Colt. He's too rambunctious for Phoebe to manage on her own."

Ben nodded. He knuckled his jaw. "Let me shave, get cleaned up. I won't be long. You're all right with this?"

"I am. Your brother said you knew I would be."

"My brother has a big mouth."

Ridley heard him grumbling all the way to the front room, where he stopped long enough to confront Remington, and then continued grumbling as he climbed the stairs. She followed at a discreet distance to check on Phoebe, and she was still smiling to herself when she returned home and informed the housekeeper to be ready to leave within the hour.

Armed with Phoebe's drawings, Remington took the direct route to Jeremiah's forge while Ben and Ridley walked the alley behind the shops until the Salt home was in sight. They took a side street, another alley, and came to the house from the rear. It wasn't until they stood on the back stoop that Ben realized there was going to be an argument.

"You can't go in with me," said Ridley. She had placed a hand on the door, barring his entrance. "You know that Lizzie and Ham will be inside, and unless they're napping, there's almost no chance that they won't say something about the visit. Today or tomorrow, it will come out soon enough, and how does it make sense for both of us to be in Jeremiah's sights?"

"Ridley," he said patiently. "No. I don't like it. This isn't what I had in mind."

"You can't examine her."

"I can distract the children and keep them away while you speak to Lily. Otherwise they'll hang on every word and repeat some version of it to their father." He paused when he saw she was wavering. He let silence fill the space between them.

"Darn it, Ben."

He was careful not to smile. "Thank you, Euphrosyne."

Ridley stared at him. "She was one of the three sisters. The Roman Graces."

"Mm, yep."

"How do you—"

"Know?" he asked, finishing her question. "I am choosing not to be insulted. I may have passed on college when Thaddeus offered me the chance to go, but I can read just as well as Remington. It's never been a problem to filch a book now and again. So, did I hit the nail this time?"

"Euphrosyne? Not even close." She lowered her arm, opened the door, and called out quietly. "Lily? It's Dr. Woodhouse. May I come in?"

It was Ham who came barreling toward her. When he got close and saw the sheriff, he leapt, arms outstretched in anticipation of being lifted off his feet. He was not disappointed.

"Where's your mama?" asked Ben.

Ham pointed up.

"In bed?" asked Ridley. When Ham nodded, she asked about Lizzie.

Ham pointed upstairs again.

Ridley looked askance at Ben. "I'll go up and escort Lizzie

to the stairs. You get her from there." She hurried off, medical bag firmly in hand.

The door to Lily's bedroom was ajar. Ridley knocked and pushed it open in the same motion. It was empty. She took the diagonal across the narrow hallway; that room was also empty. She found Lily and Lizzie behind the last door she tried. Lizzie was bedfast. Lily sat next to her daughter and held a washcloth to her forehead. She looked up when Ridley entered, her features flat with weariness.

"You shouldn't be here," she said.

"I beg to differ. Mary Cherry expressed concern for you, but perhaps I'm here for the wrong patient."

"Doesn't matter. My husband doesn't want you here, doesn't trust you. He wouldn't let me send Clay for you when Lizzie took a turn."

Ridley approached the bed at the other side, parting a pair of curtains at a window as she passed. The light put Lizzie's blotchy face in stark relief. "You know what this is?" she asked Lily.

"Measles, ain't it?"

Ridley nodded. She removed her coat and laid it at the foot of the bed. "How long ago did she have the first symptoms? Runny nose. Cough. She might have complained of feeling warm or you might have noticed redness around her eyes."

"Guess it's been five days now. The rash appeared this morning."

"Your other children? Ham looks right as rain."

"There was an outbreak when Hannah was about Lizzie's age. She and Clay took to it then. Seems like Ham is never sick." ·

"When was Lizzie out of the house?"

"Jeremiah took her and the others to church a week ago Sunday."

Ridley ticked the days off on her fingers. The incubation period for measles was one to two weeks, making the church visit the likely point of contact with the disease. Ridley opened her medical bag and took out a thermometer. She shook it out, took the reading, and then turned back Lizzie's covers. "I'm going to take her temperature under her arm. This won't hurt her."

Lily looked at the instrument suspiciously. "That's not where Doc put it."

"Probably not, but this will work for our purposes." She slipped one end of the thermometer under Lizzie's shift and then inserted it in the crease of her armpit. Ridley wore a small watch on a fob pinned to her blouse and consulted it to mark the time. "Five minutes," she told Lily. "May I look at her chest?"

Lily nodded and rolled back the covers to Lizzie's waist. The little girl's eyes remained closed, but she found her mother's hand and held it.

The telltale rash covered Lizzie's chest and belly. Ridley gently turned her on her side. The raised rash seemed to have spilled out of her scalp and spread across her back, equally distributing itself on both sides of her spine. "You know you have to keep her here until it's run its course."

"Yes."

"Ham, too, just in case he shows symptoms later. What about you, Lily? Have you had the measles?"

"Yes."

"Your husband?"

"I don't know."

Both women turned their attention to the doorway as Ben appeared. Ham was hanging upside down, supported behind his knees by Ben's forearm. "Monkey's here," said Ben. "Where's the rest of the circus?" His grin faded when he saw the somber expressions that greeted him. His gaze settled on Lizzie. "What's happened?" he asked Ridley.

"Measles. I had them young. You?"

"Have to ask Ellie. I don't remember."

Ridley used her fingers to wave him away. "Go. You don't want this, and I don't want to treat you. Adults feel worse than children, or at least they complain more." She would have said more, but she was already speaking to the air. She could hear Ben bouncing Ham down the stairs.

Lily said, "He's a good man. Always was."

Ridley murmured something noncommittal. She helped Lily straighten Lizzie's shift and then the blankets. "How are you doing, Lily? Why do you think Mrs. Cherry had concerns?"

"You'd have to ask her. I surely couldn't say."

"Will you show me that you can raise your arms over your head?"

"Now why would I do that?"

"Because I asked?"

Lily sighed, hesitated, and then reluctantly complied. When she had the arms extended, she asked Ridley if she was satisfied.

"Almost. Wiggle your fingers." When Lily proved she could, Ridley gestured to her to lower her arms. "Will you stand now?"

This time Lily did not question Ridley. She moved closer to the edge of the bed and stood. She wobbled slightly. Her flat expression tightened.

"Do you always bite your lip when you get to your feet?"

Lily pushed out her lower lip.

"Too late, Lily. I know what I saw. Where does it hurt?" When Lily became animated enough to challenge her with a fierce stare, Ridley took it as proof that all the woman's life hadn't drained away. "You're not quite steady, are you? Listing a little to the left. Did you hurt your hip? Your knee?"

"I'm fine."

"I'm not sure why I asked. That's the only tune you know."

"It's not a tune. It's the truth." She eased herself back to the edge of the bed.

"Uh-huh. What about bruises? Contusions?"

"Go away. My husband could walk in here any time."

Ridley did not explain why that was unlikely to happen. "Ham's downstairs. Do you think he won't say something if we ask him? I'm not going to suggest you leave Jeremiah, and Ben's not going to take him in for what happened here—not without you swearing out a charge against him, but please let me see if there's something I can do for you." While Lily was mulling that over, Ridley removed the thermometer from Lizzie's underarm. She read it, and then walked over to the window to read it again in the sunlight. She shook it out, returned it to her bag.

"What is it?" asked Lily. "I know she's burning up."

"Would it mean something if I told you? Isn't knowing that she's fevered enough?" She didn't wait for Lily to reply. "I'll mix something up for her fever, but we could use a bucket of cold water and more cloths to bring her temperature down. I know where your linen cupboard is. I'll get the cloths. How about you fill that bucket and bring it here?"

Lily got to her feet for a second time and managed three steps before she stopped. "I can't," she said, her voice as taut as her ashen face. "You know I can't carry something that heavy."

"I needed to make sure you knew. Sit down. I'll get everything." Ridley removed a packet of salicylate powder from her bag and took it with her downstairs. She found Ben sitting at the kitchen table playing cards with Ham. They both had a short stack of ginger snaps in front of them. "Are you teaching him to play poker?"

"Sure, but not any version that a cardsharp would recognize. We're playing by Ham's rules." He saw the powder packet in her hand. "What do you need?"

"A glass of water for this and a bucket of colder water for Lizzie."

"I'll get it for you." He pointed a finger at Ham. "Don't eat my snaps. I'll know." Hoping it was safe to turn his back, he set about pumping water at the sink.

Ridley sat down opposite the boy. "Did your mother take a spill, Ham? Maybe on the icy path outside or while she was chasing you? I know you like to run."

He nodded. "I do like to run. No one can catch me."

"That's what I thought. What about your mother taking a tumble? Did you see that?"

He nodded again, this time with less enthusiasm than before. He pressed his lips together and his expression was guarded.

Seeing him, Ridley wanted to weep. He knew, just as she had at his age, that there were family stories that could not be shared. She reached across the table, took Ham's chubby hand in hers, and squeezed it. "It's all right," she said. "You don't have to say anything." He was still wary until she stole a cookie from Ben's pile and gave it to him.

"I saw that," said Ben. He put a glass of water in front of Ridley and went to get a bucket.

Ridley mixed the powder in the water, aware that Ham was watching her closely. "This is for your sister," she explained.

"You know she is feeling poorly. I'm going to help her. I want to help your mama, too." Although he nodded, the uncertainty returned to his eyes, and Ridley vowed she was done pressing him for answers. When Ben returned with a bucket that he filled from the outdoor pump, she thanked him and took it off his hands.

"I can carry that for you," he called after her.

"Stay away."

Ben looked down at Ham, whose wide grin occupied the lower half of his face. "Told you she was bossy." When the boy nodded sagely, Ben pulled out his chair, sat, and prepared himself to be roundly trounced.

Upstairs, Ridley delivered the glass to Lily and put the bucket beside the bed. "Make sure she drinks all of it. I'll get the towels." Lily was setting the empty glass aside by the time she returned. They worked together silently, soaking the towels in the cold water, wringing them out, and then tucking them around Lizzie's fevered body. When Ridley was satisfied they had done all they could for now, she moved to the straight-backed chair beside the window. One of its legs was slightly shorter than the others and it wobbled when she sat.

Lily said, "Jeremiah's been meaning to fix that. You probably know that good intentions don't get the work done."

Ridley nodded. "I spoke to Ham." She saw Lily stiffen. "Don't worry, he didn't say anything, but I have to wonder at the harm it does him to swallow all the things he has learned that he shouldn't say. Do you ever think of that, Lily? Does it concern you more that your children are witnesses to every sort of violence or that one of them will speak up about it? Have you considered that your silence, Ham's silence, telegraphs a message almost as clearly as if you'd been honest with me? I suggested to Ham that you might have fallen on a patch of ice or while you were chasing him. There are probably a dozen or more explanations for how you hurt yourself, and neither of you offered one. I understand your boy's unwillingness to talk, but your insistence that you're fine says something else to me. I think you want me to know the truth but cannot bear to hear yourself say it. I think you want me to come to it on my own."

Lily laid her hand against the crown of her daughter's head.

She sifted through the damp strands with gentle fingertips. "You should leave." She didn't look at Ridley when she said it; her gaze was focused on Lizzie's rosy face.

Ridley glanced out the window. She wished she could see the forge, but this bedroom's view was the backyard. A smile tugged at her lips when she saw the lopsided snowman the children had built to defend the equally lopsided battlements of their snow fort. The faint smile disappeared when she cast her eyes once again on the mother of those children.

"For lack of an explanation from you, I've arrived at one of my own," said Ridley. "I think you fell because you were pushed. You might have tripped over something as you were backing away or your fall could have been as dramatic as tumbling down the stairs. Regardless of what happened, it happened because of an outside force. You could have suggested an accident, Lily, but you didn't. I appreciate that you won't say a word against your husband, but there's no reason I shouldn't."

"Don't," said Lily. "You're wrong. Wrong about everything."

"Am I? What did you do this time? Butter his bread on the wrong side? I know you must have done something because it's never his fault."

Lily remained mutinously silent.

"Was he drinking?" Ridley did not expect an answer but she waited for one nonetheless. Finally she stood, crossed to the bed, and picked up her bag. "It's all right, Lily. I'm done here. Since I won't be able to return to check on Lizzie, you should carry on as you have. You'll know when her fever's broken. The medicine I gave her will help. If you need more, you can send Clay to the apothecary." Ridley told her what Clay should ask for. "You could also ask for white willow bark tea. Mrs. Mangold will make that. You would benefit from drinking it as well, but if Mr. Salt's conscience is not bothered by the sight of you limping around, then there's no point in easing your suffering, is there?"

Ridley was already in the hallway when she heard Lily ask for her. She did not hurry back; rather she stood where she was, ticking off fifteen full seconds before she retraced her steps. When she appeared in the doorway, she saw Lily's surprise.

"I thought you'd already gone."

"Maybe you wish I had." Ridley thought it was more likely that Lily didn't know what she wished for. "What is it?"

"I want you to see."

At first Ridley did not understand, but then Lily began lifting the hem of her dress, and when she uncovered her knees, Ridley saw the point of being asked to return. Lily's right knee was swollen half again the size of her left one. Ridley looked around for something that could be used to elevate Lily's leg. There was nothing suitable but she remembered seeing a footstool in the front room from her first visit. She went to the top of the stairs and called to Ben.

"You hollered?" he asked, leaning casually against the newel post.

"You know I don't holler."

Ben glanced down at Ham, who had suddenly appeared at his side. "Sounded to me like she hollered. What do you think?"

Ham cupped his hands around his mouth and called in the hogs. "Sooie! Sooo-whee."

"See?" Ben said, grinning. "All right. What can I do for you?"

"The footstool in the front room. Can you bring it here?"

"Of course. Ham, get the footstool for me." When the boy ran off, Ben raised his eyebrows, asking his question without giving voice to it.

Ridley lifted her skirt, pointed to her knee, and then used her hands to indicate the swollen size of Lily's. She pantomimed tumbling and saw him nod his understanding. When Ham returned with the stool, he carried it to her.

"Will you be much longer?"

"No, but I need a water bottle. Ham probably knows where one is. Find it and pack it with snow, then have Ham bring it here. You still can't come in the room." She took the footstool and waved him away.

Back in the room, Ridley carefully lifted Lily's foot by the heel and placed it on the stool. She examined the knee, feeling her way around the joint to locate the area where most of Lily's pain resided. Torn or twisted ligaments had created the swelling. There was also bruising on the kneecap, which had taken the brunt of her fall. Ham showed up with the water bottle and gave it to Ridley. He stayed long enough to observe her wrap a thin towel around it, place it across his mother's knee, and then he was gone.

Ridley stepped back when she was finished. "You should keep the bottle there until the snow inside it melts and apply another cold bottle every few hours. When you go downstairs, take the stool with you and elevate your leg as much as possible. Brew Mrs. Mangold's tea when you get it and drink it every few hours. Finally, do what you can to rest the leg."

Lily looked down at her knee. Her fingers fidgeted in her lap.

"What is it?" asked Ridley.

"Jeremiah doesn't like me sitting too long. He works so hard, on his feet all day long. It pains him to see me shirking my responsibilities."

Ridley was quiet for a long moment, and when that moment passed, she decided it was better if she said nothing at all. She settled Lily's dress in place, and then placed the back of her hand against Lizzie's cheek. "She's going to be fine," she told Lily. "The worst of it will be over soon. When the fever breaks, remove all the damp towels and change the bed sheets. You should have Hannah help you. I'm not sure why Ham hasn't come down with this because it's highly contagious, but if he should, do the same as we've done for Lizzie."

Lily nodded. "Jeremiah's not a bad man," she said quietly. "He loves us."

Ridley could not hold her tongue any longer. "Then he should not be so careless."

Ben stood as soon as Ridley entered the kitchen. "What is it?"

Ridley wondered what he saw in her face that prompted him to ask the question so quickly. Were her lips bleeding from all the words she'd bitten back? She regretted her parting shot to Lily, but she equally regretted not saying more.

"We can leave," she said, getting her coat. "Ham, you help your mother if she needs you. You know where to find your father, and Hannah and Clay will be home from school soon. All right?"

Ham nodded, but it was a glum response.

Ridley squeezed the boy's shoulder. "I know you're going to miss him," she said, glancing back at Ben. "He looks as if he's just as sad to go." She finished putting on her coat and took Ben's hand. "We should leave before you both start crying."

Ham giggled as Ben made a face only partially behind her back.

"I saw that," she said, and pulled him along. She dropped his hand as soon as they were out of the house.

"What happened in there?" Ben asked.

"What do you mean? Ham was—"

"I wasn't asking about Ham. There's nothing wrong with that boy that a little attention won't fix. And I wasn't asking about Lizzie. She's on her way to mending or we wouldn't be here now. So you tell me, who does that leave?"

"Can we talk about it later?"

He caught her arm and kept her from going on when he came to a halt. It bothered him some when she didn't pull away. That at least would have given him an indication of the strength of her anger. What he felt instead was her resignation. Her head was bent; her eyes were lowered. He had to stoop to catch her eye and what he saw were tears.

"Ah, Esmeralda." He put his arms around her. He heard her soft, watery laughter as she laid her cheek against his shoulder. "What can I do?"

"This is a good beginning," she whispered.

He held her in just that manner, nudging her hair with his chin.

"I should not have been cruel," she told him. "I think I was cruel." She swallowed a sob. "I *know* I was."

Ben said nothing. He didn't tell her it wasn't in her to be cruel when he believed everyone was capable of cruelty, whether intended or thoughtless. He didn't tell her it would be all right when he didn't know that to be true. Whatever had happened, it was up to her to make peace with it, to resolve it in her own mind.

"Did Lily throw you out?" he asked.

"I wish she had that much backbone." She raised her head, looked at him. "See? I can't seem to help myself. And Lily's inadequacies are only a reflection of my own. I know that, and still I make judgments."

This time when Ridley lowered her head to his shoulder, it

was to knock her forehead against it three times. Ben cupped the back of her head, kept it steady. "Next time you want to do that, find a wall," he whispered. He heard the low rumble of her laughter. That was all right, then.

He released her as soon as he felt her trying to step back. She swiped at her tears with one tail of her scarf, and he stuffed his handkerchief back in his pocket. "Home?" he asked, though he didn't know if he was referring to his house or hers. And when she nodded, he couldn't know that she was wondering the same thing.

Chapter Thirty-five

Because of the necessity of meeting up with Remington, there was no real question of where they would end up. Whether or not it was home remained unsettled. They were sitting at opposite ends of Ben's sofa when Remington walked in.

"You two look like bookends absent of all the books between you," he said. "Is that for my benefit? I saw the kiss. You'd think that would be water over the dam by now."

Ridley stared at him. Her lips parted, but she had no words.

Remington ignored his brother's pointed stare. He removed his outerwear and blithely started up the stairs. "You don't mind if I see Phoebe first, do you?"

"You probably think you're making an advance," Ben called after him. "But I know a retreat when I see one." He could hear his brother chuckling all the way to the top. Without moving from the sofa, he raised his voice so he could be heard in the kitchen. "Mrs. Rushton! Is Colt done helping you prepare the cookie dough?"

"Indeed he is," she called back. "I only need to clean him up."

"Is he sticky? Maybe with cookie dough between his fingers and on his face, some in his ears?"

"He is surely all of that."

"Perfect. Forget cleaning him up. Sounds as if you'd have to dump him in a trough anyway. Send him directly to his father."

"But—"

"Directly to his father," Ben repeated.

A moment later, Colt was galloping through the front room. He charged up the stairs as if he were a Rough Rider reimagining the Battle of San Juan Hill.

When he was gone, Ridley said, "That was evil."

Ben shrugged. "Some might even say cruel."

From upstairs there was a bellow that could have only been Remington in the sustained grip of a cookie dough hug. They shared an easy chuckle.

"I hope some of it gets in his hair," Ben said. "He had no business mentioning that kiss."

Ridley repositioned herself in the corner of the sofa so she could see him better. "Does he know there's been considerably more done than kissing?"

"Not because I said anything."

"Hmm. Would he expect you to do something about it if he did know?"

"What do you mean?"

"Ben," she said in mildly chiding accents.

"You're talking about marriage. Am I right?"

"You are."

Ben considered what she was asking before he spoke. "I figure Remington might have some expectations about that. He did with Phoebe."

"I see."

Ben shook his head. "You probably don't, not really. Those two, well, that's a whole other story."

"Do you ever think about marriage? It's a general question; I'm not referring specifically to marriage with me."

Ben said exactly what he was thinking. "Doesn't sound like a general question. Sounds like a personal one, whether or not you're imagining yourself as the woman at the other end of the proposal."

"You're right," she said, practical and matter-of-fact. "It is. Will you answer it anyway?"

"Haven't we discussed you surrendering the bone?"

"We have."

"Will you ever do it?"

"Probably not."

Ben's mouth twisted to one side. "Yeah, probably not. So here's the answer: Sure, I think about marriage. Doc and I used to talk about it. He didn't have to say much. Just being around him made me realize I didn't want to be a curmudgeon, at least not on my own. There's something about being married, growing old and cranky together, that puts balance in your life, gives it meaning."

"Uh-huh. Old and cranky. You do have an interesting way of looking at things." Ridley looked around. "Don't you have any decorative pillows, something I can throw at you?"

"See? There's that cranky part I was talking about." He cocked his head to one side, studying her. "Have you ever actually thrown something at someone?" Before she spoke, he put up a hand. "The soup bone doesn't count. You didn't throw it."

"No, I've never done it. I'm tempted quite a bit since I met you, but my mother immediately comes to mind and that's that. Even if you'd had a pillow handy, I probably would have just hugged it."

It was the answer he expected. A smile flitted briefly before he regarded her soberly and leaned a little in her direction. "Do you ever think about marriage?"

Ridley arched a wary eyebrow. "Not often."

"Huh. I always reckoned most unmarried women thought about it all the time."

"You know we're approaching a new century in a couple of years."

"I heard."

"You might want to consider crawling out from under that rock before it arrives."

"Don't you think that's a little unfair?"

"Maybe." Her shoulders stiffened a shade militantly. She felt it. Couldn't help it. "A little. If most unattached women think about marriage, it's because it's an expectation of their parents and our society *and* because so few women have opportunities to support themselves without a husband. It wasn't so long ago that female teachers were expected to give up their positions once they married. I'm not sure that it's still not happening. Laundresses. Charwomen. Prostitutes. Seamstresses. Those are traditional opportunities. Do you know that Jim Springer owns his butcher shop because Amanda's father wouldn't deed it to her? The woman who supported suffrage for women here in Colorado wasn't seen by her own father as fit to inherit his property."

Ben shrank back into his corner and put up his hands. "Are you certain you can't find anything to throw?"

Ridley stood, turned her back on him, and walked to the window. She crossed her arms in front of her and stared out. Mrs. Vandergrift, the Butterworth's exceptional cook, walked out the side entrance carrying a long list that she tucked into her reticule.

Ben lowered his hands. He stared at Ridley's stiff back, at her self-protective stance. "I'm sorry," he said. And when she made no reply, he said it again, louder this time.

Ridley did not acknowledge his apology. She continued to stare out the front window. Mrs. Vandergrift turned the corner and disappeared. The cook had only been a watery blur anyway.

"I always wanted to be a doctor." She spoke to her translucent reflection. "Always. One of my earliest memories is sitting on my father's knee, listening to his heart with his stethoscope. My sister, and I suppose many other girls, played with their dolls as their friends or as their children. My dolls were my first patients. They contracted a variety of illnesses, most of them suddenly when my parents were fighting or Mother was inconsolable in a bout of deep melancholia. If I couldn't heal them, I took them to my father. He always knew what to do."

Ben moved to the edge of the sofa, set his forearms on his knees, and listened. Out of the corner of his eye, he saw Remington coming down the stairs. It did not seem that Ridley had heard him. Ben waved him off, and without a word passing between them, his brother turned and quietly started back up.

"Is he gone?" she asked.

So she had heard him. "Yes."

"Thank you."

Ben took a breath, released it slowly. "Ridley, I am—"

"Not now. You can say anything you like later, but not just now. I want to finish."

Though he knew she couldn't see him, he nodded anyway.

"I'm aware that I had advantages not available to many other women, but my sister had those same advantages and chose another path. While I aspired to become a doctor, she aspired to become a doctor's wife. I don't think less of her for that. What I am trying to tell you is that it was her dream, not mine. I had a different future planned, and it did not include being someone's wife. So, no, I didn't often think about marriage. I was single-minded in the pursuit of my own happiness. I had to be. But it's occurred to me since coming here that perhaps I was also shortsighted. What I could not conceive of on that train ride or any time before has lately been tickling my imagination."

Ben did not respond immediately, waiting to hear if she had more to say. When she didn't speak, but remained turned to the window, he said, "How do feel about that?"

She shrugged.

"I don't know what that means. Are you indifferent? Unhappy? Have you no words?"

Ridley swiped at her eyes before she turned around to face him. Her back was not as stiff as it had been earlier; her arms were at her sides. "When have you known me not to have words?"

Ben was encouraged that the shape of her mouth hinted at a smile. "It happens. Not often, but it happens. The kiss that Remington mentioned earlier? It happened then."

It was true; the kiss had struck her dumb. She conceded the point with a slight nod.

"Ah." He threaded his fingers and regarded her candidly. "Are you going to tell me straight, Ridley? I figure I understand it's marriage that's been tickling your imagination, but you haven't said how you feel about it." He watched her expression turn pensive and wondered if she would speak at all or if she would tuck every one of her thoughts away.

"Uncomfortable," she said at last. "Or maybe it's simply that it doesn't make me feel easy. Did you ever wade into a lake or a river and the bottom is beneath your feet and then it isn't? It's like that. You know the bottom will fall away, you just don't know when, and the anticipation is exciting and frightening and you want it to be over but not really."

"I guess I know why you shrugged."

Her short laugh was rife with self-mockery. "I guess you do, but do you understand that what's been tickling my imagination isn't just marriage and the notion that I could be someone's wife?"

"It isn't?" He hadn't just swallowed hard, had he? Ben felt as if he should clear his throat or pull his collar away from his neck. He manfully resisted the urge.

Ridley shook her head. "No, it isn't. What's been tickling me is the realization that someone could be my husband. It's merely a shift in perspective, but it means there are possibilities I couldn't see before."

Ben considered that. His collar did not feel quite as tight. "A shift in perspective. Yes, I see how that could change things."

"So?" she asked.

"So?" he echoed.

"So you're going to marry me, aren't you?"

"Well, sure, but . . ." His voice trailed away.

"But . . ." she prompted.

"I reckoned I'd still be the one proposing." He shrugged a little helplessly when she gave him an eyeful. "Yeah, well, the new century isn't here yet and I like it under the rock."

Ridley sighed, but her smile was indulgent. "So much work to be done."

Ben stood and walked over. She stepped easily into his embrace. "That work you mentioned," he said. "You were talking about me, not the wedding."

"I was." She looked up at him, met his eyes. "That doesn't appear to trouble you."

"Hell, no. I'm relieved. Ellie will take care of the wedding. We only have to show up."

Chapter Thirty-six

Colt Frost slithered down the stairs on his belly, a descent that was a far cry from his galloping climb. "Uncle Ben," he said in a whisper suitable for the stage. "Uncle Ben!"

Ben took his time lifting his head. Ridley gave him no indication that she was eager to break the kiss. Her lips moved softly under his. The hum he felt against his mouth was the sound of pure pleasure. When Ben finally responded to his nephew, he didn't shift his attention from Ridley's face. He couldn't. She was glowing.

"What is it, Colt?"

"Pa wants to know if he can come down now. I'm a spy. You want me to tell him there's kissing?"

Ben was less amused than Ridley. He put a finger to her lips as she chuckled under her breath. "You can tell him to come down." He winced as Colt hollered up the stairs.

"Uncle Ben says you can come down, Pa. There was kissing, but now there ain't."

"Isn't," said Ben.

"Isn't," said Ridley.

"Isn't," said Remington from the top of the stairs.

Their correction had no effect. Colt slithered to the bottom and jumped to his feet. "Mrs. Rushton! That's cookies I smell, ain't it?" Then he was running at a full gallop toward the kitchen.

Remington was still shaking his head when he reached the front room. "My son's too young to appreciate our grammatical chorus."

Ben noticed there was no cookie dough in Remington's

hair. He would like to have seen some of that. "Phoebe and Winnie doing well?" he asked, stepping away from Ridley. He gestured to her to proceed to the sofa and then sat beside her.

"Both are doing very well. I moved the rocker from the bedroom where Colt was sleeping to your bedroom. Mother and daughter like it there."

"Good. I wish I'd thought of it."

Remington dropped into a chair. He looked from his brother to the doctor and raised an eyebrow. "Put things right, did you? I don't think I could slide a slip of paper between you now." When Ben looked at him sharply, he said, "I'm asking because Phoebe wants to know."

"Uh-huh."

Ridley pressed her elbow lightly into Ben's side. "You can put her mind at ease. Tell her that we did indeed put things right." She looked askance at Ben. "For now."

Remington put out a hand to ward off the response that his brother was about to make. "Save it for the battle worth fighting, Ben. Everything else is a waste of your breath." Now it was Ridley who gave him a look every bit as sharp as Ben's. "My advice is the same for you. Take it or don't, just keep in mind that I said it." He smiled amiably. "Can we talk about what happened when you were at the Salts'? What I have to tell you is that Phoebe is going to acquire a handsome weather vane for our roof and some kind of elaborate wind spinner for the garden. Jeremiah swears it will scare the crows away. Neither came cheap."

"I'll reimburse you," said Ben.

"Not necessary and not my point."

Ridley seized on a moment of silence to explain what she observed while she was with Lily Salt. She left nothing unsaid so that Ben was finally able to fill in the gaps in her earlier telling. When she was done, she sat back and awaited their reaction.

Remington said, "You had the measles, Ben. I remember because I had them at the same time. So did most of the men working at the ranch back then."

"That's what you have to say?"

Remington shrugged. "I thought it was important. If I

didn't know that you'd had them, I couldn't let you anywhere near Winnie. She probably would not survive measles and you would not survive knowing you carried them into the house."

Ben paled as the consequences were borne home to him. In an odd way he felt as if his brother had just saved his life. "Thank you, then," he said quietly. "It was important."

"So is what's happening to Lily. Can't you do anything, Ben? Maybe put the Gordon brothers together in one cell and give the other to Jeremiah."

"What law has he broken that his wife will support? She denies everything. You heard Ridley. She doesn't know how Lily was hurt. There is a great deal she can infer from their conversation, but that will not stand with the judge. You know Judge Miner as well as anyone, better than most. What I know is that he plays fast and loose at the card table and never at the bench. Am I wrong?"

"No."

"In the eyes of the law, this is a matter between a husband and a wife. It would be a difficult case for a lawyer to make on Lily's behalf even if she did swear out a complaint. Not every judge is inclined to find for the wife. Ridley tells me there's a new century on the way and I'm still living under a rock. You're a lawyer. Do I really have to explain to you that these laws are living under there with me?"

Remington shook his head. "No. I know that's how it is."

Ridley rubbed her temple where a headache was beginning to take form. "We can't protect her from Jeremiah, and we can't save her from herself. There's really nothing to be done. We can rail against it, but laws change after attitudes change. I don't think Lily has that much time. The new century won't be here fast enough for her."

Ridley rose. "If you will excuse me, I'd like to return home now. I'll ask Martha to stay here with Colt and help out however she can. I have notes to write. Perhaps a patient came by while I was gone and left a message on my slate. I should attend to that."

Ben was already on his feet. "I'll walk you home."

"It's only a few—" She stopped when she saw Remington arch an eyebrow at her. "Yes. That would be welcome." And the truth of it was, she meant it.

* * *

Mrs. Rushton climbed the stairs quietly and knocked lightly on Ridley's door before she entered. Her employer was lying on her side in the bed, mostly covered by a fan quilt in deep hues of blue and green and yellow. Ridley's stocking feet peeked out at the bottom. The housekeeper eased the quilt down over them.

"You're a dear for doing that," said Ridley.

Mrs. Rushton jumped away from the bed. "Oh, I surely didn't mean to wake you."

"You didn't. Dozing more than sleeping. What time is it?"

"Half past seven. Mr. Frost sent me home, gave me something for my trouble even though I told him it weren't no trouble, only my pleasure. You don't have to pay me for today. On account of what he settled on me, you don't have to pay me for the week."

"So he's generous, is Mr. Frost."

"To a fault. I was preparing to leave when the sheriff asked me to look in on you, which was also no bother since I planned to anyway. He said you looked as if you were sickening for something when he left you on your doorstep."

Ridley pushed herself upright and leaned back against the headboard. She rubbed her eyes and reached for her spectacles. When they were settled on the bridge of her nose, she said, "I had a headache. That's what he saw. It's gone now. I took a powder a little while ago and lay down."

"A little while ago? But you were home hours before that."

"Yes, but someone left a message on Mr. Winegarten's behalf that his gout was troubling him, so I went to the Songbird. While I was there, I took out a splinter that was festering in George Hotchkiss's thumb. Hank Ketchum dropped in and complained rather loudly that he wasn't hearing as well as he used to. I removed so much wax from his ears that I believe I understand what it means to muck out a stall." She nodded sympathetically when Mrs. Rushton wrinkled her nose. "Yes, I know. It was like that. Afterward, I walked down to the jail to see how the prisoners were faring. I made Tom Gordon show me his stitches, and gave his brother some medicine to ease his aching chest."

"Land sakes, Dr. Woodhouse, you keep going like this and you *will* be sickening for something. And you, barely recovered from the last bout of whatever it was that ailed you."

"On the contrary, it felt very good to be of use. Not being able to do anything is more wearying than seeing a dozen patients. And Mr. Winegarten offered me space at the back of the saloon where I could see patients. Can you imagine?"

"Mark my words, that man wants you at his beck and call. You'd be good for his business, and he knows it. Now, is there anything I can do for you before I leave? There's a quart of vegetable soup if you want to warm it. Turnips, carrots, celery, and some onion. It will put a pleasant heat in your belly. I used one of the soup bones and some lean beef to make the stock. Did you notice there are more packages on the back porch?"

"Yes. When I came in."

"Suddenly everyone's a cat laying a mouse at your feet."

"Mm. Perhaps we can think of a less stomach-churning image."

Mrs. Rushton produced an ironic lift in her right eyebrow. "So says the doctor who treated a gouty foot, cleaned a festering sore, and mucked out an ear canal."

"It's a fair point." Ridley offered a guilty, confessional smile. "It's just that I don't like mice."

The housekeeper's jaw went slack as she stared at her employer. After a moment, she shook her head and then turned to exit, muttering something about odd ducks. She was already outside the room when she called back. "Oh, and you can expect the sheriff to drop by." Then she left, grinning ear to ear, as Ridley peppered her with questions that she pretended not to hear.

Ben paused to tap snow off the toes of his boots when he walked in his office. He was more than a little comforted to see Hitch posting new wanted notices on the wall. He would not have been terribly surprised to find his deputy relieved of his gun, trussed like an old whore in a new corset, and the prisoners nowhere in sight. He tossed his hat on the desk and pushed his fingers through his hair before he unbuttoned his coat.

"Do you think you have enough wood in the stove?" he asked. "It's hotter than Hades in here."

"The boys complained about the cold. Not much heat gets back to the cells."

"Then open the door." Ben walked over and did just that. He stuck in his head, looked over the prisoners, and withdrew just as quickly. "I don't like you calling them boys, Hitch. You'll start to think of them as less threatening. It's not a good idea."

"All right. Except for the coughing spells, I hardly heard from them. Frankie Fuller carried down their lunch and dinner from the hotel. You're keeping that boy pretty busy with some paying chores."

"Figure it helps him some."

Hitch finished tacking up the last poster and stood back to admire his work. "Rearranged them. Thought it couldn't hurt to look at them in a new way from time to time."

Ben nodded. "That's the second time today someone's telling me that a new perspective changes everything."

"Huh?"

"Never mind." He picked up the pot on the stove. "How old is this coffee?"

"Made fresh about an hour ago."

Ben poured a cup and sat down, moved some papers around on his desktop. "Anyone come in today? Complaints? Concerns?"

"Mr. Washburn was here. Wanted to thank you again for what you did at the bank. He says you can expect a letter of commendation from the main branch in San Francisco. They'll probably send Doc Woodhouse a soup bone."

Ben gave him a reproving look.

"Sorry. It seemed funny right before I said it."

"Mm-hmm."

"Mr. Salt stopped by."

Ben's head snapped up. "What did he want?"

"Did you ask him to make you some shackles for transporting prisoners?"

"I did. That was a while back. I forgot all about it."

"I guess he did, too, though that surprised me some. Anyway, he heard about the attempted robbery and the prisoners and it came back to him. He wanted you to know that he'll have them ready the day after tomorrow. He said something about doing a special request for Mr. Frost."

"He is."

The wanted notices fluttered as Hitch dropped to the bench below them. "You know, Sheriff, you can mail order things like shackles and cuffs nowadays. I can get you a catalog."

"I'm satisfied with Jeremiah's work. I know what I'm getting."

"Lots of choices in the catalogs. Might be that there's something you could use that you ain't thought of. It can't hurt to look over what's available."

"So help me, Hitch, if you tell me I'm living under a rock, I will shoot you where you sit." He was satisfied when his deputy looked sufficiently alarmed. "I'm twenty-nine years old, not eighty-nine." Ben took a swallow of coffee and scalded his tongue. "Damn. You've got the stove so hot, this is boiling and burnt."

Hitch started to rise. "I'll make another pot."

Ben waved him back down. "Don't trouble yourself. I don't need it anyway." He pushed his mug to the side and shuffled more papers.

"At the risk of you threatening my life again, Sheriff, I feel duty bound to say you're a mite on edge tonight."

"Am I?" asked Ben, but he knew Hitch was right. Lily Salt's situation was like a raspberry seed stuck between his molars. He couldn't leave it alone and he couldn't get it out. He kept hearing Ridley's voice. *We can't protect her from Jeremiah, and we can't save her from herself.* The feeling of helplessness was nearly overwhelming. Ridley had seemed resigned to it. He was not. Not yet. But short of abducting Lily and the children and secreting them away, nothing was occurring to him. *Laws change after attitudes change.* Ridley had said that, too, and it echoed in his mind. The sound of it should have vanished by now, but it hadn't. He wanted, no, *needed*, to see her.

"Did you say something?" asked Hitch. "I didn't catch it."

Ben didn't know if he had spoken or not. "Probably thinking aloud. Was there anything else?"

"Well, the doc came by. She wanted—"

"What?" When Hitch repeated himself, Ben asked, "Was

this before or after Jeremiah was here? And please tell me it wasn't at the same time."

"After. She was here afterwards. You don't look happy about that answer either."

"She was supposed be home resting. There was the robbery and then the delivery and then—" He stopped himself before he mentioned she had also tended to Lizzie and Lily. "It doesn't matter."

"What delivery?"

"You don't know? She didn't say anything while she was here?"

"Um, no. She told me that she had been to the Songbird and treated Buzz for his gout, George for a splinter, and Hank Ketchum for plugged ears. No mention of a delivery. Now, I did deliver a soup bone to her, and she thanked me for it. Is that what you meant?"

Ben felt like cradling his head in his hands or banging it against his desk. Dr. E. Ridley Woodhouse needed a keeper.

"Sheriff? You all right?"

Smiling thinly, Ben nodded. "Fine. Phoebe gave birth to a daughter yesterday. No, come to think of it, it was already today when it happened. I thought the doctor would have said something."

"Nope. She was only here long enough to examine the prisoners and leave some medicine for Mr. Michael Gordon."

"You didn't let her in the cell, did you?"

"Oh, she tried to wheedle me, but I stood fast. I think you would have been proud. She's not an easy one to resist and she knows more words than me."

"I'm learning that."

"I made both of them belly up to the bars, so to speak, so she could examine them. One at a time, mind you, and I had my gun drawn, which she didn't like, but which I thought was a prudent precaution."

"I see."

"Doc couldn't have been here more than a quarter of an hour and that includes the time she spent asking about Ma and me."

Ben just didn't want to know, and he hoped Hitch wouldn't tell him the nature of that conversation. "All right. Fine job."

When Hitch beamed, Ben gave him the less palatable news. "I need you to spend the night. I was not too worried about leaving them alone last night, but I don't want them to think that's what they can expect. I looked at the calendar. Judge Miner is in Stonechurch this week. The circuit brings him here on the Wednesday before Christmas. He'll want to make short work of this. I'm not expecting a lengthy trial."

"Mr. Tom Gordon was asking about a lawyer."

"That didn't take him long."

"Isn't Mr. Frost a lawyer?"

"Yes, but my brother writes and reviews contracts for the ranch. He doesn't defend criminals."

"Oh. Then I guess we should get Chris Whitt over here to talk to them. Or will they each need a lawyer?"

"That's up to them." He got up, went to the door, and threw his coffee outside. "You know where the mattress roll is?"

"On the top shelf in the supply closet. I don't think we gave all the blankets to our prisoners."

"If we did, take a couple back." Ben replaced the empty mug on the shelf. "Get some shut-eye. You've been awake all day. I don't expect you to stay awake all night. Keep your ear to the ground just the same."

"Don't worry."

"Not going to, Hitch. I'm really not going to."

Chapter Thirty-seven

Ridley dropped the medical text she was reading when Ben surprised her by coming in the front door. She leaned over the sofa to pick up the book and put it on the trunk. "I thought we agreed you'd used the surgery entrance."

"Did we?" He stripped out of his coat and gloves and tossed his hat at the newel post. It missed its target and landed on the stairs. He left it where it fell.

Ridley watched his careless toss and the lack of concern for the outcome. Twin creases appeared between her eyebrows. She looked at him over the rim of her spectacles. "What's happened?"

He walked into the front room. "When I walked you over here earlier, it was because you said you were going to make your notes and take a nap. I left you with that in mind. Didn't think I had to caution you not to go anywhere because you never mentioned that you would be stepping out. I took you at your word. That's an agreement, isn't it?"

"I don't know if it is or isn't, but I also said I would be checking my slate to see if anyone left a message for me."

"There wasn't a message. I looked."

"That's because the slate was turned over. There was indeed writing on the other side." She paused, eyes narrowing, and pressed a forefinger to her chest. "Are you angry with me?"

"Isn't it evident? Please, tell me what I have to do to make that clear."

"Oh, dear. I think you better sit down. This is not what I was expecting when Mrs. Rushton told me you would be dropping by."

"It wasn't what I had in mind either." He didn't sit. He remained where he was, framed in the archway between the vestibule and the front room. There was a concession of sorts when he tucked his thumbs into his belt and leaned a shoulder against the arch. The stance he struck was not as casual as he meant it to be, but neither was it threatening. "I had to go down to the jail, talk to Hitch about taking the night shift. Found out you were there earlier."

"I would have told you. It wasn't a secret. I was at the saloon before that. Mr. Winegarten's gout had flared. That's what the message was about."

"I know you were there. I know you removed a splinter from George's thumb and did something to Hank's ears so he can hear again."

"Well, then. You know everything."

"But you don't. Jeremiah Salt was in my office looking for me before you arrived."

Ridley felt some of the warmth drain from her face. Her fingertips were suddenly cold. She curled them protectively in the folds of her robe. "Hitch never said. What did he want?"

"Nothing related to Lily or the children. It was a business matter." He watched Ridley release a breath that could only have been prompted by her relief. "Do not miss my point, Ridley. He was there and you could have easily crossed paths."

"But we didn't."

"But you could have."

"But we—" She caught herself and then used removing her spectacles and cleaning them to give herself time to compose herself. "I understand that your anger is in proportion to your concern, and when I look at it in that light, it's deeply touching. At the same time, I don't think it's unreasonable to ask you to respect that I have work to do that's different from yours but no less important. You can't truly expect that I will never cross paths with Mr. Salt. Frost Falls isn't that big. We both visit the mercantile and the leather goods store and half a dozen other places. I find it uncommonly odd that we haven't had to step around each other already. The rumor that sent him into a rage is behind us because Frankie Fuller fell on his sword for you and took responsibility for what Amanda

Springer made up because she enjoys knocking over the first domino to see what will happen."

Ridley resettled her spectacles on her face. "Seeing Mr. Salt at the jail would have presented almost no risk. Besides Hitch being present, it's unlikely that he would have already learned about our visit to his home. I don't think he and I would have exchanged words beyond a few pleasantries to maintain appearances."

Ben was quiet, taking it in. "Hitch was right. You do know a lot of words."

"I'm not sure why he said that, but all right."

"You were correct about my anger being proportionate to my concern."

"I know," she said gently. "But I appreciate you saying so."

Ben's chuckle tickled the back of his throat. "And it's nice how you can take the credit and give something in return."

"Thank you."

"That doesn't mean I don't wish you'd have come to get me before you left the house."

"I understand, but you had your brother and his family with you. I wasn't about to disturb that. Do they know you're here now?"

"I told Remington I was going to the jail, and I did. I didn't tell him I was going anywhere else." He unhitched his thumbs from his belt and pushed away from the wall. "You think maybe . . ." His eyebrows lifted as he cocked his head toward the stairs.

Ridley got to her feet. She was already opening her robe as she walked toward him. "I think maybe . . . yes."

Ben caught her by the waist when he saw her intention was to walk right by him and lead him in a merry chase to her room. "Are we in a hurry?" he asked, pulling her close. He touched his forehead to hers. "Hmm?"

"You're steaming my lenses."

He removed them with the same care she always showed and fit them to the crown of her head. He anchored the ear stems in her hair. "Better?"

"I can see you now. That's always better." She laid a palm against either side of his jaw. He hadn't shaved; his stubble was agreeably abrasive. "I love your face. You have beautiful eyes. Have women told you that? I can't be the first."

Ben's features took on a stricken expression. "It would be better if we didn't talk about my mother."

Watching him, taking in that perfect balance of horror and humor that shaped his features, Ridley recognized how securely he held her with a quirky smile and mischief in his startling blue eyes. A rascal lived inside there, and she loved him. Standing on tiptoe, she kissed him hard on the mouth. "Don't make me wait," she said. Spinning away from Ben's loose embrace, Ridley hurried up the stairs.

"Hey! You stepped on my hat!" Ben paused long enough to mourn the damage to the crown and then followed his nephew's example of charging up the hill.

"I'm sorry!" In her room, Ridley backed away as Ben shortened the distance between them with his long stride. She threw out her hands to ward him off. His smile wasn't quirky now. It was wicked, the kind of wicked that made her heart thrum and her breathing quicken.

"You crushed the crown," he told her.

"I'll have it blocked again. It will be as good as new."

"I don't want it as good as new. It's taken me five years to get it good as old."

"That's ridiculous. It doesn't even make sense."

"It doesn't have to. It's my hat."

"You didn't make this much fuss when you put Colt on your shoulders and he smashed it."

"He's four. And his parents were there."

Ridley felt the bed at the back of her knees. When Ben put his forefinger against the tip of her nose, she dropped like a stone. He hadn't exerted any pressure. She just went down. She kicked off her slippers, lifted her spectacles from where he had placed them on her head, and set them aside. The robe slid off her shoulders. She didn't think he helped; it simply happened. She watched him shuck his boots, his socks, and then everything else except his drawers. He never sat. It should have been amusing to watch him hop first on one foot and then the other, but it wasn't. It was endearing, and exciting, and she didn't want to look anywhere but at him.

She scrambled back on the bed when he advanced, but it

wasn't to get away. It was to make room. Ridley threw back the covers and crawled under them, then she held them up to invite him inside.

"Lamp?" he asked.

Ridley glanced at the small steady flame under the glass globe. "Leave it," she said, and when he smiled, she knew it was what he wanted, too.

Ben got under the covers. The first thing he did was try to insert his bare feet between her calves. She made that difficult, wriggling out of his way. Once she kicked him. "Ow!"

"Your feet are freezing."

"That's because I was standing on your cold floor. You need to get a rug in here. I can't believe Doc didn't have one."

"He didn't sleep in here. There's one in the other room."

"I'm moving it in here first thing tomorrow." Ridley's quiet laughter warmed him in a way that creature comforts could not. He leaned in until his mouth was just inches above hers. He was glad for the lamplight because he could see the smile edging her lips and the gradual darkening of her eyes. Her gaze encompassed him, welcomed him, and he was not proof against the invitation.

Ridley thought she knew how much she needed him to kiss her, but when he did, she realized how little she understood her nature. Her hands slipped under his arms and around his back and she arched into him, flattening her breasts against his chest, and giving him her neck to savage with his mouth.

She twisted, fell back, and when her mouth parted on a cry that had no sound, he took her again, slanting his mouth hard across hers. Ridley thought she recognized some of his earlier anger in that kiss, but there was also a proportionate expression of caring in the way he touched her. He caressed her shoulder with gentle fingertips and sifted through her hair as though he were examining the quality of silk. Sometimes he whispered against her mouth. He knew a lot of words, too, most of them not fit for mentioning outside of a bedroom, maybe not outside of a bed. Here, though, under the cover of dim light and the shadow of intimacy, he could say whatever he liked and it would all sound as tender as yearning.

The tip of her tongue darted across his upper lip. He caught it, drew it into his mouth. He kissed her slowly, deeply, and didn't stop for a very long time. When she needed a breath, it seemed that he gave her his.

He opened the neckline of her shift and slipped his hand inside. At first it lay above her breast so she could anticipate its slow advance, and when it covered her breast, she sighed with a mixture of relief and pleasure. The rough pad of his thumb made a pass across her nipple. It swelled to attention. He flicked the rosy bud with his thumbnail, and Ridley sucked in her lower lip along with her moan.

"Don't make me wait," she said when his mouth hovered above hers.

"You said that downstairs."

"But now I mean it," she whispered. "I truly mean it."

He chuckled, and they both felt the vibration. When he moved over her, she tugged at her shift and drew it up to her thighs. Her knees lifted, parted, to make room for him. He loosened the string on his drawers. Ridley did everything else, inserting her fingers under the waist and pushing the drawers past his hips and over his taut buttocks. She wrapped a hand around his erection and returned his wicked, satisfied smile when it pulsed warmly against her palm. She used her thumbnail to score the hard, rigid length of his penis until he growled at the back of his throat.

"Don't make me wait," he said.

She didn't. Couldn't. Ridley guided him, though she suspected he knew the way on his own, and the errant thought lifted the corners of her mouth as she closed her eyes.

Ben eased into her, pushing at the very last when he couldn't help himself. He bent his head, nudged her lips. They opened on a soft exhalation of air. Now that he was snug inside her, the first wave of urgency ebbed. He kept himself still. She didn't move. Nothing happened except they felt everything in those moments. There was the weight of her hand on his shoulder, the smooth curve of her thighs against his hips. She knew the touch of his mouth at her forehead and the exquisite lightness of every breath he drew.

As it had to, this moment of simply being passed. Ridley moved, and then so did Ben, and the wave of urgency washed over them more powerfully than before. She lifted her hips as he thrust, and she contracted around him as he withdrew. The rhythm beat as a pulse in her temple, in her throat, and where she held him most securely, in her heart.

She clutched the sheet beneath her, pressed her heels into the mattress. He rocked her back hard. She felt all of him. Everywhere.

He dipped, pushed, wanted to see her undone and know it was because of him. He had seen her pleasure rise before, but this time it was different. There were no increments, no steps that were greater or fuller than the one before. She found gratification in staccato notes, quick pulses of pleasure with the first being as deeply satisfying as the next and the next and the next until the rapid firing of nerve endings could no longer be sustained. He was watching her, but he did not have to see the change in her expression to know when she was about to tumble. The violence of her release was something more than he'd anticipated, and when she shuddered hard under him, it snapped the tight rein he had been keeping on his own pleasure.

He stretched, arched, and thrust with short strokes, his entire body moving to the same swift beat that had propelled Ridley's deep pleasure. He shouted, part groan, part garbled utterance, and had no embarrassment about either, even when he heard her low rumbling laughter. That laughter grew a little louder when he rolled away, and the only explanation for the increase in volume was that he had been smothering her. It was no wonder that she didn't ask him not to move this time.

"All right," he said, once he had righted his drawers and was lying comfortably on his back. "Tell me."

Ridley shifted and wriggled and pushed at her nightgown until it was under her backside and below her knees. She turned on her side and propped her head on an elbow so she could see the whole of his face and not only his profile, although she thought there was a great deal to recommend about his profile.

"Do you have any idea what you shouted?" she asked.

"No. Do you?"

"I believe it was Eureka." She repeated it, this time with enough enthusiasm to warrant the exclamation mark. "Eureka!"

"Uh-huh. That begins with an E, doesn't it?"

"You are absurd and I adore you." She leaned over and

kissed him on the mouth. She didn't intend to linger, but as so often happens with intentions, it didn't matter. The kiss was entirely satisfactory and they were both smiling when she lifted her head. "Don't you think it's time to surrender that bone? Isn't that your advice to me?"

"Do you ever take it?"

"No."

"Is Eureka your Christian name?"

"No."

"There's your answer."

"I thought you were perhaps more commonsensical than me."

"It's probably good that you're finding out these things before we're married."

"Mm-hmm." Ridley shifted, bumped his leg with her knee, turned her hip looking for a more comfortable angle.

"What's wrong?" he asked.

"Nothing." She sat up suddenly. "I think I need to—" She threw back the blankets on her side of the bed and scooted to the edge. "I need a moment."

In the event that she was watching him out of the corner of her eye, Ben did not smile. He followed her hurried progress to the trifold dressing screen. She disappeared behind it. He heard her pouring water into the washbasin. What happened afterward was all in his imagination, and he congratulated himself on having a vivid one. When it was his turn to step behind the screen, he completed his ablutions while humming to himself, and was still humming quietly upon returning to the bed.

"'The Battle Hymn of the Republic'?" Ridley asked with a wry slant to her eyebrows. "'The Battle Hymn'?"

Ben shrugged. "'Mine eyes have seen the glory.'" He slipped under the covers. This time he was the one who turned on his side. "Are you better now?"

She nodded. "I was, um . . ."

"Sticky?"

"Damp," she said. "Perhaps you shouldn't try to be so helpful."

"Noted." He found her hand and drew it to his groin. "What do you call this?"

"Your groin."

"More specifically. You had your hand around it."

"It's a penis."

"That's what I thought you'd say. Did you feel it shrivel? That's my cock."

"I'm not a stranger to the word."

"You've never said it in your life."

"I prefer proper names."

"Yes, Eloise, I know." He moved her hand so she was cupping him. "And what about here?"

"Scrotum and testicles."

"Sac and balls." He sighed. "So much work to be done."

"I'm sure you think so. By the way, it's not Eloise either."

He nodded. "I figure if I ever hit the bull's-eye, the shock of it will render you speechless."

"A likely consequence of your cleverness and your dogged pursuit of an answer." Ridley slid her hand out from under his. "Cock and balls," she whispered. "It sounds like an English pub. Ye Olde Cock and Balls."

"If that helps you."

"Ye Olde Cock and Balls," she repeated. "Where wenches serve dark ale to men plotting to rob coaches or overthrow the government."

Ben grew suspicious. "Felicity Ravenwood?"

"No. Harmony Collingsworth. Felicity's grandmother. Felicity introduces her grandmother's story in—"

Ben leaned in. "Shut up, Ridley," he said, not unkindly.

"All right." She gave in easily, not because he said it nicely, but because she was tired. She turned on her side away from him.

He spooned against her. "You can tell me all about it in the morning," he whispered.

Chapter Thirty-eight

It was not yet morning when Ben woke, disturbed by whatever it was that was walking lightly across the nape of his neck. He flicked it away and burrowed deeper under the blankets. He had just found the indentation for his shoulder and the depression for his hip when the creature scrambled across his skin a second time. He batted at it. The third time it happened, he managed to capture it.

What he had in his tight fist turned out to be two of Ridley's fingers. "Are you satisfied?" he asked dryly. "I'm awake." He let go of her fingers and turned over. He didn't remember ever turning away from her.

Ridley shook out her fingers. "That hurt . . . a little."

He took her hand and kissed her knuckles. "Better?"

She nodded. When he released her, she tucked her hand under the covers and rubbed those knuckles lightly against his chest. "I'm an early riser." She unfolded her fingers and moved her hand lower, pressing the heel against his abdomen. He sucked in a breath, and she continued on the downward path. She cupped him through his drawers, felt the stirring of his erection. "So apparently are you."

"Uh-huh."

"Cock and balls," she whispered. "I haven't forgotten."

"Oh, Jesus." Ben caught her by the waist and lifted her so she straddled him. Her shift rode up her thighs. He pushed at his drawers. When his erection was free, he cupped her bottom, lifted her again, and then let her find her way. She did, sinking deeply and completely onto his cock.

"My," she said, her voice so breathy it sounded like a sigh. Ridley leaned forward. She looked down at herself. The shift's neckline gaped. She could see her breasts. So could he. That was all right, then. She wanted him to look. No man had ever made her feel desirable. This man did.

She watched his pupils grow wider until each blue iris was only a smoke ring. His fingers twitched on her buttocks. When she spoke, her voice was husky, taunting. "You want to touch them, don't you?"

Robbed of speech, he nodded.

"You can't. Not yet."

Ben blinked. "Who *are* you?"

Ridley's sultry smile broke into an easy grin. "I haven't the vaguest notion, but I suspect it's your fault."

"My fault?"

"When you give a person words, Ben, you give her ideas."

He stared at her. "Lord, but I'm glad I waited for you."

"Mm." She bent, kissed him on the lips. "So am I." She began to move, lifting, falling, using the rhythm he showed her, making it work for both of them. This was slow, easy, and made her think she had all the time in the world, that the sun wouldn't rise on the day until it had her permission. She liked the way Ben's hair fell this way and that because he hadn't had time to make furrows with his fingers. She did it for him. It made him smile, and she liked that, too. Always had, even when she was the target of his amusement.

She heard his breathing quicken before she saw it. The sound of his short gasps grew quieter as hers grew louder. One of his hands left her buttocks and slipped between her legs. She gave a start as his fingers separated her wet lips and found the slippery bud that excited every one of her nerves.

"My breasts," she said. "You can touch them now." To her ears, it sounded like a plea.

"I'm fine."

A whimper rested at the back of her throat. She held it until she couldn't. "I could be very angry with you."

"I know." His fingers wrested every nuance of pleasure from her, and she gave a cry and a start and held on. Ben threw back his head, bucked, and nearly unseated her as he came. It was like so many of their kisses. Long and hard and deep.

Ridley collapsed on top of him, lay there while he swept her hair to one side, and then rolled away, replete. She didn't speak until his hand snaked into the open neckline of her shift and cupped a breast. "What are you doing?"

"Figured it'd be okay now." His thumb made a light pass across her swollen and erect nipple, which he knew would be incredibly sensitive to touch.

"Well, it's n-n-n-nyeh!" She grabbed his hand and yanked it away as some vestige of previous pleasure made her shiver from head to toe. When it was over, she spoke on a thread of sound. "Not even a little okay." Ridley released his hand and raised her forearm to her eyes and covered them. "What did you do to me?"

"Trust me, whatever was done, was done to both of us."

"Hmm."

They said nothing for a time. Silence suited them; it was comfortable. He lay on his stomach, his face turned toward her, and he watched the play of her thoughts in changing expressions. She lay on her side. Her fingers gravitated once again to the nape of his neck, and she let them drift back and forth, sometimes winding threads of his dark orange hair around the tips. It was Ridley who spoke first because Ben was waiting for her. He could have told her what she was going to say. It was all there in her dark, contemplative eyes and in the fingertips that grazed his damaged skin.

"Will you tell me how you came by your scars?" she asked. "You said before that you would tell me later. Is this later? You don't have to if you'd rather not." She started to withdraw her hand.

"No, don't. It's nice. Your fingertips there are nice."

Ridley left her hand where it was. "The only thing you've told me about it is that your brother and Phoebe didn't set you on fire. I hope that was the truth."

He chuckled. "Yeah, that's the truth. They were there, but none of what happened was their fault. For a fact, they saved my life. My mother's life as well." He nodded when Ridley's eyes widened just a fraction. "That's right. She owes them, will always owe them. I don't know if that's what keeps her avoiding them when they come to town. She's a complicated lady." The muscles of his back rolled under Ridley's fingertips as she drew circles across his skin. "It happened in the barn at Twin Star. I might have been a little drunk, maybe a little more than a little. Had something on my mind that I needed to say and I suppose I thought the drink would get me there. I got into an argument with a couple of fellas who didn't want me speaking up. I knew there'd be consequences for talking but I was willing to take on the grief with the law and with my family. They weren't. Ellie had gotten herself smack in the middle of it. One of the fellas walloped me with a lantern, pretty similar to how you laid Tom Gordon out with a soup bone. I have to tell you, that's all I remember. I have the rest from Phoebe and Remington, who were foolin' around in the loft and saw it happen, and Ellie, who, like I said, had herself smack in the middle.

"The way I heard it, I went down like a pile of bricks, the glass in the lantern broke, and some of the oil spilled in my hair, more of it across my neck and back. I guess I haven't mentioned the lantern was lit. The flame followed that oil trail like a bloodhound follows a fox. It lit me up, but since I was unconscious, I didn't feel it. They say the same man kicked me under the chin like he meant to snap my neck, but I didn't feel that either. Ellie was knocked unconscious by then. There wasn't anything she could do for me or for herself. Bales of hay caught fire. Flames climbed the walls. Two of the fellas took off, barred the door. The third man, knocked senseless as he was, was no use to himself or anyone else. If Phoebe and Remington hadn't been able to escape the loft, we all would have burned alive. They dragged Ellie and me to safety while the fire was still raging, and when the doors were finally opened from the outside, they pulled us out."

"Oh, Ben, how awful for all of you."

"Sometimes I'm glad I have no memory of the events of that night, not real ones anyway, but it's in my mind so deep that I know the pain anyway." He watched a troubled shadow cross her face. "Don't feel sorry for me, Ridley. I bear a lot of the responsibility for what happened."

"When do you forgive yourself?" she asked. "I watched you with Phoebe and Remington. You're family. I have to believe they forgave you a long time ago."

"They did. I'm not sure they ever blamed me."

"Perhaps not, since you so obviously take on the blame yourself." Ridley felt his shoulders roll under her fingertips and recognized the shrug for what it was. She wanted to cuff him. Instead she leaned over and kissed his shoulder. "I never took you for a martyr. I'm not sure it suits you."

"If the cross fits . . ."

She did cuff him then, just a light touch at the back of his head, and when his response was to grin crookedly at her, it was difficult not to laugh. She asked him, "You were Doc's patient after this happened?"

"I was. He came out to the ranch and advised them what needed to be done for me. Then he'd come every couple of days to see that his instructions were being followed. There were the burns, of course, but the bigger threat was to my lungs. I inhaled a lot of smoke. Fiona was primarily the one who looked after me. Sat at my bedside for hours."

"Fiona? Not Ellie?"

"No. That wasn't possible. Thaddeus arranged for her to stay at the Butterworth. She'd already been hired there, but she couldn't work for a while. He paid for her room and board while she recovered."

"Fiona," Ridley said softly. "I didn't expect that. And yet your relationship is so strained now."

"That began before I left the ranch. I recovered and started working again. It was when I'd have to make a trip into town, usually on Twin Star business, and I'd see my mother. Fiona always seemed to know when I did, though I don't recollect ever telling her. I don't know, I guess she thought I would take a page from her script and cut Ellie out of my life. Fiona knew how to do that. I didn't."

"But isn't that what you've done to Fiona? Cut her out?"

"There's a difference, Ridley. She's not blood."

"When did that become important?" She'd put the question to him gently, but Ben looked as if she had struck him. She felt the muscles in his shoulders and back go rigid. She thought he might shake her off or leave the bed altogether. He did neither. She didn't know if she'd ever exercised the kind of restraint he showed her now, but she felt the tension slowly seep away and his breathing resume its normal rhythm.

Quietly, he said, "It's something to think about, isn't it?"

"If you like."

"I don't. Doesn't mean I shouldn't."

"Ben, I didn't say it to hurt you."

"I know."

Ridley searched his face, looking for proof that he meant it. She found it in his smile, not amused this time, but tender. Her own breathing came a little easier, and the ache that had been squeezing her heart vanished. "I love you," she said. "Have I told you?"

"No."

"Well, I do."

"I am gratified to hear it, Elsie, since we're getting hitched."

"Quaint," she said dryly. "And it's not Elsie."

"Damn."

"So why are you marrying me?"

"One reason," he said. "Maybe two."

"Oh? What's the first?"

"To see your full name on the wedding license."

"It's not on my diploma."

"I know. I looked. But a license is different, and I know a minister, a judge, a mayor, and a clerk of records who will insist that you put it there."

"And you're the sheriff."

"Right. That, too."

"What is your second reason?"

"You probably already guessed."

"Just in case I'm wrong, I'd like to hear it."

"I love you."

Ridley heard no trace of humor in his voice, saw no hint of it in his eyes. Here was sincerity to the core, and the core was his heart. She nodded faintly because just then it was difficult to speak.

"That's what you guessed, isn't it?"

It was a moment before Ridley found her voice. Even so, the words caught in her throat. "It's what . . . it's what I hoped."

"Ah, Ridley. You should have never had to hope."

"No?"

"No. Never. You got me right from the first. It was the hat, I think. Remember the one with the big pink bow, the one you arrived in?" When she nodded, he continued. "It's kinda hard to admit that I liked it on you, especially since I told you not to wear it. It was the incongruity, I think, that caught my fancy.

There you were as starched as a shirt from a Chinese laundry, wearing a hat with a floppy bow bigger than the crown. Couldn't figure out how the pieces fit. That was intriguing."

"I know how you love a puzzle."

"Uh-huh. And then there were the dime novels mixed in with your medical books. You reading Felicity Ravenwood adventures, well, that just made me want to know you better."

"Really? I don't think I liked you much back then."

"Oh, you made that pretty clear, but I put it down to you being scared because—and I say this not to brag since it's as true a fact as you're likely to come across in Frost Falls—folks like me. In spite of the challenges you presented, it never occurred to me that you might be an exception."

"You don't back away from challenges."

"Hardly ever. There's Fiona and Thaddeus."

"I didn't mean—"

"Shh. I know."

She nodded. Tentatively, she said, "If you still want to propose, that would be all right, I guess."

Ben chuckled. "You guess? I think maybe you're missing living under the rock." The militant gleam in her eye gave him pause. "Well, maybe not. All right." He took a breath and began. "Dr. E. Ridley Woodhouse, my love, my lover, will you stand at my side as I will stand at yours in the pursuit of our mutual happiness, and will you bear witness to my devotion by agreeing to become my wife as I will bear witness to yours by becoming your husband?"

When his question was met with silence, he said, "I thought it needed more work, but Remington said it was fine. Phoebe cried a little, but then she's a watering pot on account of the baby. Colt wanted me to mention him. I said I'd think about it."

Ridley put a finger to his lips. "Do be quiet. Yes. I'll marry you."

Chapter Thirty-nine

Remington was at the stove frying bacon in a cast iron skillet when Ben walked in the back door. He cocked an eyebrow at his brother. "Just getting back from the jail?"

Ben stayed by the door to remove his outerwear but the activity helped him avoid Remington's interested gaze. "Yep. Night shift. Keeping the peace."

"So no dereliction of your duties."

"No. Not a one."

"And no injury to yourself?"

Ben frowned. "No. Why do you ask?"

"Because I stepped out to answer a call of nature this morning and saw there was a lamp burning in the doctor's surgery. Then I saw you, and then I saw the doctor, and then—"

Ben put out a hand, stopping him. "I get it." He spun a chair away from the table, straddled it, and sat. "Where's Colt?"

"He just took a plate of eggs and bacon to his mother. Talk fast because he'll be back, and even when he's not listening, he hears everything."

"I don't have anything to say."

"Oh, no. Not this time."

"I didn't poke my nose into what you and Phoebe were up to in the loft."

"We were married."

"I'm talking about before that. The only reason you didn't think I knew was because I never said anything. You'd ride out. She'd ride out. None of that fooled me."

"Huh." Remington turned sizzling strips of bacon with a fork. "Well, don't mention it to Phoebe. She'll be crushed to learn we weren't as stealthy as we thought."

"And you're not?"

"Crushed? No. Glad to know you're even more observant than I thought. Makes me feel better about you wearing a badge. Don't misunderstand. It was always in my mind that you'd be good at it. I like knowing you're better than good."

Ben could feel the tips of his ears turning red and wished he'd kept his hat on. "Ridley's waiting on Mrs. Rushton to arrive and then they're both coming over. Don't worry. They're bringing food with them. You'll be able to stop tending that bacon."

Remington said, "Good. Burned the back of my hand twice now."

Ben clicked his tongue, feigning sympathy. He stopped when Remington threatened him with the fork. "You mind if we talk seriously for a while?"

"I thought we were."

"This is law serious."

"About the Gordons?"

"No, not about them. Not right now. I want to talk about Jeremiah Salt."

Remington glanced over. "Talk."

"Ridley said something to you and me yesterday that's still rattling around in my mind. She said that laws change after attitudes change. You remember that?"

"I do."

"And then last night I taught her some new words, enriched her vocabulary, I suppose you'd say, and—"

"I would never say that," said Remington. "No one would say that."

"Um, I just did."

"Well, don't say it again. I'm already trying to forget you said it once and putting the image of where you said it out of my mind, but so you know, I never figured you for spending the night at the jail." Remington's inattention to the bacon got him splashed with bacon grease a third time. He pulled his hand away and nursed it under his arm.

"Serves you right," said Ben. "Anyway, later on she got some ideas in her head, and when I pointed it out, she said, 'When you give someone words, you give her ideas.' Or something like that."

"Hmm, yeah, I bet you were distracted."

"A bit. My point is that there's nothing I can do about Jeremiah unless he breaks the law, and right now the law favors him when it comes to his home, his family, and his marriage. So it got me thinking that maybe the answer is—"

"Change the law," said Remington.

"Yes," said Ben. "Change the law. I'm not talking about state law, that can come later, but local law? There's no reason that can't change now. The mayor and the council will have their regular meeting the first week of January. I figure you can draft something that will hold up under scrutiny before you head back to Twin Star and I can start working on attitudes."

"You'll have to. The council is all men, and if there's a split vote, the mayor decides. He's a man."

"I know that, but what are you saying? They won't agree?"

"I'm saying that's a lot of attitude to change. Maybe one of them beats his wife and you don't know it. That man is going to be reluctant to support a law that could land him in jail. And there will be general resistance. The view will be that the law takes away a husband's privilege to deal with his wife as he sees fit, whether or not that includes using his fists."

"I won't be doing this alone. Jim Springer's on the council. You know his wife, don't you?"

Remington made a face. "The leader of the temperance society?"

"That's right. There are a lot of people in this town who don't have an opinion until she gives it to them, her husband included. Dave Saunders has a seat. His wife is one of Amanda Springer's most devoted acolytes. Buzz Winegarten is on the council, too, and he's not married, and even if he doesn't have a personal stake, he has a gouty foot that Ridley treats for him. She could be persuasive there, and I learned a few months back that Buzz once courted Amanda Springer, so he'll have two reasons to keep an open mind."

"That's three. There's six on the council, right? And then the mayor for the tiebreak."

"Uh-huh. Hank Ketchum is surly enough to vote opposite the others just because he can. Mickey Mangold could probably be convinced. It was his wife in the bank, so he might vote yes if he knows I'm in favor of it. There's Mr. Washburn. I dare him to vote no."

"All right, maybe it won't be as hard as I first thought, but just in case, what about the mayor?"

"Drew Abernathy will be happier if he doesn't have to vote, but whatever side he comes down on, it will be because he thinks it will sell newspapers."

"No conflict of interest there," was Remington's sardonic response. "You know this is going to rile Jeremiah when he gets wind of it."

"Maybe, but if he speaks out against it when he's never been one for making noises about town affairs, then he'd be drawing attention to himself. Whatever you end up writing won't specifically target him."

"All right. I'll do it." He said this as if it were not already a foregone conclusion. "I thought you were going to ask me to defend the Gordons."

"No. Hitch wondered if you would, but I explained you don't do criminal law. Chris Whitt could do it if they don't want to be tried separately. If they do, I should have some names to give them. Do you have any for me?"

Remington didn't have to think long. He named three attorneys practicing in the county. "I hear Colt on the stairs," he said in a hushed voice. "Tell me quick, did you propose? There were some good words in there."

"You're going to make me regret sharing that, aren't you?"

"Probably."

Ben was saved from responding by Colt's sudden appearance. The boy threw his arms wide and announced gleefully, "Here I am again in the kitchen."

"As if there were any doubt," Remington said out of the side of his mouth.

Ben welcomed his nephew by spinning his chair around again and sitting in it properly. He patted his knee and Colt happily climbed aboard.

"Where's your mother's tray?" Remington asked.

"She told me to leave it. She said you would get it later. May I have bacon?"

Remington took a plate from the china cupboard and laid

two bacon strips across it. He passed the plate to Colt. "Careful. They're still sizzling. Do you want an egg?"

"Sunshine up, please."

"Sunshine up, coming up."

Ben heard voices on the back stoop. "Cavalry's here."

Remington practically sagged against the stove. "Thank God."

Ben urged Colt to answer the door, and when his nephew's back was turned, he snapped a quarter length of one of the bacon strips and stuffed it in his mouth. "Damn, that's hot." He fanned his mouth.

Colt opened the door and then returned to his uncle's lap. "Hey! Some of my bacon's gone."

"That'd be your uncle," said Remington. "Good morning, ladies." He turned a wide, welcoming smile on Ridley and her housekeeper. Mrs. Rushton actually blushed.

"Away from the stove," she said, making a shooing gesture. She set a basket on the table and looked at Colt. "I see you have bacon. Do you want an egg?"

And thus the real morning meal got under way.

Ridley accompanied Ben to the jail so she could examine both prisoners. Ben opened the cells one at a time for her and stood with his hand on the butt of his gun the entire time she was inside. Hitch remained in the entranceway prepared to act if he had to.

While Ridley worked, Ben told the men about the attorney who would likely take their case and promised that Hitch would bring him around later. Tom and Michael decided they would take their chances together, so the names Remington provided were unnecessary. He explained Judge Miner's schedule and the likelihood that the trial would be done quickly. He had nothing to offer them regarding the judge's rulings in cases like these, but he did tell them about a train robbery some years back that didn't go well for the desperados at trial.

"Was it true what you said about those train robbers?" asked Ridley when they were alone in the front office.

He held up his right hand. "Truth."

"Desperados," she said. "That's a good description for these two. They were desperate."

"You feeling sorry for them? That's why I sent Hitch on his way. He needed the fresh air of reality."

"Not feeling sorry. But I can empathize, can't I? Tom Gordon will stand trial because he loves his brother."

"He'll stand trial because he tried to rob a bank."

"I'm speaking of his motivation."

"Tell that to his lawyer, and maybe Mr. Whitt will tell it to the judge."

Ridley glanced at her medical bag, which she'd placed on the bench beside her. "There's nothing in there for the other Mr. Gordon." She looked back at Ben. "I can't say with absolute certainty, but it's possible he won't live until the trial."

"That's only a week and a day away."

"I know, but he was diagnosed years ago. That's when he should have gone to an arid climate. The cavities in his lungs are what cause the bleeding. From what I hear when I listen to his chest, I suspect there are holes in his airway. The difficulty he has breathing is a consequence of blocked passages. The disease progressed rapidly this past year. That's when he and his brother conceived their plan."

"Ill-conceived their plan."

Ridley couldn't argue with that. She merely nodded.

Ben changed the subject. "I was speaking to Remington before you and Mrs. Rushton came by about an idea I had. It's an idea you inspired actually."

"I inspired it?"

"Mm-hmm. Laws and attitudes." He told her what he had discussed with his brother, how a difference might be made, how there might be hope for Lily. "It's not the turn of the century yet," he said. "But we are making the turn into a new year. Perhaps Lily can wait that long. What do you think?"

Ridley stood and crossed the room to where he sat. She didn't know that she put herself in his lap with the enthusiasm that was the equal of what his nephew had shown. "What I think is that you give me too much credit. This is you. You did this."

"Nothing's done yet," he reminded her.

"It's a brilliant plan."

"New words. New ideas."

Laughing, she planted swift, teasing kisses at his temple, his jaw, his chin, and finally at the corner of his mouth. When her lips moved to his, the kiss lingered just as it had that morning in her surgery when they were parting.

It was Ben who found a measure of sense first, and he wasn't particularly grateful for it. He lifted his head; his eyes fell on her splendidly full lips and the tip of her tongue, which was visible for the briefest of moments. His sigh was long and heartfelt. "I'm thinking I should board up the windows in this office so I can do whatever I like without public scrutiny."

Ridley turned her head. She half expected to find people staring through the glass panes on either side of the entrance. There were no passersby, although Dave and Ed Saunders stepped out of the land office carrying brooms. She watched them sweep away the dusting of snow that had fallen overnight. Sunlight glanced off the flakes they flung into the air.

She started to move off his lap, but he held her fast. "What about public scrutiny?"

"I've changed my mind."

"That fast? You are mercurial, Sheriff." Ridley pecked him on the cheek, and this time when she began to remove herself, he let her go. She returned to the bench, but rather than sit, she remained standing to study the notices on the wall. "You've rearranged these."

"Hitch did. He said something about looking at them fresh, but I think he was bored."

Ridley nodded absently. Photographs of wanted men were the exception, not the standard. Where a photograph existed, it was almost always because the criminal had been previously arrested and jailed, or he was so famous that he actually posed for the camera. Artists, using witness descriptions, rendered the majority of the faces on the posters. Sadly, one often looked too much like another, depending on the source of the information and the artist's talent. Some felons, though, distinguished themselves with their grooming. There were men sporting waxed mustaches and hair slick with pomade, some with wooly sideburns and eyebrows as thick as caterpillars, and finally a few men who had never been introduced to a comb or a brush, whose shaggy hair and beard were so overgrown that it would take a few swipes of a sickle to tame them.

Ben asked his usual question as he observed Ridley's interest in the posters. "See anyone you know?"

She raised a hand above her shoulder and crooked her finger. "Come here. See what you make of this." When he was beside her, Ridley pointed to the poster of one Tobias Granger, whose aliases included Toby Grant, Theodore "Teddy" Granville, and Tate Glasser. Mr. Granger's broad face was largely concealed by his unruly beard and mustache, which the artist had carefully drawn to show both salt and pepper coloring. His hair, also thick and overgrown, fell below his collar. He peered out from the poster with dark eyes.

The charges were robbery, rustling, and murder. The reward was five hundred dollars.

Ridley said, "How old do you think he is?"

"Difficult to know with mountain men. They live hard and grow old before their time."

"Why do you think he's a mountain man?"

"His appearance for one and his charges for another. A man who thinks he's carved out a place for himself in the mountains doesn't take kindly to trespassers. It's conceivable he was protecting what he claimed was his own. Cattle could have strayed into his territory, robbery might have been relieving a stranger of his gun, and murder could have been self-defense. You can't read too much into the charges until you know the story." Ben turned, tipped Ridley's chin toward him, and kissed her squarely on the mouth. When he lifted his head, he was grinning. "In this case, though, we can walk back to the first cell and ask Thomas Gordon to explain it all himself."

"You see it, too?"

"Yeah. I do."

"It's the eyes that caught my attention. The artist took pains to show the contrast of silver threads to the darker ones in his beard, but there are no wrinkles at the corners of the man's eyes and no creases across his brow. I remember looking at Mr. Gordon in the bank and thinking he was younger than he appeared at first glance." She leaned over the bench and placed her hands on the poster on either side of Tobias Granger's cheeks and jaw. She managed to cover most of his beard and give a new outline to the lower half of his face. "He has a square jaw. It takes a little imagination, but you can almost see it."

"Unbelievable." Ben looked over the posters again, all of them. "I don't see his brother here."

"I don't either. Maybe this is the first time his brother joined him." When Ben did not share his opinion, she asked, "Which one of the names do you suppose is his true one?"

"None of these. I'm betting he's Tom Gordon, and that he used his real name so his brother wouldn't have to remember a false one."

She sighed, shook her head. "I suppose even a heart hardened by robbery, rustling, and murder can have compassion for a much-loved brother."

Chapter Forty

For once, word of interest to the entire town was spread by means of Drew Abernathy's newspaper. Timing was part of it since the weekly edition was being prepared for printing, but it was Ben who supplied the story of Tom Gordon's capture and previous crimes before it could become fodder for the gossips. He also supplied a photograph to run alongside the artist's rendering on the wanted poster. Mr. Abernathy sold every paper and even printed extras to be left at the depot for visitors who only stepped off a train to stretch their legs. He was a happy man, happier when the story was reprinted in papers from Stonechurch to Liberty Junction to Falls Hollow and finally to Denver in the prestigious *Rocky Mountain News*.

That was why when he received a document, personally delivered by the sheriff, detailing a law that would "make a husband's use of force against his wife, resulting in harmful contact" illegal, Mr. Abernathy was agreeable to discussion. The understanding that the offense was subject to a fine and/or incarceration eased his mind, and he was further eased to learn the amount and/or length of time would be determined by a judge with the parameters to be set in the law by the town council.

At a hasty meeting of the council on the morning of Tom and Michael Gordon's trial, Mr. Abernathy received approval to include information about the proposed law in the next edition of his paper. The council was in general agreement that they should understand public opinion before there was a vote. The irascible Hank Ketchum was a dissenting voice. He didn't give a damn what the public thought; he'd vote his conscience.

Drew Abernathy made hasty notes about the council meeting while he was sitting in the back of the library, which doubled as the town hall and courtroom when a crowd was expected. He would have liked a seat closer to the front, but folks had started filing in while he was still in the smaller council meeting room, where the librarian kept the journals, periodicals, and newspapers.

He'd learned from Ben that the brothers had changed their minds and elected to be represented by different attorneys. It was Tom Gordon who was most insistent. His previous crimes would come to the attention of the court. His brother had none. Michael still had a chance to be shown mercy. Thomas was not expecting or asking any for himself. Chris Whitt was representing Tom. Michael's attorney was one recommended by Remington and hailed from Harmony. He wore a dark suit, a silver-threaded vest, and a stiff collar. He turned once, surveying the spectators behind him, and nodded as though satisfied the crowd was of a sufficient size to support his presence.

The sheriff had warned Drew to expect that Gideon Manchester would be full of himself, but that the lawyer's self-confidence was not unwarranted, and his bombast would make for good copy.

Ridley held on to the end of the bench to maintain her seat. With five other people squeezed on the same plank, there existed a distinct possibility that she would be pushed to the floor. Ben was seated on a slightly less crowded bench three rows in front of her. She stared at his back through the spaces between shoulders and hats and wished she could have been beside him. He wouldn't have minded having her there, but she had decided it was better for now that they maintained a public distance.

Only Remington and Phoebe knew their intention was to be married, and they had left Frost Falls three days earlier with Colt snuggled warmly between them and Winnie swaddled in blankets in her mother's arms. They carried the secret out of town along with all of their purchases.

Ridley thought Mrs. Rushton might suspect that there was a marriage in their future, for she surely knew by now that Ben Madison was no stranger to Ridley's bed. Ben did not even try very hard to escape her notice, sometimes leaving by the surgery door while the housekeeper was coming in the front.

In spite of the mild anxiety his badly timed exits produced, Ridley cherished the freedom to be with him before there was an exchange of vows. That time between a formal announcement and the wedding would be filled with a surfeit of scrutiny, and Ridley was frankly unwilling to stay out of his bed, even if he was willing to stay out of hers. And if there was the suspicion she could become pregnant, then inevitably the counting of days would begin.

Ben had not even told his mother. There were too many ways she would give them up without ever saying a word. "She'll start eyeing patterns in Mrs. Fish's catalogs and examining every bolt of cloth in the mercantile," he had explained to Ridley. "She'll ask Mr. Springer how many pounds of this will feed how many mouths of that, and she'll want Buzz to tell her how many kegs it will take to get a third of the town drunk and a third of them wobbly on their feet. Thank God the other third are children or members of Amanda's temperance society."

Ridley had laughed at his reasoning, but for her own selfish reasons, she did not disagree. Ben suggested they make their announcement New Year's Eve when the Butterworth Hotel was the site of so much revelry that no one might notice when Ellie Madison became apoplectic with joy. And if those in attendance did notice, much of the backslapping and gladhanding would be out of the way. "We'll put the cart before the horse," he told her. "Call the party our reception and then we can elope."

"If you're expecting an objection," she'd said, "you won't hear it from me. There has been little about this courtship that's been traditional. We probably shouldn't start now."

"Has there been a courtship?" he'd asked.

"You have fully grasped my point."

Since they were in bed when this conversation occurred, it only made sense to underscore that point with lovemaking that was more spirited than it was composed, more reckless than careful, and more wildly pleasurable than being tickled to exhaustion.

Ridley looked down the bench at her fellow spectators and nodded pleasantly at Hank Ketchum, who was looking her way. He was the reason she barely had room on the bench.

He'd been a latecomer. His scowl practically dared those seated not to make space for him. He did not return her greeting, and she remembered the council had been meeting about the proposal. She wondered if he thought she was in some way responsible, but since he nearly always looked testy, it wasn't worth pondering. Besides, she didn't care.

She looked around again, this time at the larger crowd. She saw Drew Abernathy several rows behind her and Buzz Winegarten in the middle on the same bench. Ridley was taken by the fact that she knew so many people. No man on the jury was a stranger to her; many of them had been in her surgery at least once.

The spectators fell silent in waves beginning with the bench directly behind the accused when Michael Gordon's thin shoulders rose and fell spasmodically as he coughed. His attorney leaned a little to the left to put distance between himself and his diseased client, but nonetheless produced a clean monogrammed handkerchief and gave it over without hesitation. People murmured among themselves about this perceived generosity, and it wasn't long before the courtroom returned to full volume, quieting only when the Honorable Judge Richard Miner took his seat at the bench assembled specifically for these occasions.

He banged his gavel, which was unnecessary since he had everyone's attention, and smiled at the assembly. He had no such smile for the defendants, their lawyers, the prosecutor, or the jury. He had words for everyone about the conduct he expected and the contempt of court charges that he would apply without fail should there be violations to the peace and dignity of his courtroom. By the time he was done, no one remembered they were sitting in the town library surrounded by walls of books.

After the opening statements, Ben was called to testify and then cross-examined. Not surprisingly, there were few questions for him after he recounted the events at the bank. Mr. Washburn was called next because he could testify to what happened in his office. He gave a clear account of the events and was supported afterward by the testimony of his employees. Mrs. Mangold took the stand shakily. No one who saw her trembling hands or heard her trembling voice doubted that she had fainted dead away before the first shot was fired. Because Phoebe had known she would be gone before the trial was under way, she wrote out a statement in the presence of the prosecutor, who went to Ben's home. It was affirmed, witnessed by Mrs. Rushton, who had no conflict of relationship, and produced as testimony for the prosecution. There was always a question as to whether the judge would accept it, but then Judge Miner had married Phoebe and Remington and trusted her without reservation.

Dr. E. Ridley Woodhouse was called last. She almost sighed with pleasure when she took her seat beside the judge and did not have to fight to keep it. The defense attorneys objected to the testimony she was about to give as biased by the testimony that had come before. They objected in the same way to everyone who came after Ben was heard. They claimed no witness should have been permitted in the courtroom while another witness was giving testimony. The prosecutor argued that since there wasn't a person in town who didn't know the story, he could call on someone outside the courtroom and they would give testimony as accurate as anything that had been heard thus far.

Judge Miner knew all about small towns because he'd been traveling the circuit for seventeen years. There was hardly any place with more than four hundred people, and that allowed for the outskirts. He favored the prosecution's argument each time it was presented and invited the doctor to stay where she was.

The prosecutor guided Ridley through her testimony right up to the moment she dreaded retelling. When he stepped back, pointed her toward the jury, and gestured for her to proceed, she explained what had occurred in a carefully modulated voice so that her actions would be seen as practical and unexceptional. She didn't say that it was what any reasonable citizen would do if he was in possession of a soup bone, but that's what every person in the courtroom heard, including Ben, and he could not have been prouder.

There was a serious breach of decorum when Ridley stood to leave the stand. The spectators applauded so hard they were deaf to the sound of the gavel. The judge looked the crowd over as if he were taking names and then let them off with the very warning he had promised to give only once. The reassuring smile that he had for Ridley when she stepped down did not bode well for the defendants.

No one present thought the outcome of the trial had ever truly been in question, although the testimony of the defendants, especially as it related to Michael Gordon's condition, softened some hearts. None of those hearts happened to be on the jury. The attorneys made powerful pleas for their clients, particularly Mr. Gideon Manchester, whose eloquence kept Drew Abernathy scribbling furiously in his notebook. It didn't matter. The jury arrived at a guilty verdict for each brother inside two minutes, and most of that time was spent bickering over who would be foreman.

No one spoke when the verdict was announced. It was what the judge would do that kept them quiet and in their seats.

Judge Miner's justice was equally swift. Tom Gordon was sentenced to two years at the state correctional facility in Fremont County. Folks in the courtroom still knew it by the name "Territorial" from the days before statehood. Since Gordon was found guilty only of attempted robbery, if law enforcement in other counties wanted to prosecute him on the more serious charges mentioned in his wanted notice, they would know where to find him. Judge Miner looked significantly at the newspaperman at the back when he said it. "Make sure you get that all down."

Drew Abernathy swallowed, touched the tip of his pencil to his tongue, and continued writing.

Michael Gordon, for all that did not want to hang, looked as if he might weep when he was sentenced to serve out his last days in the Denver jail. Judge Miner reasoned that Denver could accommodate more prisoners and would not strap the resources of Frost Falls. "Don't let me die alone," was Michael's plaintive cry when he heard his fate, and his brother reached for his hand.

Chapter Forty-one

Sunday morning, Christmas morning, Ridley attended church with Ellie and Ben. She sat on one side of Ben's mother; he sat on the other. She heard a woman weeping softly somewhere behind her, and when she stood for a hymn, she looked back and saw Louella Fuller leaning against Big Mike, dabbing at her eyes with no hope of stemming the tears. The first Christmas without Emmilou, Ridley thought, and Louella's suffering was both real and unimaginable.

After services, Ridley and Ben joined Ellie and Mr. Butterworth at the hotel. There were only two guests with accommodations, and neither was present in the dining room when Ridley and Ben arrived. The staff had hours off to be with their families, but this was Ellie's home as well as Mr. Butterworth's, and they were pleased to host dinner for their guests.

Ellie set a spread that made them push away from the table to make room for dessert. The meal began with a clear broth and a winter salad with cabbage, celery, and slivers of carrot drizzled with French dressing. The turkey was browned to perfection; the stuffing was sweetened with raisins. There were buttered roasted potatoes with onions and carrots and cranberry relish to brighten the plate. There were plump rolls for the bread and butter plates with an aroma that could be tasted before the tongue was engaged. Dessert, which no one refused, was almond cake made from a recipe handed down from Ellie's mother. She did not make it often. It was reserved for special occasions, and Christmas Day had never counted as one before.

Ben explained the significance of the almond cake to Ridley and put out a hand when Ellie tried to interrupt to serve him a second slice. "Not even a sliver. I'm serious." For once she did not persist. He regarded her expectantly. "Almond cake, Mother? Are you going to tell me, or do I have to wait until coffee is served?"

"I'm sure I don't know what you mean."

"And I'm sure you know exactly what I mean, but you can get the coffee, if you prefer."

Ridley almost groaned as she rose from her chair. "I'll get it. The walk to the kitchen will do me good." She gathered plates and utensils over Ellie's protest and carried them off. It was when the door did not immediately swing closed behind her that she realized she was being followed. She looked over her shoulder and saw Ellie. Ben's mother's handsome face bore evidence of some worry at the corners of her eyes and mouth. Her hands clutched folds of her skirt, which was only marginally better than wringing them.

Ridley put her armload of plates and cutlery into the large sink before she turned on Ellie. "What is it?" she asked. "You have no color in your face and you were beautifully flushed earlier. Please do not tell me it was the wine." She pulled out a chair and pointed to it. "Sit and compose yourself."

When Ellie was down, Ridley gave her a dry sponge to hold and squeeze before she ruined her sateen gown. "Take some breaths, Ellie. Don't you dare faint. How will I explain that to Ben?"

Ellie nodded. She pressed her lips together, which was not conducive to calm breathing. Her eyes darted to the coffeepot and then to Ridley, and there was a plea in their depths.

"All right," said Ridley, "I'll set the service." She placed dainty china saucers and cups on a serving tray and put the matching coffeepot in the middle. She found the creamer and the sugar, both treats for herself if everyone else preferred their coffee black. When she was done, though, she made no attempt to lift it. "Say something, Ellie. You can't walk back in there without telling me something."

"He's talking to him now," Ellie said in a voice hardly more than a whisper. "I couldn't be there. I just couldn't. I've never mentioned it, you see, and I know I should have, but I didn't, and now he has to ask without me."

"Ellie, I suppose you think I understand, but I don't. Who is talking to whom?"

"Mr. Butterworth. Abe. Abe is speaking to Ben."

"Yes?"

"He's asking my son's permission for my hand. He insisted. Can you imagine? He insisted."

"But that's wonderful. And romantic. I had no idea you and Mr. Butterworth were fond of each other."

"Fond? Is that what it must be for someone of my advanced years? *Fond?* I *love* him. We're in love."

Ridley wished she had kept the sponge because right now she could have squeezed water out of it and she was quite certain it was dry. She did the only thing she could. She apologized. Ellie nodded as if she'd heard and accepted, but Ridley wasn't sure that either had occurred.

"Are you telling me that Ben has no idea?" asked Ridley.

"Yes. That's what I was saying. No idea."

"Do you doubt that he will be happy for you?"

Ellie's face collapsed. She appeared mournful rather than anxious. "I don't know what he will think; that's why I kept it to myself. Abe wanted me to tell him, tried to demand it, but I told him I would not be bullied. I know he was right and that I was stubborn because I was afraid. At the very least, I should have hinted to Ben."

Ridley could not help but wonder if Ben was going to have similar thoughts come New Year's Eve. "It's done, isn't it? Mr. Butterworth is certain to have declared himself, and even if your son required time to think about his answer, he's arrived at it by now."

"Then why hasn't one of them come in here?"

"Perhaps they're sharing a drink stronger than coffee or the wine you served. Would you like me to peek into the dining room?"

Without hesitation, Ellie said, "Would you?"

Ridley did. Her stealth turned out to be unnecessary. "They're not there."

"What do you mean?"

"The dining room's empty."

Ridley picked up the service tray. "Come with me. We'll go back to the table and act as if nothing's happen. They'll have to explain themselves, but when they return with a bottle of the hotel's finest whiskey, I think you and I will know where they went."

Ridley's instincts were correct. Shortly after Ellie and she were seated and the coffee was poured, Ben and Abraham Butterworth reappeared. Ben held the bottle because Mr. Butterworth looked cheerfully dumbstruck and incapable of grasping anything. Ben walked to the table and kissed his mother's cheek. Abe floated to Ellie's side and kissed her hand. Ellie beamed, the worry lines vanishing as if they had never been, and if her cheeks flushed just a bit when Ben kissed her, and if her hand trembled when Abe finally released it, well, that was to be expected.

Watching, Ridley surreptitiously dashed away happy tears.

Ben stripped off his woolen socks and leapt into bed before his feet turned into blocks of ice. He kept promising himself to move the rug out of Doc's old room, but it never happened. Ridley, though, had presented him with a pair of fine leather slippers lined with sheepskin that morning, so moving the rug was unlikely ever to occur. He leaned over the bed to make sure they were where he wanted them. When he got up later to tend the stove, they would be perfectly situated so he could slide his feet right into them.

"You are a strange man," Ridley told him when he flopped on his back beside her.

"You've known a lot of men, have you, to make comparisons?"

Ridley was still sitting up, resting against the headboard. She plumped a pillow and stuffed it behind her. "Strange is strange. I know what that looks like."

"So says the woman wearing a stethoscope to bed."

"It's a lovely instrument." She fingered the tubing as though it were a string of pearls. "How did you know?"

"You mentioned wanting a new one when you were with Phoebe. She told me."

"It's what I would have ordered for myself if I'd ever gotten around to it." She stopped admiring the stethoscope and smoothed the delicately ruffled neckline of her nightgown instead. "Phoebe was too generous. Half a dozen nightgowns is twice as many as I gave her when she was here."

"She has her own ideas about that. In her mind she hasn't repaid you half as much. If it helps, consider how happy she made Mrs. Fish when she asked for the gowns to be done before Christmas."

"It does help." She placed the stethoscope's ear tips in her ears and leaned toward Ben until she could reach his chest with the bell. She rested it over his heart. "Shh," she said. "I want to listen."

Ben fell silent, watching her face as she concentrated on his heartbeat. Her mouth curved into a faint smile, but her eyes were unfathomable. "Well?" he asked when she finally withdrew. "What did you hear?"

"I love you."

His eyebrows puckered. "Is it you saying that or is that what you're telling me you heard?"

"Hmm," she said, removing the stethoscope and putting it on the bedside table. "Imagine that. What might have been a romantic moment is now paradise lost."

"Wait! I can do better. I didn't understand."

"Mm-hmm." Ridley slid down, pulled the covers up over her shoulders, and shifted the pillow under her head. She turned on her side away from him.

"Don't you want to take off Phoebe's gift and wear mine?" He also turned on his side, but toward her, and made himself comfortable against her curves. Although she yawned deeply, it was encouraging when she didn't move away.

"Hey, Sheriff," she said, snuggling her backside against his groin. "Holster your weapon."

But he didn't, and it wasn't all that long before paradise was regained.

"Brought you a paper," said Mrs. Rushton, placing it on the table in front of Ridley. "Mr. Abernathy must have worked himself to the bone yesterday to get it out this morning. And yesterday being Sunday *and* Christmas Day, he's probably going to hell."

"Did you tell him that?"

"No, but someone will."

Ridley examined the broadsheet's headline, which referenced the trial. It felt like old news now, coming as it did five days after the event. Mr. Abernathy's press broke and he had to wait on the delivery of a part to make repairs. She'd heard he had asked Jeremiah Salt if he could make something that would work so he could put out the edition, but it seemed that Jeremiah had already gotten wind of the proposed law and had excuses that would delay publishing it.

Ridley skimmed the information about the trial and turned the page to find a summary of the town council's meeting. She read it in its entirety and then reread it. She pointed it out to the housekeeper, who was standing by. "Did you see it?"

"Indeed I did. There's already a stir, you know. Heard some of it at church yesterday. You'll be properly shocked to learn that not all women are in favor of it."

"More disappointed than shocked, I'm afraid." Ridley turned the paper back toward her as Mrs. Rushton began her workday by firing up the stove. "Did you see Lily Salt in church?"

"No. Not her, not Jeremiah, not any of the children. And I made a point of looking for them. Not the usual thing for them to stay away. I suppose it could be on account of Lizzie's measles."

"She'd be well over them by now."

"Then maybe Ham came down with the sickness."

"Maybe."

"I saw Louella Fuller, though. Broke my heart to see her grieving so. Mrs. Springer took her to the side and talked to her real gentle-like. You could tell. Something's come over that woman. Mrs. Springer, I mean. Can't think what it could be except the hand of God. I don't know if she's had a change of heart, but she surely has had a change of disposition."

Ridley knew what had happened, but it wasn't her place to tell, and the details of the transfer of the butcher shop into Amanda Springer's name were not final. Preparation for the trial had slowed Chris Whitt's progress on every other matter in front of him. Amanda showed remarkable patience in the face of the delay.

She had confided this when Ridley sought her assistance

with the proposal before the council. Jim had not breathed a word about it to her, which did not set well, but also had the effect of guaranteeing her support and, most likely, her husband's affirmative vote.

"What plans do you have for the day?" asked the housekeeper.

"Well, now that this is in circulation, I think I'll walk to the Songbird and have a look at Mr. Winegarten's foot. No doubt it's throbbing after all the rich food he ingested yesterday."

"All the alcohol, you mean. There're folks who celebrate Christmas with rowdy drinking, and some of them will still be there. I don't imagine Buzz has had the inclination to throw them out yet."

"That's all right. If they're there, I can take their temperature, so to speak. Learn if they come down on the side of the angels or dance with the devil." She stood. "I'm going to get ready. Just tea and toast for me this morning. Do we have any of the elderberry jam left?"

"We do."

"Then I'll have that on my toast, please." She looked the housekeeper over, trying to determine what was different about her this morning. Her cinnamon-colored hair was arranged in its usual neat bun and her smile was dimpling. "You're wearing the seed pearl combs I gave you. Your hair makes them look handsome indeed."

"Go on with you. I'm sure it's the other way around. It was a lovely gift to find on my doorstep after church. I had dinner with Miss Renquest yesterday and she was full of admiration for them." She gave Ridley a knowing wink. "And wasn't I just filled with equal admiration for the navy blue straw hat she produced, one with a prodigiously elaborate pink bow. A gift from the sheriff, she said, and I didn't tell her I'd seen one like it before. I'm thinking the hatbox on top of your wardrobe is no longer there."

"The hat was never suited for doctoring. It was incongruent, the sheriff said, and he mentioned that Miss Renquest loved her hats, so I thought I'd give it a better home."

"Incongruent. Hmm. There's a word. That sheriff surprises me sometimes, but I've been of a mind lately to surprise him. Just see if I don't."

Ridley did not want to think long about that. She left the kitchen in what she hoped was not too much of a hurry.

Dr. E. Ridley Woodhouse helped deliver two infants between the day after Christmas and New Year's Eve. Ridley learned firsthand the influence the Frost name had on opinion. Neither woman had sought Ridley out before, but upon hearing that she had attended Phoebe Frost at the birth of her daughter, they independently sent their husbands to get Ridley when their contractions began. One was an uncomplicated delivery with events moving rapidly as the woman's fourth child came into the world. The other child presented in a breech position and required Ridley to turn the baby when it would not turn on its own. Ridley sent for Mary Cherry to assist her, and the woman arrived with all of her years of experience at Doc's side to help. It was a successful collaboration and a turning point in their prickly relationship when Molly Anne Saunders was placed in her mother's arms.

On New Year's Eve, standing at the sideboard in the hotel dining room, Ridley bore almost no resemblance to the physician who had attended those mothers. Her hair, lustrous with shades of autumn compliments of the candlelight, had been fashioned into a smooth coil at the back of her head and tamed by silver-plated filigree combs. She wore silver teardrop earrings that swung gently when she turned her head. Her stethoscope had been replaced for this special evening by a stiff lace collar that put the long, elegant line of her neck on display. Her gown was no fancier than any other woman's because everyone in attendance was wearing her best, but the pale champagne color was unique among the ruby, sapphire, and emerald hues, and there wasn't a person present who didn't think she looked like a flute of the bubbly.

Ben arrived late and stood at the edge of the lobby looking through the crowd to find Ridley. His eyes made only one pass before he saw her. *How like her*, he thought, the loveliest woman in the room, and perhaps the most accomplished, depending on the measure one used, and she was listening intently to Hank Ketchum as he gave her an earful. Hank's wife was dancing dizzying circles on the minister's arm, but Hank either didn't notice or didn't care. Ben had a fairly good idea what his scowl was in aid of. He dove into the crowd to rescue Ridley and get her to safety.

It took him a while to reach her. People stopped him to ask about his journey to the Denver jail, but what they really wanted to know was if Michael Gordon had survived the trip.

"Well?" asked Ridley when Ben managed to spirit her away from Hank's side.

Ben was not surprised that she wanted to know the same thing everyone else did, but she was the only one who asked the question out of compassion. "He made it. I don't know how, but he did. I expect we'll hear something soon. I asked the marshal to let me know. I knew you'd want that, and frankly, so do I."

She nodded. "I was afraid you wouldn't make it back in time to join the party."

"I got in about an hour ago. Had a word with Hitch first. He says he'd rather stay at the office tonight. Expects the Songbird might get rowdy. I didn't argue with him because he's probably right. I went home and got cleaned up." He stepped back so she could look him over and was flattered by the approval in her eyes. "Bought this suit in Denver for the wedding, I guess both of them now. Notice the long tails." She smiled, though he was aware it was restrained. "I know I'm overdressed for this shindig, but I asked myself how often would I have an opportunity to wear it, so here I am."

"And you are here very handsomely."

He believed she was sincere, but the smile was still restrained. "What is it?"

"Have you spoken to your mother?" The fact that Ben had to look around to find her was answer enough for Ridley. "Do you see how happy she is? She can barely contain her excitement. She was waiting until you arrived to make the announcement. This is her night, Ben. I know that we planned to tell her about us this evening, but do we really want to do that?"

Ben stared at her, his face devoid of expression. "Are you looking for a way out?"

Ridley's astonishment was real. "No!"

"No?"

"No!"

Ben was aware of a few heads turning in their direction. "We're attracting attention. Give me enough time to say hello to Ellie and Abe and then follow me to the lobby."

Ridley did as he asked and against her better judgment allowed him to pull her into a cupboard under the stairs when no one was looking. "You know you are behaving absurdly."

"Perhaps, but it's coming from a place of complete rationality." They were each bent at the waist because it was impossible to stand under the cupboard's sloped ceiling. He still managed to corner her against some shelves and kiss her hard and breathless.

"All right," she said after a moment to recover. "Maybe you are rational."

"No question. Now, explain why we can't tell my mother tonight."

"Because this is *her* night. She should not have to share the limelight. Whatever backslapping and glad-handing is going to happen this evening, it is going to happen to your mother and Mr. Butterworth. We'll have our night, Ben, we *will*, but it shouldn't be tonight." She waited for him to say something. When he didn't, she said, "You don't look as if you're convinced."

"I don't want to be."

"Then what do we do?"

Ben sighed and pushed his fingers through his hair. "Choose another night. I don't have to be happy about it."

"I understand, but please don't be miserable about it either."

"I have a crick in my neck. Can I be miserable about that?"

Ridley chuckled. Ben's petulance was so out of character that she could not help but be amused. "I'll make it up to you. I promise."

"Well . . ."

Ridley did not wait to hear more. She accepted that as a concession. He was close enough that she could feel his breath on her cheek. She imagined that was how he had found her mouth earlier. She brushed his lips with hers. "Tell me how we are going to get out of here without being seen," she whispered.

"One at a time."

Chapter Forty-two

Jeremiah Salt raised a foamy beer at midnight and toasted the New Year along with everyone else in the Songbird. He was aware that Buzz Winegarten was watching him, counting the number of times his glass was refilled, but Jeremiah didn't give a damn. It was a New Year, not yet a new century, but still a new beginning. He had some resolutions in mind and the beer he was holding up represented his resolve to uphold them. He liked the way that sounded and he was smiling to himself as he drained half the glass.

"You got a resolution, Buzz?" he asked, setting his beer down on the bar. He wiped foam off his upper lip with the back of his hand.

"Yeah. I'm resolved to kick my nephew's ass to kingdom come and get some real help in here." He wiped the bar in front of Jeremiah with a damp rag, including under Jeremiah's glass. "How many is this for you now?"

"You know. Been watching you count. When you tick them off on your fingers, it's kinda obvious."

"Hmm." Buzz moved away to refill another customer's glass but returned when he was done. "I guess the number don't really matter when I'm saying you've had enough."

Jeremiah used one arm to hug his beer. "You gonna let me finish this one, right?"

"Not gonna fight you for it."

"Good." He lifted his glass, saluted Buzz, and took a sip. "So what's this I hear about you maybe giving Jim Springer a job?"

Buzz shrugged. "All part of the kicking-ass plan."

Jeremiah looked around, didn't see Jim. "I guess he's hob-nobbin' at the Butterworth tonight. Him and his snooty, know-it-all wife."

"Probably better if you don't talk out of turn about Amanda."

"Wasn't out of turn. It was my turn to talk. You say something. I say something. That's a conversation, Buzz. I was holdin' up my end of the conversation."

Buzz pointed to Jeremiah's glass. "Definitely your last." He looked down the bar, saw one of the wranglers from the Double H set down two empty shot glasses, and went to refill them.

Jeremiah followed, pushing his glass along the length of the bar rather than carrying it. When the cowpoke took his shots and headed back to his table, Jeremiah said, "Do you want to hear my resolutions?"

"Sure."

"I am resolved not to spend another night in jail."

"Yeah? Well, good for you."

"I am resolved to do unto others as they do unto me."

"You might want to rethink that one. It's do unto others as you *would have* them do unto you."

"I know what it is, but I'm more of an eye-for-an-eye fella. Understand?"

"Well, if you're resolved on revenge, then you got it right. You contemplating any other resolutions?"

"I'm resolved that this is the year Clay's gonna start as my apprentice. I was younger than he is when I started workin' for my daddy. I've been watching him. He's a good boy, but it's time he was weaned from his ma. She's going to strangle him with her apron strings, if you know what I mean. Better he should spend more time with me."

"Guess it's never too early to learn a trade," Buzz said carefully. "You know, the schoolmaster comes in here regular, and he's been known to say that your son's smart as a whip. You sure you want to take him out of school?"

Jeremiah scowled, but his lips were too loose and rubbery to maintain it for long. "Now you sound like Lily." He finished his beer and pushed the glass toward Buzz. "Another."

Buzz shook his head. "I know you heard me. That was your last."

"Dammit, Buzz. Ain't you heard what I said about how others do unto me?"

"I did. I was hoping I was an exception."

"There can't be exceptions. Breaks my resolution otherwise." He nudged the glass forward. "C'mon. One more. Promise I'll leave after."

"I made promises, too." He swept the glass away and put it on a shelf under the bar. "You've had your fill and then some. Go home, Jeremiah."

Jeremiah pushed back from the bar and straightened. He studied his reflection in the mirror behind Buzz. He looked like a man who had had his fill of a lot of things, but beer wasn't one of them. "It's the sheriff, right? You're sayin' I've had enough because of the sheriff, but I'm telling you, Buzz, what I've had enough of is our damn sheriff. I don't care who his pa is or who his pa ain't, or how long he was deputy before he got himself elected to the big job, he's still wet behind the ears, and he has no business tellin' folks how much they can drink or suggestin' laws for this town that cut off a man's balls in his own home."

"Ah," said Buzz. "You heard about the proposal."

"I *read* about it. Every word."

"So, and this is a guess, you'd be against it."

"Now you're just tryin' to rile me. You figure you can make me fail at my first resolution. Well, I'm not spendin' the night in jail no matter how much I wanna smash your mirror or your face. I'm leavin'."

"You want someone to walk you home? My nephew will walk with you. You can kick his ass and I won't press charges."

Jeremiah didn't turn on his way out, but he spoke loudly enough that it didn't matter. "Go to hell, Buzz."

When Jeremiah was out of sight, Buzz crooked his finger at his nephew, who was returning to the bar with an empty tray. Buzz snatched it out of his hands when Lincoln finally arrived. "Why does it take so long for you to get here when you were already on your way?"

"Could be that inviting Jeremiah Salt to kick my ass slowed me down some."

"That was just talk. I can do it myself, gouty foot or not."

He put the tray aside. "I want you to go down to the jail. Sheriff's probably at the Butterworth, but Hitch should be there. Tell him Jeremiah drank more than I promised the sheriff I'd let him, and I'm sorry for it, but couldn't be helped. Here's the important part. Tell him Jeremiah was talking a little out of his head. No specific threats, just talk, but it didn't set right with me. You can remember that?"

"Hmm. Let me see. You served more beer to Mr. Salt than was good for him and now you want to relieve yourself of the responsibility by informing the law about his crazy talk. That about it?"

Buzz struck with the speed of a rattlesnake but without that reptile's polite warning. He seized his nephew by the collar and pulled him in until they were eye to eye. "Yes, that's it, and I'm definitely going to kick your ass now." Satisfied when the young man gulped, Buzz released him and smoothed the collar. "You go on, think about what I said."

Chuckling, he watched his nephew hurry to the door. He drew a beer for himself and then gave it away, recalling that his true resolution was to treat his gout with more respect. Besides, he was beginning to like his nephew.

Ben did not know he was expected to make the announcement until his mother told him while they were dancing. "I probably didn't hear you right," he said, but there was no getting around it when she repeated herself and it sounded exactly the same. "Why is now the first time I'm hearing this?"

"Because you had to escort that poor prisoner to Denver and I thought all your attention should be on that. You know how you fret."

"I don't fret, Mother. You're confusing me with you. Is Mr. Butterworth all right with this?"

"He wants you to call him Abe. Can you do that?"

Ben sighed. "Is Abe all right with this?"

"He thinks it's proper that it should come from you. No one will doubt that you approve; that's important to him. You do approve, don't you?"

"I'm not sure how many more ways I can say it."

"Just one more. Make the announcement."

So he did. Timed to exactly two minutes before midnight—Ellie's suggestion—he pulled everyone's attention away from the clock by inserting his two little fingers into his mouth, setting his lips and tongue just so, and giving one sharp blow. The whistle was loud and shrill, and he suspected that as far away as the livery, Lady Macbeth had stirred in her stall.

"I promise not to do that again," he told them, "if you will hear me out. I am privileged and proud to announce the engagement of my dear mother, Eleanor Madison, to the estimable Mr. Abraham Butterworth, who I will be honored to call Abe from this point forward. They are happy beyond words, as I am for them, so I ask you to raise your glasses and wish them well in what's left of this year and in all of the years to follow."

Ben raised his glass. No one required encouragement to follow his lead. There was a general murmur of approval, warm and polite at first, then a smattering of applause and cheers that soon became a steady percussion that increased in strength and volume. A chant for the couple to kiss started in the back and rose in a crescendo until Ellie and Abe obliged their audience. The humor was sometimes ribald but always good-natured and the clamoring stayed at a rowdy pitch until the twelve o'clock hour arrived. There was marginally less noise then as the other couples in the room exchanged kisses and wishes, mostly with each other. It was encouraging to Ben that so few liberties were taken and that retribution for offenses, real or imagined, would probably occur outside the hotel. If he could avoid breaking up a fight, it would be a fine start to the year.

Ben kissed his mother again, clapped Abe on the back a second time, and then wended his way through the dancers, sometimes around them, until he reached Ridley's side. She had a glass of champagne in her hand, the perfect complement to her gown.

"You did Ellie and Mr. Butterworth proud," she said, raising her glass and touching it to his beer. "How did your mother convince you to do it?"

"Equal measures of guilt and guile. She knows I don't like speaking in public."

"You ran for office. How could you avoid it?"

"My opponent was long winded and boring. People were relieved when I got up and down in a hurry."

She laughed.

"Swear to God it's true. Now tell me that I imagined Mr. Washburn planting his lips on you."

"It was my cheek."

"It would have been your mouth if you hadn't turned in time."

"He was thanking me."

"He could have shaken your hand. Where was Mrs. Washburn?"

"In the corner behind us with that bank teller. The tall one."

"Todd Lancaster?"

"Yes, if he's the tall one."

Ben rubbed the back of his neck as he shook his head. "You want to go home soon?"

"I do."

"You know, if we'd told everyone about us, we could be kissing right now."

"Go dance with someone," she said.

"I want to dance with you."

"I'm promised to Hank Ketchum."

Ben came close to choking on his beer and just managed not to spill any from his glass as his hand jerked. "I'm going to find Mrs. Rushton."

Smiling to herself, Ridley watched him go in search of her housekeeper and then went to take the perpetually sour Hank Ketchum in hand.

Hitch stood in deep shadow as he watched Jeremiah Salt lurch from his forge to home. Jeremiah had spent a fair amount of time banging around the forge before leaving it for his house, which was what allowed Hitch to catch up to him and follow his progress now. The larger problem for the deputy was that Jeremiah was not empty-handed. Hitch was familiar with the size of Jeremiah's fists; the man had shaken them at him more than once. When Jeremiah clenched his hands, they were like anvils, and as best as Hitch could determine, he was carrying a hammer in one and tongs in the other.

It was hardly a crime to be carrying tools of his trade, but Jeremiah was drunk and, according to Buzz Winegarten's nephew, talking nonsense that had Buzz worried. That was at least enough for Hitch to give Jeremiah a holler, wasn't it? Wish him happy on the New Year and ask him what he was going to do with the hammer and tongs? Anyone seeing him would put the same question to him, wouldn't they? And Hitch was a deputy, making his rounds, so it wouldn't be peculiar to ask or expect an answer.

Hitch shook himself loose, shoulders and arms and wrists. He unbuttoned his coat, took a deep breath, exhaled slowly, and stepped out of the shadows. The full moon was on the wane, but on this cold, clear night it illuminated sweeping crests of fallen snow and made the shoveled path between the forge and the house a dark artery that Hitch had no problem following.

"Hey, Mr. Salt," he called. "Hey! Happy New Year!" Jeremiah turned slowly, so slowly in fact that Hitch suspected he was having trouble with his balance. "Did you get up to the Butterworth tonight?"

"Who is that?" he said, peering bleary-eyed at the figure approaching. "That you, the sheriff's whelp?"

That offended Hitch, but he answered good-naturedly, "Sure is. Deputy Hitchcock Springer." When he had closed the distance to ten feet, he stopped. It was clear now that Jeremiah Salt was indeed in possession of a hammer and tongs. "Did you hear the guns going off at midnight? I guess there will always be folks who mark the New Year that way."

"Guess so."

"Dave and Ed Saunders promised fireworks but I didn't see any. Maybe they didn't arrive."

"Maybe not."

Hitch couldn't think of anything else to say in the way of general conversation. "So I'm noticing the hammer and tongs, Mr. Salt, and I gotta tell you, I'm curious. If you were still in the forge, I wouldn't have given a thought to them, but out here, well, you probably understand why I'm finding it odd."

"I don't understand. Don't understand at all. But if you

have a question, you should probably ask it straight out. It's cold. I haven't been drinking so hard or long that I don't notice that."

The deputy supposed it was good to hear Jeremiah himself confirm that he had been drinking. "All right. Why are you carrying the hammer and tongs, Mr. Salt?"

"Gotta carry them. They can't get to the house on their own."

Hitch chuckled and hoped it didn't sound forced. "I meant what are you going to do with them?"

"Then you should've asked that. My boy's got a toothache. Complainin' about it for days. The hammer's to knock it loose. The tongs are to remove it."

It was so patently absurd that Hitch had to believe Jeremiah was pulling his leg. Maintaining a straight face, he asked, "Is it Clay you're talking about or little Ham?"

On any other night, Jeremiah's belly laugh would have awakened the neighbors. Tonight that sound was merely part of the larger celebration. "Maybe you're not so green after all, Deputy. Hard to tolerate your ma, but I like your father well enough. Could be you got more of him than her in you."

"I've heard that before."

"Maybe you'll run for sheriff someday."

"Maybe I will." He pointed to each of Jeremiah's hands in turn. "About the hammer and tongs . . ."

"Gotta rat problem. There's maybe a family of them, living between the walls. I've had enough of their scratchin' and scrabblin'. Getting rid of them tonight. Knock 'em out with the hammer. Remove 'em with the tongs."

Now Hitch was not sure if his leg was still being pulled. In Jeremiah's inebriated state, what he was proposing might seem reasonable. "Maybe you should wait until morning, Mr. Salt." He glanced toward the house, where only a single window remained lit by a lamp. "Looks like your children are sleeping. Mrs. Salt might be as well. Do you really want to wake them?"

"Got you that time," said Jeremiah.

It was evident to Hitch that Jeremiah was clearly enjoying himself. "Guess you did."

"I'm feelin' just that much sorry for you, so here it is. The boys sleep in an iron rail bed. I got no idea how they shook it up, other than them being boys, but it needs some straightening. It's a little tippy. Besides that, Ham stuck his head between the head rails the other day and Lily had to call me in to get him out. I aim to fix that problem."

"Right now?"

"Do the marbles in your head rattle when you walk, son? Never mind. I'm not doin' anything but fallin' into my bed once I get inside. Thought about Ham and the rails on my way home and figured I'd take in the tools I needed so I could attend to things in the morning. That satisfy you?"

"You could have said so straight off."

"You're right, Deputy. I could've. Now, if you don't have another asinine question for me, let's end it at good night."

Feeling vaguely unsettled, Hitch nodded reluctantly. "Good night, Mr. Salt. If you don't mind, I'll wait right here, make sure you get in."

Jeremiah Salt shrugged. "Suit yourself."

Hitch did. He not only waited until Jeremiah was inside, but walked the perimeter of the house afterward to assure himself that the interior remained quiet. He felt marginally better about leaving but not so easy that he could let it go without saying something to the sheriff. With that in mind, he headed straight to the Butterworth.

"Excuse me," said Ben, easing himself away from the tight circle of the Fishes and the Hennepins the moment he saw his deputy standing at the entrance. He hurried toward Hitch, apologizing as he squeezed past folks on his way to the front. "Let's step outside before your mother sees you, unless you're here for her. Are you?"

Hitch shook his head and ducked back out. He stared at Ben, taking in his attire from neck to tails to toes. "Well, aren't you turned out like Mrs. Astor's pet horse?"

"You want to keep your job? Shut up."

Hitch grinned. "Guess you heard that a couple of times tonight." When Ben merely raised an eyebrow, the grin vanished. Hitch cleared his throat and launched into the reason for his visit.

Ben listened to the whole of what Hitch had to say and then he moved them to the boardwalk in front of the hotel as Sam Love and his wife stepped out onto the porch for some fresh air. The couple did not attempt to engage them in conversation, which suited Ben but prompted Hitch to frown. "Plenty of time to chat later," said Ben.

"Chat? No. Seeing Sam reminded me I need to get a haircut."

"Jesus."

"Sorry."

Ben simply shook his head. "What do you want to do, Deputy?"

"I'm not sure. Maybe make a couple more passes by the house?"

"Couldn't hurt." Ben was struck by how young his deputy looked in the silvery blue moonlight. He thought of Amanda and Jim inside, both of them perfectly, blissfully ignorant of the danger their son had faced tonight. One throw of the hammer, one swipe with the tongs, and Hitch could have had his skull crushed. "Listen, how about you give me a minute to get my gun belt and an overcoat and I'll go with you?"

"Didn't come here to trouble you," said Hitch. "Just thought you should know what happened."

"And you were right. I need that minute now." He was on the point of leaving when he realized that Hitch was no longer listening to him. The deputy's head was raised at an angle and he was peering narrowly into the distance. "What is it?" Ben asked even as he turned to look for himself. Hitch didn't answer, probably the shock of recognizing what he was seeing left him speechless, but Ben had no such difficulty. He saw the orange and yellow flames licking the night sky and immediately raised the alarm.

"Fire!" he yelled. "Fire at the forge!" It made no difference that the flames were at the far end of town; Ben experienced them as if they were licking his skin. A thin line of heat parted his hair all the way to the scalp and spread across the webbed scars on his neck and shoulders. This pain, this fraying of every nerve ending, the smell of burnt hair and burnt flesh, this was what he had known only in the aftermath of the barn blaze, but he was conscious now and it felt as if he were being burned alive.

Sam Love separated himself from his wife and charged back into the hotel. "Fire!" he yelled above the din. "Sheriff says there's fire at the forge!"

Ben sent Hitch to the church to ring the bell. It had rung in the New Year, and Ben had to hope people would understand this was not more of the earlier celebration. Every hand would be needed.

He glanced behind him when he reached the apothecary. Men and women were exiting the hotel like army ants on the move, organized and driven for a single purpose. Ben slipped inside the Songbird to pass on the alarm. By now he knew the fire was not at the forge. Not yet. The angle was wrong and the flames were too high. It was the Salt home that was burning, and the fire was likely rising from the second story. The bedrooms, Ben thought. The children, Lily. He ran faster.

Ben had wanted to be wrong about what he would find, but his worst fears were realized when he arrived. Flames were spilling out of the upper-floor window at the front of the home and had broken through the roof. He ran to the back of the house and was astonished to see Clay leaning out a window holding his brother by the hands and preparing to drop him. The drift of snow beneath the window was as good as anything Ben could provide to soften the fall. He cupped his hands around his mouth and yelled up to Clay. "Let him go! Now!"

Clay did.

Ben scooped the terrified boy out of the way and hollered to Clay to make the same jump. "Your turn! Come on."

Clay shook his head and didn't waste a breath to explain. He ducked back inside and disappeared.

Ben's heart dropped to his stomach, where it churned until bile burned the back of his throat. He set Ham down and tore off his coat, swaddling the child. He hunkered in front of Ham and took the trembling boy by the shoulders. "Help is coming! Go around to the front of the house. Tell them I went inside to help Clay." There was no time to wait to see if his instructions were understood, but this was a boy who walked on broken glass, and Ben kept that in mind as he pushed Ham in the direction he wanted him to go.

To his surprise, the back door was locked. He shouldered and kicked his way inside and ran through the empty kitchen to the stairs. He didn't open the front door for fear of drawing the smoke and flames toward it and making any chance of reaching the upper floor impossible. He might not have been a witness to the barn burning at Twin Star but he'd heard plenty of stories about it to know what to do. He kept his head down and stayed under the smoke as he climbed. The last bits of snow clinging to his shirt and trousers melted. He tried not to think about his own terror as he climbed; he tried to think about theirs. Sometimes the two were confused.

He found Clay lying on the floor outside his sisters' room. As quick as that, the boy had been overcome by smoke. Ben heaved him onto his shoulder and carried him to his bedroom, where he unceremoniously dumped him out the window. He heard shouting from below but couldn't make out what was being said. It was more important knowing that help had arrived. He hoped it came with a ladder and buckets.

Ben tore a sleeve off his shirt and wrapped it around the lower half of his face as he hurried to the girls' room. Smoke leaked out from under the door but the door itself wasn't hot. He opened it, crouched low, and worked his way blindly to the bed. He reached it just as flames ate their way through the ceiling and crawled across it to the open door.

Ben felt for the girls and found them huddled together as he imagined they had been in sleep. He used the sheet under them to drag them toward the edge of the bed, covered them in blankets, and carried them through the sheer curtain of fire that shimmered and twisted in the doorway. The stairs were invisible to him now. He took the girls to Clay's room and laid Hannah down while he eased Lizzie through the opening. He was too blinded by smoke and tears to see who was waiting to take her. He let her go and then did the same for Hannah.

Ben wanted to make the jump himself, God knew he did, but Lily was still in the house, and perhaps Jeremiah as well. Hunching his shoulders, using his shirtsleeve—the one he was still wearing—to wipe and shield his eyes, he got as far as the open door before he admitted the impossibility of his task. The girls' room was fully engulfed in flames and they were leaping and dancing toward him. Fire was shimmying down the stairs. He could never reach Lily's room. He backed away until he felt the windowsill behind him.

He knew there was a snowbank below, a flawless white pillow made silver by moonlight, so why when he jumped did he feel as if he were falling into darkness?

Chapter Forty-three

Ben woke because he was coughing as hard as a consumptive, that, and because whatever was in the dark pit with him was pushing him out. Apparently the devil didn't want him.

"Mm," he said, looking up at Ridley. He swiped at his eyes but then realized the tears he was looking through were hers, not his. He raised his hand, touched her cheek. "Ah, sweet Eudora, are you the one that pushed me out?"

Ellie was on her knees in the snow beside Ridley, huddled in Mr. Butterworth's coat. "Why is he calling you that?"

"He thinks it's my name." She smiled. "It's not."

"It's not?" asked Ben. "I was so sure . . ." His hand fell away from her cheek. He frowned when he saw the sooty fingerprints he'd left behind. A memory returned with the force of a blow to his head, but instead of staying put, he started to rise. The pressure of Ridley's hand on his shoulder pushed him back. "No. I need to—"

"There's nothing you need to do," she said gently. "You've done enough. You've done it all."

"I want to see the children." He was aware of other faces looming around and above him. He recognized Hitch and Abe and Louella Fuller and Big Mike. He looked past Ridley and between the legs of those gathered close by and could see that the fire was still burning in places but wouldn't for much longer. Buckets were still being passed up and down the brigade. The pumper truck was there, but no one was manning it any longer, and the hose lay on the ground as useless as a bullsnake for getting water to the fire when the pumper was empty.

By morning the house would be charred wood, embers, and a chimney.

"Let me up," he said. Ridley did. For the first time, Ben realized that his evening jacket was spread over him like a blanket. He held up one of the tails and looked to Ridley for an explanation.

"Ham gave it back to you." Tears lay at the rim of her lashes. She pushed her spectacles to her head and knuckled the tears away. "He insisted."

Ben smiled weakly. "You know I had to go in there."

Ridley nodded. It took her a moment to find her voice again, and when she did, it was little more than a smoky whisper. "Of course. How could you not?"

There were chirps of agreement; at least Ben heard them that way. Like house cricket invaders in the summertime, the sound swarmed in his head. He was tired, unbelievably tired, and breathing deeply made his chest ache. "The children," he said again because they came and went in his mind.

"Sam Love and his wife took Ham and Clay away because they have boys and room for two more. Mary Cherry and Mrs. Rushton are caring for the girls in my surgery, and Mr. and Mrs. Springer are there to take them as soon as I say it's all right. I promised I would be along directly."

"You were waiting for me." It wasn't a question.

"Of course I was. You have to come with me. Hitch is here to help. And Big Mike."

Ben nodded. He was dizzy, and the acrid smell of smoke still filled his nostrils. He coughed into the shirtsleeve that he had used as a mask and was now wound around his neck. "Lily?"

Ridley shook her head. She started to speak and then fell silent as the things she needed to tell him were trapped in her throat.

Hitch observed her distress. "Big Mike? Louella? Would you mind stepping away? Give me a couple of moments to speak to the sheriff and the doc? I'll holler for you, Mike, when it's time to get Ben on his feet." When the Fullers obliged, Hitch hunkered beside Ben opposite Ridley. Taking no chances that he might be overheard, he spoke quietly.

"We don't know where Lily is." He put out an arm to block Ben's attempt to get to his feet.

"Don't," said Ridley. "Just sit and listen."

Ben exhaled sharply, coughed, and stayed where he was.

Hitch withdrew his arm and continued. "Some of us started searching for bodies as soon as it was safe. I found Jeremiah under a smoldering rafter. He had been in bed when the floor collapsed and fire ate away the roof. He was still in bed, more or less. The iron bedrails were there but not much else. Now, I have to tell you that it's possible that the falling beam is what crushed his skull, probably is for all I know. That's what I had in my mind as I poked around a little more. Mostly I was trying to make sure the burning embers didn't pose another danger so I was just toeing through the rubble.

"Doc was trying to be everywhere at once, looking after the children, keeping an eye on you, but when she saw me hopping around on one foot in the middle of the burnt shell of the house, she was suddenly right there beside me. I stubbed my damn toe. Hard. I tried to shoo her away because it was embarrassing, but she wouldn't go, and then we both poked around some, and that's how we came across the working end of Jeremiah's hammer. The wooden handle was gone, of course, but the head was still there. I understood what it meant, or at least what it could mean, so I told the doc about seeing Jeremiah carrying it earlier, then I asked her to look at Jeremiah's body, and she says the way his skull was caved in, it could have been a beam."

Ben looked from Hitch to Ridley. "And not the hammer? You're satisfied with that?" When she nodded, he turned back to his deputy. "You?" Hitch also nodded. "All right, then." No one spoke for a long time. This silence, deeply secretive and significant, felt as though it had weight and substance, and there was mutual understanding that they would never speak of Jeremiah's death occurring in any other manner.

Ben asked, "What do you know about Lily?"

"Nothing," said Hitch. "Nothing except that we can't account for her. There's no body in the house."

"Then she wasn't there when the fire started. She would have never left her children. She'd have died trying to save them."

Ridley nodded. "Hitch and I think so, too. The fire must

have started after she left. It might be that Jeremiah wasn't in as bad a way as Lily thought and that he knocked over the lamp trying to get up."

"The way we're piecing it together," said Hitch, "is that Jeremiah took to his bed soon as he got home because all the drinking he did earlier finally got to him. He passes out so deeply that Lily gets worried because she can't rouse him. Or maybe he gets sick and she can't turn him on his side and she's afraid he'll drown in his vomit."

Ben regarded the two of them again, each in turn. "So you're thinking she went for help. Is that it?" When they nodded simultaneously, he played devil's advocate. "Why didn't she send Clay?"

Ridley answered. "She didn't want her boy to know that Jeremiah had been drinking, or maybe Jeremiah hurt her again and she didn't want Clay to know that either. She left on her own because in her mind it was what was proper."

Hitch said, "I figure I'd get a few men to help me search. She would have known about the party at the Butterworth so she could have been heading there. Or maybe she was on her way to Doc's surgery or Mr. Mangold's shop."

"My fear is that she's injured," said Ridley. "I don't think she can know about the fire or she would have returned by now. It makes me wonder if she's collapsed somewhere. It's too cold for her to survive long if that happened."

Ben listened. He understood very well that their thinking was predicated on the story they all wanted and agreed to believe, but it was unlikely to help them find Lily. Better to put themselves in Lily's shoes, if only briefly, to follow in her footsteps.

"I have an idea," said Ben. When he started to rise, Hitch called Big Mike over for assistance. "I can get up on my own."

"Uh-huh."

Before Ben could make another protest, Hitch got him by one elbow, Big Mike by the other, and they had him on his feet so quickly that he wobbled unsteadily. In spite of that, he told them he could manage. He did not miss the uncertain looks that were exchanged all around and had to hold firm. Hitch released him but stayed close. Big Mike, at Ridley's suggestion, returned to his wife's side.

"If you fall over," said Ridley, "we are going to leave you there."

Ben ignored her. "Hitch, how about you staying here and overseeing the last of the work? Make arrangements with the undertaker for Jeremiah's body. If it's a question of payment, tell him I said we'd work something out. Thank everyone for their help."

"What about organizing that search for Lily?"

"Leave it for now. I have a pretty good idea where she is. If I'm wrong, I'll let you know."

"But—"

"Let me handle it, Hitch. Doc's coming with me." He clapped his deputy on the shoulder. "Good job tonight. Oh, and don't let my mother follow me."

Ridley easily kept pace with Ben. Occasionally he took a step sideways and bumped into her, but mostly he held to the straight and narrow. He'd put on the evening jacket that Ham had returned to him. It was hardly proof against the cold. Hitch had offered his overcoat, which Ben had stubbornly refused. "We're not going far," was all he would say, and then they were off.

His steps slowed as they neared his office. "Did you forget something in there?" Ridley asked. Ben shook his head, stopped altogether, and opened the door for her. Seeing no point in asking another question, she preceded him inside. "Go warm yourself at the stove." It was no longer a surprise that he acted as if he hadn't heard her, but that did not mean that it set well. She was on the point of telling him he had no business being on his feet at all when he put a finger to his lips, silencing her.

Ridley stood still, listened. She heard a faint rustling in the back where the cells were. She cocked an ear in that direction. Out of the corner of her eye, she saw Ben nod. When he headed for the cells, she followed.

Her lips parted on a sharp intake of air when she saw Lily sleeping on a cot in the first cell. Ben had no such reaction. He had come here in anticipation of finding her.

The cell door was wide open. And why wouldn't it be when

Lily's incarceration was voluntary? Ridley thought she might weep at the gentleness in Ben's voice when he said Lily's name. Instead, she brushed his hand with hers as they stepped inside.

Lily Salt stirred, moaned softly. Watching her, Ridley expected her to come out of her deep sleep slowly, which surely had been Ben's intention, but then Lily's eyes suddenly opened wide and she bolted upright. If there had ever been horror, it had come and gone. Lily stared at them through haunted eyes.

Ridley took off her coat and put it snugly around Lily's shoulders. The woman was wearing a thin robe over her nightgown and slippers with no socks. Ridley counted it as something of a miracle that Lily had made it this far, and then had to come to terms, as Ben already had, that the jail was Lily's destination all along. Ridley stepped out of the way as Ben came forward and dropped to his haunches in front of Lily.

Lily turned her cheek into the collar of Ridley's coat. "Smells like smoke," she said, her voice husky with the remnants of sleep. "And you. Look at you. Did someone dump an ash pan on your head?"

"Something like that."

She nodded, satisfied with an answer that was no answer at all. "I was waiting for you. Or Deputy Springer."

"Mm-hmm."

"I fell asleep. I didn't mean to fall asleep. Have you been to the house? Are my children all right?"

"Yes, Lily."

She went on as if she hadn't heard him. "When you weren't here, I figured you were at the Butterworth, and maybe Deputy Springer was, too, so I thought it'd be better if I waited. The cot's more comfortable than it should be. I fell asleep."

"I know."

"Is this where Jeremiah stayed when you arrested him?"

"Mostly."

"I wondered about that." She took a deep breath, glanced at Ridley, and then locked eyes with Ben. "He came home drunk. I don't think he was at the hotel. He was probably at the Songbird." When Ben confirmed her suspicions, she continued. "I know what to do when he's been drinking. I help him upstairs if he needs it and point him to the bed. Sometimes I help him undress. I didn't know what to do tonight. I was already in bed. I heard him stumbling on the stairs so I got up. I didn't get very far before he came in the room. Oddest thing about it, though, he was carrying a hammer and tongs from the forge. Couldn't imagine what he was going to do with them, or rather I could. Do you understand? I *could* imagine, and I don't think I've ever been so scared. He set them down beside the bed. I remember staring at them for a long time after he collapsed. Just staring at them and then at him and then . . ."

When her voice trailed away, so did her gaze.

Ben said, "Look at me, Lily. I'm going to tell you a story and you're going to make it your own. Don't worry if you don't understand me now. You will." And then he began by starting at the end, telling her once again that her children were safe. That news, rather than reassuring Lily, made her increasingly anxious. She peppered Ben with questions that left no doubt in his mind that she hadn't known about the fire.

"Whatever you think you might have done, Lily," said Ben, "you didn't. Here's what happened." He described the events as Hitch and Ridley had described them to him, how Lily left to get help for her husband because she was worried about him, and how he must have come around briefly after she was gone and, in his inebriated state, knocked over a lamp. The fire erupted and spread too quickly for him to be able to manage it. He passed out again, and this time the fire consumed him and the room and threatened the children. Ben told her about Clay's heroics and almost nothing of his own. She wept for her children, but not her house or her husband. She had no tears for herself.

Ridley sat beside Lily and pressed a handkerchief into her hand. When Lily merely squeezed it in her fist, Ridley took it back and used it to wipe Lily's face. "Tell us you understand," she said. "We need to know that it's your story now."

"I know what you want, but—"

"No," said Ridley. "No buts. There can't be. A beam fell on Jeremiah. That's what crushed his skull."

Lily nodded slowly, taking it in. "Are you sure you want to—"

Ben interrupted her, holding up his hand. "We only need to hear that you understand that it's your story now."

"I understand." She hardly did more than mouth the words. "It's my story."

"That's right." He took her hands in his, squeezed them gently. "How about we take you to see your children and figure out your sleeping arrangements for the night. We can do better than a cot."

Ridley knelt beside the tub in her kitchen and squeezed a soapy sponge over Ben's shoulders and back. "Can you lean forward just a little?"

"My knees are already propping up my chin."

She laughed because it was true. "We'll get a bigger tub after we're married."

"We'll get a trough."

"If you like." She sluiced more water over his shoulders. He had washed off most of the soot and ash before he stepped into the tub, but there were still places that required the attention of another pair of eyes. Besides, Ridley thought, he deserved the attention and she wanted to give it to him.

She used the sponge to draw a spiral on his back and later on his chest. He closed his eyes. She didn't think it was possible, but it seemed to her that he sank more deeply into the water. "How did you know that Lily would go to your office to turn herself in? You must have realized it immediately. I didn't understand until we were standing in the cell."

He shrugged almost imperceptibly. "I suppose because I've known her most of my life, and in this job you get a feeling for what people will and won't do. It's not exact, because I sure as hell never thought that Lily would lay a hand on her husband, let alone smash in his skull, but once she'd done it, it wouldn't occur to her not to take responsibility."

"It was self-defense."

"I understand."

"She felt threatened."

"I agree, but it wasn't the first time. Probably not the hundredth. I keep turning it over in my mind. Why now?"

"Maybe because he finally gave her a weapon that would

end it. What else had she ever had that would assure his death? A knife? A gun? Her fists?"

"Well, it doesn't matter because we know what really happened. Jeremiah Salt burned in hell."

Ridley nodded. "And God dropped a hammer on his head."

Chapter Forty-four

The town council met in January. Their first order of business was to vote yea or nay on the proposal that the sheriff had put before them weeks earlier. They expected more than the usual number of folks to participate in the proceedings and set out benches in the library to accommodate them. It was often remarked that the room was half again as crowded as it had been at the Gordon brothers' trial. People were permitted to stand in front of the council and weigh in on the law before the councilmen voted. There were a few who thought it was unnecessary to put a law on the books that anyone with common sense and kindness was already following and a few more who railed against it because they considered it contradictory to the Bible's teachings, but the overwhelming majority of those who stood and voiced their opinion were in favor of it, and as many men came to the front to speak as women.

The law passed unanimously because even tetchy Hank Ketchum argued in its favor, and although it was hardly ever said in more than a whisper, folks took to calling it Lily's Law.

Ridley and Ben had imagined announcing their engagement immediately following the council meeting when so many townspeople were still gathered in the library. By mutual agreement, they changed their minds, as neither wanted to step on the celebration that followed the passage of Lily's Law.

The town rallied in the wake of the fire to help Lily and her children. The Springers took her and the girls in while the Loves kept the boys. The arrangement lasted until the debris from the fire was carried away and volunteers constructed and furnished a new home for the family. Mr. Washburn found a buyer for the forge and struck a good deal for Lily that made it worth selling. Mrs. Fish learned that Lily was a better than competent seamstress and hired her to do piecework for the dress shop. The work would be steady and would not require Lily to leave her younger children. Clay Salt and Frankie Fuller teamed up to hire themselves out for odd jobs around town. Pennies earned here and there sometimes bought candy from the mercantile, but mostly they filled the family coffers.

Ridley was not the only one who noticed when healthy color returned to Lily Salt's face and the last vestige of a limp disappeared. The family appeared in church every Sunday, where young Hamilton Salt sang with gusto even though he was only beginning to learn the words.

Ellie and Abe Butterworth's wedding reception at the end of February was the first event to bring people together in the town's new meeting hall. The vote to approve the construction of a hall was the second order of business the day Lily's Law was passed. Hank Ketchum was the only dissenter. He thought squeezing six people onto a bench meant for four was just fine, and if folks had to rub shoulders against stacks of books, well, maybe they'd be smarter for it.

The day following the reception, the newlyweds boarded a train for Chicago, where they intended to spend a week seeing the wonders and touring hotels with an eye to modernizing the Butterworth. Visiting hotels had been Ellie's idea, not Abe's, but he was so pleased to get her out of Frost Falls that he didn't care what they did. The capable but unconventional choice to manage the hotel in their absence was Amanda Springer. In the short time since taking over the reins of her family's butcher shop, she had improved the selection and the service and knew to the penny how the profits were being spent. She hired Big Mike Fuller as her butcher and reluctantly agreed with her husband that Big Mike was better suited to the job than James had ever been. Jim Springer was behind the bar at the Songbird almost daily, but he promised the departing Butterworths that he would help Amanda at the hotel if she asked. It was an easy promise to make because he knew his teetotaling wife would knock back three fingers of whiskey before she'd come to him.

Neither Ben nor Ridley wanted to announce their engagement before Ellie and Abe returned, but they both agreed that an announcement had become ridiculously anticlimactic.

Ridley sat on the edge of her bed, removing her stockings, while Ben hunkered in front of the stove and added wood to the fire. "It's not possible," she said, "that people don't know we are—"

"Lovers?"

"I was going to say 'a couple.'"

Ben turned away from the stove so she couldn't miss the face he made. "A couple of what?"

"Don't be difficult. You know what I'm saying."

"I'm not sure I do because there's something you're not saying." He stood, brushed himself off, and went to the basin to wash his face and hands. From behind the dressing screen, he said, "I'm right, aren't I?"

"Yes."

"What? I couldn't hear you."

"Yes!"

"You might as well tell me, Eugenia. You know I'll persist. I learned that from you."

"It's not Eugenia."

Ben peered over the top of the screen. "You're sure?"

"Sure enough."

"Then what's the thing you're not saying?"

"I've been thinking that we could elope."

Ben still held a sopping wet washcloth in his hand when he stepped out from behind the screen. The dripping water was distracting so he tossed it back in the basin. "Elope? Did I hear that right?"

Pressing her lips together to maintain her mien, Ridley nodded rapidly several times.

"How long have you been carrying around that thought in a poke?" When she didn't reply immediately, he became suspicious. "Don't pretend you have to think about it."

"I'm thinking about a thought in a poke. Sometimes you divert me."

"Hmm. Answer the question."

"I suppose it occurred to me when you said you'd be my husband."

"So even before I proposed."

"Uh-huh."

Ben's expression turned puzzled; he rubbed the back of his neck. "Why didn't you say anything?"

"You have family around that would be disappointed if you eloped, and I never thought we'd still be participating in a charade of our own making at this late date." She held up a hand. "Not that the charade isn't without its rewards. There is a certain excitement to an illicit affair."

"There is nothing illicit about it."

She shrugged a little sheepishly. "I know, but sometimes I like to pretend."

"Let's call it a secret affair."

"That's just it. I don't think it's a secret any longer."

Ben walked over to the rocker, dropped into it, and began removing his boots. "Is there talk? I haven't heard any. Not even a whisper."

"I think the silence speaks for itself."

"Huh?"

"They're having fun with us."

"You think so?"

"I do."

"Does it bother you?"

"No. It's sweet in a way. They're colluding."

"I don't know if I would call that sweet, but it's tolerant of them."

"So . . ."

"You're asking about eloping?"

"I am."

"Have you told your parents?"

"Yes. And my brother and sister. I wrote them before Christmas."

"And?"

"Nothing. At least not yet. I'm not certain anyone believed me. I told you that marriage was never much on my mind when I lived at home. They're probably trying to decide how to respond."

"Did you tell them how I earn my living?"

"I did."

"Well, that goes a long way to explaining their silence."

"Not as long a way as you think." She shimmied out of her gown and hung it in the wardrobe. "What would your mother think if we eloped?"

"She knows I don't like standing up in front of people, so she'd blame me."

Ridley smirked. "Well, that's good."

"Yeah, you don't want her cuffing you."

Chuckling, she slipped her nightgown over her head. When she emerged, she asked, "What about your father and Fiona? You didn't leave it to Remington and Phoebe to tell them, did you?"

"No, but I haven't done anything about it."

"Hmm."

Ben was quiet as he stripped down to his drawers and nightshirt. He looked over his shoulder at Ridley, who had moved to warm herself close to the stove. "I've been thinking about something you said."

"Oh?"

"About family and Fiona and cutting her out. Do you remember that conversation?"

Ridley turned around to face him. "I do remember."

Ben took a breath and said, "I'm going to ride out to Twin Star tomorrow. It's been too long. I need to make amends."

"You didn't do anything wrong, Ben."

"Yeah, but I didn't do anything. That's what you were telling me."

Ridley left the stove to walk around the rocker and stand between his splayed legs. She leaned forward, rested her palms on the rocker's arms, and stopped it from moving. "What you're going to do, it's important."

He nodded. "I know."

"You've thought about what Ellie will say when she returns and finds out?"

"She'll have a lot to say, but she has no say. I had to get that clear in my head." Ben placed his hands on either side of Ridley's waist and toppled her so that she was snug in his lap. "Do you still want to elope, Euphemia?"

"Not Euphemia."

"Effie?"

"No."

"All right. Do you still want to elope?"

"No, I don't suppose I do."

"It's because of your name, isn't it? You want to torture me as long as you can."

She laughed. "Of course you'd think that. No, it's because I want to meet your father and Fiona before we're married, not after."

"You can come with me tomorrow."

"No. That's a terrible idea, and you'd realize it if I lost my bearings and said yes. Besides, I'm going to press you to invite everyone from Twin Star to our wedding." She placed a finger across his lips when he groaned softly. "Don't act as if you didn't expect it, and you know it's the right thing to do."

She kissed him then, which was also the right thing to do, and for as long as it lasted, Ben forgot that he could have eloped.

They were married on the first day of spring, which in Frost Falls meant that there were still pockets of snow on the ground and a chill in the air in spite of clear skies and a butterball sun. The bride wore a silk gown the color of pale pink roses. The low décolletage and sheer puffed sleeves highlighted her bare shoulders and the graceful line of her neck. She thought it was too daring when she studied it in one of Mrs. Fish's design books, but the three women hovering close by—Ellie, Phoebe, *and* Fiona—all of whom had firm opinions and had yet to reach consensus on anything to do with the wedding, finally did just that. Ridley seized on their agreement, told Mrs. Fish that she would have this gown, and closed the book to prevent further discussion.

She felt a slight tug from behind and looked back over her shoulder. Hannah and Lizzie Salt, turned out beautifully in silk dresses with high collars and pointed lace yokes, were fussing with her train so that it draped like a sheer waterfall from her waist to the floor. She smiled at them, but they were so earnest in their fussing that they didn't notice. Ridley turned that same smile on the man at her side, dear Abraham Butterworth, who had been so honored when she asked if he would escort her that he had to pluck a handkerchief from his pocket and dab at his eyes.

When he held out his elbow for Ridley to take, there was no question as to who was supporting whom. For her part, she couldn't wait to reach the groom, and Mr. Butterworth's real purpose was to help her keep her dignity by preventing a mad dash up the center aisle. He did his job very well.

Ben had eyes for no one but Ridley. It was easy for him to forget that the church was crowded with family and well-wishers, so he didn't mind standing up in front of them. Remington was at his side with the ring, which Ben had asked about nearly a dozen times before they left the house. His brother finally drove him into a corner and threatened to give the ring to Colt and what happened to it after that . . . Remington's careless shrug was all that was required to punctuate his threat and it was the last time that Ben asked.

Ridley carried a spray of purple crocuses tied with a pink lace ribbon. They were unceremoniously presented to her by Clay Salt and Frankie Fuller, who thrust them into her hands and took off so quickly to find their seats that she suspected the flowers were not plucked from the wild but more likely from someone's garden. She did not want to think about whom that someone might be. She handed the flowers to Hannah Salt when she reached the front of the church. Hannah unbundled the spray and gave half to Lizzie along with the ribbon.

The minister asked who gives this woman, and Ridley hardly bristled at the question. She was sure Ben knew what she was thinking because she glimpsed his brief smile, the one that told her that in spite of the solemnity of the occasion, he was amused. It warmed her heart to know it.

Abe Butterworth answered the minister's question in a surprisingly steady voice and then took his seat beside Ellie. In the interest of maintaining the fragile peace in Ben's larger family, Ellie and Abe sat on the groom's side, while the Frosts—all of them except Remington—sat in for the bride's family. Thus far, the only chill in the air was outside.

Ridley could not keep her attention on the minister, not when Ben took a sideways step toward her. He looked splendid in his black wool suit and black satin vest. The coattail was spoon-shaped with two large fabric-covered buttons at the small of his back. She wondered how many times his fingers had raked his hair before someone—Thaddeus perhaps—had told him to stop. Except for one thatch of orange hair at cross-purposes with all the other darker ones, there was scant evidence that he had indulged in his most endearing habit.

Side by side, they listened to the minister's words, and when it came time to make their vows, Ben took Ridley's hand in his and whispered, "You'll have to tell me now, Emilia."

"Not Emilia," she whispered back.

"Edie?"

Ridley shook her head.

"Elspeth?"

"No."

"Enigma? Because that would make sense."

He looked so disappointed when this last guess failed that Ridley did not care that she had not been instructed to kiss him yet; she did it anyway. And when he beamed at her, she did it again.

This break in tradition caused a happy hum to hover over the congregation and the minister to pointedly clear his throat not once, but twice. It was never certain to anyone that Ridley and Ben heard the reprimand coming from the minister's throat. It seemed more likely that they turned to face him again because they were done kissing.

Ben went first. "I, Benjamin Franklin Madison, take you, E. Ridley Woodhouse, to be my wedded wife, to have and to hold, from this day forward . . ." And so it went until it was Ridley's turn.

"I, Easter Ridley Woodhouse, take you, Benjamin Franklin Madison, to be my—"

"Easter?" Ben said under his breath. "What kind of name is Easter?"

"Wedded husband," she went on. "To have and to hold, from—"

"That's not a name. It's a religious observance."

"This day forward, for better, for worse, for richer, for—"

"I could have guessed until death do us part and never arrived at Easter."

"Poorer, in sickness and in health, to love and to cherish, till death do us part."

"Uh-huh. That's what I was saying."

Ridley's mouth curved in that splendid, swallowed-the-sun

smile that he loved while she stepped hard on his foot. Only those in the pews at the front observed it, and not one among them, including the groom's mother, found fault with the bride.

Remington encouraged Ben and Ridley to leave the reception while the revelry was still at a civil pitch. It was not a suggestion they had to hear twice. They bade good night to family and dearest friends and escaped the town hall through a side door.

Ridley hooked her arm in Ben's and leaned into him as they walked. She held him back only once when he veered away from their houses. "I didn't have my mind set on one bed or the other," she told him, "but they're both back that way."

"Wedding gift from Abe and Ellie." Ben pointed to the hotel. "Tonight we have the finest suite in the Butterworth, and tomorrow we have a private car on the train to Denver."

"Oh, but—"

"The car is compliments of Thaddeus and Fiona. Remington and Phoebe are giving us two nights in the city. We can be gone that long. Hitch will see that peace in the town is not compromised, and Mary Cherry will do the same for the health of your patients."

Ridley didn't know what to say except that he had thought of everything.

"I knew you wouldn't want to be away too long, and frankly, neither did I. C'mon." He escorted her up the hotel steps and signed the register at the front desk.

She stared at what he wrote. "Mr. Ben Madison and Dr. Easter Ridley Woodhouse Madison. It's a mouthful, isn't it? And it took up two lines."

Ben picked up the pen and drew a line through "aster" so it now read, "Mr. Ben Madison and Dr. E Ridley Woodhouse Madison." "Better?"

She smirked, nodded, and this time she escorted him up the stairs.

The suite was on the third floor, and when Ridley stepped inside, it was clear to her that somebody—more likely somebodies—had been very busy. A lace-trimmed diaphanous nightgown lay draped across the bed, and a pair of ice blue kid slippers sat on the floor below it. The bedcovers were turned back, the pillows plumped, and on the nightstand were two empty glasses beside a champagne bucket.

Ridley turned to Ben. "Was this you?"

"You don't know how badly I want to lie, but no, not even my idea."

She kissed his cheek so she wouldn't laugh at his forlorn expression. "It's all right. I wouldn't have thought of it either. The wedding elves left you a new nightshirt on the wing chair. Look, your slippers are there. They didn't forget anything." She looked around, saw that small trunks had been packed for each of them, their train tickets resting on top. "What's in there?" she asked, pointing to an adjoining room whose door was a few inches ajar. "Is it—" She stopped because she didn't want excitement to take her away and disappointment to bring her back. She grabbed his hand and pulled him along but stopped short of pushing open the door. "You do it," she said.

Ben did, and they stepped inside together.

"It's a bathtub," said Ridley.

"It's a trough," said Ben. "This must be how Abe is modernizing."

Nodding, Ridley pointed to the taps. "Do you think they work yet? It seems impossible they could have managed the renovation so quickly." She caught Ben giving her a jaundiced look. "Oh, right, your mother."

"Uh-huh. Why don't you try them out? It's the only way to know for sure."

The sensuously curved porcelain bathtub rested on large claw feet. The double-handled faucet was polished brass and was mounted to the wall equidistant from both ends of the tub. Just taking in the whole of it made her sigh.

Ben nudged her. "Stop admiring it and see if it works."

She bent over the tub and twisted one of the handles. The gush of water was so powerful that she leapt back. "Oh, my."

"Well, there we go." Ben adjusted the tap, turned on the hot water, and then removed towels from the linen cupboard and soap and sponges from under the washstand. He set everything on a footstool and pushed it within easy reach of the tub.

Ridley was still standing over the porcelain behemoth when he was done. "Aren't you going to take off your clothes?"

"Don't you want to do that?"

That made him laugh because she was so rarely patient enough to allow him the pleasure. In the end this evening was no different although it started well enough. He untied her train, unfastened the silk-covered buttons at her back that she could not have possibly managed on her own, and loosened the laces of her corset before she shooed him away. It was not the worst thing that had ever happened to him to straddle the ladder-back chair and watch her remove her shoes, peel away her stockings and garters, then shimmy out of her gown, her corset, three petticoats, a bustle, and finally a camisole and drawers every bit as delicate as the nightgown waiting for her on the bed. The tub was halfway filled when she finally stepped in. Her smile was beatific as she lowered herself into the water and she had the most delicious little shiver for him that was like a siren's call.

Ben almost tipped the chair over as he scrambled to his feet. He shucked his clothes with careless disregard for the sharp creases and stiff collar. If something fell over the back of the chair, that was fine, but if it landed on the floor, he didn't pick it up. He would have worn his shirt into the tub if she hadn't pointed it out. He yanked it over his head, whipped it around like a lasso, and captured the hat tree in the corner.

"Impressive." Ridley closed her eyes, rested her head against the lip of the tub. The water rose almost to her shoulders as Ben eased himself down. "I'm never getting out," she told him.

Ben turned off the water and leaned back. "Neither am I."

But they did . . . eventually. They dried hastily, picking their way around their scattered clothes, and fell into bed in a tangle of arms and legs and towels. Ridley was barely able to sweep her wedding nightgown out of the way before they rolled over it.

Slippery with soap and water, they made love with mad frenzied abandon. For a while laughter ruled, and when it didn't, it was because it was replaced by words, some of them naughty, some of them nice, all of them spoken with a gravity that made them imperative.

"We're not under the blankets," Ridley said when she'd recovered her breath. It seemed perfectly reasonable to point that out.

"Our heads are at the footboard. That might have something to do with it."

Ridley reached under her, found a towel, and pulled it across her.

"That's damp." He dragged it off her and used it to cover himself. "You'll catch your death."

"So will you."

"No, because I'll have you to tend me."

Snorting, Ridley turned on her side and backed into him. He cradled her butt against his groin. There was plenty of heat there. She fisted some of the blankets that she was lying on and pulled them over her. He got rid of the towel and arranged the blankets so they were both covered.

Ridley snuggled, spoke softly. "I thought it would be different somehow, making love to you, I mean, now that we're married, and it was but in a good way. In a very good way. It felt complete, as if I was embracing all of you, touching you more deeply than I've ever done."

He said nothing for a time, then, "That's the way I recall it."

She tried to turn her head to see if he was amused by her confession, but he tapped her cheek and turned her back. He wasn't amused at all, she realized, he was moved, and that's why she decided to make a second confession. "It was supposed to be Esther."

"Pardon?"

She could imagine he was frowning slightly as he tried to follow the shift in subjects. "Esther. Not Easter. It was misspelled on my birth certificate and again in the family Bible. My father thinks it was my mother's mother who was at fault. My mother thinks it was my father."

"Does someone have to be blamed? It's a lovely name."

"You say it."

"Easter."

"Yes, it's lovely when you say it."

Ben said it again, this time against her hair, parting strands of it with his breath. It wasn't long before he realized she had fallen asleep. It made him smile that it came to her so easily.

Someday he would ask her how she did it, but tonight he was content to drift off as he often did, whispering each name as it occurred to him. "Eudora. Esmeralda. Eve. Evangeline. Eos. Elspeth. Eris. Emma . . . Eleanor . . . Evelyn . . . Esther . . . Easter . . ."

Ridley made him love them all.

Turn the page for a preview of Jo Goodman's

A Touch of Frost

Available now from Berkley

"He's got eyes for you. I know about these things, and I'm not wrong about this. Just see if he doesn't."

Belatedly, Phoebe Apple's attention was drawn from the window where the landscape passed at a measured, hypnotic speed, to the fellow traveler on her left. "Pardon?" she asked, turning slightly in her seat to address the older woman. There had been precious few words exchanged since they had boarded together in Denver, and Phoebe had a desire to keep it that way. As a rule, she favored conversation, but found it more comfortable when it was going on around her.

She offered an apologetic smile. "I'm sorry. Woolgathering. I didn't hear what you said."

"I see that plain enough. You've had your nose pressed to that window for the better part of the last hour. Like a beggar at the bake shop." She presented this with a hint of amusement, no reproof. "Deep thoughts, I take it."

Phoebe presented a light shrug but made no comment about the depth of her thoughts. She required a moment to recall the woman's name. There had been introductions at the point of taking their seats, but Phoebe found herself struggling to bring forth a name.

"Amanda Tyler," the woman said. "Mrs. Jacob C. Tyler."

"Of course." Having been caught out, Phoebe felt herself flushing. "Phoebe Apple."

"Oh, I remember." Mrs. Jacob C. Tyler leaned a few degrees

toward Phoebe and whispered in confidential tones, "Don't look now, but he's glancing your way again."

Startled, Phoebe's chin came up a fraction and she cast her eyes in every direction except behind her. It was the hand suddenly covering one of hers and squeezing gently that grounded her. She dropped her head and stared at her lap, aware now of the softness of Mrs. Tyler's palm, the pressure of plump fingers, and that comfort and admonishment were being offered simultaneously.

Under her breath, Phoebe asked, "Who is watching me?"

"I didn't exactly say he's watching you. More like he's got an interest."

"Why would he be interested in me?"

Mrs. Tyler sat back again and released Phoebe's hand in order to give it a few light taps. "You have a passing acquaintance with a mirror, don't you?"

Phoebe turned fully sideways to regard Mrs. Tyler and was confronted by the woman's clearly entertained expression. "I know what I see in the mirror, Mrs. Tyler, but that is neither here nor there." She wiggled the fingers of her left hand, drawing attention to the gold wedding band. "I am married." She widened the opening of the pale gray cape she was wearing, modestly exposing her rounded belly. "And then there is this." She splayed her fingers across her abdomen. "There is every possibility that I will give birth before I reach Frost Falls. It is that imminent."

Mrs. Tyler chuckled appreciatively. Creases radiated from the corner of her eyes like rays of sunshine, adding lines to what was otherwise a seamless face. Her smoothly rounded countenance made her a woman of indeterminate age, certainly north of forty given that there were silver threads in her sandy-colored hair, but how far north was impossible to know.

"He entered this car after we were seated," she said. "I can't imagine that he saw your ring or took note of your condition. The way he looks at you suggests to me that neither would be an impediment. I have the sense that he's a man who enjoys looking."

Phoebe frowned, troubled. It was difficult not to seek out the man.

Mrs. Tyler's smile faded along with the lines at the corner

of her eyes. Two small vertical creases appeared between her eyebrows. "Oh, I see that I've done harm. Nothing I said was meant to worry you. I thought you would be flattered or at least diverted. It seemed to me you were in need of a bit of diversion, but clearly I mistook the matter." She twisted the brilliant cut pear shape diamond ring on her finger. "My husband will tell you that I frequently say what's on my mind with no sense that my observations might not be well received. I do apologize."

"There's no need that you should." Force of habit had Phoebe responding quickly, too quickly perhaps to give her words the weight of sincerity. "Truly. You aren't wrong that I am in need of a bit of diversion."

"Well, if you're sure." Mrs. Tyler said the words uncertainly, but she did not wait for confirmation before she plunged ahead. "Four seats in front on the left. He is in a seat facing this way, though how he can ride backwards on the train is something I will never understand. He's wearing a black duster and a black, silver-banded hat. Quick. Look now."

Phoebe did. It was only possible to glimpse him in profile before his head began to swivel back in her direction. She could not be sure that he meant to look at her again—if Mrs. Tyler's observation could be trusted—but she did not want to take the chance that she would be spied studying him. The wide brim of his hat shaded his face, making it difficult to see much more than sharply carved features set in a fashion that could most kindly be described as grim. She had the impression of dark, unkempt hair, overlong so that it curled at the collar of his duster, and at least a day's growth of stubble defined his jaw.

Oddly, neither his hard, forbidding expression nor his lack of interest in barbers diminished Phoebe's sense that here was an attractive man.

"Do you know him?" asked Phoebe, speaking out of the side of her mouth.

"No. Never saw him before, but then maybe you don't recall that I told you right off that I'm not from these parts. Saint Louis born and raised."

"Yes. I remember now. You're going to Liberty Junction. That's farther along the line than Frost Falls."

"That's right. My son and daughter-in-law just settled there. He's managing the hotel and gambling house."

"Hmm."

Mrs. Tyler surreptitiously nudged Phoebe with her elbow. "I take it you don't know him. The man watching you, I mean. Not my son."

Phoebe shook her head. "I think I might have seen him at the station in Saint Louis, but I don't know him."

"Don't know as you could have any question one way or the other, so it probably wasn't him. His good looks stick in my mind the way hot porridge sticks to my ribs."

"I suppose."

Mrs. Tyler shrugged. "Maybe it's different for you. Maybe you only have eyes for your husband, which is nice on the face of it. You're young. Time yet to discover that there's no harm in looking or being looked at."

Phoebe risked another glance four rows up and on the left. The gentleman—and Phoebe was resolute in naming him as such—had reclined in his seat as much as space would allow. He had shifted his long legs into the aisle and rested one boot across the other. His arms were folded against his chest and his head was bowed. She imagined that beneath the brim that obscured his face, his eyes were closed. Phoebe felt completely at ease studying him until she noticed the bulge under the duster at his right hip.

"He's carrying a gun," she said.

Mrs. Tyler nodded and amusement crept into her features again. "I do believe you're right, but I hardly imagine he is alone. Surely you've read some of the popular dime novels. Nat Church is a favorite of mine, and I don't mind saying so."

"Mine also, but I believe the tales of gunfights and entanglements at high noon are exaggerated for dramatic effect."

"Perhaps." One of Mrs. Tyler's eyebrows arched in its own dramatic effect. "And perhaps not."

Phoebe's quiet laughter changed the shape of her mouth, lifting the corners, revealing a ridge of white teeth resting on her full lower lip. Her eyes darted to the beaded bag wedged between her hip and the side of the train car. She slipped a hand through the reticule's strings and pulled it onto her lap.

"That's a beautiful bag," said Mrs. Tyler. "May I?"

Phoebe held it up for the woman to examine more closely but she did not release it. "Seed pearls and jet beads. It was a gift."

Mrs. Tyler tentatively ran her fingertips across the bead-work. "It's exquisite. Wherever did you find it?"

"Paris. But I didn't find it. As I said, it was a gift." Phoebe regarded the bag with more careful study than it deserved and said in a low voice, "He's looking this way again, isn't he?"

"Mm-hmm."

"Perhaps he's admiring the bag," she said.

"Lord, I hope not. It would be so disappointing."

That made Phoebe laugh again. She lowered the reticule and Mrs. Tyler withdrew her hand. She was still smiling, carefully avoiding eye contact with the stranger, when she felt a subtle change in the train's rhythm. "Did you—" Her question remained unfinished because the next variation in the clackety-clack cadence was not at all subtle. Engine No. 486, a powerful workhorse of Northeast Rail, regularly carrying passengers, mail, and cargo from New York to points west by way of Chicago, Saint Louis, and Denver, jerked, juddered, stuttered, and squealed, and began to slow at a rate that threw people forward or pushed them back into their seats.

Mrs. Tyler threw an arm sideways in aid of protecting Phoebe and Phoebe's swollen belly. It was of marginal helpfulness, keeping Phoebe from becoming a projectile that would have landed her with considerable force against the empty bench seat across the way, but not keeping either of them in place. They both dropped to the space between the forward and rear seats, banging their knees and landing in an awkward brace of limbs. Mrs. Tyler's arm was squeezed between the lip of the forward seat and Phoebe's abdomen. There was time enough for her to give Phoebe a curious look before the train bucked and buckled and they were thrown sideways into the aisle. Mrs. Tyler took the brunt of the fall, supporting Phoebe's slighter weight in the cushion of her plump bosom, arms, and thighs.

"Don't try to move yet, dear," Mrs. Jacob C. Tyler said. "I'm fine. You're fine. No sense—" She stopped because men were shouting, a woman was weeping, and at least two children were caterwauling in a forward car. There was no point in talking when action was what was called for. She held Phoebe close, keeping her still until she realized that Phoebe was not moving. "We need some help here!" she shouted. "Help here!"

She was in no expectation that help was coming. She could not be sure that anyone had heard her above the din. The train was moving but still slowing; the floorboards vibrated against her spine and backside. "Mrs. Apple?" She raised her head as far as she was able in an attempt to reach Phoebe's ear. "Mrs. Apple?"

Phoebe groaned. Her eyelids fluttered. "I'm here. I'm fine."

"How's that? Did you say something?"

This time Phoebe nodded. It was more effective than trying to speak. She managed to place her hands on either side of Mrs. Tyler's shoulders and push herself high enough to create some space between her and her comfortable cushion. She slid a knee between Mrs. Tyler's, found more leverage, and was finally able to sit up. She scooted backward, took Mrs. Tyler's hands in hers, and pulled her to a sitting position as well.

They stared at each other for what felt to be several long moments but was probably no more than a couple of pounding heartbeats. Nodding simultaneously, they yanked at their skirts, untangling them from under their knees so they could rise unimpeded. Using the seats for purchase, they lifted themselves just far enough to collapse into their respective places.

The train stopped. The silence was eerie. It was not that people were no longer shouting or weeping or caterwauling, it was merely that the train had ceased to be the steady, comforting percussion that meant there was forward progress. There was none of that now.

Phoebe looked around to see where she could help. Behind her, passengers were getting to their knees or coming to their feet. One man held a handkerchief to his nose. Blood speckled the white cotton. He waved her on, indicating he was fine or that he would be. A mother was huddled in one corner of a bench seat, her young daughter in her lap. They were locked in a fierce hold that looked to be reassuring for both of them.

Phoebe moved her gaze forward, four rows up and to the left. Her lips parted on a small, sharp intake of air. He was not in his seat. "He's hurt," she said, no question in her mind that Mrs.

Tyler would know to whom she was referring. Without communicating her intention, she sidled past Mrs. Tyler and stepped into the narrow aisle. She started forward, felt a tug on her skirt, and looked back and down to find Mrs. Tyler holding a fistful of mint green broadcloth. "It's all right. I think he's unconscious. Someone needs to attend to him."

Mrs. Tyler unfolded her fingers. "Fine. But have a care. Handsome doesn't mean he's not dangerous. Sometimes they go hand in hand."

Phoebe knelt at the stranger's head and put one hand on his shoulder. She shook him gently. There was no response. Out of the corner of her eye, Phoebe saw his hat lying under a seat. She leaned sideways, pulled it out, and set it on the flat of his abdomen. His duster lay open, and what she had suspected was a gun was exactly that. Without knowing why she did it, she raised the right side of the duster and drew it across the weapon, then secured the coat by tucking part of it under his hat.

"Ma'am?"

Phoebe raised her head. The man who had addressed her was peering over the back of his seat. His bowler sat at an angle on his head that might have been jaunty once but was now merely askew. He regarded her out of widely spaced gray eyes that indicated he was experiencing some pain. He did not ask for help. There was a trickle of blood at one corner of his mouth and another just below his left ear. He alternately dabbed at the wounds with two fingertips and then patted the breast pocket of his jacket for a handkerchief. He merely shrugged when he came away empty-handed.

"He was trying to move toward your end of the car," he said. "Perhaps to go to that mother and her child. I don't know what he hit when he went down, but I heard a crack. Or at least I think I did. You might want to look for a bump. I'm going to go forward. Seems to be the heart of most of the commotion."

Phoebe reached into her reticule, felt for her handkerchief, and passed it to him. "For your lip."

He thanked her for it and smiled unevenly as he pressed it to his mouth. He got to his feet, wobbled a bit before he found his bearings, and then began to move to the forward car.

Phoebe watched his progress to make sure he didn't stumble and fall. At the same time, she made a careful search of the stranger's thick thatch of dark hair. She found no obvious lump and her fingertips were clean when she removed them from his scalp. She located the contusion at the side of his forehead, just above the gentle depression of his temple. There was no laceration and that made her suspect that he had not fallen against anything sharp. More likely he had banged his head on a wrought iron armrest.

She was on the point of trying to rouse him again by taking his shoulder in the cup of her palm when she heard the first shot. She remembered thinking that the sudden silence of the train had been eerie, but that silence was nothing compared the dead quiet that followed the gun blast. Phoebe quickly looked over her shoulder at Mrs. Tyler. That worthy was wide-eyed but still as stone. The man who had been nursing a bloody nose was sliding back into his seat. The mother and daughter continued to clutch each other. Phoebe could not see the child's expression, but the mother was clearly terrified.

Another shot.

Phoebe jerked. While the sound echoed in her ears, the man under her hand never stirred. Oh, to be unconscious. She envied him his oblivion and could not call herself a coward for wishing that state had been visited upon her.

Two male passengers at the very front of the car had taken cover under the seats and were now belly-crawling toward the rear. As a strategy for escape, it was not a bad one. It lacked speed and dignity, one of those being infinitely more important than the other.

Phoebe gestured to Mrs. Tyler to flee the car, and when the older woman stood and turned, Phoebe believed she had been successful in encouraging her. It was not the case, however. Mrs. Tyler took only as many steps as necessary to reach the mother and daughter and slipped in beside them.

"You really should wake now," Phoebe whispered to the stranger. "Whatever is happening is coming this way. I can feel it." The words had barely left her lips when the forward door to the car was flung open.

The first man to enter was not dressed so differently from the unconscious man she was trying to rouse. Black hat. Black duster. Black boots. All of it was a little more battered, more weather-beaten, but essentially indistinguishable. She wondered if there was a uniform for men in the West or only men on trains in Colorado. Phoebe recognized the absurdity of the errant thought but that did not help her tamp down the nervous laughter that bubbled to her lips.

The man's broad shoulders filled the doorway, but he had enough room to bring up his gun and point it at her. The way he did it was not a menacing gesture, merely a casual one. Phoebe instantly felt cold and the placement of her lips was frozen on her face. That was perhaps unfortunate, but at least she was no longer laughing.

Jo Goodman is the *USA Today* bestselling author of numerous romance novels, including *A Touch of Frost*, *The Devil You Know*, *This Gun for Hire*, *In Want of a Wife*, and *True to the Law*, and is also a fan of the happily ever after. When not writing, she is a licensed professional counselor working with children and families in West Virginia's Northern Panhandle. Visit her online at jogoodman.com or facebook.com/jogoodmanromance.

Ready to find
your next great read?

Let us help.

Visit prh.com/nextread

Penguin
Random
House